AN AMERICAN TRAGEDY

A PETER O'KEEFE NOVEL

DAN FLANIGAN

Publisher:
Arjuna Books
5301 Pawnee Lane
Fairway, Kansas 66205

ISBN Paperback — 979-8-9855614-6-3
ISBN eBook — 979-8-9855614-7-0
ISBN Audiobook — 979-8-9855614-8-7

File version: 202401001.031

Dan Flanigan's Books ⁓

Peter o'Keefe Series
Mink Eyes

The Big Tilt

On Lonesome Roads

Other Books
Tenebrae: A Memoir of Life and Death

Dewdrops

WARNING ∰

This story contains content that might be troubling to some readers, including graphic descriptions and references to childhood trauma and childhood sexual abuse.

AN AMERICAN TRAGEDY

"Preschools in this country in some instances I think we must realize have become a ruse for larger unthinkable networks of crimes against children."

Testimony of Key Macfarlane,
Director of Children's Institute International,
U.S. House Committee on Ways and Means and
U.S. House Select Committee on Children, Youth, and Families,
98th Cong., 2d Session,
17 September 1984

CHAPTER ❧ 1

"THEY BASHED HIS face in with a tire iron. Then they slit his throat. Then they collected some of the blood in a bottle. Not to drink it. As a trophy kind of thing."

"Gruesome."

"Star athlete. Voted by his classmates as most popular and most likely to succeed."

"Who killed him?"

George Novak lowered the newspaper. "Just the opposite. This hotshot wasn't the victim. *He was the killer.* Leader-of-the-pack type guy. But this was a devil's pack, a 'Satanic cult' supposedly. The victim was some poor unpopular schlub that wanted to be in the group. They lured him to a supposed initiation ceremony. They dubbed him alright, but with the tire iron."

"Where?"

"Some small town downstate. So much for country values, eh?"

"So much."

George read from the newspaper: "'One of the killers, asked to explain why this happened, said, 'drugs, violent rock music, and Satan worship.'""

"Meth?"

"Probably. But this devil-worship stuff is getting weirder all the time. All over the country. That Richard Ramirez 'Night Stalker' guy out in Los Angeles that broke into all those houses and killed people … He's supposedly a Satan worshipper. His trial's starting in July. Offers from would-be groupies to join him in everything from menages to marriage are pouring in."

Peter O'Keefe took another spoonful of cereal, then bit into a slice of cinnamon raisin toast. They met almost every Monday morning for breakfast at this friendly spot down the street from their office. It was early June, but the broiling heat and suffocating humidity had not yet locked itself in for the summer, and they were still able to sit outside at one of the tables lining the sidewalk.

Karma, former police dog, O'Keefe's dog—though O'Keefe insisted the dog was "owned" in common by everyone in their private investigative agency—lay on the ground between them, head up and observing everything around him, ears occasionally twitching in response to some sound that he'd apparently registered as quiver-worthy, seemingly ready to join the conversation if invited.

Lowering the paper again, George said, "One of the boys who pleaded guilty claims it had nothing to do with devil worship. And get this: For several months now, there's been a task force on Satanic and other cult-based or ritual crime—there's a mouthful for you—organized by one of the local suburban police chiefs. Local law-enforcement officers—*fifty* of them—and a few other professionals, mostly shrinks. Concerns children mainly, and mainly in day-care. Hard to believe. It's 1988 for Christ's sake. You'd think it was 1700 or whatever. When did Salem happen?"

O'Keefe finished his coffee. "Can't remember. But around 1600-something, I think."

"Wonder if it's true, or just crazy talk?"

"No clue, but I guess where there's smoke, maybe there's some fire? Just because there's no Satan doesn't mean there aren't Satan worshipers."

"One of the task force cops says the first local case might be coming soon." George ruffled his paper, straightening the pages. "Kelly went to day care, didn't she?"

"Almost from birth. Annie went right back to work."

George raised his eyebrows.

"Don't be trying to scare me," O'Keefe said, squirming. "If somethin'd happened, we'd know about it. Let's get back to our own business."

George put down the paper. "I'm drowning in new deals. Meetings all day today. Everyone wants security. Business people, homeowners. Nobody feels safe anymore. Serial killers poppin' out of every bush."

"Good for us, I guess," O'Keefe said with a touch of rue.

"But it's hard as hell to find good people for the job, even halfway-decent people. I mean, a lot of these security guards are *armed*. You can't give that job to just any bozo that fills out an application."

"An embarrassment of riches."

"Why do you do that shit to me?" George said.

"What?"

"What's that mean?"

"Something like too much of a good thing."

"Spare me the fancy talk, Boss. I was a C-student."

"At best."

CHAPTER ⇜ 2

AMANDA HAYNES, AGE thirty-one. In her hand, the so-much-smaller hand of her daughter, five-year-old Misty.

Amanda squeezed gently, feeling the resistance, the uncertainty. She led Misty into the elevator that would take them to the offices of the Children's Clinic. Waiting would be Betsy Mortimer, the clinic director and designated leader of the interview process in the Operation Go! investigation.

Mortimer had already conducted a brief interview with Amanda to discuss a disturbing letter she'd received, signed by a police detective and an investigator from the state Child Protective Agency about Operation Go! and certain of its employees. The two women had agreed on a follow-up interview with Misty. Since the interview would likely be lengthy, Amanda would call in after two hours to check on the progress, and if the interview wasn't finished, every hour thereafter.

They entered a brightly decorated waiting room with cartoon posters on the walls, child-size chairs, and on the small tables picture books, coloring books, and crayons. Amanda was slightly relieved when she felt the small hand in hers relax.

They didn't have to wait long. Mortimer greeted them, squeezing Amanda's arm and bending over so that her eyes were only slightly above Misty's. "Hi, Misty. I'm Betsy Mortimer. But you and your mom can call me just Betsy."

Misty recoiled slightly, her eyelids fluttering.

"Your mom tells me you love dollies. Is that right?"

Misty looked down and nodded slowly.

"Puppets too?"

Misty, surprised, seemed to not fully understand but looked curious about that.

"Come on into the Safe Room."

Mortimer guided them into another whimsically decorated room. Carts packed with dolls and puppets stood beside a conference table lined with several swivel chairs and a single straight chair with a booster seat. The table was long and much narrower than most conference room tables. An adult on one side of the table could reach across and touch the person on the other side. A long mirror extended the length of one wall.

Amanda had already explained to Misty about the interview and that just like on regular school days, she would be leaving Misty there and returning later to pick her up. She helped Misty into the booster chair, then drew Mortimer aside. "I can't get her to admit anything," she whispered. "It's crazy. If it happened to the other kids, surely it happened to her."

"We'll get to the bottom of it. Trust us."

Amanda tried not to flinch. The horror of what secrets might soon be disclosed in this room hovered just below the surface, but she put on what she hoped was her sweetest smile and said, "See you soon. Have fun!"

As she left the offices, she silently scolded herself. "Have fun"? The comment now seemed stupidly inappropriate, even callous. *Oh, my little girl. Have I failed you?*

In the Safe Room a man emerged from the side of the wall that contained the mirror, walked to the conference table, and sat down next to Mortimer and across from Misty. He introduced himself as Ken Brinkley. "But you can call me 'Uncle Ken' if you want."

Some getting-to-know-you talk followed, and when Misty seemed at ease, Mortimer said: "So, Misty, you were in Miss Ginny's class, yes?"

Misty nodded eagerly, smiling.

"Do you remember when?"

"Until"—Misty searched for a word—"soon … ago. I was still five, like now."

"Do you remember when you started?"

"When I was three. My mom told me on the way here."

"Do you know what jail is?"

Misty nodded again, less enthusiastically this time.

"What do you think jail is?"

"My mom told me that too. Time out for big people."

Mortimer nodded. "We think Miss Ginny will be in jail soon."

"My mom said so. Why?"

"Well, some of the kids you went to school with—"

"Who?"

"Several. Like Mark Caller, Jeannie Norris. You know them?"

Misty's head bobbed vigorously.

"Well, Mark and Jeannie and some of the other kids told us that Miss Ginny did some yucky things to the kids."

"Yucky?"

"Let me show you." Mortimer took two dolls from the cart and pulled her chair closer to Misty's. "This one's a child doll. A girl child. Like you. This other one is a teacher doll. Like Miss Ginny."

"Miss Ginny didn't have a black face."

"Let's pretend anyway. You can do that, can't you?"

Misty took the teacher doll and examined it. It had breasts with nipples, a vaginal slit covered with pubic hair, and buttock cheeks with a hole in the center. Mortimer pushed the child doll toward Misty. It too had a vaginal slit but without pubic hair.

"Like I said, Miss Ginny will be in jail soon. She can't do anything to you or your parents now—"

"What would she do?"

"Hurt you."

"No."

"Some kids, like Mark and Jeannie, said Miss Ginny made them lick her … here."

"No. You're bad."

"That's what they told us."

"They're bad."

"And Mark and Jeannie and the other kids also told us that Miss Ginny did some things to *them*. Like in this place." Now she pointed at the girl doll. "What do you call that?"

"My mom told me. Virgin…"

"Vagina. So, she did something to you there too."

"Not to me."

"Mark and Jeannie said she did."

"To me?"

"Yes."

"Not to me."

"You're really saying they would lie?"

"I don't know. What did she do?"

"They told us she put her fingers in there."

"Ooh!"

"And other things," Mortimer said. "Spoons. Even a knife."

Shaking her head vigorously back and forth, Misty said, "That would hurt. She never hurt me."

"But if it was a plastic knife—"

"No."

"How about a spoon? That wouldn't hurt, would it?"

"I don't know."

"Her fingers? That wouldn't hurt."

"I don't know."

"She helped you go potty, didn't she?"

Misty nodded.

"So she did touch you there?"

Misty seemed to contemplate the question. Finally, she said, "I guess so."

"Do you ever tell lies?"

"Maybe. A couple times."

"Are there good lies and bad lies?"

"I don't know."

"Like when your friend does something bad, and you lie to protect them so they won't get in trouble?"

Silence.

"Maybe you think it would be okay to lie about Miss Ginny hurting the kids."

"She never hurt me."

"How about Marvin Smith?"

Misty appeared confused.

"A black man. The janitor."

Slight recognition.

Mortimer took a black adult male doll from the cart. It had a penis and pubic hair. She placed it in front of Misty, who seemed frightened and pushed the doll away. Mortimer withdrew it and exchanged knowing looks with Brinkley.

"And," Brinkley said quickly, changing the subject, "you said she touched you when she was helping you go potty?"

Misty slumped, looked around the room, eyeing the toys. "I don't know. I forgot. When do I get to play?"

"Soon. Try to remember first."

"I can't."

"Maybe we could play with the puppets," Mortimer said. "Detective Puppet might be able to help us find out how Miss Ginny hurt the kids."

Misty shook her head. "I don't think so."

"Let's try. You take Priscilla Puppet, and I'll take Detective Froggy. Maybe Detective Froggy can help you remember." Mortimer spoke in a deep exaggerated tone and wagged Froggy at Misty. "I'm Froggy the Detective, and I'm trying to keep Bad Ginny and Bad Mr. Smith in jail because they hurt some kids. I think you can help, Priscilla Puppet."

Misty slid her hand into the toy and awkwardly manipulated it until the puppet appeared to bow.

"That's it, Priscilla Puppet. Detective Froggy wants you to remember how Miss Ginny might have touched your vagina."

"I don't know, Mr. Froggy."

"How about with a knife?"

"That would hurt."

"So, she would hurt you by putting a knife in your vagina?"

"Yes."

"And in your hiney? How about in your hiney?"

"Yes, there too," Misty said, her brow furrowed in confusion. "That would hurt too."

"So, Detective Froggy says that Miss Ginny put the knife in your vagina and in your hiney.'"

"Okay, Froggy."

"Yes, yes," Mortimer said in the puppet voice. "You're a smart one. I knew you'd help."

So fearful was Amanda by the time she arrived to pick Misty up, she could barely breathe and thought she might throw up.

Betsy Mortimer came into the waiting room without Misty.

"We made some progress," Mortimer said, "though not much."

Amanda looked confused.

"I'm afraid Misty is deeply in denial. But that's typical at this stage."

Confusion turned to disappointment.

Mortimer continued. "I do have to advise you . . . there's no doubt she was abused."

Amanda thought her heart might explode. "How can you know?"

The director explained that when a child had been in a confirmed abusive environment but wouldn't disclose it, it meant that the trauma ran especially deep.

"My God, what should I do?"

"It's not hopeless. I've brought other children out of this kind of deep denial. And as I said, we did make a little progress today. She came very close to admitting that Ginny did some things to her."

"Like what?"

"Stroking … and, I'm afraid, insertion."

Amanda groped for the nearest chair, grabbed the arm, and sat down. She didn't want to ask, but had to. "With what?"

"Fingers. Likely also a plastic utensil. Maybe something else."

"Something else?"

Mortimer described certain suspected activities of Miss Ginny and Marvin Smith.

"Marvin Smith? The janitor?"

"I'm afraid so. Those were the two employees mentioned in the letter you got from the police."

It was too much, and the tears came. "What do I do?"

They agreed that Amanda would continue to probe, that Misty should come for another session the following Tuesday.

"And," Mortimer said, "Dr. Carlyle needs to examine her right away. It's critical."

"I'll make an appointment."

"I'll make one for you," Mortimer said. "His office is right here with us. Dr. Carlyle's exam will remove any possible doubt, let alone a reasonable doubt. We might even be able to use it to bring Misty to tell us what really happened."

Amanda tilted her head back and looked at the ceiling, tears pooling in her eyes. She would have to tell Mitch what might have happened to their daughter. It would crush him.

When Misty came into the waiting room, Amanda pulled Misty to her into a tight hug.

"Mommy, let go. You're squeezing too hard."

Mortimer returned to the Safe Room. Two women entered from a door in the side wall that led to an observation room behind the mirror—police officer Sally Hicks and Rhonda Tarwater from the District Attorney's office.

"Tough one," Hicks said. "Good job though. As usual."

"If you can get her there," Tarwater said, "she'll make an incredible witness."

CHAPTER ⇝ 3

RALPH MERKEL LED his son, Terry, just turned seven, into the Safe Room. It wasn't their first appointment.

By the time Terry had turned three, Lori, his mother, had been wilting from stress. There never seemed to be enough time. Not time for herself—forget that—just time enough to run the household, be a decent mom to Terry, and help Ralph with bookkeeping and other clerical chores for his business so he wouldn't need to spend the money to hire another employee.

Ralph had sensed and sympathized with Lori's increasing desperation, and it had been his idea to enroll their son in preschool. At first they'd been hesitant about putting Terry in the care of strangers, but many of their friends were doing exactly the same thing in response to the same stresses. It must be alright. "Plus," Ralph had said, "it might give him a head start if they really do teach 'em something."

They studied all the opportunities available within a reasonable commute from their house. Operation Go! had been the best ("Hands down," Ralph had said). Their interview with Marie Dreyer, the school's principal, and Virginia Montrose ("Miss Ginny" to the kids), who would be Terry's primary teacher, had reassured them. Plus, it gave them comfort that the preschool was on the grounds of the Saint Stephen's Episcopal complex, though Ms. Dreyer had made clear that there was no actual affiliation. Operation Go! was just a tenant of the building the church had previously used as an elementary school. The Merkels were Catholics, "but," Ralph had said, "the Episcopalians are the next best thing."

Terry had attended the school until he was five, and Ralph and Lori had enjoyed their son's "graduation" ceremony. Ralph had even given a short speech recounting Terry's progress, showering special praise on Miss Ginny.

But a couple of years later, the rumors had started. Followed by open accusations.

Child abuse. *Sexual* abuse.

Rhonda Tarwater of the DA's office had organized a meeting for the parents and the Child Protective people where Ralph had met Betsy Mortimer from the Children's Clinic and Chief McGraw from the new task force. Several parents reported disgusting stories of horrifying abuse by Miss Ginny and Marvin Smith, the school's janitor and handyman. They stressed how the parents must "believe the children" if they reported incidents of abuse, and Mortimer provided a list of sexual-abuse indicators including bed-wetting, masturbation, and nightmares.

Terry was exhibiting some of those behaviors.

Ralph and Lori sat Terry down and talked gently to him. But Terry denied that anything "icky" or "yucky" had happened. To him at least.

How about to others?

No.

They asked about Mr. Smith.

Some of the kids were afraid of him and wouldn't go near his "office"—the boiler room in the basement—but other kids liked him. But he had never touched Terry or, to Terry's knowledge, any of the other kids.

Ralph read everything he could find on what appeared to be a new and frightening trend in American life: Satanic worship, witches and wizards, terrible rituals including sacrifice of animals and even human babies. He read several times the sensational best-selling *Michelle Remembers,* in which Dr. Lawrence Pazder, Michelle's therapist, told of his heroic work to recover repressed memories of the girl's parents' Satanic cult activities and her resulting horror-filled childhood, during which she'd been kept in a cage crawling with snakes and forced to witness and participate in gruesome sexual practices and Satanic rituals.

As Ralph continued to participate in the parent meetings, hear the increasingly numerous and detailed stories the children were telling, he continued to interrogate Terry. Was he sure Miss Ginny hadn't done this or that? At nap-time maybe? Or right across the hall there in Mr. Smith's boiler room? "Or when she babysat you for us those times?" His classmate Maggie Baker had said that she had seen Terry with his pants down, frolicking around in some sort of strange "ceremony" at Miss Ginny's house. Terry denied it all, but Ralph couldn't accept Terry's denials. If it had happened to so many of the other children, it must have happened to Terry too.

Then, two days ago, there'd been a breakthrough. Terry, who'd been indifferent, even hostile in some of his previous interviews, even occasionally telling Ken Brinkley to "leave me alone," seemed like a different boy altogether.

Ralph put his hand on his son's arm. "Okay, Terry, tell these people what you've told me about Miss Ginny."

Terry recounted what had been done to him, and what he'd seen done to other kids in the basement of the school, in Mr. Smith's boiler room, and at Miss Ginny's house. Ralph would occasionally remind Terry of things he had told him and was now failing to tell.

Ralph said, "Tell them why you didn't tell any of this before."

"I was afraid," Terry said.

"Why?"

Terry looked at Ralph as if for instructions. Ralph nodded. Terry continued, "She said Mr. Smith and the devil would come in the night and cut our throats."

Again, Terry looked at his father, who looked intently back, locking him in his gaze, an unspoken act of willing.

"And our parents' too."

"How about those nights when she babysat you?" Brinkley asked.

Terry looked at his dad again, who nodded.

"She had an altar-like thing she set up. She would get naked and make us get naked, and she would say some kind of prayers, and she had a big cup that was full of blood of a baby that she and Mr. Smith had killed … at least that's what they said they did."

"Mr. Smith was there too?"

"Sometimes."

"Did he get naked too?"

"Yeah. They would call us up one at a time, and do things to us, and make us do things to them."

And they took him through all those things, which he described without tears or even a catch or trembling in his voice.

"Did you ever see them kill a baby?" Brinkley asked.

"No, but they cut the throat of a little bunny and told us that would happen to us if we told."

Mortimer handed Terry the boy doll, and he showed them exactly where Miss Ginny and Mr. Smith had inserted various things.

"That's where he put his dick," Terry said.

"In you?" Mortimer said, her voice breaking. "He put his penis in you?"

"Not me. But some of the other kids."

"Girls and boys?"

"Both."

"Which boys and girls?"

He thought for a few moments, then said, "I don't remember."

"Between now and next time, try your best to remember. Your dad will help, right, Dad?"

"You bet."

"Do you remember anything else?"

"Yeah," Terry said, eyes wide. "She flew."

Brinkley frowned. "Flew? Ginny?"

"Yeah. Around the room."

After the Merkels left, Brinkley said, "Most of that sounded right. The bunny part was interesting. Let's see if we can get confirmation on that. But that flying around the room was too much. He'll lose all credibility with that one."

As they left the office building, Ralph said, "Son, I'm extremely proud of you for being brave enough to tell those things. Make sure you keep thinking about it and tell me anything else you remember. We need to make sure those evil people stay in jail forever."

He took Terry's hand. "How about an ice cream?"

Terry's step quickened.

IN FORT SMITH, ARKANSAS, FOURTEEN WHITE SUPREMACISTS, ACCUSED OF PLOTTING TO OVERTHROW THE U.S. GOVERNMENT AND CONSPIRING TO ASSASSINATE FEDERAL OFFICIALS, ARE ACQUITTED. ONE OF THE JURORS LATER MARRIED ONE OF THE DEFENDANTS AND ANOTHER SAID HE AGREED WITH MANY OF THEIR VIEWS.

CHAPTER ☙ 4

AND WHAT ABOUT the people who ran that school, the people who had allowed all that to happen, the people Ralph and Lori and other parents had trusted with their children and who had betrayed that trust?

Ralph had contacted his corporate lawyer, who referred him to Perry Slotkin, one of the leading plaintiff lawyers in town. Ralph hired him to pursue civil claims against the school. Slotkin, considered something of a legal wizard, quickly obtained copies of the school's insurance policies.

"It's fantastic, better than I could've hoped," Slotkin said. "The liability policy is great for us. Seven hundred thousand dollars of coverage. Per child. No overall limit."

Slotkin asked Ralph to introduce him to other parents. Ralph had been instrumental in organizing those parents into an informal but well-coordinated group. They called themselves "Save Our Children!." He arranged a meeting at which Slotkin made a presentation. Almost all of them signed an engagement agreement with Slotkin on a contingency fee basis—nothing for Slotkin if the claim failed but forty percent of any recovery.

Too late Ralph realized he may have passed up a chance to share in the windfall he had arranged for Slotkin. Wishing he'd had the good sense to raise the issue with Slotkin *before* he'd introduced Slotkin to the parent group, he now carefully broached the subject with the lawyer. "I was so interested in helping everyone out, I didn't even think to ask for something for myself."

Slotkin looked at him quizzically. "You mean like a finder's fee? I couldn't have agreed to that anyway, Ralph. That's ambulance chasing. I can't pay someone to find cases for me."

Ralph's sullen silence telegraphed a wounded resentment.

After an uncomfortable pause, Slotkin said, "Let me think about it."

A few days later, Slotkin called and asked Ralph to meet at the lawyer's office.

"I've thought and thought about how to go about this ethically, and here's the only thing I could come up with. You've done a lot of investigative work, and you intend to keep doing it, especially for the criminal case, right?"

"Yes. I'm trying to help the prosecutors every way I can."

"That investigative work should help our civil cases too. I'll put you on a monthly retainer. But you'll have to do real work, report your hours and provide a weekly summary of what you've done. If your work results in something especially valuable, I'll give you a discretionary bonus."

"Will you give me ideas, instructions?"

"Maybe occasionally, but not much," Slotkin said. "You're closer to all of this than I am. You're in the best position to know what needs to be done."

Ralph felt quite satisfied that the arrangement would enable him to receive some benefit from all he was doing for the cause: organizing the parent group and working with the group and individual parents; digging the truth out of his own son who would now be a vital witness and assisting the prosecutors in every other way he could think of; finding Slotkin and thus the insurance policy and introducing the lawyer to the other parents. Now he felt nothing short of deputized. But none of these things dampened the rage and fear that had been building in him since he'd realized how badly he'd misjudged that devil's den and that devil's spawn lurking within it. None of the usual obscenities—bitch, slut, whore—could come close to describing her monstrousness. Surely she had seduced that janitor, Marvin Smith, into assisting her in those dreadful rituals. And, compounding her evil, she was now denying it, calling these innocent children liars. She'd even found lawyers who intended to join her in smearing these children—not only brutalizing the kids in the first place but blighting their futures as well, portraying them to the world as bad seeds, maybe even planting seeds of doubt in their minds about whether they'd really experienced these terrible things. Some things in the world were indefensible, and those, like the despicable defense lawyers, who allied themselves with such evil must themselves be so. They would say anything, do anything to get their slimy clients off the hook. What kind of system of justice was it that allowed that kind of shit? They all must be stopped—and punished.

How strange that a battle, even a war, between good and evil had erupted in this unassuming town in the unassuming life of Ralph Merkel. But they said that you should live for things greater than yourself, and what greater cause could there be than this holy mission that had now been thrust upon him?

CHAPTER ꙮ 5

"I'M HEADING TO Harrigan's," O'Keefe told Dagmar Sibelius from the phone in his Jeep Grand Wagoneer. "I'll drop Karma off in two minutes. Can you come down?"

No introductory pleasantries, but she didn't mind. Dagmar had quickly grown used to his all-business style and mostly adopted the same manner in her dealings with him, though sometimes her true self shone through: bright, beaming, buoyant, brave, and brash. And he seemed actually to appreciate that.

"Love to," she said. "Grady Runyon from Global Insurance just called. Wants to meet with you soon. Has a couple of cases he thinks you might be interested in."

"Nice. Tell him I can be there anytime from noon on today. Can you take Karma for his exercise?"

She laughed. "You know how I hate that."

Sara Slade, who, along with George Novak, O'Keefe had recently made a partner in Peter O'Keefe & Associates, sat next to Harrigan at his conference room table in a haze of Harrigan's cigarette smoke, intently studying papers spread out before them. Initially, she'd disliked Harrigan, regarding him as blunt and unfriendly, even conceited, resisting O'Keefe's assurances that this was merely a mask his best friend from childhood had seemingly unconsciously fashioned to survive, then thrive, in the perpetual conflict of life of the legal profession despite his true nature: soft, sensitive, and sympathetic to the underdogs of the world. Once she'd started working more closely with him, she'd discovered those things for herself.

Harrigan had hired the agency to help investigate the affairs, collect the unpaid loans, and liquidate the assets of Enterprise Bank, which had collapsed amidst the so-called S&L Crisis, the mass insolvencies of savings and loans that was causing financial havoc throughout the country. The assignment provided a welcome opportunity to establish the agency's expertise in financial forensics, one of the pillars on which O'Keefe wanted to build his future business. The other pillars would be George's division, corporate and personal security (i.e., body-guarding) and corporate "investigations," including everything from background checks on prospective key employees to due diligence on potential acquisitions and merger partners. This last pillar was O'Keefe's responsibility and not exactly taking off, its development slowed not least because he'd only recently tracked down those who'd almost killed him— twice——while he simultaneously struggled to make peace with the local Mafia, whose now deceased boss, Carmine Jagoda, had on his deathbed decreed that O'Keefe be exterminated.

Harrigan, ever able to deftly poke at any bruise, said, "So, now that you're through palling around with Rose Jagoda and her Mafia buddies, are you ready to help us get some real work done?"

Sara was enjoying that snark. *Too much,* O'Keefe thought, and said, "I guess you two called on me because you need some real expertise."

"We'd be looking in a more likely place for that," Harrigan said. "What's the deal?"

"She's the one who discovered this. Sara?"

O'Keefe could tell Sara was trying to disguise her pleasure in Harrigan's compliment, as, with most serious manner, she pointed to a pile of papers in front of her. "I think we've got a daisy-chain deal."

She outlined how a series of sales of the same property—a big hunk of land in the western suburbs—had been made to various entities for increasingly higher prices, supported always by increasingly higher valuations from a local appraiser, the same one every time.

"Which," she continued, "therefore justified correspondingly higher loans from our favorite friendly failed bank. And then, when the final owner/borrower in the chain—a shell company, of course—stops making payments, it turns out to be worth even less than it was before the first transaction. In fact, one wonders if in the current real-estate depression it can be developed at all. Best result is gonna be a fire sale to some bottom feeder, at a big loss of course."

She looked at Harrigan, expecting him to pick up the story, which Harrigan promptly did. "A lot more investigation needs to be done," he said, "but as we've turned over a few rocks here, the appraiser turns out to be one of the bank's favorite go-to boys. The original seller in the chain was Pomerantz Development. And guess what? Lance Pomerantz was one of the bank's directors. So we might have a real snake pit here, excuse the metaphor, maybe a little painful in your case. The client wants us to jump on this before Pomerantz and everyone else involved comes crashing down in our current national real-estate debacle."

"You guys get all the fun," O'Keefe said.

"You're personally invited to join in," Harrigan said. "We need all the help we can get. And you can bet there are more where this one came from."

CHAPTER ⚜ 6

O'KEEFE LEFT HARRIGAN'S office and walked the two blocks to Global Insurance.

The company had traditionally sent most of its work to Ray Sorenson, who'd been in business for decades and was considered the dean of the local private detective community. But Sorenson had retired, and the work was up for grabs. O'Keefe had worked on several Global Insurance matters as Sorenson's subcontractor and also worked directly for Global on a few occasions when Sorenson had been too busy and in the process earned the trust of Grady Runyon, the local office's senior claims examiner.

"I've been wanting to send some things your way," Runyon said, "but I wasn't sure you'd be able to finish the job. You think the Mafia, bombs, and venomous reptiles are all behind you now?"

"I really do."

"Well, clearly, you're the survivor type. So far anyway. And this one shouldn't be dangerous."

Like a schoolboy eagerly awaiting instruction, O'Keefe straightened up in his chair.

"How's your Spanish?" Runyon said.

"Hola, Paco. Que tal?"

Runyon waited for more.

"Grade school lesson number one. 'Hello, Paco. How goes it?' That's about it for me."

"You might want to work on that. *El futuro es en Espanol.*"

"The future is in Spanish?"

"You bet."

"I'll take that under advisement."

"On this one you'll probably need to hire a translator. I have a list."

"Intriguing."

Runyon explained. Global had a pending claim on a life-insurance policy that was troubling them. The insured, name of Bart Yarborough, had disappeared several weeks earlier during a solo kayak excursion in Panama. The guy was an adventurous type. Liked to go without a guide. They'd found his kayak washed up on a small barrier island, close to where the Chiriquí River met the ocean, a water bottle and an empty dry bag attached to the top of the kayak with a bungee cord. No body found. No sightings of Bart since. No word. Nothing at all.

"Wife is the beneficiary," Runyon said. "She's made a claim and is getting impatient. Says she's about to hire a lawyer."

"Why not pay?" O'Keefe asked.

"It's too soon, and there's too much mystery. Exotic locale. Hostile to U.S. right now, so it's hard to get info. We've done a little checking, and he had some financial problems."

"And?"

"We're between the old boulder and hard place. We don't want the wife suing us for a bad-faith failure to pay. But we can't just pay out stupidly. We're hoping you can do a quick check on him. Creditors. Other background. Get at least some kind of handle on what went on down there. Talk to the place he stayed, the place he rented the kayak. No reason to travel down there yet. Not until we turn up something that makes us suspicious."

"Start now?"

"You bet." Runyon used both hands to slide a couple of stuffed-full accordion files across his desk. "And interview the wife ASAP. We want her to know we're not just ignoring her."

O'Keefe stood, picked up the files, which required both hands, and thanked Runyon.

"Easy work," Runyon said. "All you have to do is keep the wife from suing and us from pissing away our money on a fraudster. The old boulder and hard place. Your favorite spot."

CHAPTER ❦ 7

"**A** LAWYER NAMED Scott Hartley called," Dagmar said.. "Says he needs to see you ASAP. It's a matter, he says, of the utmost importance."

The name was only vaguely familiar. "When?"

"As close to now as possible. I made the mistake of telling him you planned to be here later, and he's on his way over. I couldn't stop him."

O'Keefe called Harrigan.

Harrigan answered with, "As usual, I'm leery about picking up the phone when you call. What's up now?"

"Lawyer named Scott Hartley. What can you tell me?"

Harrigan paused, then said, "Not much. He started out in Legal Aid. Met him at a couple of alumni functions. Now he has his own small criminal-defense operation. He seems to be building a good rep. Want me to ask around?"

"Please."

"What's the deal?"

"He's demanding to see me on what he claims is some earth-shaking matter."

"Tell him to go away. Sara needs your help on this daisy-chain deal."

"You'll ask around though?"

"Yeah, but tell him to get lost. I mean it."

Entering his office suite, O'Keefe found Dagmar at her desk and a sandy-blonde-haired gentleman, knees bouncing up and down nervously in a waiting room chair he was uncomfortably occupying. He was in his early thirties at most and looked even younger, with eyes of pale blue, long and prominent forehead, the top button of his white shirt undone, his tie loosened, his suit wrinkled, his shoes needing a shine.

He sprang up as soon as he caught O'Keefe's eye, stretched out his hand, and declared, "Scott Hartley. I'm so sorry, but I need your help. Can we talk?"

"I guess," O'Keefe said, wondering how he'd get rid of the guy.

When they entered O'Keefe's private office, Karma broke away from chewing the face off a new stuffed toy that Dagmar had given him, stood up, gave a single wag of his tail, and looked curiously at Hartley.

"Dog," Hartley blurted, shrinking backward. "Is it friendly?"

"He won't bite you." *Unless,* O'Keefe thought, *I tell him to, and I might before this is over.*

Without being invited to, Hartley occupied one of the chairs in front of the desk, rested his forearms on top of the desk, and thrust his face toward O'Keefe's. "I have a new case. Very delicate. Very difficult. I need a good investigator. I followed the Harrigan case pretty closely and your work on that—"

"Whoa!" O'Keefe said. "First, I'm not really a criminal-defense guy. Harrigan's not only my primary client, but we also go back to grade school together. Blood brothers and all that. Second, I can't afford to get pinned down in a trial right now."

"Would you at least listen?"

Hartley looked to be on the verge of tears.

O'Keefe weakened. "I guess. But no promises, express or implied."

"Thank you," Hartley said, and launched in as if even a momentary lull might provide O'Keefe an opportunity to escape. "Maybe you've heard about these day-care child-abuse cases that've been popping up around the country lately—McMartin out in California, or Michaels in New Jersey, or the Jordan, Minnesota cases, or others?"

"A little."

"Wild stuff. Unbelievable stuff. Including Satanism, witchcraft. And it's come to town. You know about the local law-enforcement task force they've formed?"

"Just that it exists."

"Well, they've been busy. The first indictment is coming out, literally any minute. You ever heard of Operation Go!?"

Hartley seemed to recognize the sudden surprised and troubled look on O'Keefe's face as he slowly nodded his head and said, "I have." But Hartley was in full-bore narrative mode and didn't seem to fully absorb O'Keefe's reaction.

"They're located in a building on the grounds of the Saint Stephen's Episcopal complex, where a long time ago the church operated an elementary school that closed when white flight emptied out the neighborhood. This Operation Go! isn't church-affiliated, they just rent the building. Been operating there for I don't know how long, at least several years though. My client is … was … a teacher there: Virginia Montrose. The kids call her Miss Ginny. Been teaching there since the school started. She's been accused by several children and their parents of all kinds of horrible stuff."

"Like what?"

Like performing oral sex on the children and forcing them to perform oral sex on her. And other wild, disgusting stuff. Sometimes even inserting utensils—spoons, forks, even knives—into genital areas, front and back. And, in her home, while babysitting them, forcing them to engage with her in sexual games and even Satanic rituals, devil worship, including sacrificing, killing, slitting the throats of small animals and, in one case, even, supposedly, a human baby. One kid claims that in one ceremony she turned him into a snake and back again, which was right after she levitated herself off the ground and flew around the room. And who knows what else? The stories build on themselves, get wilder by the minute."

Kelly loved those babysitting nights … And she loved Miss Ginny.

"And they claim Virginia's partner in a lot of this was the school janitor and handyman—a black guy, by the way. Marvin Smith. He's supposed to have sodomized both girls and boys, including five-year-olds."

"The police are believing this stuff?"

"I don't know about the police, other than Sam McGraw—"

"Don't know him," O'Keefe said.

"Police chief of Prairie Township, rinky-dink burg on the outskirts of the city. He's head of the new task force. He's been the local, self-declared expert on this kind of stuff for a while. Lecturing about it all over the state and beyond. No actual cases, just stories and speculation. But the real people behind this are the District Attorney's office. There's only one real cop assigned to this: Sally Hicks. It's a half-hearted gesture by the metro police so they won't be accused of not cooperating. But it's mainly the DA's chief trial counsel, Donovan Dolinar, and his chief deputy, Rhonda Tarwater. The DA's investigators and lawyers have built the whole insane case. They're all in."

"Crusaders?" O'Keefe said.

"Worse. I call Dolinar 'The Commissar.' Like one of Stalin's boys. He'd send millions to their deaths if someone told him it was his job. Too bad he's so fucking smart. Tarwater, she's the crusader. Worse than Dolinar on this. They've got a crew of supposed child-abuse experts interviewing the kids and parents. It started with a statement to the authorities by the mother of a three-year-old—"

"Three-year-old?"

"Yes," Scott said. "Can barely talk. But from there it's spread like 'The Blob.' It's threatening to devour everyone in its path. They've focused on Virginia and Mr. Smith, but Virginia's female housemate might get named too. By the way, there's a sort of snide, eyebrow-raised suggestion of lesbianism there. Tarwater's an expert at snide."

"I'm surprised it's stayed out of the press."

"It's gonna blow any minute. They've scheduled a big press conference. The investigation's ongoing, and they intend to add victims and counts later if they find them. And I shouldn't say 'find.' I should say 'manufacture.'"

"I have this feeling you think they're innocent."

"'Innocent' ain't the word. There's no crime to be innocent of. This is the worst thing since Salem."

O'Keefe said, "These kids would just make this stuff up?"

"Wait until you get into the facts. You'll agree. And here's the ultimate: She passed a polygraph."

Hartley let that sink in, then said, "Their own propaganda says there's supposed to be something close to a ninety percent chance that a person cannot pass a polygraph if they're guilty. So what do they do? They bring in a"—he made air quotes—"'more experienced' examiner for a second opinion. And what does he say?" More air quotes. "He says the results are 'inconclusive.' I've seen them pull some ugly stuff, but this is the worst."

"You really believe in polygraphs?" O'Keefe said. "And they can't go into evidence at the trial either way, good or bad, right?"

"The important thing is that *they* believe in them. They had to nullify that positive result to justify all this to themselves."

"What do the Saint Stephen's people say?"

"They just lease the building to the Operation Go! people. Regardless, they're running for the exits. Like everyone else, they're afraid they'll be accused next and get sued to high heaven, excuse the reference."

"Well, here's a small-world item. My daughter spent several years there. From age three to five. And Miss Ginny was her teacher."

Hartley flattened his back against the chair. "Unbelievable. When? How old is she now?"

"Eleven."

"I assume she never reported anything like this to you."

"No."

"And you've never had any suspicion of any abuse?"

"Hell no, and excuse *that* reference. Just the opposite. She loved the place. She loved Miss Ginny. Still does. Her favorite teacher ever."

"Most of the original accusers are either current or very recent students. But I think they're also interviewing previous students now."

"But doesn't that disqualify me for your job?"

"Not at all."

"Not at all? You must be desperate."

"If you believe in her innocence, given your personal experience with her and the school, you could be the best choice possible."

"Doesn't seem like a smart thing to get involved in," O'Keefe said. "Defender of pederasts and pedophiles. Not sure I even understand the difference."

"A pederast is an adult male sexually attracted to young boys. A pedophile is an adult of any sex who's sexually attracted to children of any sex. Virginia and Marvin are accused of being pedophiles."

"Satanists, witches, child abuse," O'Keefe said. "The peasants'll be stormin' the castle with torches and nooses."

"They're already there."

"Wouldn't seem smart to get in the way of that."

"Seems to me if we're in the middle of a witch hunt, we have some duty to defend the innocent. Posterity won't be kind to the cowards."

O'Keefe shrugged. "I'm sorry, but I don't live for posterity. I have a hard enough time surviving in the here and now. You think you might be the next Clarence Darrow or Atticus Finch?"

"That would be nice," Hartley said, "but not worth the risk of this. Truth is, I signed on when I thought there was no way this could go anywhere. She'd already passed the lie-detector test then. But I misjudged the insanity. And now I feel it would be just too rotten to quit. But my firm is tiny. I need all the help I can get. I hear you're sort of the hero type, so I thought I'd reach out."

O'Keefe laughed. "Who did you hear that from?"

"My paralegal sings your praises."

"I don't think I know any paralegals."

"Maura Davis. She's working almost full-time for me and going to law school too. She says you were one of her inspirations to do that."

Maura. He'd pretty much suppressed the memory of her. Attractive as she was, physically and otherwise, she was a complication, one he didn't need in his already messy life.

"I wish you well," he said, "but the answer is no."

Hartley looked like his eyes might pop out of his face.

O'Keefe continued. "Much as I'd like to justify Maura's compliments, actually *be* the Grail knight and all that, I'm not. I'm just a schlub who's managed, mostly by accident, to survive some things I didn't deserve to. And now I owe it to myself, my partners, and my little broken family, such as it is, to work on building my business, not sacrificing myself to 'the Blob' as you call it."

"Grail knight?"

"Long story."

"We've got a decent-sized retainer," Scott said. "Virginia's lifestyle has been very frugal. She has an ample savings account."

O'Keefe flushed with anger. "I know how this will end. We'll bankrupt her, and it still won't be enough to pay us in full. Can't do it, even if I wanted to, which I don't; even if I was right for the job, which I'm not."

Hartley collapsed back into the chair. "Will you at least think about it?"

"No."

Hartley stood, but not in surrender. "I have to go meet Virginia."

At the office door, he turned and asked again, "Will you at least think about it?"

"No."

OFFICIALS CLAIM MAFIA IS "ON THE DEFENSIVE."

CHAPTER ❧ 8

HE CALLED ANNIE.

"I need to talk to you about something."

She hesitated, then said, with suspicion, "About what?"

"Can I come now?"

"I guess. But I'm like you. I can't stand suspense. What is it?"

"Ten minutes," he said, and hung up before she could interrogate him further.

She was already at the door when he arrived, her face a mixture of fear and suspicion.

"Why so secretive?" she said.

"Where's Kelly?" he said.

"Upstairs. Doing homework."

"Did you tell her I'd be coming?"

"No. Was I supposed to?"

"Let's go in the kitchen."

At the kitchen table, which had seemingly become the unofficial venue for their summit meetings, he told her what he'd learned.

"That's insane," she said. "It can't be true."

"I know the *wildest* stuff can't be, but maybe there's a kernel of truth in it somewhere. Did you ever have any reason to suspect anything? Did Kelly ever say anything?"

"Never. I loved that place. And I admire that woman. Kelly adored her. We've stayed in touch. I still have coffee with her sometimes. Kelly comes with us. It can't be true."

Another voice. "It's lies."

She appeared in the doorway, tears glistening on her face.

You little sneak, he thought. She was an expert eavesdropper, but this was no time to scold her for it.

"Well," he said, "I guess you should take a seat."

She remained standing. "Miss Ginny would never do those things."

Then she was full-out bawling, struggling to catch her breath between sobs.

O'Keefe looked at Annie, his eyes quietly but desperately passing her the baton.

"You're sure?" she said. "Nothing? Not even something that could be misinterpreted somehow?"

"No way, Mom."

"How about the other teachers? Any of them do anything … strange?"

"No way."

"How about Mr. Smith?"

"No way."

"It's said that children who've experienced terrible things sometimes bury the memory way down somewhere, so they won't have to think about it anymore."

"No way," Kelly said. "They're all liars. Why would they say those things? Why would they believe those little kids anyway? Are they gonna put her in jail?"

Neither parent responded.

"Are they?"

"It looks like they're gonna try," O'Keefe said.

"Are you gonna help her, Dad? You have to help her."

"I've got too much else to do. I have to make a living. For us all."

"You can't get paid?" Annie asked.

"I could. Until her life savings run out. I don't want that money."

"Well, she'll have to pay someone. Might as well be someone who cares."

"And once we've taken everything she has, it still won't be enough, and I'll still end up with a bunch of unpaid bills at a time that neither I nor, by the way, you guys, can afford it. These things can ruin everyone involved."

"Please help her, Dad."

"I can't. It would be totally irresponsible. Somebody will, but it's not me."

"They're all liars!" She ran out of the room.

Annie looked at him, though whether in sympathy or disapproval he couldn't tell, and didn't really want to know.

CHAPTER ⌘ 9

A FEW DAYS LATER, Annie called back, her voice thick with stress.

"I received a call from a Rhonda Tarwater in the DA's office, wanting to know if we'd be willing to allow them to interview Kelly."

"How did we get so lucky?" O'Keefe said.

"No blame intended, but I think it was you. Your exploits are pretty well known, and they recognized your name."

"Are we willing?"

"I'm reluctant to put her through that," Annie said, "but if Ginny really is innocent, and surely she is, Kelly's testimony might help her. I don't think we can just sit by."

"Okay." He'd already determined that the decision would be hers.

"And if," she continued, "Kelly has suppressed something, maybe the interview would bring it out. It would be horrible, but I can't bear to think of her dealing with it, consciously or subconsciously, all by herself ... Would you go with us?"

"Of course," he said. "But how about we ask Kelly?"

Kelly wanted to do it. She insisted.

Two days later, at 9 a.m., the O'Keefes reported to the offices of the Children's Clinic where they sat in the waiting room in adult-size chairs while Mortimer pulled up a kid-size chair facing them and smiled sweetly. O'Keefe noticed that that pupils in her green eyes were disarmingly big, as if dilated.

"So, we have here Kelly and Annie and Peter—"

"Pete," O'Keefe said.

"Pete, yes. Thanks to all of you, and especially you, Kelly, for coming. Our small kids really need help from the big ones."

"How long do you think we'll be?" Annie asked, curt, all business.

"Well, Kelly's likely to be here all morning, maybe a little longer. We've got a nice little lunch here for her, several choices." As if noticing and already prepared for the concerned, questioning looks on the parental faces, she continued, "Yes, just Kelly. We've found that these sessions are almost useless if the parents attend."

The O'Keefes, uncomfortably surprised, glanced at each other.

"So what should we be doing?" Annie said.

They could go about their daily business, she told them, and call in periodically.

"You don't need any information from us?" Annie said.

"Not now. Maybe later, after we've gotten to know Kelly a little better."

Annie looked at Kelly. "Okay with you?"

"Yeah," Kelly said. "But it won't take long because I've got nothing bad to tell."

Scorn flashed across Mortimer's face before she could suppress it. "We'll take it a step at a time," she said, then looked at O'Keefe and Annie. "Okay?"

They stood. Mortimer reached for Kelly's hand, but Kelly didn't reciprocate. Quickly recovering, Mortimer said, "Okay, Kelly, let's go to the Safe Room," and to the parents, "See you soon. And thank you again for being willing to help the children."

In the corridor, waiting for the elevator, Annie said, "I wanted to tell her that we never saw any sign of anything bad happening at that school."

"Probably exactly why they don't want the parents in there," O'Keefe said. "The kids might be uncomfortable telling things with the parents hovering around."

"You're not thinking there's anything to this, are you?"

"I doubt it. But I do understand the rationale."

But he wasn't as sure as Annie that all was well. It could be a wicked world, and wickedness often hid in the most unlikely places.

CHAPTER ᷾ 10

IN THE SAFE ROOM, Mortimer introduced a man sitting at the long table as Ken Brinkley, the chief investigator for Child Protective Services.

"Ken will be helping us out today."

"Are you a detective?" Kelly asked him.

"I'm not called that," Brinkley said, "but we do pretty much the same thing."

"My dad does that. He's a private eye."

"Yes, we know. Works for the good guys going after the bad guys, right?"

Remembering that her dad had told her more than once that his clients were not always 'good guys,' she said, "Sort of."

Mortimer initiated what became a long, meandering series of questions—about Kelly and her life; how much she remembered of the time when she was younger; about her parents, their divorce, the current living and visitation arrangements, and where she slept at home and at her dad's; whether she liked school and how she was doing there; about friends and boyfriends; whether she'd ever wet the bed; what she was most afraid of and if she had nightmares when she was at Operation Go!, and later, and now.

Kelly didn't mind all of that. It was kind of interesting to examine herself and her life, not something she usually did other than through quick flashes of memory, soon themselves forgotten.

Then Mortimer said, "We're hoping you can help the little kids, like some of the other bigger kids have."

"What bigger kids?"

"Kids like Nate Shapiro and Tricia Ferguson. They were in your class. Do you remember them?"

"Not right now. But I'll think about it."

"Can you sometimes remember things if you think about them for a while?"

"Maybe." But right now she couldn't remember any of the kids in her class except for those she'd continued to be involved with in the years after. And if she couldn't, how had those other older kids remembered all the things they claimed to be able to?

"How did the bigger kids help the little ones?" Kelly asked.

"By being brave enough to tell us about some of the yucky things that happened to them back when they were at the school … the same things the little kids have been telling us about."

"Like what?"

"First, let me ask you a couple of things, okay? Mr. Smith was pretty scary, wasn't he?"

"Not really. He was a black man, and that scared some of the kids."

Brinkley said, "We hear that he's done some bad things, a lot of bad things, to a lot of kids."

"Like who?"

"A bunch of kids have told us about it."

Mortimer took over again. "He hung around in a room down in the basement, didn't he?"

"Yeah. He had it all fixed up. A desk. Even a cot."

"Miss Ginny took you down there sometimes, didn't she?"

"No."

"But you know what it was like. Somebody must've taken you in there."

"No, we sneaked in there sometimes."

"Who's 'we'?"

Kelly thought about it but nothing came to mind. "I forget now."

"And what did he do to you in there?"

"Nothing. He wasn't there."

"But he did do some yucky things to kids in there, didn't he?" Mortimer said.

"Not that I know of … or ever heard anything about."

"Are you sure Miss Ginny didn't take kids in there sometimes?"

"The music and art room was across the hall from his room. She'd take us down there sometimes for those things. It was the nap room too, so she took us down every day for that."

"And to Mr. Smith's room, right?"

"No. I already told you that." *What is it with these people? It's like they didn't hear what I already told them.*

"If a person did something bad, you wouldn't protect them, would you? You wouldn't lie for them?"

"What do you mean by 'bad'?" Kelly asked.

Mortimer took a doll from the cart and pointed at its crotch.

"What if someone touched you down there?"

"I wouldn't let them."

"But when you were three or four or five, you wouldn't have been able to say no."

"Oh, yes I would. I did."

"You did? So someone did touch you there?"

"No. I just meant I wouldn't let them."

"Even when someone was giving you a bath?"

"Well, my parents, yes."

"Your mom?"

"Of course."

"Your dad?"

"Sometimes, yes. Not very often."

"Touched you down there?"

"No. I meant he gave me a bath."

"He never once touched you down there?"

Kelly's eyes narrowed, and her face tightened in suspicion. *What are they doing?* "I don't know. Probably. It was a bath. He might've had me do it myself. I don't remember."

"Do what?"

"Wash myself … down there."

"It can be hard to remember."

"Sometimes." Certainly she didn't really want to think about it.

"But like we discussed, sometimes you think about things for a while, then you remember what you couldn't remember at first."

A moment of silence as the adults looked knowingly at each other.

Mortimer resumed. "Did Miss Ginny ever give you a bath?"

"We didn't take baths at school."

"How about at her house? She babysat you sometimes, didn't she?"

"Sometimes."

"What did Mr. Smith do there?"

"What do you mean? He wasn't there."

"Didn't he work around there some?"

"I don't know. I never saw him there."

"You saw some of the special ceremonies, didn't you?" Brinkley asked.

"What do you mean?"

"Where she set up the altar, dressed funny, said strange prayers … and sometimes did other things—"

"Never," Kelly interrupted. "Who's telling you these things?"

"Lots of kids."

"They're liars."

Brinkley leaned over the table toward Kelly. "You went there a long time ago. You can't speak to what's been happening the past few years. We don't think that all these smart, honest kids can be lying."

"I don't care. I know those things didn't happen. She was the nicest, best teacher I've ever had."

"Your parents were having trouble then, weren't they?" Mortimer said.

Something told her to lie about this. "I don't remember that."

"Surely she undressed you those nights you stayed there … changed you into your pajamas?"

"Probably. I don't really remember."

"I bet she undressed in front of you."

"I don't remember." The questions were tiring. It was like they were trying to put words in her mouth. Responding with "don't know" to anything else they asked her was more than tempting.

"Did you sleep in the same bed with her?"

"No."

"Not even when you got scared?"

"Not that I remember."

"You know how that is. I'm sure your parents let you climb into their beds when you were afraid at night or having nightmares."

"Sometimes."

"Does that still happen?"

"Yeah, even now I can still convince myself sometimes that there's monsters under my bed or behind the shower curtain."

"With your mom?"

"Yeah."

"Your dad?"

Kelly thought about that, then told them no.

Mortimer's eyes narrowed. "You seemed hesitant. Are you sure?"

"I was trying to remember if there's ever been a time, that's all. And I can't think of one."

"And not Miss Ginny? I bet it was scary sleeping in a strange house."

"Not that I remember."

Brinkley butted in. "Where did Ginny sleep?"

"Not sure."

"With her roommate?"

"I don't know."

"You didn't ever see them sleeping together?"

What's that about? "No."

"Did you know the roommate?"

"Not much. Just to say hello to. She wasn't around much when I was there."

Brinkley looked at Mortimer, silently turning things back over to her.

"Did Miss Ginny give you baths those nights you stayed with her?"

"I don't remember. I was little. I don't think I had a bath every day back then."

"You know, sometimes we bury things really, really deep. A lot of the other kids *do* remember. Boys and girls. They've been very honest and brave. We hope you will be too."

"How many? What do they remember?"

"Things like Miss Ginny pulling down their pants, touching them. What do you call your private parts?"

Kelly recoiled slightly. "I just say 'down there.'" They looked at her skeptically, so she offered, "Boobs, I guess. Vagina, I guess … Butt. Toosh."

"Did she ever touch you in any of those places?"

Kelly scoffed. "No!"

"Not even when you needed wiping after you went to the bathroom?"

Kelly flushed in embarrassment. "I don't know. Maybe. I don't remember."

"She never put things in any of those places?"

"Like what?"

"Her fingers?"

Kelly shook her head emphatically. "No."

"Anything else? Spoons. Forks. Knives?"

"No way. That's crazy. Are kids telling you that?"

"Yes. And kissing and licking them there, and making them kiss and lick her."

"Don't be disgusting."

"You really think all those kids are making that up?" Brinkley said.

"What kids?"

"You wouldn't know all the little ones, but, like I said, Nate and Tricia from your class."

"They're lying."

"We don't think so," Brinkley said. "Children don't make up things like that. If you told us something like that, you wouldn't want us calling you a liar, would you?"

"If I was a liar, I should be called that."

"Why would they lie?"

"I don't know."

"Do you ever lie?"

"I have."

"When do you lie?"

"When I'm in trouble, and I think I can get myself out of it."

"How about when you're ashamed?"

"Of what?"

"Of something bad you did."

"I guess."

"Sometimes, when kids have things done to them like Miss Ginny did, they feel guilty and ashamed."

Kelly said nothing. The adults glanced at each other, and gave each other that look like they'd uncovered a secret.

"How about Mr. Smith?" Mortimer asked.

"What about him?"

"Did he ever do any of those things?"

"No."

"If not to you, how about to other kids? Did any of them tell you about that?"

"No."

"Did you ever see his penis?"

"Gross. Of course not. No way."

"Many of the kids have said that Miss Ginny threatened them—that if they told anyone about these yucky, awful things, she'd send Mr. Smith and the devil to kill them and their families."

"That's ridiculous."

"Well, like we've told others, you need to know that they're both going to jail soon, and we've made sure they can't get out and come to hurt you or your parents."

Kelly began to cry. "That's terrible," she said.

"We know. Such terrible things they did—"

"I mean putting them in jail."

This back and forth continued for a while. It was relentless. The same questions over and over. Kelly began to respond the same way each time: "I don't think so," "I don't know," "I don't remember."

Eventually, Mortimer seemed to realize that any further dialogue would be fruitless. Instead she said, "You know, Kelly, after helping children for many years, we've learned that sometimes the more a child can't remember, the more they deny that something's happened, the more likely is that it did. But it was so traumatic … Do you know what that word means?"

Kelly nodded. "I think so."

"It was so traumatic, so disturbing, so shocking that they try to erase it from their minds, bury it deep, like it never happened, because it's too hard to face it."

A long silence ensued, ultimately broken by Mortimer, "We talked before about how sometimes we don't remember something right away, but then we think about it, and it comes back to us. Will you think about these things and meet with us again soon?"

"There's nothing to think about."

"Won't you even help us, help those little kids, just a little, Kelly? Like the other older ones are doing? Can you be brave and at least think about it?"

Agreeing seemed the only way to end this, so that's what Kelly did.

CHAPTER ❧ 11

THEY CALLED ANNIE to tell her she could pick Kelly up.
But she was a real estate broker in the midst of an open house showing she couldn't abandon. She called O'Keefe and asked him to substitute for her. When he arrived, Mortimer met him and led him toward a small conference room while a man escorted Kelly into the waiting room. O'Keefe managed to exchange glances with Kelly. She looked stricken and shook her head, slightly, almost imperceptibly, but that gesture and her eyes and face were strongly signaling "no"—about what he wasn't sure, but it was alarming.

In the conference room with Mortimer, O'Keefe said, "How many of you questioned her?"

"Just me and a colleague. That's for the child's protection."

"Who's the colleague?"

"Ken Brinkley. Chief investigator at Child Protective Services. Lots of experience."

O'Keefe said nothing.

"Kelly either denies that abuse happened or says she doesn't remember. I have to say, she's one of the most resistant children I've ever interviewed. We're very familiar with that situation. It's called Child Sexual Abuse Accommodation Syndrome, and it means the child has been the victim of severe abuse."

O'Keefe made no effort to hide his scorn. "It *always* means that?"

"In my personal experience, yes, always."

"Isn't that a sort of Catch-22? If she admits there was abuse, there was abuse. If she denies it or can't remember it, there was abuse and probably even worse abuse."

"That's correct."

"Excuse me?"

That's how it almost always was, she told him. And almost always the children begin by denying the abuse or saying they can't remember. It's just too traumatic to admit because the abuse implants a sense of guilt and shame in the victims, and they don't want anyone finding out what happened to them. In this case, that impulse to suppress and deny was compounded by threats of harm to the kids and their families. They wanted to help Kelly remember by scheduling another interview a week or so from now "so we can try to gently break through her resistance."

O'Keefe said he'd discuss it with Annie—and Kelly.

"Please ask her mom to call me," Mortimer said, smiled sweetly, and held out her hand. "Nice to meet you. So glad we can help."

At the door, he turned and said, "Just like you tend to believe certain children, I'm likely to believe mine."

That flash of hostility on her face again, quickly suppressed again. He followed her out of the small conference room. Kelly broke from Brinkley, ran to O'Keefe and hugged him so violently it seemed more like an assault than an embrace.

Hicks and Tarwater emerged from the observation area and sat at the conference table with Mortimer and Brinkley.

"You think she might be right?" Hicks said. "Maybe this evil only started recently."

"No," Mortimer said. "It's been going on for a very long time, as some of these older kids are revealing to us. That whole O'Keefe family is in deep denial."

The three others nodded in unison as Mortimer continued, "I'm sure Kelly was abused as much or more than the other children, but it's gone beyond that. You saw what happened with her and her father just now. I have to wonder about him. Can Child Protective open an investigation? Quietly?"

"I sure can," Brinkley said, "and I will. Among other things, they allowed their child to remain in an abusive situation."

In the car on the way home, Kelly tried to convey to her father exactly what had happened in the interview, but it was hard for her to express it. She could only say, "They don't believe me. They've made up their minds. They believe all the lies they'd been told. I think they were trying to get me to lie too."

He'd let her talk all she wanted, tell the whole story. Then she asked if she had to go back. When he told her the clinic had suggested that, she said, "Don't make me. Please don't make me."

Later that evening, her mom interrogated her thoroughly, prying out of Kelly as much as Kelly could remember. After Kelly went to bed, Annie called O'Keefe.

"Why did we let that happen?" she said. "They've made up their minds. They refuse to believe she wasn't abused. They actually think Ginny is a witch or something. They took her through some gross stuff. Talk about abuse. That interview was pornographic. And they were asking about us, about you, about whether you gave her baths and where you might have touched her. They'll be after us next. There's no way she's ever going back there."

He didn't respond, and she wasn't done. "When I put her to bed, she was still crying, and the last thing she said was, 'They're gonna put her in jail, Mom. Dad's got to help her. Please ask him to help her.'"

O'Keefe had a hard time sleeping that night.

The next day he called Scott Hartley. "You still need an investigator?"

AN EDITORIAL STRESSES THE NEED FOR MORE AND BETTER DAY CARE DUE TO SO MANY PARENTS NOW WORKING OUTSIDE THE HOME.

CHAPTER ⟞ 12

HARTLEY DID STILL need an investigator, and O'Keefe could take a bit of satisfaction from making at least one person happy that morning.

Now he needed to deal with the consequences.

First, he called George and Sara into the conference room and told them about his decision. "I promise I'll work like a dog," he said. "But there's no doubt this will limit my time for the work we really want to do and hustling for more business."

George said, "Why do they say, 'work like a dog,' anyway? No offense to Karma, but dogs are about the laziest bums around."

O'Keefe and Sara impatiently acknowledged the attempt at humor with tight smiles and abbreviated chuckles.

"But, more serious," George said, "you ain't exactly gonna be on the popular side of this thing."

"No doubt," O'Keefe said, "You say 'child abuse,' and they reach for the rope. We could lose business now and in the future. I guess I can't do anything but quote Scott Hartley: 'Posterity won't be kind to the cowards.' And my daughter won't either."

The subsequent silence was painful. He wanted to fill it with more words, and more reassuring ones, than those he'd just uttered, but better to leave it to them now.

George came somewhat to the rescue. "I don't need any more business anyway. I've got too damn much to do already."

Sara laughed but turned quickly serious. "Harrigan wouldn't fire us, would he? He wants you full-time on this daisy-chain deal."

"I haven't talked to him yet," O'Keefe said. "I'm sure *he* won't, but it might not be his call. He's not the boss. His client is."

"How sure are you that the lady is innocent?" George said.

"Pretty sure. And if at any point I conclude she's not, I'll quietly resign."

George said, "I don't get it though. You can make it up to Kelly over time. And piss on posterity. Why would you want to stick your neck out on somethin' like this?"

"Not sure. But I think I learned that you can try to ignore it all you want when it's happening to somebody else, but eventually they'll come for *you*."

The second item: Harrigan, who said, after hearing the story, "No matter what I do, I can't seem to keep you out of trouble. Your deep-seated longing for pain and death is just too strong."

"They need to be stopped," O'Keefe said.

"And who appointed you to be the crossing guard?"

"I was trying to mind my own business, but they made theirs mine."

"There's no slack cut to child molesters. Guilt is assumed. Their defenders become pariahs themselves. It'll be a media circus. Can you accept the consequences if all the world hates you?"

O'Keefe laughed. "Actually, I was wondering if you'd be willing to give us some help on this."

It was Harrigan's turn to laugh. "I've got enough things besmirching me at the moment. Have you forgotten that only a hung jury saved me from prison just a few months ago?"

O'Keefe felt a little ashamed. "Okay. I do recall that. But I also recall that the Grail knights often set out *together* into the forest."

"Ouch. But this Miss Ginny's already got a lawyer. Can you honestly say you need me?"

"You told me yourself Hartley's a bit of a greenhorn. He might need help."

"How 'bout you leave me on the bench until I'm really needed?"

"Fair enough."

Harrigan wriggled uncomfortably in his chair. "There's another problem. I just found out the client wants us to take that daisy-chain deal on a contingency, so not only will there be no cash flow on it, we could even be working for nothing."

O'Keefe just sat and looked glum.

"I'm sure I can get someone else," Harrigan said.

"No. But I'll need you to help me talk one of your banker buddies into making me another loan."

Third item: Maura. He'd been tempted to do it over the phone but had bowed to the world's judgment and corresponding expectation that things like this needed to be done in person. He gave her a choice of lunch or a drink after work. "Lunch it'll have to be," she said. "Got to get home to my kid and my studies right after work."

It shouldn't have been a big deal. A year earlier, O'Keefe had lured the divorced mom-cum-paralegal out of semi-hiding and enlisted her to be a powerful witness in the criminal case brought against Harrigan for alleged bank fraud. And she'd been quite a find: vivacious, disarmingly open and honest, and, inexplicably, single, with a history of ill-advised broken relationships.

Their own relationship, if you could even call it that, was a touch-free mutual admiration society involving mild flirtation, nothing more. They'd deliberately kept their distance. Now that gulf was about to close, and the result would be uncomfortable—two people powerfully attracted to each other but resisting the attraction would now be forced to encounter each other on a daily basis.

"So you did decide to go to law school," O'Keefe said. "You were on the fence last time we talked."

"I started in January, but I'm not gonna thank you until I've actually managed to finish. And then I'll *really* thank you."

"You'll finish."

"I have to. I'm terrified I'll have to drop out with a ton of student debt and nothing to show for it."

"I'll help if I can."

"What I hope you'll do is help on this insane case. She's a sweet preschool teacher."

"There's only one thing keeping me from signing up."

"And that is?"

"You."

She straightened, shook her strawberry-blonde curls, opened her lapis-blue eyes extra wide. "*Me?*"

"At the risk of sounding both conceited and presumptuous," he said, "the last thing you said to me was something like, 'You'll be hearing from me.'"

She blushed. "Yeah. But I decided that was too forward, even for me. I thought maybe *you* would call." She looked down. Shame. "You didn't."

"But not because I didn't think about it or didn't want to, and more than once. But I needed to resolve some things before I could be in anyone's company."

"I understand. I read the papers."

"And now I'm trying to put my family back together. Make no mistake though, you're damn near irresistible."

"But not quite."

He paused, trying to dig up a suitable response, but it didn't come, and she finally intervened with "Just kidding, go on."

Relieved, he obeyed. "We'd be working together. That's unavoidable. Constant temptation for me. I'd need your one hundred percent cooperation to keep anything from happening."

She looked at him, a little angry, all resolute. "I would never knowingly try to get in the way of something like that. I would never hurt your former wife, or your daughter, or you … or myself either."

When he didn't respond, she said, "Do you believe me?"

"Based on our prior experience, I don't think there's anyone I'd be more likely to believe."

Her face was a question mark.

"Because you're surely the most open, transparent, candid person I think I've ever met, whether it serves your interests or not."

"You said you were divorced. I'd never have come on to you otherwise."

"I wouldn't call that a come-on."

"Well, let's call it a signal of availability. A damn strong one." He smiled.

"But no more," she said. "You're off limits now." A bleakness rose in her face. "I really know how to pick 'em."

"And now I'm regretting that I got what I wanted."

"The truth is," she said, "I have no time for a relationship anyway. Kid, work, school. All that already takes more than twenty-four-seven. And I'm not quitting. I'm gonna finish. And then *I'll* be the one hiring *you*. How about that?"

They both were quiet for a bit, absorbing what had just happened. Then she said, "But now you have to take the job. You can't put me through that for nothing."

"You realize there's no upside for me in this? None. And it could be a disaster."

She blushed. "I swear I didn't think about that. I guess I should have, but I didn't."

"It's not like the upside your boss is looking at—being the next Clarence Darrow or Atticus Finch."

"You wouldn't get the same benefit?"

"Only if I'm looking for accused child molesters to be lining up outside my door."

"God, I'm so sorry. I didn't think … But you haven't really agreed yet, right? You can back out."

"No. And I'm ashamed. I shouldn't have said that. Just making sure you understand the situation." He smiled. "And that you're aware how heroic I'm being."

"Fear not. I'm very aware."

No, this was not going to be easy.

CHAPTER ☙ 13

HOW DEEP HAD she buried it? And what would leaving it there do to her?

That's what Betsy Mortimer had emphasized and why she and the other clinic people had insisted that it had to be unearthed, brought out from the darkness and into the light. Otherwise it could blight the rest of Misty's life, and she'd never know the source of her suffering. And that was unthinkable.

Dr. Carlyle had validated Mortimer's conclusions. The Save Our Children! parents were equally certain that the abuse had occurred and must be exposed. Ralph Merkel, the group's informal leader, had even visited Amanda at her house, to "offer support" according to Ralph.

At one of the parent meetings, Ralph had introduced the lawyer Perry Slotkin, who'd emphasized that the amount of damages he'd be able to extract from the school's insurance companies would ultimately depend on the extent of the abuse and the certainty that it had occurred. Any expression of doubt could cost them hundreds of thousands of dollars. Misty deserved that money to pay for therapy, didn't she? And she and Mitch deserved their own settlement for the pain and suffering that had been inflicted on them. Yet Mitch seemed so strangely unmotivated by the whole thing. It made her angry, but maybe it was shock, or even shame, that had paralyzed him. Regardless, Amanda would do all she could to make up for his disinterest. If something horrible had happened to her little girl, she intended to get to the bottom of it and help Misty overcome it.

But Misty persisted in her seeming cluelessness, until Mortimer, frustrated by Misty's incomprehension and indifference, had suggested that all three of them meet so therapist and mother together could gently but insistently press Misty in "a special effort to break through," as Mortimer had called it.

Together they'd developed a scenario to open the session with.

Amanda hugged Misty hard and long and said, "I'm so sorry I put you in that school and let that woman babysit you. Tell us what she did to you. Please tell us."

"Okay, Mommy."

"Do your best to remember, okay?"

Mortimer then took Misty on a journey—more dolls and puppets, more genital organs, more suggestions of incidents that might have occurred. But each time that Misty seemed tantalizingly close to disclosure—of *something*, they weren't sure what—it slipped away.

At the end of the session, as Misty played with the Legos she'd been so looking forward to, Mortimer drew Amanda aside.

"She's close, I can feel it. Are you willing to keep working on this?"

"Oh, yes. Nothing is more important."

CHAPTER ⇒ 14

ALL THE LOCAL print and broadcast media attended, even some of the nationals.

They'd scheduled the event for 11 a.m. on a Monday so there'd be plenty of time to flood the evening newspaper and radio and television slots with the sensational story. Donovan Dolinar, the DA's chief trial counsel, and Chief Deputy Rhonda Tarwater, head of the recently formed Child Abuse Unit, sat at a long table in front of a massive screen in the county courthouse's auditorium. Arrayed on either side of them: representatives of the city police department, the metropolitan task force on Satanic and ritual abuse, Child Protective Services, and the therapist and medical advisers from the Children's Clinic.

Dolinar was made for TV. Tall, dark, and lithe. Perfect looking in his perfectly fitting suit. Some said he was downright beautiful. Growing up, he was called "Don" or "Donnie." He put a stop to that after high school when he embarked on a campaign to be called only "Donovan," not Don and *never* "Donnie," saying frequently, "I'll be damned if I'll be a full-grown adult and have people calling me 'Donnie.'" And, like most things he undertook, it had been successful, even with his resistant parents who were reluctant to let go of their beloved little "Donnie."

Dolinar took the podium and introduced Tarwater, who nodded sternly. She might have been considered "handsome," or at least "pleasant looking," if she ever showed to the world a face that was anything but an imperious mask of disdain. She'd finished at the top of her law-school class, was probably the smartest person on the stage, never mind in the DA's office (and that included Dolinar), but her quick-to-judge, censorious nature often clouded her reason and judgment.

Dolinar explained that he wished the child victims could be present, but Betsy Mortimer of the Children's Clinic—he gestured to his left—had advised otherwise. She sat forward slightly, like an eager schoolgirl ready to raise her hand when the teacher asked a question, then acknowledged his gesture with rapidly blinking eyes and bobbing head.

The children, Dolinar said, had already suffered horrific trauma. Publicity around the trial might exacerbate this, and they and their parents should be shielded to the fullest extent possible. He implored the media to respect privacy, protect identities, use pseudonyms, and refrain from physical or other descriptions that might expose them.

Next he announced the indictments, reciting each count's detailed descriptions of how Virginia Montrose and Marvin Smith, sometimes separately and sometimes conspiring together, had sexually assaulted multiple children over a number of years. The children were aged three to six at the time of the molestations. He asserted his belief that there were many other victims who'd either moved out of town or were too afraid to come forward, and *so many more* who had repressed their memories of the traumatic abuse they'd suffered, a typical defensive psychological reaction that required careful therapeutic work to break through.

As he spoke, the auditorium hummed with a constant murmur and even a few outcries from the audience. After finishing his presentation, he gestured toward a small group of people standing to the side. Several carried signs, and said, "We're also working closely with the Save Our Children! parent group, who are assisting with the investigation. And of course we're all doing our utmost to help these children and parents overcome the trauma of these experiences."

A reporter asked, "Will the children be required to testify?"

"It's not appropriate that we discuss our trial tactics at this time, but the children's testimony will likely be essential in order to bring these defendants to justice."

Dolinar then gestured toward the reporter from the *Herald*, who identified himself as Paschal McKenna. Dark Irish. In all respects. Black hair and olive-skin but with a faint but noticeable reddish whiskey sheen on his face. He wore a black leather jacket, dappled with white spots from long and hard use, and a gray string tie cinched with a block of turquoise at the neck of a black shirt. One side of his shirt collar poked up over the lapel of his coat as if standing at attention. Adding to his unruly appearance, his thick, wavy hair had clearly not received that morning the benefit of comb, brush, hair cream, hair spray, or even a sprinkle of water.

"Is it true," he asked, "that there have been extensive interviews of the children by your investigators and therapists?"

"Well, they're not 'our' therapists. They're completely independent."

"Who's paying for their work?"

Taken aback by this cheeky creature in the unusual attire, Donovan hesitated, his typical aplomb momentarily disturbed, seeming uncertain for a moment whether to answer or just brush the guy off, but he finally said, "Child Protective Services, I believe."

"Another government agency, right?"

"Of course."

"And that's the agency that initiated the original investigation and involved your office, correct?"

"Yes."

"Are there tapes of those interviews?"

"I don't believe so," Dolinar said, and looked at Tarwater and then Mortimer for confirmation. Both shook their heads vigorously.

"If," McKenna said, "any do exist, will we be able to review them?"

"If any exist, and you've just been advised that they do not, they would be protected as trial evidence."

"So not released to the press?"

"No."

"But wouldn't you be required to show them to the defense?" McKenna said.

"Maybe. Maybe not. Under the Supreme Court's *Brady* case, as you may already know, that would be required only if they contain evidence that might be favorable to the defense. But we're talking about something imaginary. As we've just confirmed, there are no tapes."

"Is it true that all or most of the children initially denied any molestation?"

"We can't comment on evidentiary details, but if that were true, it wouldn't be surprising. In fact, it would be expected. As any qualified therapist will tell you, denial is a natural response by children who've been traumatized—what the professional literature calls Child Abuse Accommodation Syndrome. But, again, these things aren't appropriate for discussion at this time. Thank you for your attention."

And that was clearly all Donovan Dolinar was going to say.

As soon as the legal team left the room, the reporters descended upon the Save Our Children! group. One parent had positioned himself at the front. McKenna shoved his way through the throng and said, "Is your child one of the victims?"

"Yes," he said. "My son."

"Are you willing to give us your name, sir?" McKenna said.

"Yes, Ralph Merkel. I don't believe I can be an effective advocate for our children if I hide my identity. My son is a strong young man. He will come through this … is already coming through this."

"Is this an organized group?"

"Yes. Our name is a call to arms: Save Our Children!. We meet regularly to share information and otherwise contribute to the investigation. There are forces that would very much like to strangle this in the cradle by casting doubt on the children, claiming the children are liars. But we believe the children, and we intend to advocate for them to the end of the world."

CHAPTER ॐ 15

IN LATE JUNE the heat descended and locked down on the city, the region, the country, and refused to budge.

They called it a wave. If so, it was a wave that refused to break. Temperatures routinely reached above 100 degrees, sometimes 110. Heat deaths soared. By August, 62.5% of the continental United States was officially in drought, "burning away" the country's corn crop. At a heavy metal rock concert at the local stadium, dozens collapsed from the heat and had to be carried out on stretchers. On August 6, Harvard University closed for a day, the first time in its 353-year history that it had closed due to heat. Manhattan suffered massive blackouts. An Amtrak train derailed due to heat-warped tracks. When rain occasionally fell, it poured, usually accompanied by hailstorms and devastating tornadoes. A conference convened in Toronto on global warming and the pernicious effect of fossil fuels. Newspaper articles referred to the "ozone problem" and "the greenhouse effect" that was warming the earth, and warned of an impending global environmental crisis. Planet Earth itself was described as saying, "I'm tired as hell and I'm not going to take it anymore."

O'Keefe spent two days preparing for the next few months as if for a military campaign, mapping out the days, weeks, and months ahead in order to spread himself necessarily thinly but as effectively as possible across his various responsibilities: Ginny's case, the daisy-chain deal, consulting with George as needed to ease his burdens, somehow continuing his efforts to build the agency's business, and spending time with his daughter.

He met with Hartley and two of his associates. One, Rob Nugent, only a year out of law school. The other, Ben Lerner, the "veteran," out of law school for only four years. Plus paralegal Maura Davis. The waters, it seemed, were muddied. In civil cases, discovery rules and associated procedures—written interrogatories and depositions primarily—allowed both sides to greatly reduce if not eliminate the element of surprise from the trial.

Not quite so in a criminal case, Hartley explained, "States vary, but in this state, no depositions, so no way to talk to prosecution witnesses except under exceptionally extraordinary circumstances unless they voluntarily agree to be questioned—which they usually don't. Yeah, it's true that the prosecutor has the duty to hand over anything in the prosecution files that's favorable to the defense. But that lets *them* decide what *they* think is favorable, and that leaves a lot of room for abuse. It means that the investigative work is more critical in a criminal case."

Wonderful, O'Keefe thought. *Even more of a burden, and not just with someone's pocketbook at risk, but their freedom, maybe their entire life, or the quality of it anyway.*

"So, what do they have that we know about?" Hartley said. "The testimony of the children. That buries us in a deep hole right there because people won't believe that children would make this stuff up. And even if some of it does lack credibility, they'll argue that there must be some truth to at least some of it."

"'Where there's smoke,'" O'Keefe said. "I said that very thing myself when I first heard about this."

"And that's close to a stake in our heart right from the get-go," Hartley said. "How could kids just make all that up? They don't know enough to make up that kind of stuff. We have to"— and he raised his arms to indulge his penchant for making air quotes— "'believe the children,' especially when there's a courtroom full of parents demanding blood. How does a juror tell those parents through a not-guilty verdict that they think their kids are liars?

And the hell of it is that a lot of the kids *aren't* liars. Not in the usual sense anyway.

"They've been brainwashed by these so-called therapists and sent to a doctor who's guaranteed to confirm that they've been abused. So the parents can't help but continue to interrogate the kids, frown at them or worse, and demand they tell them the so-called truth, and then reward them accordingly."

He stopped—a theatrical moment, as if in the courtroom, playing to the jury. "And on top of that, we'll face the parents' testimony about how the kids had exhibited 'behaviors' supposedly signaling they'd been abused even though such behaviors are quite common to non-abused kids as well. And worse, the parents might be allowed to repeat what the kids supposedly told them about the abuse, even though it's hearsay. But in other cases around the country, they've found ways to get it in front of the jury anyway. And the legislatures are passing laws that make it easier to get this particular type of hearsay into evidence for the specific purpose of making it easier to convict child molesters."

O'Keefe said, "Never understood that 'hearsay' thing."

"Most lawyers don't either, and sometimes I'm one of them."

He went on to explain that hearsay is a statement made outside of the courtroom by *anyone,* "including even the witness that's on the stand—and here's where it starts to get weird—it's only hearsay *if* the statement is being offered to establish *the truth of the content of the statement.*

"That concept might seem simple, but it's actually incredibly complex, often misunderstood, and subject to a litany of exceptions, creating a conceptual thicket that even experienced trial lawyers sometimes get lost in."

O'Keefe looked no less confused than before. "'Offered for the truth?'"

"If you, Pete, tell me, Scott, that Rob here made a pass at my wife, if you're offering that to prove that Rob actually made a pass at my wife, it's inadmissible hearsay. But what if Rob got shot soon after that and I'm being accused of killing him? You're not offering it for its truth that Rob made a pass at my wife. You're offering it to show why I might've had a motive to shoot Rob."

"Got it … I think, sort of," O'Keefe said.

"Good," Scott said, "but as soon as you get it, you'll probably lose it, because even if something *is* hearsay, there's more than thirty exceptions to the rule, so it might be allowed in anyway. The big one for us is the exception for statements made in connection with a medical diagnosis, physical or psychological. Not just statements to doctors. Could be to a social worker or other therapist, like Betsy Mortimer, or even maybe to the parents. They'll probably claim the whole process was about diagnosing and treating the kids, which means everything the kids said can come in."

"And," Rob said, "those stories were the ones those very therapists had planted in the kids' heads in the first place.

"Exactly," Hartley said.

Hartley continued on in this vein for a while until O'Keefe's head hurt. By the end of Hartley's presentation, O'Keefe was impressed by Hartley but depressed about Ginny's chances. "So what's our winning strategy then?" he said.

"There's no corroborating evidence for any of the children's stories. Why? Because the crimes never occurred. They couldn't have occurred without someone seeing or at least suspecting something. The kids have been brainwashed. The therapists terrified the parents into hysteria. The parents then either further terrified or rewarded their kids for faithfully repeating the stories, being good puppets for the therapist ventriloquists. The medical people are just rubber-stamping the therapists. The evidence of abuse doesn't exist except in the minds of the therapists, but they successfully triggered these kids' fantasies."

O'Keefe felt a little bit better, even if it hadn't quite been a Knute Rockne halftime rouser. "How do you prove the brainwashing?"

"Not sure. They didn't tape the interviews. In the McMartin case out in California, they taped all the initial interviews so the jury out there will be able to see how the brainwashing worked from the initial tapes to the final courtroom testimony. In our case, they say they taped nothing, so all the jury will see is the final finished, spit 'n' polished product."

"When do I get to talk to Ginny?" O'Keefe said.

"Yes, you should hear directly from her, not just through my filter. We'll go together, but I'll try to be quiet. She knows you've signed on to help her."

"What'd she say?"

"It was over the phone, so I don't know what she was thinking. Working that out is hard enough even when she's right in front of you. She's reserved, opaque. I worry about what impression that'll make on the jury."

"Will you put her on the stand?"

"Too early to tell. But I'm making her think she'll have to."

O'Keefe had barely spoken to Ginny outside of parent-teacher conferences. They were alike in many ways. Quiet, shy, uncomfortable with small talk. She would hardly even say "hello." Even her smile was barely more than a suggestion. She was tiny, her hair short and dark, her eyes darker, solemn, cautiously curious and framed by thick, black-rimmed glasses. Her skin tone suggested Southern European or South Asian ancestry. She somehow transmitted a preternatural calmness that Kelly seemed to have understood and appreciated right away.

The interview would occur in the jail, Hartley said, because bail had been set at an amount that was impossible to pay.

"Why so high?" O'Keefe asked.

Hartley's jaw tightened and his eyes flashed. "At the bail hearing, the parents testified that their children had told them that Virginia and Marvin had threatened that if they ever revealed to anyone what had been done to them, they, and Satan himself, would come to their homes in the night and slit their throats."

RAMBO III IN THEATRES.

CHAPTER ॐ 16

IT WASN'T THE first time O'Keefe had visited this place— but that other time he'd been on the other side of those steel bars.

Cocaine could be such a wondrous thing. Until it wasn't.

Almost five years ago. The second day—or was it the third?—of a coke binge. Thundering along in his car. Everything blasting—the engine, his head, the tape deck playing Steppenwolf's "Born to Be Wild." His hands pounding the steering wheel, alternating hands—right twice, left once, right twice to the thump of the music. The goddamn light turns red. He slams on the brakes, slides sideways into the intersection. No cars coming. Wipes his fingers through the powder he's spilled onto the console, thrusts them into his nose, rubs whatever might be left on his nostrils. On the corner a mother and her little girl, maybe six or seven years old. The mother is frightened, disgusted. Yanks the daughter against her body and bends down, sheltering her. Sheltering her from that awful man. Him. The daughter was about Kelly's age.

A few blocks later, he stops, tires screeching, in front of a sign. *Harvey's Bar & Grill*. He's in a delivery zone, no parking. But he doesn't know or doesn't care. Rifles through the console, tossing items here and there, extracts a baggy. Not much powder left in it. Fuck. The last one. He stuffs it in his jacket pocket.

Harvey—grizzled, aging hippie—is tending bar. He eyes O'Keefe warily. O'Keefe is his friend, but not always welcome.

O'Keefe locks eyes with a customer swaying on a bar stool. Ugly fucker. Just emerged from a cave. Caveman. Fucking Alley Oop … Boop Boop.

O'Keefe climbs onto a stool a couple of stools away from Caveman. He looks at Harvey. Neither speaks for a long time, like two combatants sizing each other up before they engage.

Eventually Harvey says, "You in trouble?"

"I am become death, the destroyer of worlds."

Harvey—confused, irritated, on guard—says, "Well, not in here. Take that shit outside."

Caveman smirks. O'Keefe notices.

O'Keefe is on his second beer with Wild Turkey back when Harvey cautiously ventures some small talk, "I haven't seen your pal Harrigan lately."

"Probably at work right now."

"On Sunday night?"

"Workaholic."

"Worst kind of 'aholic there is. I like your kind better."

"He's one of my kind too. Just hangin' on for dear life to a shred of respectability."

"Yuppie," Harvey said. "Whole world's becomin' fuckin' yuppies. I remember you two the first time you came in here. Not even of age. Fake IDs. I served you anyway. Never would've guessed he'd end up a yuppie."

"Me neither. Back then we were poets ... and Grail knights."

"Silly fuckers," Harvey says.

"Goofy fuckers," the swaying Caveman says.

"Who invited you to this party?"

"Nobody. I'm crashin' it anyway."

"Nobody'd let you come to their party. You're too fuckin' ugly, Caveman. I mean, really fuckin' ugly. Unforgivable ugly."

Off the stool the Caveman comes. O'Keefe meets him with full force, bowls him over, smashes him to the floor. They roll over and over.

"Shit, here we go again," Harvey says, reaching for the phone.

They'd come to get him the next morning, told him he was being released. He didn't know why, but there was no alternative but to go along as they escorted him into the public waiting room where Michael Harrigan stood jingling his car keys and slicing O'Keefe with razor eyes, dressed all in blue: suit, striped shirt, tie, cufflinks, Cartier watch with a lizard-skin band, all of it blue. Even his shoes were navy. Even his underwear was probably some shade of blue.

"Well, Sir Gawain," Harrigan said with a sour smile and in sardonic tone, "looks like you haven't found the Grail yet."

O'Keefe shrugged.

They left the jail and walked to Harrigan's car.

"I'm hungry as hell," O'Keefe said.

"Coke binge'll do that, eh? Wish whiskey had the same effect. I just wanna puke in the morning."

On Harrigan's windshield, a parking ticket.

"Fuck. That'll cost me fifty bucks. On top of the thousand for your bail."

"Add it to my tab."

Harrigan gestured toward a building down the street. "Let's walk over to *Bonnie's*. I already got the ticket, might as well leave the car here."

At *Bonnie's*, O'Keefe studied the menu while Harrigan studied O'Keefe.

Without looking up, O'Keefe said, "Sorry about the thousand. I'll pay you back."

"How might you go about doing that?"

The waitress arrived, looked skeptically at O'Keefe, and cocked her head to focus on his swollen and discolored left eye.

"Who won?"

"I don't remember."

Harrigan said, "Just black coffee for me."

O'Keefe said, "Is your sausage link or patty?"

"We got both."

"Two eggs basted. Patty sausage. Hash browns super well done. Crispy, crispy. Near burnt. Same with the toast. Wheat. What kind of jelly?"

"The standard. Strawberry. Grape."

"Nothing else?"

Harrigan squirmed impatiently.

"Something called 'Mixed Berry.'"

"I'll have that. And a pancake."

"Jesus!" from Harrigan.

"Pancake," she said, emphasizing the singular. "We don't serve just one."

"I'll pay for a short stack, but I only want one."

Harrigan again, "He means *I'll* pay. He hasn't got a pot to piss in."

Now O'Keefe: "Don't pay any attention to him. I'm a ventriloquist. He's my dummy."

"Then both of you are in a really bad way."

"But just one pancake. Extra jelly. I do jelly on pancakes, not syrup. And really well done. All the way through. Not soft and gooey in the middle."

She addressed herself to Harrigan: "Your ventriloquist is quite special, isn't he?"

"Oh, yes. A Knight of the Grail."

She left. O'Keefe looked around, searching for enemies.

"Nobody's after you here," Harrigan said. "That shit's making you paranoid."

"Paranoids have enemies too."

"You weren't even smart enough to get rid of the coke. Now you're facing a possession charge."

"Thought I'd give you a chance to see if you're a real lawyer, not just an office pogue."

Harrigan was fed up with smart-ass banter that disguised the real problem and its gravity. "This is it, man. They've repo'd your car, your landlord is evicting you, no gainful employment, though the cops think you're probably dealing now to support your habit. You've thrown away your family—"

"'Freedom's just another word for nothin' left to lose.' I thought that was our motto. I guess not yours anymore."

Harrigan noticed O'Keefe eyeing a middle-aged male diner a couple of booths down and across the aisle who was likewise staring at O'Keefe. Having fixed his gaze on the man, O'Keefe said loudly, "What're you lookin' at?"

"Shit," Harrigan said, "don't get a brawl goin' in here. Switch places."

Harrigan stood up and gestured to O'Keefe to switch places so O'Keefe would have his back to the customer. O'Keefe grudgingly complied.

After switching places, Harrigan said, "So you're just gonna go and slide off the end of the world, is that it? What's wrong with you? Is it Vietnam again?"

It flashed. Men. Bloody, wounded, dying, groaning, screaming men. Scratching, scrambling, being loaded, stuffed, dumped into a helicopter. O'Keefe inside, eyes bulging, firing his M60 over the heads of his comrades, firing blindly into whomever and whatever else might be in the vicinity—beast, man, woman, or child, it didn't matter.

"You're headed for real jail this time," Harrigan said. "Prison."

A long silence.

"But it just so happens that one of the main guys in the prosecutor's office was a law school buddy of mine. I told him your story. Vietnam, etcetera. And our story. Blood brothers, Grail knights, all that stuff. I said I would take a modicum of responsibility for you if they would just give you a pass on this."

"Don't stick your neck out for me. Maybe I don't want a pass."

"What else do I have a neck for? I told them I'd give you a job and work my ass off to keep you straight. They'll hold on the prosecution. If you stay straight long enough, they'll dismiss it."

"I'm not exactly in the best position to start on my law degree."

"No law degree. I need an investigator. I can't afford a real one, but I can probably afford a semi-slave, being you. I'll give you enough to scrape by on and pay for the drug tests you'll be doing frequently. And eventually you'll be able to go out on your own."

O'Keefe started shaking his head in protest and denial.

"Don't shake your fucking head. Surrender. Give it up. Marx and Engels, man: 'You've got nothin' to lose but your chains.'"

"What bullshit. Chains. How 'bout your chains, Mr. Yuppie? I thought we were gonna be dead by thirty-five anyway. 'Only the good die young.'"

"I guess I had the misfortune to grow up … slightly."

"Grow up to be what? Some slickster who doesn't believe in shit anymore Drinks like a fish and would likely fuck a rock if he sniffed a snake under it? You're about two steps behind me, and it's comin' for you too."

"Does that rebel despair shit really make you feel better? What wonderful things are *you* believin' in these days? What about Kelly? Her father not only abandons her. Now he's a jailbird too. In what fucking world do you live in where Kelly deserves *you* as a father?"

No answer for that one. That one's not to be shrugged off. A slight nod to Harrigan. The barb has stuck in his heart.

Harrigan noticed that the customer who had previously been staring at O'Keefe was now staring at Harrigan.

"What the fuck are you lookin' at?" he said.

The customer looked quickly away.

Harrigan looked back at O'Keefe.

Raucous laughter.

The jailer came out and gestured to them to follow him back to visit Ginny. O'Keefe had been guilty, but been saved. Ginny was innocent, but would she?

CHAPTER ≋ 17

IN THE SPECIAL interview room, O'Keefe examined the ceiling and walls, then the metal chairs and the metal table at which they sat.

"Any suspicion they might be bugging this place?"

Hartley shook his head. "Plenty of smart and paranoid lawyers visit their clients here. I've never heard one of them even suggest that possibility. I guess it could happen, but if it got out, a whole bunch of cops would end up on the wrong side of the bars here."

"I don't suppose they'd let me bring in my tech guy to check the place?"

"Not a chance."

A hulk of a guard, more than twice her height and breadth, escorted Ginny into the room. She looked like his tiny child. She wore a prison jumpsuit surely worn by many before her and faded by countless launderings to the same soul-depleting gray as the prison walls themselves. The pathos of that scene almost overwhelmed O'Keefe. He had to struggle mightily to stifle tears.

O'Keefe stood to greet her, a deliberate gesture of respect. Hartley seemed surprised by that and, after a brief hesitation, also stood.

O'Keefe had no idea what to say. Certainly not "how are you?" Even "hello" seemed inappropriate. So he only tendered his hand. She took it, pressing so gently he could hardly feel it. Her dark eyes had lost any spark, any life they had ever expressed, now just dead embers of shame.

They sat down, and the guard receded to a space within line of sight but out of earshot.

"Kelly said to give you her best," O'Keefe said. "Annie too. All the O'Keefes are with you."

She lowered her head. "Thank you, Mr. O'Keefe," she said, as if she were still a teacher and he a parent to whom respect must be tendered. "And please tell them 'thank you' for me."

He thought she might weep, but she didn't. She seemed to have shrunk even further into herself, more distant than ever.

"To get things underway," Hartley said, "I'll start with the most obvious question. Are you innocent?"

She looked at them as if the question was ridiculous, then said softly, "I am."

O'Keefe asked, "Is there any truth to *any* of it? If there is, I won't judge you"—a lie—"but you have to be completely honest with us."

"None of it's true."

"Maybe something innocently intended that was misinterpreted?"

"No."

"Virginia," Hartley said, "tell Pete about Randy Lowe." He looked at O'Keefe. "That's the source. That's where it all began."

She looked at Hartley, her face still impassive, but those dead eyes sparked for a moment, with pain. "Do I have to? Can't you?"

"You need to get used to telling it, Virginia. You'll have to on the witness stand."

Her voice when she spoke was so low that O'Keefe had to lean forward to make out the words.

"Randy came to school one day with a bruise on the side of his face, near his eye. I asked him what happened. He said he'd fallen down. He said it angrily, like he wanted to close down the conversation. So I left him alone. When his mother came to pick him up that day, I asked her about it, and she answered the same way. Said he'd fallen down. Said he was 'a klutz.'"

"These Lowe parents were nothing but trouble," Hartley said. "Frequently late bringing him and picking him up … and paying the tuition. The school had to send letters almost every month threatening to expel him if they didn't pay. Right, Virginia?"

She nodded but said nothing more until he coaxed her. "Go on."

"A couple of weeks later, Randy came to school with a sprained wrist. Again, I asked him about it. He said the same thing as before. So did his mom. They used the exact same words, like it was rehearsed. I watched them out the window as she led him to the car. He was dawdling, and she grabbed his arm and yanked him. Hard. Too hard, I thought. She was sort of dragging him along. He resisted, and she yanked him even harder."

O'Keefe tried to recall if he or Annie had ever yanked Kelly like that. He had to acknowledge that was possible.

"The next day I noticed him favoring that arm and wincing on occasion," Ginny said. "When she came to pick him up, I took her aside and told her about my concerns—the injury and what I'd seen in the parking lot. I told her that I wouldn't report it this time, but that if there was another incident, I would have to, that I would have no choice.

"And what did Mrs. Lowe say to that?" Hartley asked.

"She said, 'What are you accusing me of?' And I said, 'I'm not accusing. I'm just telling you that I have a legal duty.' And she said, 'I told you what happened. It wasn't us. It was him.' And I told her again what I'd seen. And then her eyes got really big and her face really red, and she grabbed Randy by the arm and yanked him. Not as hard as before, but obviously, and she stared at me, like she was daring me. Then she marched out, him running along to keep up with her…"

She had trailed off again. It seemed like she was having a hard time catching the next breath.

"And?" Hartley prompted.

"I got a phone call. From her husband." She looked imploringly at Hartley. "Do I have to repeat what he said?"

"Yes," Hartley said, his tone sternly commanding.

"He called me a … fucking bitch. Said I was fucking around with the wrong people. That if I kept it up, they'd destroy me."

Scott prompted her again, and she continued.

"It was a while after that I began hearing that Mrs. Lowe was saying some bad things about me. Then Mr. Brinkley from Child Protective Services and Ms. Hicks and another police officer came to my house and took me to the station."

"For what reason?"

She didn't answer.

Most women O'Keefe knew would have wept at that point, maybe even before. Not Ginny. Instead, she seemed bewildered. Like she couldn't believe the horror story she'd found herself living in from the moment she'd answered that knock at her front door.

Hartley answered his own question. "For sexual assault and molestation of one Randy Lowe. So her misguided act of mercy or kindness—"

"Wrong," Ginny said.

Her emphatic tone caught O'Keefe off guard.

"I was wrong," she said. "I should have reported it. I had a duty."

"That's the last time I want to hear you say that," Hartley said.

"If I would've just reported it …

"You would still be exactly where you are," Hartley said.

"Did you tell them about the abuse incident?" O'Keefe asked.

"Yes."

"And?"

Ginny just shook her head.

"It made things worse," Hartley said. "Remember, these are the guys that wouldn't accept her clean polygraph. In fact, Hicks said to me later: 'Your client is the worst of the worst. Concocting that abuse story, accusing those parents to try to cover her own disgusting crimes.' Then the other accusations and charges started. And here we are."

O'Keefe asked, "How are you doing in here?"

"They have her in isolation," Hartley said, "supposedly for her own protection."

"They hate me in here," she said.

"The guards?" O'Keefe said.

"All of them. The prisoners too. They scream at me, call me a monster, curse and spit at me, and throw things at me when I walk by their cells."

Addressing both of them, O'Keefe said, "Anything we can do to make things better?"

An involuntary half shake of Hartley's head. "I'll make a complaint, but I doubt it will do much good. I'll keep at it."

She only looked hopeless and said, "I don't know what it could be. Other than keep bringing me things to read. Maybe some of these?"

She handed over a note she had been squeezing in her hand. O'Keefe took it, glanced at it. One of the items was the King James Bible. *So it's that bad,* he thought.

"We can do that. How about if Annie and Kelly bring them when they come to visit?"

"Oh, no. They shouldn't come to this place."

"Oh, no. Even if I wanted to, I couldn't stop them … with an army."

CHAPTER ⚜ 18

IN THE CAR and continuing in the conference room at his office, Hartley filled in more of the story.

"A few days after the confrontation with Ginny, Heidi Lowe began her campaign. She called every parent she could and told them, 'They're doing horrible things at that school. My son's teacher, that Ginny witch, started by fondling him, playing with his pee-pee when supposedly helping him go potty.' And that was only a start. According to Mrs. Lowe, Virginia supposedly moved on to performing oral sex on Randy and enticing him to perform the same on her."

And she claimed Randy told her Virginia's been doing all this to other kids too. From Randy who can barely talk? No way. But in the panic nobody bothered to consider that. The parents started interrogating their children. In the meantime, Mrs. Lowe also had the gall to report Virginia to Child Protective Services and the police."

The police department itself seemed not to know what to do with her complaint, at least until the Child Protective people intervened. Ken Brinkley of Child Protective had been attending seminars on Satanic and ritual abuse for several years and was a member of the task force. "And Ken was rarin' to go. He covered every base he could, lobbying not only the police but the District Attorney's office, which had recently formed its own Child Abuse Unit, which also has responsibility for prosecution of Satanic crimes. And our friend, Chief Deputy Tarwater, is in charge of both units and serves as the office's delegate on the task force. That's where she buddied up with Ken Brinkley.

"Enter Sally Hicks, the city police rep on the task force. The mighty triumvirate of Brinkley, Tarwater, and Hicks interviewed the Lowes, who'd initially refused to let them talk directly to Randy. But eventually they allowed it. When they did talk to him, he apparently did nothing more than bob his head up and down a couple times."

Realizing they had no competence to interview such a young child, they hired the Children's Clinic in the person of Ms. Betsy Mortimer, another task-force member, who was rarin' to go herself. After several hours with her dolls, puppets, and Randy, she concluded that the boy had indeed been sexually molested by Virginia on multiple occasions.

"Not that Randy himself recounted these things. He was incapable of that even if those things were true. I can't wait to cross-examine him—gently of course. He won't be able to credibly confirm those lies.

"But the ever-resourceful Ms. Mortimer managed to get around that by basing her conclusions not on what he actually said, but instead on certain reactions that Randy exhibited during her interrogations and by recent behaviors recounted by his mother. Bed-wetting, for example. Nightmares, for example. No, I'm not kidding you. Those had now become evidence that he'd been molested."

The squad then moved on to other parents identified by Heidi Lowe as those with children who'd been similarly abused. A few had questioned their children, all of whom had initially denied that any molestation had occurred. "Can you tell that's a constant refrain? Denial, denial, denial. The kids say it never happened. And most of the parents initially"—air quotes again— "'believed the children.'"

But a few families had expressed concerns about their children's "disturbing" new behaviors, the very type of behaviors that Mrs. Lowe had described and Ms. Mortimer had ferreted out. And some of the children had given evasive responses when questioned about what might have happened at the school. "These children were taken to the Children's Clinic, and guess what—Mortimer and her puppet detectives concluded they'd been molested."

"By Ginny?" O'Keefe said. "No other teachers?"

"Not then. There were some accusations against other teachers, even the school principal, floated later, but they didn't go anywhere. I think that was Donovan Dolinar's influence. He wanted to keep the thing manageable, not a circus like the McMartin case out in California and some others."

"How about Marvin Smith, the janitor?"

"One set of parents reported that their four-year-old son was especially afraid of 'the Negro janitor,' as they described him. Then our inimitable sleuths unearthed some especially damning evidence. Virginia often went out of her way to be nice to him, like bringing him cookies and other treats for his lunch. And, further, it turned out he'd done some handyman-type work at her home. Hmm. Suspicious. That really made them stroke their chins.

"Mr. Smith's role rapidly expands from there. In short order it occurred to our Inspector Clouseau group that they might have uncovered a pattern of sexual molestation going on for the entire time Virginia had taught there. That speculation led Hicks and Brinkley to recommend to their respective agencies that any parent with a child who'd been to Operation Go! during Virginia's entire tenure, all those years, be contacted.

"So every child that was ever in Ginny's class was now a possible victim," O'Keefe said.

"Exactly," Scott replied, "and some of those kids are now as old as twelve."

They obtained records from the school, compiled a list of names and addresses of all children who had attended during those years, whether they were in Virginia's class or not, and sent a letter to the parents.

"And here was the fateful moment. The letter."

Hartley slid a piece of paper across the table to O'Keefe. "Have a look."

It was on the letterhead of the Metropolitan Police Department. O'Keefe read:

To: Whom It May Concern:
Re: Operation Go! Preschool

Records indicate that your child or children attended the Operation Go! preschool. Based on complaints we have received from several parents, we have initiated an investigation involving alleged child molestation by two employees of the school—one female, one male. We are taking this extraordinary step to make sure our investigation is complete.

Both male and female students are alleged to have been victims. Allegations include a broad range of molestation from the fondling of genitals under the pretext of helping children go to the toilet or taking their temperatures to sodomy including oral, vaginal, and anal sex.

Some of these were allegedly committed on school grounds, especially in the napping area and in the basement boiler room, but also at the home of the female employee.

It has been reported that some of these activities were accompanied by what are commonly called "Satanic rituals," such as praying to Satan and other devil-worshipping activities, blood-drinking (animal and human), and even animal and perhaps human sacrifice.

We have consulted child-development and psychology educators, who have indicated that the following behaviors are often indications that sexual abuse has occurred: nightmares, biting, spitting, bed-wetting, masturbation, constipation, vaginal and anal redness, and bladder infections.

Please question your child about whether they may have been witnesses to or victims of such crimes.

Sincerely,

Myra Hicks
Detective

CHAPTER ☙ 19

O'KEEFE FINISHED READING, and Hartley said, "You didn't receive that letter?"

"No, but we'd long since moved … Divorce."

"What's your reaction to that list of behaviors?"

"Biting, spitting, constipation, etcetera. They just seem like part of growing up. Spitting? Is that a joke?"

"But I submit that receiving that letter would have at least got your attention. You might even have been scared shitless. And you'd've at least questioned your kid some."

"That was my exact reaction when I did hear about this," O'Keefe said.

"Of course. And now those behaviors you thought might be attributable to normal child development could be attributable to someone else's nefarious interference.

"And while all of this initially produced only denials from the children and negative or inconclusive findings by almost all the professionals, Brinkley, Hicks, and Tarwater referred all of the concerned parents to the Children's Clinic. Well, that was all she wrote. Literally. Betsy Mortimer never met an Operation Go! kid who wasn't molested."

"What about the parents who didn't buy in?"

"Shouted down, shunned, and shamed into silence. They were branded as negligent parents, dupes, or maybe even abusers themselves. There were even threats of physical violence," Scott said. "You should listen to some of the voicemails they've left on my phone."

"I should," O'Keefe said. "For your sake, your staff's sake, maybe even mine. And make sure those aren't erased."

"We'll arrange it."

"And what about Mr. Smith?"

"The prosecutors loved that development. A conspiracy, a cabal, someone to provide the muscle, and, oh how delicious, a possible interracial sexual thing, still distasteful to a lot of people."

"And you're not representing him?"

"No. Too much possibility of conflict between their interests. In fact, first thing I'm filing is a motion to try their cases separately."

"So who is?" O'Keefe asked.

"Legal Aid. My old employer. They didn't assign their best person. An old friend of mine named Lou Rockwell. They're scared to death like everyone else."

"Nobody standing up?"

"A couple of parents, like you, are hanging in, but they have no impact. I went to the ACLU. They clammed right up. They're willing to defend the rights of the Klan to go on TV and spew hate but won't speak a single word of caution against lynching an accused child abuser."

"When will this go to trial?" O'Keefe asked.

"As fast I can get it there while still doing the right thing for Virginia. And, no, it's not because I'm afraid we'll run out of retainer. As long as we put together the best defense case we reasonably can, there's no reason to have this drag on for months or years like some of the other cases. Ours is a lot simpler. And you saw her today. So sad. Let's get her out of there as fast as we can. If we can't, what difference does it make? There won't be much left of her."

"What a clusterfuck," O'Keefe said. "How about hunkering down and letting the witch hunt panic run its course and die down?"

Hartley squinted. The issue obviously troubled him. "It hasn't done that anywhere else. The parents and the prosecution have been as fanatical at the end as at the beginning. There's no sentence other than death that'll satisfy them, and I'm not so sure about even that. They'd burn her at the stake if they could."

Back at the office, Hartley called his tiny working group together. Ben Lerner, the most senior associate, needed to be left out of Ginny's case as much as possible so someone in the office could be available to deal with other matters, which left only Maura, still in law school, and Rob Nugent, a year out of law school. Hartley introduced O'Keefe, brought everyone up to date on latest developments, and laid out the strategy going forward.

Rob and Maura left the meeting, each bearing a list of research and drafting assignments, leaving O'Keefe and Hartley alone in the conference room.

"What about me?" O'Keefe said.

"What would you put on your list?" Hartley said.

"First," O'Keefe said, "how about a thorough site visit and scene reconstruction? That might reveal a number of things. Like how all these terrible things could've been done in that physical space without anyone knowing about it."

"Good," Scott said.

"How about background on the prosecution's therapists and doctors?"

"My people are supposed to be doing that, but we might need help at some point."

"And," O'Keefe said, "background on all the parents whose kids are named in the indictment, especially the Lowes."

Scott nodded. "Yeah. And next that maniac Ralph Merkel."

When O'Keefe rose to leave, Hartley said, "And speaking of bankrupting the client, can you send me weekly bills so I can stay right on top of that? I have to manage the retainer very carefully."

"I'll send you the bills, but you can wait until the end to pay me."

"That's not smart."

"I know. But let's see where we end up."

80,000 FARMERS ARE SCHEDULED TO RECEIVE FORECLOSURE NOTICES.

CHAPTER ⇛ 20

"**H**ERE'S THE LATEST," Hartley said at the beginning of their daily phone conference.

"The famous Reverend Billy Bitson is on his way here from Baton Rouge.

"'Why?' might you ask … Answer: to perform an exorcism.

"'On whom or on what?' you might ask … Answer: the building that until so recently housed the darling and dynamic little forward-thinking preschool known as Operation Go!."

O'Keefe listened with growing irritation, then disgust, and finally anger as Hartley verbally painted Bitson's garish portrait.

In his twenties Billy had discovered that he'd been vouchsafed a special personal relationship with God. By the early 1970s, God had revealed to the now "Reverend" Bitson (though he and everyone else still referred to him as "Billy") that America had given itself over almost entirely to Satan and thus become a sewer of corruption and depravity. Wasn't the evidence everywhere in that evil decade? Hence, Billy's God had directed Billy to seize the sword and smite the doers of such evil. Billy had enthusiastically obliged by embarking on a career as a popular radio and television preacher, dedicating himself in fanatical particular to the sacred mission of warning the world of the spreading Satanic contagion and calling out the devil's disciples everywhere he could detect them.

It had taken considerable time, but a decade later, in the early 1980s, people began to pay attention, and Billy believed he deserved some credit for that. His audience first alerted to the raging heavy-metal rock bands and their vile, nihilistic, drug-fueled lyrics and stage and video performances. The publication of *Michelle Remembers* had advanced Billy's cause yet further. The police began noticing strange things at murder scenes, such as hand-drawn pentagrams. The FBI formed a special unit to investigate such activities. Atrocities committed by the likes of Richard Ramirez, the feared "Night Stalker" in Los Angeles, who claimed to be a Satan worshipper, spurred on the law-enforcement initiatives including the formation of the local Satanic and ritual abuse crimes task force. And Billy's cause seemed to be further validated by the McMartin preschool sexual-abuse case in California, followed by similar cases around the country, many of which had Satanic overtones.

And now the devil had even invaded property owned by St. Stephen's Episcopal Church, which did not entirely surprise the Pentecostal Reverend Bitson. The recently announced indictments had moved Billy to embark on a special mission to evict Lucifer from the Operation Go! premises.

The media met Billy at the airport and followed him to the school. Vehicle access to the grounds, with its ghostly jungle gym, sand boxes, and teeter-totter rusting away, was barred by a droopy chain stretched across the driveway. Billy and the reporters simply stepped over it.

The church had refused to provide access to the locked building, prompting Billy to wonder if sinister forces might be at work here. In the event, he was forced to perform his ablutions in front of the barred doors. With pens and pencils scribbling, flash bulbs snapping, video cameras whirring, and microphones humming, Billy bowed his head and summoned the angels of heaven to smite the fallen angels of eternal darkness.

"Lord God, we humbly beseech you to rescue us from the terrible calamity that has befallen us … a calamity that we have, to our everlasting shame, brought down upon ourselves, by opening a door, many doors, inviting the Prince of Darkness and his legions into our wicked world."

It went on for some time, and the scribbling slowed, then stopped, though the video cameras continued to roll and the radio microphones to crackle. Billy seemed to sense he might be losing his audience and conclude it was time to close the show. He raised his right hand and intoned, "We drive you from us, whoever you may be and in whatever guise you may appear ... all unclean spirits, all Satanic powers, all infernal invaders, all wicked legions, assemblies and sects, the principalities and the powers, especially the physical bodies and lingering soul-stench and corruption of those human familiars of Satan, those imps of the Devil who have infested and fouled this building and laid their filthy hands on our children, and who now, in the very nick of time, are being brought to justice before the tribunals of both God and Man."

That done, the reporters from each of the city's four television stations vied for Billy's attention. Did he think the crimes of (they forgot to use the word "alleged") of Virginia Montrose and Marvin Smith were linked to broader national and international Satanic groups? Were they possibly connected to Richard Ramirez in any way? How about the Kelly Michaels trial in New Jersey where, just a few months earlier, a young preschool teacher in her twenties, an aspiring actress from a Catholic family, had been convicted of hundreds of counts of sexual abuse of the children in her care?

A wave rippled through the crowd as someone pushed his way to the front row and identified himself as Paschal McKenna of the *Herald*.

"Why here, Reverend?" McKenna asked. "What caused you to travel all this way from Baton Rouge to visit us?"

"I go where Satan goes," Billy said. "I've been chasing Him down in this country for almost twenty years, and I will not rest until he is thrust back down into Hell where he belongs."

"Isn't it true, Reverend, that there've been a number of recent public complaints from female congregants in your church that you've made unwanted sexual advances on them?"

Billy pointed at McKenna and raised his voice several notches. "So you've dug up that slander, have you? Satan will not rest until he silences me, just as I will not rest until I thwart His evil designs. As Saint Paul said, Ephesians 6:12, 'For we wrestle not with flesh and blood, but against principalities, against powers, against the ruler of the darkness of this world, against spiritual wickedness in high places.'" He stared at the reporter, paused for a moment, then said, "'High places,' yes, sir. So I have to wonder why you and your newspaper are doing *His* work instead of helping to further expose the evil in your town here. Obviously, this is exactly the place I need to be."

CHAPTER ෯ 21

FOR HIS FIRST visit to the site, O'Keefe wanted to be alone. No distractions. He told Hartley to hold off on the photographer until next time.

"All by your lonesome, huh?" Hartley said. "Spooky."

"No worries now that Bitson's cleansed the place."

He hadn't visited the building for years, not since the last time he'd been the one to pick Kelly up at the end of the day, which he'd done only rarely, in part because he couldn't always be depended on to arrive on time—or sometimes at all. Annie and he had still been married then, though they seemed to have taken up permanent residence on the bitter cusp of imminent divorce. They'd never seemed particularly "made for each other." Just the opposite. But in truth, it had been mostly his fault: the drugs, the drink, and the idiotic idea—one he'd not been fully conscious of at the time—that if a marriage wasn't near-perfect, it wasn't worth preserving.

He had obtained and studied the building plans. Typical of its era, it was brick, two stories, plus a semi-finished basement. Double entry doors opened into an abbreviated foyer where another set of double doors led to the building proper, a long hallway with four classrooms, two on each side. At the end of the corridor, a staircase led up to a second floor with administrative offices and a teacher's lounge. In the basement was an unfinished room, now infamous, containing the boiler and other utilities over which Marvin Smith had presided. Across the hallway was the also now-infamous large multi-purpose room used for naps, art, music, and special programs and gatherings.

A security guard greeted him. It would be ironic, O'Keefe thought, if the guard refused him entrance and turned out to be one of George's people, his own employee. But the guard was not his employee and did let him in. They'd turned enough lights on for him to see but not to see well. He wondered how his photos would come out and made a mental note to request proper lighting when the photographer came on site.

Ginny's classroom was the first one on the left. He switched on the lights. Nothing noticeably different from the last time he'd seen it six years earlier. A bit scuffed up and shabbier than the fanatical festive spic-and-span orderliness of Betsy Mortimer's Children's Clinic, but far more comforting … the miniature desks, the clutter of toys, the crude drawings pinned haphazardly to the walls, the goofy uplifting slogans on banners and blackboard. *Here is the Eden from which we fall.*

He'd forgotten about the window in the doorway, though not the four windows spaced evenly along the opposite wall. Those looked onto the parking lot, where parents and others came and went throughout the day, and onto the adjacent building used by the church for administrative offices and various parish support functions and meeting areas.

The church people had initially denied vehemently that such abuses would be possible given the busyness of the area, all the comings and goings, and insisted they'd never witnessed anything remotely suspicious, nor heard one complaint of any kind of abuse in all the years the school had operated.

That was before some of the parents announced their intention to sue the church as well as the school. After that, it had been "no comment."

Between the two classrooms were restrooms, the boys' on one side of the hallway, the girls' on the other. Crimes were alleged to have occurred in both. Some of the children were barely toilet-trained when they started at the school. Others occasionally had accidents or just needed help. Money for teachers' aides was scarce and volunteers sparse. If kids needed help, their teacher might ask a colleague across the hall to take an occasional look into her classroom while she accompanied the student to the bathroom. The female teachers—and they never seemed to be male—had to help the boys as well as the girls. The bathrooms were alike except for urinals in the boys' and two additional stalls in the girls'. There were windows, but they were frosted. Both rooms had stalls. *Unfortunate,* O'Keefe thought. While it was difficult to believe that the alleged abuses could have occurred without detection given the number of windows and doors and fairly constant and unpredictable traffic in this environment, the partitioned toilet areas allowed for concealment. The prosecution had already picked up on that theme, and the children's stories had begun to emphasize it.

But the real problem for the defense was the basement, where most of the alleged horrific events had occurred. Sliding his hand along the banister, O'Keefe felt his way down the steps, wondering if they'd deliberately left the basement lights off. As he felt along the wall for a light switch, he noticed the clicking, whirring, and bumping sounds that since childhood had made him anxious when he found himself alone in dark places. He felt the light switch, flipped it, and tensed, anticipating a revelation of something in the hallway to be afraid of. Of course there was nothing. The hallway just looked old, bruised, defeated.

He found the multi-purpose room. Kelly's graduation ceremony had taken place there. She'd been five then, and blushingly proud of her achievement, even if not quite sure exactly what she'd achieved other than a vague but somehow special marker of progress toward the cherished goal of "growing up." In the boisterously decorated room, each set of parents had received a hand-decorated program made by their child. Annie still probably had theirs stored away somewhere.

Now, in this quite different present, he noticed the complete absence of windows. No lock on the door either. Marvin Smith could easily have come in, but so could others—teachers, administrative staff, parents. Surely the other teachers and administrative people would travel back and forth to the room at will and unannounced, and maybe the parents too, when picking up their children.

Marie Dreyer, the school's principal, had greeted the abuse allegations with contempt, and had been vociferous about it, using words and phrases like "insane" and "hysterical idiocy" and "witch hunt." The authorities had responded by promptly opening an investigation of Marie Dreyer. Not long after, a couple of children identified her as an occasional witness to the abuse, and it was rumored that she might even have been an active participant.

"That didn't silence her," Hartley had said, "but it sent everyone else involved with the school rushing for cover. None of the other staff had supported the accusations against Virginia and Marvin, but they aren't saying anything publicly in their favor either." O'Keefe intended to try to interview them but couldn't force them unless Judge Snyder could be persuaded to order depositions, which was unlikely. It was enough to hope that during the remaining proceedings Snyder wouldn't maintain the unmistakable initial hostility to the defense he'd shown at the preliminary hearings. Certainly he'd do nothing special for them, nothing out of the ordinary that would allow the parents and the media to paint him as a black-robed abettor of the depraved.

At the back of the larger room, behind a wall extending the width of a room, there was a nook with hooks in its walls that had served as a cloak room. There was no door, just openings at both ends. Vile things were said to have occurred here. If any of it were true, the evildoers must have been seized with a desperate, insane courage to take the risk, so easy would it have been for someone to come through the unlocked main door and through to the nook and behold the shocking scene. Ginny seemed the opposite of a risk-taker.

He crossed the hallway to the boiler room and opened the door. The door was a little too large for the doorway, and the floor squeaked, as if in pain, as the door dragged across it. Since the place had been untended for weeks, the spiders had wasted no time asserting their dominion. But aside from the webs and the crumbly stuccoed walls and ceiling, the place was surprisingly clean and Mr. Smith's nook tidy.

On his worktable were a couple of pencils and a small, crumpled notebook with writing on it that appeared to be a to-do list. There was a cot, a dark-gray pillow, a thin mattress covered by a sheet, and a soft, thin blanket. Very comfy. Dainty, even— disturbingly so. He wondered what that might mean, and whatever it really meant, how the prosecution might spin it.

On his way out, he spotted a padlock latch at eye level on the inside of the door. Why would anyone want to lock the door to a boiler room from the inside? Had this been installed at the time the building was constructed, probably in the 1930s at the latest? It didn't look that old. If Marvin Smith had installed it, that could be a problem. Hartley would need to ask Marie Dreyer about that.

He climbed back to the main floor. At the far end of the hallway toward the entrance, the security guard was shifting from one foot to another, broadcasting an air of hostile impatience.

"Almost done," O'Keefe called out. "Just need to do the second floor."

He waited for the guard to say something, which didn't happen. O'Keefe mumbled, "Okay," and headed up the stairs, pretty sure he'd find nothing of interest since there'd been no mention of anything untoward occurring on that floor.

The man navigated his van through the streets adjacent to the St. Stephen's complex. It was now a mostly commercial zone, older buildings of the same vintage as the Operation Go! structure, most of the businesses closed on this Sunday afternoon. Only a single bedraggled block of houses and a shabby two-story brick apartment building indicated that the area had once been residential, and those stragglers looked like they were only barely managing to hold on for dear life against the commercial onslaught. But the whole area had so deteriorated that they now risked little danger of anyone even bothering to want to tear them down. Which worked for him just fine. It was unlikely that some resident would notice him circling and report a suspicious vehicle to the police. The people who lived here were the type likely to still be snoring in bed, even on a Sunday afternoon, and even if awake, they probably wouldn't care enough to call anyway.

He found three available spots around the St. Stephen's quadrangle where he could position his van inconspicuously and still be able to observe the Operation Go! building entrance and the Jeep Grand Wagoneer parked in the lot. To minimize the risk of attracting unwanted attention, he could stay for a while in each place, then move to another. But even if someone challenged him, he'd simply explain that he often came here to observe this horrible place where his son and the other children had been violated. It was part of his grieving process, approved and even encouraged by his therapist.

He'd used only two of his observation posts when the man exited the building, walked around to the side and into the parking lot, checked out each of the windows of the witch's classroom and took photos. He understood the man to be Peter O'Keefe, a private detective hired by the witch's lawyer to assist her in thwarting justice. He'd begun following O'Keefe, thinking that the PI might be doing the same to him and other parents of the violated children, sneaking sinisterly around, maybe even stalking the children themselves. Would he be trying to dig up dirt on the families? Maybe do even worse?

No way was that going to happen. He would turn the tables. He'd already visited O'Keefe's office, taken the elevator to the man's floor, walked up and down the hallway, ready, if challenged, with a story about looking for a business that was apparently no longer a tenant.

But this was the first time he'd observed the detective in the flesh for more than a few seconds. Taller than the average man, above six feet for sure, slim, dark hair worn a bit longer than most people were wearing it these days, short-sleeved polo-type pink shirt, jeans, loafers, no socks.

As he watched O'Keefe climb into the Wagoneer, Ralph's revulsion, turning physical, rose in his gorge.

Keeping what he calculated was a safe distance, he pursued.

Ralph congratulated himself. He was getting good at this.

CHAPTER ❧ 22

IT WAS ALMOST full dark when O'Keefe arrived in front of the small house where Ginny had lived prior to her current residence in city jail. This was the house where she'd provided occasional babysitting services for the children in her classes, an arrangement perfect for those one-night trips out of town for some wedding or athletic or other event, or just a night *in* town when the O'Keefes or other parents suspected the party might go on hard and late.

Ginny had a female roommate, infrequently encountered. He could conjure up only a fuzzy image of her. The same roommate all these years. More than a roommate? He couldn't recall any talk of a boyfriend or even a date. But so what? What did that have to do with child molestation? But the fact that his thinking had even drifted in that direction meant that it might be an issue with more than one juror, as well. If you were one kind of nonconformist or "deviant," why not another?

Ginny had paid the rent several months in advance to keep the landlord at bay, and on the assumption—delusional, it turned out—that she'd quickly be freed on bail. That deposit was almost exhausted now, and soon her things would need to be moved out. The police and prosecutors had thoroughly inspected the house several times, and this would likely be the defense's only chance.

A cute, cozy little place, landscaping neat but sparse, as might be expected from young women, at least one of them earning wages only slightly above the poverty level, who tried to make up for their lack of funds with diligent yard work on weekends. Now, it had all grown ragged and unkempt, what with Ginny in jail and her roommate gone. Gone abruptly—not just from the house, but all the way out of town—soon after the authorities had begun wondering how such atrocious things could have transpired in that small space without the roommate's knowledge … or maybe even participation? The police had questioned her several times, without a lawyer present because she couldn't afford one. Word leaked out somehow that she'd refused to take a polygraph. Eyebrows arched, mutterings ensued, rumors abounded.

What hadn't leaked was her reasoning: "It didn't do Virginia any good even when she passed a polygraph." In the face of that, and with no legal obligation to stay, she fled. But her flight only made things worse for the one who remained—more squinting of eyes on stern faces and judgmental head-nods affirming Ginny's certain guilt: "We knew it. We told you so."

The front door opened onto darkness. O'Keefe ran his hand along the wall until he found a switch. The ceiling light flickered on in the tiny living room, revealing only two small chairs with minimal cushioning, an overstuffed couch not much larger than a loveseat, a couple of small end tables, another small table that might have once held a television. No lamps, just the fixture in the ceiling, which gave off only a meager light because one of its bulbs had burned out.

To the right, a short hallway, leading perhaps to a bedroom and a bath. Just beyond the living room, a small dining room to the right, a kitchen to the left. The furnishings and accessories remained, except for bare spots where the roommate had apparently taken items that belonged to her, such as an empty spot where a dining-room table had likely once stood.

But what struck him most was the books. He couldn't find a bare wall. Bookcases, some built in, others free standing, covered every square inch not occupied by furniture. If there were a prize for books per square foot in a residence, this one would surely have been a contender.

Some of the books had yellow Post-It notes on their spines. He inspected the titles of some of those tagged books: *Lolita; The Wretched of the Earth* by Frantz Fanon; *The Second Sex* by Simone de

Beauvoir; works of Henry Miller, D.H. Lawrence, Anaïs Nin, and others in that vein. And there it was: *Life Against Death,* Herbert Marcuse's "polymorphous perversity" by way of Norman O. Brown, surely read by many thousands of college students of O'Keefe's generation, maybe Ginny's too. He wondered if the police, or more likely the prosecutors, had affixed those notes, marking those books as evidence that suggested politically radical, countercultural, and oversexed owners. The prosecution might go in that direction. Had these two women, seeking maximal liberation, thrown off their bourgeois, philistine shackles and crossed well-established boundaries? Experimenting with the forbidden? Lesbianism. Interracial sex. Polymorphous perversity. Only a step or two from there to pedophilia. Hadn't there even been a cult back then whose leader had engaged in and publicly glorified sex with young children? Only a further small step to the black arts, witchcraft, devil worship?

Outside, just after O'Keefe had entered, the van drove by, turning at the corner and into an alley running behind the houses on both sides of the alleyway. A few of the houses had only driveways. Others had driveways that led into garages underneath the houses. A couple of them, including the witch's house, had a detached garage. He had enough room to park up against the back of it without jutting out into the alley. The garage prevented anyone in the house or backyard from seeing the van, but it also blocked his view of the house. He rolled down the window, hands trembling so much he could barely accomplish it, and listened. A dog barked, but it sounded far away. He wondered if the police and prosecutors knew about O'Keefe's visit to this place. Didn't he need permission? And what was he doing in that house? What was he finding, or hiding? The authorities and others needed to be made aware of this. Slotkin too.

He opened the van door. The dome light switched on, startling him. Panicked, he slammed the door shut and the light went out. He cursed himself for forgetting about the dome light and then stupidly slamming the van door. He waited for the sound waves to fade and the silence to settle back on him while he gave himself a moment to settle. No harm done? Or had the light and noise alerted O'Keefe? Regardless, he would not flee. He would proceed, be brave against the forces of darkness, rise to this occasion.

On one side, the garage extended up to the neighbor's property line. On the other, a six-foot-high and tightly packed row of bushes blocked the way to the backyard of the witch's house. He eased through the bushes as best he could but received what he feared might be a nasty looking scratch on his face. He'd need to concoct an explanation for that. Best for Lori not to know about these special initiatives of his.

The slam of the car door outside faintly registered in O'Keefe's consciousness, but just as quickly dissipated as he trained his flashlight on the bare, unfinished basement walls. Spooky place. Two of the children had said that Mr. Smith had taken them down here, where they could see nothing but the blackest dark, and he warned them that if they ever reported what happened in that house, they would be flung down and locked in here, and down here was the fiery mouth of Hell itself, where devils waited with their pitchforks, eager to stab and snatch them on the prongs and toss them into the flames.

Back upstairs, he took careful steps along the dark hallway and found a door frame. He opened the door, felt the smallness of the room, smelled soap and perfume. Bathroom. His eyes kept slowly growing more accustomed to the darkness. No more than two or three steps down the hallway were two bedrooms abutting each other.

Approaching the window, Ralph peered in. The back of the house was dark. He could see nothing. Suddenly, light! He'd been exposed! O'Keefe was standing in the room, looking around, but not yet at the window. Ralph froze, afraid that any motion, even the blinking of his eyes, would draw the PI's attention. O'Keefe turned and opened the closet door. Ralph ducked, hoping his movement would go unnoticed. The light went off, but he stayed in a crouch and snuck to his left around the side of the house. A light came on above. He wanted badly to stand and see what the detective was doing now, but he stayed put. He'd already tempted fate too much.

The first bedroom, the one O'Keefe had just left, contained a double bed, a dresser, a small chair, three full bookshelves (of course), and clothes in the closet. This second bedroom was slightly larger. Another double bed. An empty dresser. An empty closet. Likely the housemate's room.

The light above Ralph went off. He crab-walked along the side of the house and the small front porch. He heard the front door of the house open. What if O'Keefe came exploring around the side of the house, directly into Ralph's path? The man was a PI. Good chance he was tough. But Ralph would have the advantage of surprise, could attack first, knock O'Keefe over, then run like hell. So much could go wrong.

He pressed himself against the side of the house and lay on his side, hoping O'Keefe didn't have a flashlight and would just walk by him. If he continued this, and he would continue it because there was no one else guarding against the evil's spread, he would need to arm himself. Some brass knuckles, perhaps. A switchblade, maybe. Or a small pistol, like a derringer.

He listened. Heard footfall across the porch and down the porch steps. Where was O'Keefe now? Coming around the house?

The seconds dragged. Excruciating. Your heart really did pound. He'd been sweating all along, but now the volume seemed to triple.

And then a car door opened, an engine started.

He couldn't remember ever feeling such relief. He'd been lucky this time. Next time, he would be better prepared.

REACTING TO MEDIA REPORTS THAT THE PRESIDENT AND MRS. REAGAN HAVE CONSULTED ASTROLOGERS ON VARIOUS ISSUES, A CHRISTIAN CONSERVATIVE GROUP PETITIONS THE WHITE HOUSE TO STOP CONSULTING ASTROLOGERS AND INSTEAD PUT THEIR TRUST AND FAITH IN GOD.

CHAPTER ❧ 23

"**Y**OU'VE HEARD ABOUT my latest excursion?"

"Is she innocent?" Paschal McKenna said.

"I sure hope so. What do you think?"

"I think she probably is. In fact, I'm sure of it."

"Is that why your byline hasn't been on the last couple of stories?"

"*Harvey's?*" Paschal said.

Neither man trusted the phone lines. Harvey's was the bar long frequented by O'Keefe, and the place that—drunk or sober—he favored for meetings, especially sensitive ones.

"When?" he asked.

"Cocktail time?"

"Isn't that *any* time for guys like us?" O'Keefe said.

"Lately I've been trying to hold off until five."

Several minutes before the appointed time, Paschal entered and exchanged nods with Harvey himself.

"He's in the back, as usual," Harvey said.

"What's he drinking today?"

"Iced tea," Harvey said, his tone slightly mournful.

"Let's have one of those, and my two Jamesons with a Moosehead back. At five on the dot."

"You trying to save on tips?"

"No. Have her bring it. But no delay."

As Paschal passed the waitress, he said, "I already put the order in. But bring it exactly at five, okay?"

She nodded and looked a bit reluctant and sad. "Any food?"

"Way too early for that."

She raised her eyebrows and moved on.

O'Keefe stood as Paschal reached the table. They shook hands and smiled, happy to see each other. O'Keefe craned his neck in search of the waitress.

"I already ordered," Paschal said. "One for you too. You're a cheap date."

"So they pulled you off the story?"

"Why are you so sure this place isn't bugged?"

"Three reasons. First, Harvey would never allow it. He's still counterculture, even now."

"It's not like they always ask permission."

"Second, I'm not important enough to bother with."

"Maybe. Maybe not. Somehow that doesn't make me comfortable."

"Third, I send my guy in to de-bug it every once in a while."

Paschal laughed. "There you have it."

Now it was Paschal who craned his neck, looking for the waitress.

"Five o'clock on the dot," O'Keefe said.

"Yeah, pumpkin time," Paschal said.

Paschal had downed the first of his two shots before the waitress even had her back turned. "Another round," he said. She nodded, again with that gloomy look that Paschal either didn't notice or deliberately ignored. To O'Keefe he said, "about my vanishing byline, yes, they pulled me off it. Said I'd lost my journalistic objectivity. They put Karen Todd on it. She's already slanting toward the prosecution. That'll get worse real fast. They'll be at the front of the mob, claiming journalistic objectivity but tossing logs on the fire themselves, hoping nobody's smart enough to notice but not really caring if they do."

O'Keefe said, "I'm still kind of in shock. What the fuck is going on?"

"You're not much of a follow-the-news guy, are you?"

"I try to avoid it."

"It's been going on for five years, all over the country. Isolated pockets, but a lot of them. Manhattan Beach, California; Kern County, California; Chicago; Memphis; Jordan, Minnesota; Florida too. New Jersey just a couple of months ago. And there's more. And now us. It's like a virus that makes people go crazy. Prosecutors, therapists, legislators, judges, jurors. The shrink types are the worst. They're not even shrinks. Half-baked shrinks like social workers and people calling themselves 'therapists' and 'counselors.' Not that the real shrinks have done any better. They've become vigilantes. The so-called Child Protective people are the very worst."

O'Keefe's look said, "Tell me more."

"And that's from personal experience. When I was six years old, they invaded my house on some rotten neighbor's phony complaint, declared my mother unfit because she left me alone so much. That was because she was out working her ass off to feed us, goddammit. They put me in foster care with some of the nastiest people you can imagine. Those so-called "protectors" from Child Services do some good things but a lot of really bad ones too. Why can't they just do the good?"

After the separation from his mother, Paschal's life had spiraled downward. Lots of juvenile delinquency led eventually to an amateurish, bungled armed robbery, more done for the hell of it than for the money, which sent him to the penitentiary. In prison, he decided to do some writing and sent his work to Oswald Malone at the *Herald,* who recognized a possible major talent. They helped him achieve parole and hired him, on a probationary basis initially, and he'd risen to become the leading crime reporter at the paper.

"Maybe here we could stop it," O'Keefe said. "There's no way she did any of this stuff."

"That's a pipe dream, buddy. Believe instead that you're caught up in something that'll wound everyone it touches, assuming it doesn't destroy them altogether, and that has nothing—*nothing*—to redeem it."

"Anything you can tell me that might help?"

Paschal said, "I remember right here at this table, not that long ago, you made quite a big deal about going off the record with me. Can I do the same with you now? Can you protect me?"

"I'll do my best … as long as it doesn't hurt the client. But I can't guarantee it."

"Don't know if I care anyway"— he tossed down his second shot— "so fuck it."

"Stop it," O'Keefe said. "I know where you're headed. It's the deadest end."

"Better to end with some integrity left."

"Better to live to fight another day."

"That's worth drinking to," Paschal said, and signaled the waitress for another round. Her look now was more like despair. He sat silently for several seconds, looking at O'Keefe, then said, "The prosecutor's office is leaking."

O'Keefe leaned forward.

"Most of it's just their propaganda, but something else slipped out … something they haven't given the defense like they're supposed to. I'm not sure, but it might be a tape or maybe even several tapes."

O'Keefe turned his face into an excited question mark.

Paschal continued. "I do know this. When the investigation started, they taped at least one of the children's initial interviews. As soon as the prosecutor found out they were doing that, he squelched it. No more. Maybe even told them to destroy what was there. In some of those other cases I was telling you about, tapes like that showed that the kids denied anything had happened, but the therapists kept at them, suggesting things, showing them anatomical dolls with actual sex organs, and telling them that 'Johnnie' and 'Jennifer' had already told them about this or that 'icky' thing that happened."

"Any idea how to get that, or them?"

"I don't know, but whatever it is, I intend to get it."

"I thought you were off the case."

"That's what *they* think. I'm on it, maybe not as a journalist, as just a human being. But it was a real loss. It was my chance to play Emile Zola"—he raised both his voice and his right arm, his index finger pointing in mock denunciation, "J'accuse!"

O'Keefe looked puzzled again and glanced stealthily around to check whether people were staring.

Paschal lowered his voice and said, "That's French for 'I accuse.'"

"Duh. That I could figure out all by myself."

"1898. Famous open letter he published in the Dreyfus case."

"I happen to know that one too. The Jewish officer they framed as a spy."

"Yes. Court-martialed him. Banished him to solitary confinement on Devil's Island for life. But Zola turned it around with that letter. 'J'accuse,' he proclaimed, over and over again, denouncing each of the malefactors, including the 'gutter press' as he called it, all of the people that had put Dreyfus on that Island. And for that, they hounded Zola into exile. He had to flee to England for a couple of years. But eventually it turned around. They finally exonerated him, and Dreyfus too."

"I can't sit on this. Maybe Hartley and I can figure out a way to dig out that tape."

"Wait. Fools rush in. Give me a chance first. A wrong move, and we could lose it forever."

O'Keefe frowned. This was what they called "the horns of a dilemma."

CHAPTER ~ 24

AS THE TRIAL date approached, the case demanded more and more of O'Keefe's time, meaning less help for Sara on Harrigan's daisy-chain case or the Global Insurance missing-person matter.

But he had managed to schedule interviews with some of Bart Yarborough's business partners, investors, employees, friends, and creditors, and was on his way to meet one of them when the car phone rang. "You won't believe this," Annie said, "but that woman, Mortimer, called. Asked about scheduling a follow-up visit with Kelly."

Taken aback, O'Keefe didn't respond.

Annie continued, "I didn't know what to say. I don't know what they know or don't know. I said I had to discuss it with you. Then she said their records show that I have primary custody. What the hell? ... Their 'records'! What 'records' should they be keeping on us? I said, 'So what.' And she said they were hoping I would come with her this time. Just me. It's weird. And scary. I think you should call them."

He did. When Mortimer answered, he said, "Are you aware I'm now working for the defense in this case?"

Her cheer had disappeared now. Her voice had a hard and wary edge. "Yes ... We know that's a little awkward, but not really. I know Mr. Hartley believes we're working for the prosecution, but we're only working for the children. *All* the children. We thought we owed you the opportunity for the second interview. To make sure we give Kelly, and your wife, and you too, every chance to know what really happened."

"I think we do know. She insists that nothing happened."

"We feel we have a duty to Kelly. We've seen that stubborn resistance so many times, when just a little more work can lead us to the truth. It's such a horrifying experience. The little ones can't bring themselves to acknowledge it, or sometimes even remember it, without help. Too many times we've seen it blight the rest of their lives. I would think a parent would want their child to have that opportunity, just to make sure."

O'Keefe detected a vague threat lurking in her words. And they'd wanted Annie to come in with Kelly, just the opposite of what they'd said previously about the parents not being present during the interview.

"I'll call you back."

He hung up, dialed Hartley, and described the problem.

"Strange," Hartley said. "I bet they're afraid she'll testify for the defense."

"Seems unethical," O'Keefe said.

Hartley made a scoffing noise. "They're probably hiding behind what Mortimer said to you—that the Clinic is independent, not working for the prosecution. What a crock. Neither side can get discovery depositions in a criminal case, so this is their ethical, I guess, but definitely sleazy way around that. They must think seeking a special order for a deposition would be a sign of weakness. While it's tempting to send Kelly back and give us some further inside scoop, it wouldn't be right to use her that way."

After a silence, O'Keefe said, "I've been wondering if she ought to testify."

"I've thought about bringing that up but didn't want to put you in that kind of vise. It could be pretty traumatic for her."

"She's pretty tough."

"Plus, the jury would likely discount her testimony because her father's working for the defense. Might be traumatic to no purpose. Let's not decide until we have to identify our witnesses. Meanwhile, see if you can find some other parents who might be willing to help us. If only we had tapes of the interviews, we could show how they manipulated those kids."

Those dilemma horns were poking him damned hard right now.

O'Keefe called Mortimer and told her Kelly would not be coming for a second visit.

"I guess you don't trust us," she said, "but I hope you'll think about it and maybe reconsider. For Kelly's sake. It would seem like a caring parent would want to make absolutely sure."

CHAPTER 25

TRENT LOWE WASN'T Randy's biological father.

Heidi had been a single mother when she'd met him. And O'Keefe could find no evidence that Trent had ever adopted the boy. They had just given him Trent's last name without bothering about legal niceties. So Trent was not a father but a stepfather to Randy. That seemed like just an oddity of marginal, if any, relevance until O'Keefe also learned that Trent had a former wife, Patricia, who, like Heidi after her, had brought a child to the marriage. In her divorce papers, Patricia had accused Trent of mentally and physically abusing her and the then-four-year-old child.

He located her, including her phone number, called her and played it straight. "I'm a private detective investigating some child-abuse allegations against your former husband."

"No surprise there," she said. "He's a vicious, violent prick." She was eager to provide details. The bastard belonged behind bars, she told him. He was her second marriage. A whirlwind thing. She'd been desperately poor with a young kid and an estranged former husband who barely made enough money to feed himself, "never mind me and the kid."

She learned too late that Trent's father had been very strict, regularly beating on the whole family. Trent thought that was the way you raised kids. To top it off, Trent was a drunk, and not a happy one. "When he came home from the bars, the rest of us had hell to pay."

"Would you be willing to provide an affidavit on that?"

"Is he beating on some other kid now?"

"We think so. We have reports of injuries to the child that are consistent with parental abuse."

"If it might help the helpless kid, I'd be glad to do it."

"Did anyone else witness what he did to your boy?"

"Some of the neighbors saw some of it. Some of our friends saw it when they visited. I haven't forgotten the look on some of their faces when he started whalin' on my boy."

The testimony of an ex-spouse would be good, but corroboration from friends and neighbors would be even better. Following up with several of them, he experienced a couple of doors shut in his face, but one person agreed to provide an affidavit, and another said they'd think about it. O'Keefe worried about the hostile people. Would they report his visits to Trent Lowe?

Probing the world of Ralph Merkel was a different sort of experience. Despite O'Keefe's almost romantic attachment to his big black Wagoneer, it was far too conspicuous to be an effective surveillance vehicle. For a while he had borrowed George's or Sara's cars, but their cars weren't well equipped for surveillance and both of them chafed at the inconvenience and let him know they didn't like it. So he reluctantly laid out the cash for a used "blandmobile," as he called it, and installed a car phone and other mobile-surveillance essentials. He looked forward to the day he could do the same for his two partners.

Merkel was a very busy man. Two clerical employees handled his office while Ralph devoted most of his day to sales calls and other marketing initiatives, and to such things as Rotary Club and other volunteer activities that Ralph considered to be just another form of marketing ("getting his name out there"). To what extent all this was for his business or for his organizational and amateur gumshoe efforts on behalf of the Save Our Children! group, O'Keefe couldn't be sure.

Merkel made frequent visits to Perry Slotkin, one of the city's top plaintiff lawyers. And when Slotkin accompanied Ralph to Save Our Children! meetings, he was accompanied by a middle-aged female who exhibited a sartorial splendor and a commanding physical presence. With Harrigan's help, they figured out she was a local public-relations standout who'd worked with Slotkin on his personal branding initiatives and lawsuits, especially in situations where her efforts might engender sympathy for Slotkin's cause from the general public and beyond—the press and the likes of Judge Harold Snyder, and maybe even the jurors who would ultimately decide the case.

O'Keefe managed to arrange a few visits with parents whose children had attended Ginny's class but who had not participated in the Save Our Children! group. Some had scoffed at the allegations. Some, like Ralph Merkel himself, eventually became zealous converts with all the fanatic zeal so often displayed by the converted nonbeliever. Others were simply intimidated by Merkel and the other Save Our Children! people who did not hesitate to publicly and loudly dismiss the doubters as fools—or worse, as possible participants in the ritual-abuse conspiracy, accusations and innuendoes that the media, though careful not to actually name names, were only too eager to publish.

CHAPTER ॐ 26

"**H**ARTLEY CALLED AND asked me to give you a message right away," Dagmar said on the speaker phone, interrupting his meeting with Sara regarding her initial findings in the daisy-chain case and where she should look next. "He has a meeting with Marvin Smith's lawyer in an hour and hopes you can come."

Sara, obviously disappointed, picked up her papers, said, "I'll report back next time you're here," and left his office.

When O'Keefe arrived, Hartley was pacing around his conference room. "The first thing I need to do," Hartley said, remaining in motion as he often did while talking, "is try to sever Virginia's case from Marvin's. Odds aren't good, but I have to try. It could be the key to an acquittal. Or a conviction. They need her to've had a partner. It's hard to imagine that tiny creature accomplishing all of that all by herself. And a man being involved taints it so much. They'll be sitting right there together at the defense table the whole time. And a black man at that. It's still a racist world. Who knows what the jurors really think, whatever they said at voir dire?

"I've been trying to convince Marvin's lawyer to file his own motion along with mine, but he's lukewarm—like he is about everything else. I won't be able to tell him that *he's* a big reason I desperately want the severance."

"What's that mean?" O'Keefe said.

"Just watch and listen. You'll see."

When Rockwell had not arrived by approximately the fourteenth minute after the scheduled meeting time, Hartley strode over to the open door and barked at the receptionist. "Call Lou's office and find out where he's at."

He stood waiting, his thumbs hooked onto his belt.

"No answer," the receptionist said.

He turned back to O'Keefe. "Unbelievable. I'm gonna have to carry that guy through the whole damn trial."

Approximately six minutes later, Lou Rockwell shuffled into the conference room mumbling an apology and wearing a rumpled sportscoat, baggy double-pleated khaki pants, faded Hush Puppies, and a garish, floral tie loosened at the neck.

Other than a look of disgust, Hartley controlled himself and introduced O'Keefe.

"Private investigator," Rockwell said. "Wow. Impressive. Who's paying for him?"

Hartley ignored the comment and launched into an impassioned speech on the importance of the severance motion, but Rockwell interrupted him. "Aren't you gonna offer me a cup of coffee or somethin'?"

O'Keefe disguised his amusement as Hartley struggled to keep himself in check. Despite the vigor with which he advanced his legal positions, he was usually a pretty mellow guy, but Rockwell seemed to trigger something rageful in him. He jumped up, opened the door, and said, "Hey, can you get us a pot of coffee in here?"

Returning to the conference table, he resumed his argument that separate trials were "absolutely and without question" in the best interest of both parties and how prejudicial it would be for them to be tried together.

After he finished, Rockwell defensively pushed himself back in his chair as if preparing for a blow and said, almost inaudibly, "I don't quite see it that way, Scotty."

"What?" Hartley Scott snapped.

"In a separate trial, all I've got is a black guy"—he nodded toward O'Keefe—"and no private investigator…"

"We've got to stand together on this motion. It'll be hard enough even if we're united."

"That's another reason I'm reluctant. Judge Snyder'll never grant it. Two trials is too much work. Why piss him off for nothin'?"

"Don't tell me you're afraid of Snyder, Lou. We're in a big hole here. He's against us right out of the chute. Judge Roy Bean. We're gonna have to risk pissing him off a whole bunch of times."

"Better rethink that, my friend. He ain't that old. You and I'll have to be in his court how many times in the future?"

"I'll worry about that then. Right now we owe our duty to *these* clients."

"I think we're better off together."

"*We?* What about the clients?"

"You know that's what I mean."

"What if Pete worked on your case too? Maybe my side could cover the expense."

O'Keefe almost flinched at Hartley's presumption in negotiating with Rockwell using the currency of O'Keefe's services without the consent of the service provider, i.e. O'Keefe.

"Or," Hartley said, "are you resisting because you don't want to do the work you'd have to do if you had to try this all by yourself?"

"It won't do you any good to insult me, Scotty. It's simple, like I said. All I'd have then is a black guy."

After Rockwell left, O'Keefe said, "Don't ever do anything like that again or neither of you'll have an investigator."

Hartley shook that off. "I was just smoking him out. He's a lazy wimp too much of the time. I'll have to carry him the whole trial and worry about him selling us out the first chance he gets."

O'Keefe kept his thought to himself, which was that Rockwell might be lazy, but he wasn't stupid. Because what he had said was true. Without Ginny, all he had was a black guy.

CHAPTER ⇜ 27

RAYLEE REYNOLDS.

They decided, reluctantly, that they needed to track her down, interview her, and try to persuade her to return for the trial. It didn't take O'Keefe much effort to discover where she lived now. She'd fled across the state, back to the town where she grew up, and moved in with her parents.

"I know she doesn't want to come back to this gone-crazy town," Hartley said, "and who knows whether she'll help or hurt us, but it's likely to be worse if she doesn't show up at all. Dolinar and Tarwater will work that every way they can, and the jury won't be able to help but conclude there must be something very wrong if she isn't willing to take the stand and speak up for her longtime friend and roommate. They'll regard it as proof that she's afraid of being put under oath. She must have guilty knowledge, likely even participated in the crimes."

He picked up the telephone receiver and punched a button. "Can you come in here right away?" Hanging up, he said, "It's gonna be really delicate. Need to give it our best shot."

Maura entered uncertainly and took a chair at the side of Hartley's desk, looking alert, expectant, and lovely.

Hartley explained the situation and the mission. "I'm worried about just sending a man to interview her. I want you to go with him."

Maura's eyes widened. O'Keefe hoped his own face remained more stoic. Slowly—he hoped not too slowly—he said, "Okay."

"You don't resent that, do you?" Hartley asked O'Keefe.

"Not at all."

"In fact," Hartley said, "I think Maura ought to set up the interview." Turning to Maura, he said, "You think you can handle that?"

She hesitated, then slowly nodded and said, "But what if she refuses?"

"Start out by telling her I was planning to subpoena her to force her to testify," Hartley said. "Since she's still in the same state, I can get that done. But you talked me into a softer way. Then tell her you're just a paralegal so you have to bring our investigator with you, but you promise to keep him on a leash."

"She could still refuse."

"If so, then you'll have to go down and waylay her somehow. We'll prepare a subpoena to give you some authority."

Maura looked confused. "Don't we need a court order for a subpoena outside this county?"

"Yeah, but she doesn't know that."

"Do you want to listen in to the call?"

"No. Don't want to cramp your style."

"When?"

"As close to now as you can. And, guys, when you get down there and are talking to her, don't forget the 'L' word.' It's essential. Get the truth on that if possible, but second best will be how she reacts."

As they left Hartley's office, she looked up at O'Keefe with that same semi-amused dread as when Hartley had given her the assignment. O'Keefe did his best to mimic her.

"It'll be alright," she said. "We can do this. Cool and clean."

She called him the next day. It had been a helluva lot harder than Scott had let on that it would be, but dropping O'Keefe's name had actually helped soften Raylee up some. She'd remembered the O'Keefe's and said that Virginia was quite fond of them all.

CHAPTER ᵗ³ 28

RALPH THOUGHT HE was getting better at this.

Following. Watching. He'd staked out O'Keefe a few more times and checked out his office and employees: Dagmar Sibelius, the tall skinny girl with the scramble of red hair who he guessed had been the one who answered the phone when he'd called and hung up; George Novak, the tall husky jock with a receding blond hairline; Sara Slade, the shapely, dark-haired woman who seemed to work harder than the others, arriving before dawn and sometimes not leaving until well after dark.

He had followed each of them, knew where they lived and which cars they drove. But none of them seemed to be working with O'Keefe on the witch's case. Nor did the men in uniform who came and went from the place, guards from the security line of O'Keefe's business. Ralph was considering the idea that he might obtain a similar uniform, wait for the Slade woman to leave for the evening, get access to the premises somehow, and install a listening or recording device.

He'd also become quite familiar with O'Keefe's neighborhood and his house. Painted a dainty yellow. Lori would have called it "cute," which didn't seem right for a private eye. It set well back in the lot, mostly shrouded behind hedgerows, trees, and other vegetation, so that once a person made his way onto the lot, he wouldn't be seen from the street. Seemed like it would be easier to get inside O'Keefe's house than into his office. But it would have to be at night and when there was no chance that O'Keefe's German

Shepherd would be there. And surely, given O'Keefe's profession, there'd be an alarm system.

He'd also undertaken surveillance on some of the law-firm people working on the case. Scott Hartley, Enemy Number One, had two young boys and a wife who seemed frazzled and desperate every time he saw her. Ralph could understand why. She got no help from her husband, who seemed never to be at home, always at the office, including weekends and evenings. She seemed to have no help—no cleaning woman, no babysitters. Hartley apparently didn't make much money. His house—peeling paint and a weedy yard—and cars—his was an older Ford Escort, hers an ancient rusty van—looked ready for the junkyard.

Hartley employed a couple of punk associates and a paralegal, Maura Davis. She lived in a small house with her young daughter. Good-looking woman. The most vulnerable of the whole group, Ralph thought, her home probably the easiest to access and install one or more bugging devices. But what good would that do? He doubted her job required her to be on the phone any significant amount of time. She'd more likely be paying attention to her daughter in the few hours she got to spend with her.

Whether any of this would prove useful, he couldn't know. But if he prepared well, and practiced at it, there might just come a moment…

His quarry on today's early morning drive-by was Maura Davis. And there she was! Standing on the curb. Apparently waiting for a ride. And soon a vehicle stopped and picked her up. A big black Grand Wagoneer.

He trailed them and ended up at the airport, parked in the same lot as they did, and followed at a safe distance into and through the terminal until they boarded a plane bound for a city on the other side of the state. Was this some shack-up deal? Or maybe it was on some mission connected with the case. Or both.

He thought about hustling to buy a ticket on the same plane. Sure, they might recognize him, but why would they think it was anything more than an innocent coincidence? But by the time he figured that out, it was too late. The departure gate had closed.

BIONDO SAID HER BODY WOULD NEVER BE FOUND. "DON'T BUY NO BOLOGNA THAT WEEK."

CHAPTER ఴ 29

JUST AFTER DAWN, Maura was waiting for him at the curb.

No standard-issue lady-lawyer matching skirt and top and low heels today. Instead, moccasin-style loafers, no socks, faded jeans, a peasant-style blouse that gathered in pleats under her breasts. Strawberry-blond hair a little more tousled than usual. Earrings turquoise hoops, not too large but a statement. A backpack instead of a briefcase.

She must have noticed him looking at her a little too long because she said, "Why not the professional lady lawyer? It's because of our witness. I got her background from Virginia. She's on the moderately alienated side of bohemian. No fuss, no muss."

"What's her job?"

"Some computer thing."

When they landed, Maura found a pay phone to call Raylee about the meeting place. Returning, she said, "We are to report, and I'm not joking, to picnic table number seven in Randolph Park."

They rented a blandmobile and found the Park where the city blended into its oldest suburb, a three-block-square oasis with several picnic tables, a couple of shelters for larger gatherings, a rose garden, four empty tennis courts, and a small duck pond. The park was fairly crowded, mostly by female joggers, power walkers, and strollers. A few groups of young mothers sat on blankets and chatted as they watched their children play nearby.

From the parking area, they could see in the distance a picnic table occupied by what appeared to be a lone female. As they approached, O'Keefe recalled his fleeting meetings with Raylee the few times he'd dropped off or picked up Kelly. There had been the occasional forced smile and mumbled hello as she made her way to another part of the house, a door quickly closing behind her.

The years hadn't changed her much. She was still alarmingly thin, her nose and chin finely chiseled. Her black hair was Louise Brooks all the way, a short, crisp bob that fell to just below her ears and short bangs straight across her forehead. Her light-black cotton jacket was unzipped, revealing a black tube top, skin exposed below and above, her collarbone protruding alarmingly as if it were about to poke out of her skin. She had the look of a starving she-wolf in the woods—gaunt, wary, and dangerous.

O'Keefe smiled in recognition. She acknowledged him with a nod but no smile. He noticed on the table a pack of Marlboros, a red BIC lighter, and two stubbed-out butts. She noticed him noticing, glanced down at the table, and said, "This damn circus has driven me to take up cigarettes again … and worse."

Maura introduced herself in her usual effervescent way that could cause a new acquaintance to mistake her for a phony. O'Keefe hoped Raylee would quickly realize that it was sincere and heartfelt, but these two women seemed like peas who would never mix in the same pod.

"Okay," Raylee said, "take your best shot."

"Do you call her Virginia or Ginny?" O'Keefe said.

"Only the kids called her Ginny."

"Okay. First things first. Do you know anything, anything at all that would support the charges against her?"

"Of course not. The only place any of those kids were molested was in their own homes."

"What'd you think about the babysitting?"

"I didn't get involved in that. Didn't like it much. I'm not a big fan of kiddies. Looks like I was right."

"But they were there at night, right? And often stayed overnight? Sometimes multiple nights, three-day weekends, etcetera?"

"Yeah. But I stayed out of the way. I worked a lot anyway. Nights and weekends too. All the time. My to-do list back then was infinite. Or I'd go to a movie. Or to my room and read. She didn't shove them at me, or me at them. She knew my feelings about that."

"Did she babysit more than one kid at a time?"

"Sure. Quite a bit. Like multiple kids from the same family."

"How about more than one family?"

Raylee thought for a moment. "Yeah. Quite a bit. It was quite popular with a lot of the parents. Two or three might ask her for the same evening. She always got their okay for that. And some of those parents were close friends. They would do things or go places on the weekend together."

"Do you know of anything that could've been mistaken for a religious-type ceremony?"

"No. She'd ask them if they said prayers before bed, and if they said yes, she'd say 'em with 'em."

"Anything like an altar?"

Raylee rolled her eyes. "This is the devil-worship bullshit, right?"

"I'm asking," O'Keefe said, "because if there was something that could've been mistaken for that, it might help her case to know what it was."

She quickly shook her head, then cocked it, and a few seconds later said, "She sometimes organized little theatrical things, playlets, song-and-dance stuff."

"Any costumes?"

"Maybe. I'm not really sure."

"How about a devil's costume?"

"I doubt it, but maybe a Halloween costume. She was a big fan of Halloween."

"I assume you've met Marvin Smith," O'Keefe said.

She lit a cigarette, and he thought her fingers trembled as she did so. She pursed her lips, then blew a line of smoke to the side. "He did a lot of odd jobs for us when we couldn't get the landlord to do what he was supposed to."

"Can you estimate how often?"

"Pretty often. It was an old house. Virginia and I were pretty good at that stuff, but we could only take it so far."

"Once a week? Once a month?"

"I don't know. It was over a lot of years. Sometimes a lot of things broke or had to be installed, sometimes not. I'd say maybe six times in an easy year, more in a bad one."

"Did he ever work at night?"

"Sure. He worked at the school during the day. Some things couldn't wait for the weekend. And he had his own family stuff on weekends."

"How late did he work?"

"I don't know. Sometimes pretty late."

"How did you pay him?"

"Cash."

"Why cash?"

"He asked for cash, and we wanted to keep him happy."

"I bet you did."

"What the fuck does that mean?"

"That," O'Keefe said, "is exactly the kind of dig a prosecutor might try while you're on the stand. I wanted to test it out."

"No more games. I'm not gonna be on any witness stand."

"Was there ever anything romantic or sexual between Marvin and Virginia that you know of?"

No hesitation, no flutter, not even a blink. "Nothing."

"Anything that a kid could mistake for something romantic?"

"Not at all. We all would banter with each other. Joke, tease, and all that. Especially him. He was a funny guy."

"How about you?"

"What about me?"

"You and Marvin."

Her look was sufficient answer.

He continued for a while, moseying along, wandering around, trying to find something that could help or hurt the cause.

"Do you believe she's innocent?"

"Of course she is. It's not a matter of belief. It's a fact."

"Then why won't you come and help her?"

Raylee toked hard on her cigarette. "I don't believe in throwing my life away for no reason or purpose. They're gonna lynch her no matter what. I went up against them at the beginning, and it was clear to both of us they were angling at prosecuting me too. What good would my testimony do? None. She knows that. She's told me not to come. Why would they believe her best friend, her roommate, her—"

O'Keefe wondered what she'd been about to say.

"How long have you and Virginia known each other?"

"Since we were eighteen. Freshmen in college."

It was time for the "L word" question.

"How about between you and Virginia?"

"What?"

"Romance. Anything romantic?"

"Why is that pertinent, or germane, or relevant, or whatever the legal word is?"

"It shouldn't be, but lawyers are creative, and judges can be stupid or even malicious ... So, was it romantic?"

A pause, then, "No."

"Not ever?"

"Never."

Her face had changed. If he had to say one way or the other, he'd have said she was lying. Would the jury see it the same way?

He said, "I'm not sure Ginny ever had a boyfriend."

"She had a few dates."

"But nothing steady. Did one ever stay the night?"

"No."

An uncomfortable silence. Raylee broke it: "Nor did mine."

"So you've had boyfriends?" in a surprised tone that he immediately regretted.

"More or less."

"But yes?" this time in a tone expressing something he hoped was a corrective to the previous and encouraging her to amplify.

"They can be a chore. Sisterhood's easier. I think she understood that sooner than I did."

Maura leaned forward. "Raylee, don't believe Virginia when she tells you she doesn't want you to come. She's being the foolish, brave martyr. If you, her own best friend and roommate, won't testify for her, the jury could only believe that you're afraid to testify because you believe or know she's guilty. Don't kid yourself. The prosecution will make a big deal of that. Your testimony may not get her acquitted, but your failure to testify might guarantee a guilty verdict."

Raylee winced. There was moisture in her eyes, but no tears fell.

"If I did agree to testify, who'll pay for my lawyer when they prosecute *me?*"

O'Keefe and Maura didn't answer, neither willing to try to persuade her with false hope and reassurances so empty they amounted to lies.

"Any more questions?"

They had none.

Raylee looked toward the horizon. "Getting nasty up there. It'll storm like hell soon. Hope your flight goes."

She stood, pocketed her cigarettes and lighter, said, "Good luck, and tell Virginia I love her," and walked slowly out of the park.

CHAPTER ⁓ 30

HEADING BACK TO their rental car, Maura said, "This storm is gonna be somethin.' Hope we make it to the car."

On the way to the airport, she kept an uncharacteristic silence for a long time, then said, "Well, what do you think? Will she or won't she?"

"I think not," O'Keefe said. "I think her assessment of the downside versus the upside is accurate."

"You don't think we can win?"

He thought for several seconds, then said, "That's not the point. The point is what *she* thinks."

"But what do you think?"

"Unfortunately, I think it might be a tossup."

"That's scary. It would be terrible to lose this. For Ginny and Marvin ... but for so many others too. We have to stop it right here."

O'Keefe let that sit for a moment, then said, "What did you think of her answer to the 'L' question?"

"You first."

"I think she was lying ... a little bit anyway ... maybe about their relationship at the beginning, maybe just a couple of encounters, then they let it go. Or it just passed into some version of a dull 'marriage' sort of thing."

"I agree. If she doesn't take the stand, it might be just to avoid that question."

After another silence, he said, "What's our ethics here?"

"That we think she might be lying? Nothing. If anything, the ethics go the other way. We owe it to Virginia not to be making something out of nothing. If we *know* a witness is lying, that's different—for lawyers anyway. About someone like you, I don't know. But anyway, we *don't* know anything for certain."

As they neared the airport, large, noisy plops of rain began hitting the windshield. The electronic message board in the terminal told them that various flights were delayed and one canceled though the storm hadn't yet begun in earnest. For now, theirs was still on time. But what if that changed? What if they had to stay overnight? They had promised each other, but had either of them really meant it enough to survive a real test?

Fifteen minutes later, the storm broke hard and loud. Swirling winds, driving rain, and hail battered the terminal's windows and roof. Not long after, their flight was canceled. They'd be staying overnight. Maura flashed him a look much like the one when Hartley had announced they'd be taking this trip together.

As they waited for a taxi, O'Keefe's thoughts drifted to the evening ahead. Dinner. For her a drink and maybe some wine, which would only stoke her unfeigned, endearing enthusiasm about pretty much anything she was talking about. Saying goodnight at the doors of their adjacent rooms might be awkward, and he could think of four possible outcomes: abrupt muttered "see you tomorrows" and quick escapes into their rooms with mixed feelings of relief and guilty regret; or him making a shy move that she rejects, to his shame, her keeping her promise after he had broken his; or her making the move, which he doubted he'd be able to resist; or both giving in to it and gambling on their ability to deal with the consequences.

He thought he knew enough about her eager embrace of the world that her every pore would dance with invitation and promise. Naked so quickly, lithe and tan. She beckons, and he goes to her, and her eyes say, "yes, this is exactly what I want to do. Yes, let's go there, together." Holding each other, bodies slightly apart, lips and tongues rehearsing what would happen next. She pulls him down to her and into her. Clutching her hair. Her sparkling lapis eyes…

At dinner she glanced at him now and then across the table, her eyes almost merry, as if she knew what he was thinking. As for what she was thinking, he could only guess. He neither believed nor indulged in one-night stands. Never had, even back in the old days when he'd been running hard, loose, and insanely high. Perhaps it was his puritanical Catholic boyhood, or something deeper and more important that he couldn't quite understand. Whatever it was, he couldn't keep himself from believing that something profound occurred in those moments that should be respected. Therefore, he had to consider consequences.

He'd tried to persuade Annie to take him back, at least for a trial run. She'd rejected him. He could easily rationalize that she'd had her chance. But he also thought he might have seen a softening in her, and with it a possibility that she might reconsider. What if that happened?

And how about Maura? What next after that night? She might tell herself it had just been some well-deserved fun, but she'd still long for something more meaningful even if she didn't expect it. And that wasn't possible until he'd given up hope of reconciliation with Annie.

And then Maura made it easier by saying, "I've got to call home. They were expecting me tonight."

At their respective doors, they muttered their "see you tomorrows." As he closed his door, locked it, and engaged the dead bolt a little harder than necessary as if to make sure he would stay in the room, he felt relief, and guilty regret along with it …

CHAPTER ⇝ 31

HARASSMENT, RHONDA TARWATER called it.

Hartley and Rockwell had made what they'd thought was a routine request to the DA's office for an examination of the children included in the indictment, but this time by a physician and a child psychologist retained by the defense. The DA's refusal, adamantly seconded by the parents, required the defense lawyers to file motions requesting that Judge Snyder order the medical examinations under appropriate conditions and limitations. The DA's office hit back with affidavits from Betsy Mortimer and Lawrence Marsden, a psychologist on the task force, swearing that further examination could cause irreparable harm. The defense responded with affidavits from their experts contravening the prosecution affidavits.

Hearings on motions were usually lightly attended. Not so this time. The courtroom was packed including numerous journalists and television and radio newspeople.

Hartley said, "Judge, I thought the District Attorney's office couldn't do any more to shock me, but their opposition to this motion truly flabbergasts me. I'd understand if they'd filed an opposition designed to impose some conditions and controls on the examination, but to try to keep the defense from any examination at all is preposterous."

"Preposterous?" Judge Snyder said. "I find that word is more apt to describe your position. The rules don't provide the defense a right to that type of discovery."

"They've had these kids in their clutches for months now. It's time to let someone else talk to them. Gently. Of course gently, very gently. But the defendants should have that opportunity. We shouldn't have to do it through cross-examination where we'll be walking on eggshells the whole time to keep from offending the jury by being too harsh with the children. The defendants deserve to have unbiased experts—"

"Unbiased?" Snyder interrupted. "The defense experts are unbiased?"

"They *are* unbiased. That's why we chose them. They're here today and ready to testify. We welcome examination by you or the prosecution concerning their lack of bias and how they intend to conduct their examinations."

Tarwater moved to stand and rebut, but Snyder saved her the trouble. "Motion denied. These children have already been through a hellish experience, and they deserve to be protected from yet more poking and prodding in private places."

Back at the defense table, Hartley muttered, "So much for the presumption of innocence."

Aware that Hartley had said something under his breath, Snyder said, "You have more to say, Mr. Hartley?"

Hartley only wearily shook his head.

The next motion was what Hartley called "a long shot but worth a try." Acknowledging the rule prohibiting evidence of the results of a polygraph, whether passed or failed, he argued that the defense should be allowed at trial to present evidence of the polygraphing process imposed on Virginia. "Our position," he said, "is that all these authorities—the Child Protective bureaucrats, the police, the task force, and the Children's Clinic people—were desperately looking for, actually drooling over, any chance to catch Satanic conspirators or other abusers of children. And the false claims of the Lowes provided them that opportunity. Once they had Virginia in their sights, they weren't going to let her escape, no matter what. And that became apparent as soon as they hauled her in and requested that she take a polygraph. Which she wholeheartedly agreed to.

"And what happens? Their own expert *concludes that she passed;* that her responses, denying everything, were *truthful.*"

He paused for a moment, then continued. "And that was a disaster for them. One that might stifle this great crusade of theirs from the get-go. Leaving them with no option but to at least try to neutralize it somehow. So they called in another of their experts, who looked at the same test results and concluded they were … *inconclusive.* Not as good as a fail, but it at least allowed them to ignore their first expert's findings. And that whole thing was in bad faith.

"In this unusual case, due process demands that this highly questionable process be disclosed to the jury. Yes, the law generally says that polygraph results are inadmissible. But it's not our purpose to offer them to demonstrate Virginia's innocence, and we will agree to an instruction that tells the jury they cannot be considered for that purpose. Rather, we have the right to show how tainted this so-called investigation was—a literal witch hunt. It's the police who believe so strongly in the efficacy of the polygraph as an identifier of truthfulness or deception. Time after time, they clear suspects who've passed a polygraph. The jury needs to know the lengths these people went to in order to burn Virginia Montrose at their stake."

Again Tarwater stood. Again Snyder saved her the breath.

"Very creative, very cute, Mr. Hartley. But no. Your theory is just a Trojan horse designed to smuggle in the polygraph results."

LOCAL PROSECUTOR DECRIES U.S. SUPREME COURT RULING THAT ONE-WAY SCREEN TO SHIELD A CHILD FROM ACCUSED ABUSER VIOLATES THE DEFENDANT'S SIXTH AMENDMENT RIGHT TO CONFRONT THE ACCUSER.

CHAPTER ⇜ 32

GINNY'S CASE WAS demanding more of O'Keefe's time than he'd planned for, more time than he had.

His support of Sara on the daisy-chain deal had been minimal at best, which not only overworked her but left her no time to give George any help. It may have been merely his own conscience, maybe they were just bent down and focused on work, but he seemed to have lost something valuable in his relationship with both of them. His one source of some help to the cause and to his own self-worth was the Global Insurance case. At least he'd managed to assemble a preliminary dossier on Bart Yarborough.

The seasoned adventure traveler seemed to have "done it all," including wilderness hiking, whitewater rafting, and of course the solo kayaking that had possibly now led to his demise after many such experiences without misadventure. He called himself an "entrepreneur," which as far as O'Keefe could tell, in Bart's case translated as "unsuccessful businessman." He had pursued various enterprises, losing money in most of them or barely selling or liquidating them for the capital he and his backers had invested. His investors expressed a variety of emotions about him, from resignation to anger, including threatened litigation against him should he be found alive, against his estate if dead. Two banks were chasing him for business debts he'd personally guaranteed. The multiple mortgages on his house likely exceeded its value. His only unencumbered asset was the Global Life Insurance policy, which was unusually high in the first place and had been substantially increased a few months before his Panama trip. The proceeds would clear all his debts, with a substantial chunk left over.

Complicating things further was the nation he'd disappeared in or from. General Manuel Noriega—the strongman who'd turned Panama into his own private fiefdom, funded by a spectacular drug-trafficking operation—had gone from the CIA's pet dictator under then Director George Bush, to an embarrassment, to a biter-of-the-feeding-hand, and finally, to all-out enemy. Earlier in the year, two grand juries in Miami had indicted him for his drug-running activities, and the White House and Congress had imposed economic sanctions on the country. A month later, Noriega had stifled a coup, claiming with at least some truth that the U.S. "gringos" were behind it. There were increasing reports of harassment of U.S. citizens living in Panama. Yet Bart had blithely parachuted himself into this maelstrom.

Mary Yarborough had provided Global the name of the hotel her husband had checked into on arrival and of the outfitter who'd supplied the kayak and other provisions for his trip. Luis Delgado, the proprietor of the kayak shop, "spoke English," but O'Keefe could barely penetrate the man's accent to understand all of this words, let alone capture any critical nuances of meaning. He'd learned in Vietnam that it was not so much what you couldn't understand as what you mistakenly thought you did understand that could bring trouble and tragedy. He interviewed several translators, practicing briefly with each of them until he found one he believed could well handle both interpreting Spanish and properly expressing O'Keefe's English into Spanish. They set up a conference call on the speaker phone in O'Keefe's office.

According to Delgado, Señor Yarborough had multiple interests and had obviously read extensively about the country and enquired about several possible itineraries. He showed up at Delgado's establishment in a bare-bones, rugged-looking jeep, showing much enthusiasm about river and ocean kayaking opportunities. Delgado had discussed whitewater adventures on the Chiriquí River with him. Señor had inquired as to whether the river drained into Chiriquí Gulf and about a possible route downriver that would end there. But he'd shown a special interest in the San Blas archipelago, 300 small islands populated almost exclusively by the Guna, an indigenous people who fished from dugout canoes, lived in thatch huts among the palm trees, and governed themselves, having successfully resisted all attempts at interference,

It disturbed Delgado that Señor desired to gather up all the things he needed for a number of possible itineraries and intended to pursue one or more as the mood took him. This was a very large number of items. As a result, Delgado had insisted on a cash deposit for the full amount of the rental plus the replacement value of the items in case Señor failed to return them. Bart hadn't quibbled, just pulled a large wad of U.S. dollars from his pocket—an unwise amount of cash to carry around, Delgado remembered thinking at the time—and bounced off down the road, his jeep loaded to and on the rooftop with kayaking and camping gear.

"I recall thinking, this guy is, as you say in English, bonkers."

Delgado never saw the jeep, Señor Yarborough, or his equipment again.

Following the call, O'Keefe thought about what he'd learned. He tried to gather his thoughts and identify the possibilities, but the thoughts refused to gather, and the possibilities were too many and too murky.

It was time to visit the grieving widow.

Both the neighborhood and the house appeared to be worth more than Bart Yarborough could afford on his best entrepreneurial day—similarly with his wife Mary. Younger than her husband, and handsome if not beautiful, with a shapely figure that her fashion choices did nothing to disguise. Once upon another time, she'd been Bart's receptionist. One or the other of them had seduced the exceedingly willing other. He abandoned his former wife and two kids, lugging into the new marriage a crippling load of child support and alimony.

The second Mrs. Yarborough invited O'Keefe in with a look somewhere between suspicious and hostile. She led him through a living room, a dining room, and into the kitchen, and offered him a glass of water, which he declined. They sat opposite each other at the kitchen table.

"Why Panama?" he said. "It's complete chaos down there. Isn't there a travel ban?"

"An advisory, not a ban. And even that wasn't in place at the time he went."

"But still chaos."

"Yeah. But by then he was in chaos himself. He'd talked about going down there and kayaking in the canal, but this time he hinted at some business opportunities there. He was a big believer in taking advantage of other people's financial distress."

She rolled her eyes toward the ceiling, then stifled a sob. "I guess he didn't quite get that *we* were the ones in distress now."

Her reaction seemed authentic enough.

"This is delicate, I know," he said, "and I'm sorry, but I have to bring it up. Noriega has been a major cocaine trafficker for years. It's not often that the head of state runs their country as a criminal enterprise. I can't tell you how many times I've seen legit businessmen give in to it. Quick score, and all that."

She considered that, then said, "Actually, I've suspected as much. Tried to tell myself that he'd never do that, but then I had to admit ... he was desperate."

He'd expected her to take umbrage, come to her husband's defense, at least regarding the suggestion of criminality. So maybe this was an honest reaction. It could equally be a way to leave open the idea that Bart had been engaged in potentially fatal activities. Perhaps she believed in good faith that he was dead, or as good as. Or maybe she'd given up on him and his feckless ways and cared only about the life-insurance proceeds that might rescue her. Or was it that she'd been taken in yet again by one of his pipe dreams and was conspiring with him to fake his death, collect the insurance, and pursue a new life elsewhere? Despite being alert to every tic of body language, voice modulation, and emotional expression, he remained unsure whether she was an Oscar-worthy actress or a confused woman worn-out from years of sleeping with a Don Quixote.

He wondered if she and Bart might've talked, might've rehearsed all this, a skilled director coaching a skilled actress. How could he get hold of her phone records? Legally. A local PI had been prosecuted for bribing a phone company employee to get hold of such records. It would probably take a lawsuit and a subpoena. He would check out the legal situation with Harrigan. Anyway, surely they'd have been smart enough to do something like that on public pay phones.

"So what's your conclusion?" she said. "You gonna make me file a lawsuit?"

"A lot more needs to be done before it would be reasonable to conclude anything."

"I don't have time. I made the mistake of becoming a housewife. I've got no income. In fact, I've got negative income. The charge cards are maxed out. His creditors are pounding on my door."

"I urge you to be patient."

"Easy for you to say."

"I know you don't trust me, but I'll try anyway. My client is not acting in bad faith. They know their business is about paying out on life-insurance policies, and they're actually happy to do it. You can't get new customers if you develop a reputation for screwing over your existing ones. But they can't just give away the money. They're used to having a corpse and a death certificate. We don't have those, and the circumstances are otherwise way out of the ordinary, involving a foreign country not known for the rectitude of its governance. And your husband, as you've indicated, was not in the best financial shape. Add the fact that he knows his way around the world. Maybe you can at least understand the situation."

"I can't *afford* to understand the situation."

"Have you hired a lawyer yet? And if so, may I ask who?"

"Perry Slotkin. Know him?"

"Oh, yes."

"So now you'll trash him to me, right?"

"Not at all. He's probably the best you could get."

That surprised her. She seemed to reappraise him.

O'Keefe asked if she'd got as far as signing an engagement agreement.

She shook her head. "But it's sitting on my desk, and my pen is clicked open right next to it."

"And I'll bet it's a forty percent contingency, or even more."

She said nothing.

"That's a lot of money to give up by being in too much of a hurry."

"I don't have time or money enough not to be in a hurry."

CHAPTER ❧ 33

LATE THAT EVENING, when even Sara had gone home, he put on a CD of Bach's violin concertos, hoping the composer's gift for birthing stately order out of clashing melodic lines would somehow inspire him as he began writing the preliminary report that Grady Runyon had requested. No way could he make time to do it, but the truth was that the only way to figure out what had happened—or didn't happen—to Bart Yarborough was to go to Panama. He'd need a guide, a translator, probably even a local private investigator.

So many possibilities:

One: Bart heads to a put-in somewhere on the Chiriquí River and at some point his kayak overturns in the turbulent water. His body hadn't been found. Or it had been found, but by someone who didn't care or didn't know what to do about it. Result: Bart Yarborough had been left to rot.

Two: Bart had ventured not into the river but into the ocean instead, to explore some of the hundreds if not thousands of islands off the Panamanian coast. There too, he'd come to grief. Result: Food for the fish or left to rot on a deserted beach.

Three: Like Kurtz in Conrad's *Heart of Darkness* or Coppola's *Apocalypse Now,* he'd plunged into the realm of the Guna and established his own small kingdom. Likely result: He'd offended the wrong people and been relieved of his belongings and his life. His bones now lay buried in a shallow pit scraped into the sand.

Four: He'd offered to mule a load of cocaine back to the mainland, marking himself as a fool. Result: Someone had separated this oaf from his wad of dollars and shuffled him off his mortal coil.

Five: He'd ditched the jeep and its cargo and made his way without leaving a trace out of Panama and toward somewhere lush, warm, and sandy. Result: No more bad memories and bad debts once his handsome wife collected the insurance proceeds and joined him in their new life together.

Six . . . Many other variations were possible, but with Mrs. Yarborough threatening to file a lawsuit brought by a lawyer well known for persuading juries to award large verdicts against insurance companies, it would be clear to Grady Runyon that an investigation in both the U.S. and Panama needed to begin immediately.

And that investigation couldn't involve O'Keefe—not with the Operation Go! trial looming.

No good deed goes unpunished, they said. But the punishment for undertaking Ginny's case was getting to be too much. He'd taken on the burden at Kelly's tearful request without thinking it all the way through. He doubted he'd be able to collect much, if anything, for his work on the case. And there was a lot more at stake than dollars. His partners were increasingly restless. His failure to support them was affecting their productivity. He was missing opportunities to create more business for them and to set existing relationships on a firmer footing. Global, for example. A pipeline crammed with future work.

Maybe the smart move was to fund the cost of a substitute investigator who could take over Ginny's case.

He imagined Kelly's and Annie's reaction to his bailing out. And finally, inescapably, there was that face in the mirror.

Something had to give. Whether Global continued with O'Keefe or he brought in someone else, the Panama investigation would take considerable time, and Mrs. Yarborough's bank balance and patience were both exhausted.

An interim solution came to him, one that might just purchase some time and keep the dreaded Slotkin in his cage.

A nonrecourse loan to cover her expenses while the investigation was ongoing. The loan would be secured by the insurance policy proceeds. And if Global didn't pay out, the company would agree—absent proof of participation by Mrs. Yarborough in a fraudulent conspiracy with her husband—not to collect the debt. If they did pay out, the loan would be deducted. A reasonable approach, he concluded in his report, one that if the wife refused would surely heighten suspicion of fraud.

A few days later, Runyon left a voicemail: "Nice idea about that policy loan. No matter what happens, that was worth your billings so far."

O'Keefe was happy with the compliment, but "no matter what happens"? That gave him some pause.

CHAPTER ⚜ 34

THE BAILIFF ANNOUNCED the two motions that would be heard that day.

First, the prosecution's motion to shut down the Lowe investigation and similar investigations of parents of the children named in the indictment.

Second, the defense motion to sever the trial.

Rhonda Tarwater handled the first motion. She put O'Keefe on the stand and had him designated as a "hostile witness," enabling her to ask leading questions.

She quickly brought out that he had watched the comings and goings to and from the Save Our Children! meetings.

"Did any of your operatives attend the meetings under the guise of being concerned parents?"

"No."

She scowled at him like a parent catching a child telling obvious falsehoods. "How about electronic eavesdropping, or recording conversations?"

"Not yet."

"What do you mean by that?" Judge Snyder barked. "You don't know that it's illegal to record a conversation without the person's consent?"

"Actually, Your Honor, I think I know otherwise from the Mafia cases I worked on recently."

Hartley grinned at O'Keefe's reminder to Snyder that the defense professionals weren't always on "the wrong side of the law."

"How so?" the judge said.

"There's a brand-new statute. If one party to the conversation consents, it can be recorded without the other party's consent or even knowledge."

Looking both embarrassed and angry, Snyder said, "Is that true, Ms. Tarwater?"

"Under some circumstances, yes, Your Honor."

Turning to O'Keefe, Snyder said, "Do you have plans to arrange any such recordings?"

"Not at this time."

"'Not yet' ... 'Not at this time,'" Snyder snarled. "Mr. O'Keefe, you won't do it at *any* time in this case without my permission."

Anticipating an objection, O'Keefe looked toward Hartley. Hartley hesitated, then stood. "Your Honor, I don't believe you have the authority to order that."

"Oh, Mr. Hartley, I think I do have the authority to control the proceedings in my courtroom."

Hartley sat down.

Tarwater continued. "And isn't it true, Mr. O'Keefe, that you approached former neighbors and even employers of Mr. Trent Lowe and accused him of physically abusing his former wife and stepson?"

"It's not true. I told them—"

"Objection, Your Honor," Tarwater said. "He's answered the question. The rest is not responsive."

Hartley leaped up. "Her question not only suggested but assumed *as a fact* that the witness 'accused,' her exact word. He should be allowed to say what he really said instead of leaving that false impression with Your Honor and"—he gestured to the audience—"the rest of the world."

Snyder said in a reluctant tone, "I don't see how I can sustain your objection, Ms. Tarwater."

O'Keefe hurried forward before Snyder could change his mind. "I told them I was investigating the possibility that something like that had occurred, and several of them confirmed—"

"Objection, it's hearsay," Tarwater called out, but O'Keefe managed to finish before Snyder could rule. "Several of them confirmed that such incidents had occurred," O'Keefe said, "and have provided affidavits saying that Mr. Lowe physically abused his former wife and stepson."

Tarwater made a couple of efforts to repair the wounds she'd inflicted on herself, then gave up.

Not that it mattered. To O'Keefe's disgust, Snyder announced that he would grant limited relief to the prosecution on its motion. "These children and their parents have had to endure a lot, and they don't deserve to have their privacy invaded by an unsupervised private investigator. Any further investigations of the children, their parents, any of their relatives, or anyone else associated with them cannot be undertaken until and unless the defense obtains my permission."

Hartley looked weary as he rose to protest. "Your Honor, again, I don't believe anyone can point to anything giving you authority to order something like this."

"Mr. Hartley, you can throw that in with all the other issues you'll be raising on appeal, but I won't risk putting these children and their parents through any more hell than they've already been subjected to."

Appeal. The word hit O'Keefe hard. The judge had all but assumed the defense would lose.

CHAPTER ⚡ 35

THE DAY DIDN'T get any better. Snyder quickly disposed of Hartley's motion to sever the trial, reminding Hartley that such motions were rarely granted, and that even Mr. Rockwell, his co-counsel, was only half-heartedly supporting him.

After Snyder left the bench, there was a smattering of applause from the Save Our Children! people in the audience, and the prosecutors smirked condescendingly toward the defense team.

Hartley remained in his seat until the courtroom had been cleared, only the defense team remaining. O'Keefe approached, put his hand on Hartley's shoulder, and said, "You okay, Scott? You said you couldn't expect to win this motion."

"Yeah," Hartley said, "but we needed to win it anyway. It's a disaster."

Judge Snyder scheduled the exchange of witness lists as part of a pretrial conference.

Hartley and O'Keefe decided they might as well list Annie and Kelly as character witnesses even if they ultimately chose not to call them. They first discussed it with Annie, explaining that her testimony would likely be discounted, maybe even ignored and repudiated altogether by the jury given her relationship with the chief investigator for the defense.

"Relationship?" she said. "You mean a broken marriage and a divorce? Come on."

O'Keefe shrank slightly into his chair.

"Still," Hartley said. "I don't want to ask you to suffer through it for what may be no upside."

"I absolutely want to testify. It's the least I can do."

"What about Kelly?"

"She's more important than I am, isn't she?"

"Probably, yes."

"I'm sure she'd be eager to do it."

"It could be a tough go. All those people staring at her. Those hostile parents."

"She's tough enough. And she spends every other weekend with her father. Couldn't be tougher than that. Ask him sometime to tell you what happened two Halloweens ago."

But she did smile slightly when she said that. O'Keefe made sure to suppress his own.

"Seems," she said, "like we have to put forward everything we can. The town's convicted them already."

Hartley handed Tarwater the defense witness list. She studied it, huffed, and looked up in amused contempt. "You've got to be kidding. The whole O'Keefe family? Do you really believe anyone would give even the slightest credence to the wife and daughter of the investigator hired by the defense?"

Hartley shrugged.

"I wonder if we can just disqualify them," Dolinar said.

"Why bother?" she said. "Bring it on. It'll help our case, not theirs."

Dolinar didn't seem so sure.

Hartley finished reviewing the prosecution's list. Puzzled, he said, "You forgot the Lowes."

They both smiled, and Dolinar said, "No, we didn't."

"What's up?"

"We'll be taking the Fifth on that for now."

Which was odd, Scott thought. O'Keefe too.

And it got odder. The next day, Maura burst through the closed door of Hartley's office, almost breathless, and tossed a document on his desk. "They just filed a motion to drop the Lowe charge from the indictment … Good news?"

Hartley sat reflecting as Maura stood waiting for his response, which eventually was, "I can't figure out exactly why right now, but I guarantee it won't be good."

CHAPTER ⚜ 36

TWO DAYS AFTER the witness lists became public, Paschal called.

"There's an article coming out tomorrow or the day after. About you. And your family. From what I hear, though I haven't seen it, it's not terrible, but you won't like it."

O'Keefe had received mostly good press from the *Herald,* deserved or not. Two years earlier, Harrigan had mobilized his political contacts and PR people to transform O'Keefe in the *Herald* and other local media from a possible bumbling clown to a hero following his firefight with Carmine Jagoda's Mafia soldiers in the mountains of southern Arizona. Later, O'Keefe developed a mutually supportive relationship with journalists Oswald Malone and Paschal McKenna, one that had raised his profile following other sensationally publicized adventures and near-death experiences.

Dagmar brought him the paper along with a sad face, and said, "Enjoy."

Now it was Karen Todd writing about him, and as far as she was concerned, he had become an eager volunteer soldier in the legions of evil. Someone had leaked information on a couple of his arrests in earlier days for brawling in various bars. In one arrest, they had found a packet of cocaine in his coat pocket, confirming their suspicions that he had morphed from addict to sometime pusher. The case had mysteriously faded into the fog—again, Harrigan's handiwork.

The article also effectively conveyed, without saying exactly so, that he had abandoned his wife and young daughter several years ago. Further, it probed his relationship with Mafia Princess Rose

Jagoda, and implied that he might be somewhat of a double agent, part police informant, part Mafia fellow traveler. It mentioned too that Annie O'Keefe was a real-estate broker and named the company she worked for, that his daughter Kelly had been a student at Operation Go!, that the O'Keefes had a rather close relationship with Virginia Montrose, and that it was still unclear whether Kelly was a victim or had played some "other role" in the activities of Montrose and Smith.

Later that morning, Sara didn't drop by his office but only called him and said she was sorry about the article. That was all. Not like her to be so terse and not to tell him that in person. He heard nothing from George that day. His previous exploits had enhanced their reputation and attracted business. But this case was damaging them—how much so was still unclear—and the trial hadn't even begun.

Annie called in the afternoon. "Well, that was fun," she said. "The head of my office stopped at my desk and said, 'Really wish I wouldn't've had to read that article today. I thought you were long rid of that guy.'"

He called Paschal, who answered with the voice of a man enduring a deathly hangover. "Don't say it," Paschal said. "Way worse than I thought it would be. Unbelievably chickenshit. I'm getting to hate these people. They've become a lynch mob with a pen for a noose."

"What about Oswald?"

"He can't do any good, and he's not stupid. He won't stick his neck out when there's no chance of it helping."

"How about that other thing?"

"What thing?" Paschal said wearily.

"Your source at the prosecutor's office?"

"You know where."

"I do. What time?"

CHAPTER ⚔ 37

As USUAL, O'Keefe called Harvey enroute to check on the availability of his favorite table.

"Planning another teetotaling orgy?" Harvey said.

"Paschal will be there."

"Sad case, there. Hate to even serve him. Have you ever in your life made friends with a mere social drinker?"

"Maybe we'll eat something. Well, maybe me at least. I'm sure you gouge your customers as much or more on the food as the drink."

"I try my best."

Also as usual, O'Keefe arrived a few minutes early to survey the situation and position himself.

"Here," Harvey said, holding a coffee pot over an empty cup. "I'll pour for you. No use wasting a perfectly good waitress on you. And I'll get the double Jameson's ready for Paschal."

Paschal arrived even later than he usually did, a waitress trailing him with his double whiskey plus a draft beer back.

"Why does life have to suck so much?" he slurred and sat down.

"Hard to sneak out early?"

"Not at all. They don't seem to care what I do anymore as long as I stay away from your case."

"Make them happy. I need you there."

After watching Paschal down the first Jameson shot, O'Keefe said, "So what's up on your source inside the DA's office?"

"Our usual agreement on no recording devices is in place?"

"Certainly."

"Have you done your fancy bug check on the place recently?"

"You bet. Eleven or so days ago."

"Pretty big interval."

"I don't *live* here, Paschal. Besides, I have my own little checking device. Not as good as my gadget wizard Terry Lecumske's full-bore approach, but probably good enough for one table."

"Is that why you always sit at the same table?"

"No. But it's an added benefit … You're not avoiding my question, are you?"

"Not really. But maybe I'm reluctant. Our ethical obligations aren't matching up here. I have an obligation *not* to reveal my source. But you have *no* obligation to protect me or them."

"I guess that's part of why life sucks so much. So far, I haven't told Hartley, but I can't keep that from him much longer."

Paschal said, "The answer is that it looks like there's a tape. At least one. I'm worried about it disappearing somehow. I'm told several more were taped over or just went poof."

"That might be prosecutorial misconduct."

"The story is, the employees who taped over them didn't realize they might be evidence as opposed to the live testimony."

"Sounds like a crock."

"The backup story's maybe better. They didn't think the tapes could possibly be favorable to the defense."

"Horseshit. Any idea when you might get it?"

"Can't say."

"Trial's starting real soon," O'Keefe said.

"I have to be cool about it. My source is scared to death." Paschal gave O'Keefe a long look, and O'Keefe let him take as long as he wanted. "You've noticed, I'm sure, that I'm deliberately not identifying my source to you."

"I respect that entirely. Now at least. Someday I might have to ask you."

"Bad moment that will be."

Every receptacle in front of Paschal that might hold an alcoholic drink was bone dry. He signaled the waitress, held up two fingers, and said, "Bring two. They're small. And the beer."

As they waited for the drink delivery, it was O'Keefe's turn to do a hard study of Paschal, which Paschal was not tolerating as well as O'Keefe had tolerated Paschal's.

"Okay, so what is it?" Paschal said as the drinks arrived.

"I've held my tongue on this, and I really hate letting it loose now. But you can't be doing yourself any favors with your employers"—he pointed to the drinks—"with that stuff. It's got to hurt your credibility—wreck it, maybe. And I guarantee you that your life won't suck as much without that stuff in it. And whatever life you have left just might not last all that long."

Paschal's smile was faint, brief, bitter. "Speaking of that, my honey girl finally couldn't take it anymore. Packed up and left last week. But here's the truth. I don't want to live without it. 'Til death do us part."

CHAPTER ༂ 38

DAGMAR BUZZED HIM to tell him that Grady Runyon was on the phone.

"What's next?" O'Keefe said.

Grady was silent. For too long. A small stone plopped into the previously placid pool of O'Keefe's consciousness, and troubling waves began rippling outward.

Finally, Grady said, "I've been trying to come up with a way to sugarcoat this …"

Yes, now it seemed obvious. *If I was worth shit as a detective, I would've seen this coming.* "The article?" he said.

"'Fraid so. The last straw. They've been after you since they heard I hired you … after me too. Believe me, I don't agree with them, and I told them so. But it didn't do any good, especially not after that article. Send me a bill for what you've done, and I'll get it paid, plus any follow-up you might need to brief the new man on the case."

"Who'll that be?"

"Niles Panderman."

"Do I have to? Anybody but him."

"Don't like him?"

"Hate him, actually."

"Curious … why?"

"I detest his tactics, all of them, both investigative and competitive."

"Yeah. I have to say he's poured salt on your wounds with my superiors. I'll try to keep the contact to a minimum."

"Keep it to one. And can I charge double or triple for that?"

Hanging up, he knew George and Sara needed to know right away. *I promised them no more secrets.*

CHAPTER ⇟ 39

THE INDICTMENT COULDN'T be amended to drop the Lowe charges without the court's permission.

Still unsure about the implications, Hartley filed a terse objection. Judge Snyder held the hearing in chambers rather than open court despite grumbling from some of the media. Since it was the prosecution's motion, Dolinar spoke first. "It's simple. While we wouldn't be allowed to add charges against the defendants and expose them to additional charges and jeopardy, we can certainly amend it to *reduce* charges, to *reduce* their jeopardy. That's all we're doing."

Snyder said, "He's right, Mr. Hartley. The law is clear. And why would you not want to consent to an amendment that eliminated counts and charges, especially ones so damning as these?"

"It comes as no surprise that the prosecution would like to avoid having to deal with the Lowe scandal, but Mr. Dolinar left something out. The law not only requires that an amendment must not add new charges, but also that, and I quote, 'the defendant's rights are not prejudiced.'"

Snyder frowned. "How could this possibly prejudice you?"

"This way. We intend to show this investigation was tainted from the start. They leaped from those Lowe lies right onto our clients like lions on baby antelopes. And we don't want the prosecution's dropping of the Lowe charges to keep us from arguing that."

"Well, assuming that's even a valid point in theory, you're not showing any prejudice now."

Floundering, grasping for some alternative, Hartley said, "So I assume I'll be able to renew my motion at such time as the prejudice arises?"

Snyder looked at Dolinar as if searching for permission.

Dolinar said, "He has to show it now, Your Honor."

Hartley said, "I think I've shown it. The amendment does us no favors and contains the potentiality of prejudice."

"No favors? Dropping charges isn't a favor?" Snyder said and looked at his law clerk, who only opened his eyes wide in a profession of ignorance. Snyder tucked his chin into his neck and said, "This has to be the first, and will surely be the last, time in this court that a defendant has objected to the dismissal of charges from an indictment. The prosecution's motion is granted. We'll deal with the prejudice issue if and when it arises."

EDITORIAL: IN OUR COUNTRY, THE RICH KEEP GETTING RICHER AND THE POOR POORER.

CHAPTER ❦ 40

HARTLEY SET UP a meeting in his conference room with O'Keefe, Lou Rockwell, Maura Davis, and Rob Nugent, the young associate working on the case, to finalize the strategy to pick the jury, a process known as *voir dire,* French for "speak the truth."

As usual, Lou was late. As usual, Scott was disgusted: "That fucking guy is taking years off my life. But however irritating Lou might be, he's a damn good lawyer some of the time, and he's especially good on voir dire. Not that it's any kind of science. But it might be the most important thing in this entire case, and you have to do it with minimal information and insufficient time. It's like playing pin the tail on the donkey at a sprint."

While they waited, Hartley explained to his inexperienced crew, which he had taken to calling the "Greenhorn Brigade," the general issues and strategy around voir dire. To start with, a jury wasn't so much selected as *de*-selected. A group of potential jurors substantially larger than the fourteen (twelve plus usually two alternates, sometimes more at the judge's discretion) that will serve at trial is assembled in the courtroom for questioning. In some jurisdictions, the rules provide that jurors fill out questionnaires giving some basic information about themselves, in other jurisdictions, not. General questions designed to tease out possible biases would be asked, sometimes only by the judge depending on applicable state or local rules, and sometimes by both the judge and the lawyers.

During the course of the voir dire, each side could challenge particular jurors they think might be biased in some specific way that could affect their ultimate vote. There was no limit to the number of those challenges. Judges didn't like to grant those, preferring instead to rehabilitate the seemingly tainted juror by asking if they'd follow the law in spite of their views. Which of course they almost always said they would.

"After all the for-cause strikes are dealt with, each side receives a limited number of what are called *peremptory* strikes, which, until recently, were completely arbitrary and required no showing of cause whatsoever—"

The door opened, and Rockwell hesitantly entered in his typical sartorial disarray, looking furtive and guilty and muttering, "Sorry, guys, sorry."

Rockwell and Hartley went through their standard drill: the former requesting coffee; the exasperated latter calling out instructions to the receptionist to fetch it; the former saying, "Why don't you just have some coffee out when I get here? Why do we go through this every time? You know I live on that stuff."

Once they settled, Hartley said, "I'm explaining voir dire to my Greenhorn Brigade here. Okay, gang. Pop quiz. What'll be the most important issue in the voir dire in this case?"

He stared demandingly at his associate Rob Nugent for an answer. The silence hung heavy as Nugent pondered nervously, then ventured, "Victim of child abuse?"

"Important, but not the most important."

Maura offered, "Race?"

Rockwell and Hartley nodded. Smart woman, O'Keefe thought, even if he did say so himself, since he'd come up with the same answer but held back, reluctant to volunteer, always the kid at the back of the class who never raised his hand.

"Right on," Rockwell said. "Maybe not the most important, but damn close. We've got to get as many black people on the jury as possible. But we may not get any. The prosecution'll do everything possible to keep them off."

"But there's the Supreme Court's *Batson* case," Nugent said, recovering from his previous lapse and earning a look of commendation from his boss.

"*Batson?*" Maura asked, again mirroring O'Keefe's own thoughts.

"Go ahead." Scott nodded to the associate.

Rob took the cue, straightened himself, and addressed the small crew as he might someday in the future address a courtroom audience. "Supreme Court case two years ago. The prosecutor used his peremptory challenges to knock all the black people off the jury panel. The Court said that was unlawful discrimination."

"You got it," Lou said, forcing himself into the discussion. "And they adopted a rule—one that basically means that if anyone uses a peremptory to knock off an African American from the jury, they have to give a satisfactory reason that's not based on race. In short, as far as race is concerned, there's no such thing as a peremptory strike anymore. Not really. And that gives us a chance, because if we can get one or more black people on the jury, they might think Marvin Smith is being railroaded, and they'll hang the jury."

"How does that help Virginia?" Nugent asked,

"Because," Hartley said, "if they think he's being railroaded, there's a good chance they'll think it's also happening to her."

"That's the good news," Rockwell said. "Here's the bad. Prosecutors have learned to be cagey. They now try to strike black jurors for reasons that aren't race-based on the surface but are in the real world. And the Judge Snyders of this world have been accepting them: lower socioeconomic status, prior arrests of the juror, prior arrests of the juror's relatives or friends, expressing hostile attitudes toward the police. Those are just four examples. Snyder is the kind of judge who'll accept that kind of crap. But we'll fight like hell and at least try to preserve it for appeal."

"Lou," Hartley said, "can you get some of the civil-rights people involved to support Marvin ... so the Save Our Children! people won't be the only ones demonstrating in front of the courthouse?"

"I'll try. But ... you know ... child sexual abuse. Nobody wants to take any risk of ending up on the wrong side of that."

"It's even worse than that," Hartley said. "There's another way that race is an issue here and dangerous as hell for us."

Maura again. "Miscegenation."

"You got it, kid," Rockwell said.

O'Keefe recalled, shamefully, his own involuntary negative reaction to the interracial sex aspect of the story.

Hartley said, "Scratch an American just a little bit, and you'll find a racist."

"And," Rockwell said, "scratch an American a little deeper, and you'll find a fascist."

"Whoa, Lou," Hartley said with a mock-horror face. "You've been working at Legal Aid too long."

Rockwell laughed. "That's for sure … And on this miscegenation issue, we have to be careful even with black jurors. A lot of them share that prejudice."

Despite his reluctance to volunteer, O'Keefe thought there might be another important issue lurking over them. And even if he was wrong, he owed it to Ginny to make sure it was identified and worked through. "There's something else."

They all perked up, all of them interested in what this quiet, odd-man-out type had to offer.

"No boyfriends. Long-term female roommate."

Nugent, startled, said, "Virginia's a lesbian?"

"Not saying that, but it's a possibility, and there are facts that might lead the man or woman in the street to conclude that. You can bet Dolinar and Tarwater will insinuate it every chance they get."

Nugent looked flabbergasted. "But she's supposed to've been diddling with little boys and screwing Marvin Smith."

"All are welcome in the devil's kingdom," O'Keefe said.

The discussion continued for hours, identifying the seemingly infinite possible juror biases and how they'd ferret them out in an incredibly short time. Which ones believed that children never lied about something like sexual abuse? Or that adults could convince children to believe in things that weren't true? Who worked in the medical field? What was their experience with law enforcement, and did they trust it? Had they or their relatives or friends been accused of sexual abuse, or been a victim of it? Had they read *Michelle Remembers* or other books on "recovered memory"? Had they viewed *The Oprah Winfrey Show, The Sally Jessy Raphael Show, Geraldo,* ABC's *20/20,* or other sensationalist, often hysterical national television shows about child sexual abuse or recovered memory? What knowledge did they have of other child sexual-abuse cases, such as McMartin and Kelly Michaels? Did they believe the devil actually operates as an active force in the world and on individual lives? Does Satan have human partners in conscious and active league with him?

Rockwell added a list of questions aimed to unearth pervasive racism and assess how virulently it ran in particular jurors.

At the same time, they would be trying to fend off what they knew would be the campaign of the prosecution to ensure not only that no black person would end up on the jury but that it would include as many racially biased and "law and order" white people as possible ("Yeah, fascists," Rockwell said).

Finally, how in voir dire and through the rest of the trial would they handle all the shocking sexual words and actions that would be constantly assaulting the jurors?

O'Keefe felt overwhelmed by the impossibility of it. They would have an hour, maybe two or three at the most, in order to probe the psychic depths of fourteen or more prospective jurors, who might or might not be giving honest answers, to try to uncover possibly deeply held, even unconscious bias and prejudice in the people who would hold in their hands the fates of Marvin Smith and Virginia Montrose.

It was pin the tail on the donkey at a sprint alright—for the highest of stakes.

CHAPTER ❦ 41

THE VOIR DIRE occurred a few days before the trial.

A large group holding Save Our Children! signs packed the sidewalk in front of the courthouse, ensuring that everyone, including especially the arriving potential jurors, would see them. When the courthouse opened to visitors, a large number of them proceeded from the sidewalk to fill most of the benches on the prosecution side of the courtroom. A smattering of civil rights activists also appeared on the sidewalk and in the courtroom sitting behind the defense table. "Lou's finally done something useful," Hartley said.

Virginia and Marvin were led in separately. They were allowed to wear their civilian clothes instead of prison garb, but they were escorted by officers, branding them as in-custody. It was O'Keefe's first opportunity to meet Marvin Smith who shook his hand with a strong grip and a furtive, hunted look, and quickly lowered his eyes. By all accounts he had been an exceedingly cheerful man, always smiling except when intensely concentrating on a project he was working on. But no smiles now. He had a similar look of disbelieving shock as Virginia did, but while hers was the dazed look of the deer in the headlights, his was of the angry buck ready for battle. But he had no adversary to lock horns with, only a mob of hostile white people on the other side of the courtroom. His face softened only once, when he saw his wife in the first row behind the defense table. O'Keefe had overheard her tell Rockwell, "I can't always come. Work, you know. But I'll be here every chance I get. Please help him."

The event proceeded about as confusingly and opaquely as O'Keefe had feared it would. By the time it was done, he had no clue what kind of jury had been chosen. But one thing was clear. The prosecution intended to do everything it could to ensure that the trial jury would not include a single black juror.

Intentionally or not, Judge Snyder and the courthouse officials had already done Dolinar and Tarwater a great favor by accepting without question from numerous potential black jury panelists their disqualifying stories of hardship, prejudice, and police brutality, dismissing them even before the voir dire, leaving only four African Americans on the panel.

Dolinar promptly went after the stragglers. His first target was Lester Spencer, who conceded that in his youth he had not himself been a member of the Black Panthers but did think "they'd done some good, forced some long-past-due respect to be paid."

Dolinar asked to approach the bench and, once there, requested that Mr. Spencer be excused on the grounds of hostility to law enforcement.

"Here we go," Rockwell said. "Mark my words, Your Honor, he's gonna try to knock every black person off this panel. And it can't be allowed under *Batson.*"

"Well," Snyder said, "that can't be true, Mr. Rockwell. What if every one of these black jurors is a blood relative of Marvin Smith?"

Rockwell shot him a look of disgust. "Not quite likely on this particular planet, Your Honor."

Snyder said, "I know, but you get my point, I'm sure. We take them one at a time." He turned to Dolinar. "The Supreme Court has spoken, like it or not. I don't think you've got quite enough yet."

Dolinar returned to Mr. Spencer who testified that he had been arrested a couple of times himself, though never prosecuted, and several times stopped for no reason while driving in or near white neighborhoods. He also conceded that he was not at all pleased with the way the officers treated him on a couple of those occasions. And he had relatives and friends who'd experienced similar unpleasant encounters.

"Do you think," Dolinar asked him, "that your experiences with law enforcement might affect your ability to follow the evidence and render a verdict of guilty in this case?"

"Depends."

"I sympathize with your situation, Mr. Spencer," Dolinar said with maximum feigned empathy, "but as you've heard and seen here today, this is about assembling a jury that doesn't have any automatic going-in distrust of either side. So, do you think it might be harder for you to trust the prosecution side of the case given your experiences and the experiences of your relatives and friends?"

"Probably so."

This time Snyder allowed the challenge. Both Rockwell and Hartley put their objections to its allowance on the record for appeal purposes.

The questions continued. Dolinar explored every possible avenue that might result in eliminating the other black panelists—their experiences with law enforcement, that of their friends and relatives too, the impact on their ability to trust the prosecution. He succeeded in digging deep enough with a second black male panelist to bring out a milder but similar negative historical experience with law enforcement. Again, the challenge was allowed.

But Dolinar couldn't dig up enough from the remaining two black panelists to convince Snyder to dismiss them for cause. But those two were on Dolinar's peremptory challenge list. The defense lawyers duly objected based on *Batson*.

"So we are kind of new at this *Batson* thing," Snyder said. "I need a reason from you, Mr. Dolinar. It doesn't have to be as strong as would justify a for-cause exclusion, but it has to be other than because they're Negroes."

"Sam Jordan was clearly hungover and nodded off at least twice during the questioning."

"I can accept that, I think."

Rockwell said, "I saw a couple of white jurors dozing off too. They're not on his list."

"Did they look hungover?"

"Well, I honestly can't say, Your Honor."

"Mr. Rockwell, we can't make this inquiry into a trial all of its own. I think I have to accept his challenge."

"We're heading, Your Honor," Rockwell said, "toward an all-white jury, here."

There was muttering among the civil rights people in the gallery, garnering hostile looks from the Save Our Children! group. Snyder lifted his gavel but seemed to think better of it and laid it back down.

They moved to the last of the black panel members, who was a church-going Baptist woman of what appeared to be unassailable rectitude and no admitted bias against law enforcement. Dolinar could offer only that she seemed skeptical about the qualifications or wisdom of psychologists and therapists generally and had been "evasive" and sometimes "downright hostile" in her response to some of Dolinar's questions.

Snyder looked apologetic. "Mr. Dolinar, I'm going to protect you from yourself. I really fear that if we have an all-white jury, and especially if we reject this upstanding Negro lady, any conviction here will be overturned, and we'll be back here years from now doing all this over again."

Dolinar looked ill.

Rockwell and Hartley, and especially Marvin Smith himself, were relieved and delighted that "the Negro lady" had managed to survive the prosecution's assault.

"One might not be enough," Rockwell said. "But better than none. Maybe even if we can't get a not-guilty, at least she might hold out and hang them."

When O'Keefe asked Hartley and Rockwell how they thought the jury selection went otherwise, Hartley just shook his head, and Rockwell said, "Who the fuck knows?"

CHAPTER ❧ 42

DAY ONE OF the trial.

The children included in the indictment, carefully selected from the many that claimed to have been abused, occupied the first two rows on the prosecution's side of the courtroom. Behind them sat other parents of the Save Our Children! group. Still others, as they had done during the voir dire, lined the sidewalks outside the courthouse from sunrise on, carrying *SAVE OUR CHILDREN!* signs for the enlightenment of the press and the jurors. The media had squeezed themselves into the benches on the prosecution's side of the courtroom until there was no room left and they were forced to sit in the mostly empty rows behind the defense.

There too were Annie and Kelly. Annie had called and asked if O'Keefe could arrange seats for her and Kelly the opening day of the trial. "As far as I can tell," she said, "the parents and other people against her will jam the place. She ought to know that someone in the world is on her side. Hartley says, since we're witnesses, we won't have a chance to come back until after we testify."

"You sure you want to expose Kelly to that? Or, for that matter, yourself?"

"Of course," she said, decisively dismissing his concern.

Also on the defense side, Marvin Smith's wife and adult daughter, and Marie Dreyer, the school principal who remained an unwavering and vocal but lonely supporter of her former employees. Ginny's fellow teachers, wanting to attract no attention to themselves, stayed away. Some had been questioned by the police, some had been actually accused and subjected to desultory but continuing investigations, and all of them hoped to somehow find jobs somewhere despite the black mark of Operation Go! on their résumés.

O'Keefe had approached several parents who'd originally publicly mocked the allegations and asked them to testify as character witnesses for Ginny. They refused, so he asked if they would at least attend the first day of the trial so that jurors could see that there were parents who didn't believe the accusations. All gave excuses, but O'Keefe guessed that one mother and father spoke for the rest.

They were afraid. Of the police, the prosecutors, the child-protection people. The parents too. Especially the parents. "Vicious," the father had called them. "And why would we want to expose our kids to that?"

O'Keefe was unaware that, jammed along with the rest of the crowd in the hallway as they waited for the bailiffs to open the courtroom, Annie and Kelly had been subjected to exactly that as they tried to keep looking straight ahead to evade the glares from the openly hostile crowd, some of them seeming barely able to restrain themselves from physically attacking.

"Don't look at them," Annie said.

"I won't," Kelly said and opened and began reading her Nancy Drew book so she wouldn't be tempted.

Once the visitors had been seated and settled, the prosecution team came in, then the defense, O'Keefe walking a little stiffly and self-consciously in a new suit, shirt, tie, and shoes. He had purchased several new suits—a black, a navy, a light gray, and a dark gray—and accompanying shirt and tie combinations to wear for the trial proceedings. It all cost more than he could afford, but he wanted to do his part to help the defense present its best professional face to everyone in the courtroom, especially the jury. He lobbed what he hoped was an "I'm proud of you" look at Kelly, who returned the favor with enthusiastically raised eyebrows and forehead and the short wave of her stiffened right hand that had become one of her trademark gestures. Ginny tried to smile back at her but failed to bring it off.

Judge Snyder addressed the jurors: "Your duty will be to determine whether the defendants are guilty or not guilty based only on facts and evidence provided in this case. The prosecution has the burden of proving the guilt of each defendant beyond a reasonable doubt. This burden remains throughout the trial to its very end."

He went on to explain the sidebars that would frequently occur—objections to a particular testimony or other item of evidence discussed by the lawyers and the judge quietly at the bench out of the jurors' earshot until the judge ruled on the issue.

Now he called on Dolinar for his opening statement.

The lawyer stood and turned around to the packed courtroom, eventually resting his gaze on the front rows at the children named in the indictment, ranging in ages from five to twelve, accompanied by their parents. He nodded his head slowly as the parents nodded back. He turned to the side and stared with cold contempt at the defendants and their professionals.

"Ladies and gentlemen of the jury, thank you for being here today, having the courage and fortitude to serve justice in this wrenching, harrowing, awful situation."

Hartley looked hard at Snyder, poised to object. An opening statement was supposed to be non-argumentative, just a summary of what the prosecution's evidence would show.

Snyder looked away.

Dolinar introduced himself and his team. Each stood, nodded or bowed slightly, and sat down again.

He raised his intensity several notches. "And, of course, the victims. The little ones. Over there in the first row with their parents. It began a long time ago. One of those children is now twelve, another eleven, another nine. Two are seven, and two more are only five years old. Each of these courageous children will climb up there on that witness stand and tell you what these defendants did to them. It will be very painful, and I'm sorry you'll have to listen to it. Things like fondling the children's private parts, performing oral sex on the children, and manipulating the children to perform oral sex on the defendants. It's been hard on all of us. But it's our job to face these things and do our duty as citizens to protect our children from and punish their predators."

And O'Keefe understood why Dolinar was reputed to be a great courtroom lawyer. It was his manner more than the substance of what he said. He seemed to radiate a magnetic field that captured his listener and held them there until he was done with them.

"And you will hear about penile penetration perpetrated by Marvin Smith, in the presence of and enthusiastically assisted and cheered on by Virginia Montrose, on boys and girls as young as three and four years old."

Dolinar stopped. Let the horror sink in.

The facial expressions of the jurors said it all. Shock. Outrage. One woman had her hand to her mouth and seemed to be choking back the urge to vomit. A shroud of despair engulfed O'Keefe. Had they lost the case already?

O'Keefe also glanced unobtrusively at the defendants. Ginny looked mournful. The veins in Marvin Smith's temples pulsed and his face had a bluish red sheen to it, as if his head might be about to burst.

"Yes," Dolinar continued, "from the mouths of these babes you will hear those things ... and how"—he pointed at Virginia, which surprised her and she flinched—"under the guise of babysitting services, this woman enticed these children into her house, where, sometimes alone, sometimes with Marvin Smith—I won't call him her lover—her occasional sex partner, she swept these innocent children into sexual orgy-like games, even sometimes Satanic practices, devil worship, including slitting the throats of small animals, baby bunnies...

"...Yes, these innocents will be climbing up on that witness chair and telling you these atrocious things that happened to them. We hate to put them through it, but justice, indeed basic human decency, demands it. Certainly we, the prosecution, will be very gentle with them."

"Objection," Hartley said, and approached the bench. "I've waited as long as I can, but he has to be stopped. This is an improper opening statement. Not only is he grandstanding, he's also trying to put the defense in the trick bag on cross-examination of the children. He's probably coached them to cry the moment we open our mouths."

"That comment about coaching is uncalled for, Mr. Hartley," Snyder said, but then addressed Dolinar. "You *are* getting awfully close to improper, maybe more than close. I'll let this one go, but this is a warning. No more. And, Mr. Hartley, since you're so sensitive on this issue, I'll expect the same from you when it comes your turn."

Hartley said, "Will you instruct the jury that his last two sentences were improper, and that the jury should disregard?"

"Don't be overreaching, Mr. Hartley."

"I move for a mistrial. He's been allowed to prejudice the jury, likely irrevocably."

"Denied."

Dolinar and Hartley resumed their previous positions. Dolinar continued as if nothing negative had occurred. "And the parents of these children will be telling you about certain things the children told them at the time all this was happening about their physical and mental situation, and about some unusual and disturbing behaviors their children were acting out.

"We will also bring to the witness stand Ms. Betsy Mortimer, head of the Children's Clinic, who will testify that such behaviors are typically exhibited by sexually abused children.

"She will also tell you how she conducted multiple in-depth interviews with each of these children and concluded that each of them had been molested by these defendants.

"We will also be presenting the testimony of Doctor Norman Carlyle, a specialist in pediatric medicine, with a long history of examining and treating child victims of sexual abuse. He examined each of these children, and he will tell you that, based on his physical examination and the children's statements to him, these children were in fact molested."

Hartley's jaw tightened. His pretrial motion to exclude the hearsay statements the children had supposedly made to the parents and these so-called experts had failed. He couldn't stop that now, only maybe on appeal if it came to that, but he'd identified something else objectionable in what Dolinar had just said and headed for the bench once more.

"He's misrepresenting the evidence," Hartley told Snyder. "It's our understanding the doctor will only be testifying that the physical examination was 'consistent with abuse,' which is decidedly *not* a finding, to quote Mr. Dolinar, that the children were in fact abused."

Dolinar didn't even need to defend himself this time. "Well," Snyder said, "we won't know that until the doctor testifies, will we? If the testimony isn't what Mr. Dolinar says it's going to be, you can point that out on cross and in your closing, right, Mr. Hartley?"

"Move for a mistrial."

"Denied. I hope you're not going to be moving for a mistrial every five minutes in this case. That's bush league."

A NEWLY PUBLISHED STUDY INDICATES THAT, IN THE PREVIOUS YEAR, THERE WERE 187 INCIDENTS OF CHILD SEXUAL ABUSE IN DAY CARE SETTINGS AND 2,462 SUCH INCIDENTS IN THE CHILDREN'S HOMES.

CHAPTER ⇝ 43

HARTLEY HAD TOLD his colleagues that he would not hold back in his opening.

He intended to go to the edge and beyond until Snyder reined him in. The problem the defense had faced from the beginning and still faced and would always face was the great difficulty—near impossibility, actually—of believing that the children would, even *could,* lie about such things. It was almost inconceivable they could even *know* about such things, let alone make them up. "So I have to go as hard and as strong as I can, even at the risk of overstating, that these kids have been brainwashed, made into little puppets or robots regurgitating what adults have jammed into their heads."

Rockwell and Hartley had decided that Hartley would generally go first and take the main laboring oar in the case. "After all, you've got the investigator," Rockwell joked.

Hartley didn't project Dolinar's magnetic field, but he did effectively project his sincere belief in his client's innocence and measured outrage at the falsity and unfairness of the accusations against her. "Ladies and gentlemen, I assure you that what Mr. Dolinar told you is in large part *not* what the evidence will show. What the evidence will show is this:

"My client, Virginia Montrose, lovingly known by her students over many years as 'Miss Ginny,' has never had any mark against her in her entire career. Not one. We will be putting people on the witness stand who've known her for a long time and who will tell you what kind of person she really is.

"And Mr. Marvin Smith, the other accused. His lawyer, Mr. Rockwell here, will tell you more about him. But, like Virginia, there is nothing, not one negative thing in his employment background. He is just a man trying to scratch out a living as a school janitor to feed his family.

Not a single one of these horrible things the prosecution is accusing Virginia or Marvin of, things that supposedly occurred over *eight* years, was ever reported at the time they supposedly occurred. Not one. Then, suddenly, we have this volcanic eruption of accusations. Many of them simply defy belief. Like these incredible accusations about spoons and knives and pens that would certainly have caused visible injuries to these very young children. Not once, during all this time, all these years, was an injury reported.

"Am I accusing these children of lying? No. Not intentionally."

Dolinar was stirring, as if about to object. Snyder was frowning and fidgeting. Hartley ignored them.

"But the evidence will show that these children were subjected to a series of intense interrogations by intimidating authority figures, including"—he pointed at the prosecution table—"the District Attorney's office, in the form of Ms. Tarwater over there; the police, in the form of Officer Myra Hicks sitting with the prosecution over there; Mr. Brinkley, the lead investigator from the state Child Protective Agency, also sitting with the prosecutor over there. Those interrogations were both intensive and extensive. The evidence will show they amounted to brainwashing of these impressionable young children.

"We can trace this to the first moments of the investigation.

Again, Dolinar started to fidget. Again, Hartley continued. "This case started with a family—"

"Objection."

At the bench, Dolinar said, "Judge, this is irrelevant. With your permission, we dropped all of the Lowe-related charges. So all of that is irrelevant."

Hartley said, "Well, here we are. Here's the prejudice. You'll recall our discussion that an amendment to an indictment should not be allowed if it prejudices the defendant. I couldn't identify at the earlier argument exactly in what way it might prejudice us, but

I knew this wasn't an act of mercy or charity by Mr. Dolinar. I knew he had something up his sleeve though I wasn't sure what. And here it is. They're using it to keep us from showing the tainted origins of this investigation. That's prejudice, for sure. We must be allowed to proceed with our opening argument without further interference."

"Not if I ultimately don't allow you to put the whole thing in evidence," Snyder said.

"Absolutely right, Your Honor," Dolinar said. "And we're sure you won't. We have case law on that."

"Then," Scott said, "we'll ask you to reconsider your previous ruling allowing the amendment of the indictment."

Snyder looked flummoxed. "I can't force them to add counts to their indictment."

"Then you have to let us get all this evidence in."

"A lot to deal with here. I need some time to consider. We'll take a break."

During the recess, the Save Our Children! people trickled out to the hallway as well, only a few staying behind. O'Keefe joined Annie and Kelly, who remained in the courtroom.

"Don't you want to go out and get a drink of water?" O'Keefe said.

Kelly shook her head slowly "no," and Annie said, "I don't want to be near those people. What's going on?"

"Prosecution's trying to squelch any mention of the Randy Lowe story."

"I thought this process was supposed to be about establishing the facts," Annie said. "Seems like it's more about suppressing them."

An hour later Snyder summoned them to chambers. Flanked by a law clerk on each side of him, note pads and law books open in front of all three, Snyder waved off Dolinar when he tried to speak and addressed Hartley. "It's just not relevant. The Lowes aren't in the case anymore."

"But there wouldn't *be* any case without the Lowes," Hartley said. "It was tainted from the beginning, based on a false premise. We should be allowed to show that."

Dolinar intervened. "Just because their investigator discovered things in Mr. Lowe's background that are less than praiseworthy doesn't mean the defendants didn't commit these atrocious acts on other kids or even the Lowe kid. And even if Mrs. Lowe made the whole thing up, so what? They still found what they found. Nobody was probably more misguided than Columbus when he set out in the wrong direction to discover India. But he sure did find something, didn't he? And that's what happened here."

Hartley persisted. "The jury is entitled to know what initiated this investigation."

Snyder held up his hand. "I'll let you make a general statement about how the complaint that triggered the original investigation was dropped from the original indictment. And perhaps the initial interaction between Montrose and Mrs. Lowe, but even that may be subject to a valid hearsay objection, which we'll deal with if and when it comes up. No other details though. We'll let the jury draw its own conclusions."

Hartley hung his head. "Judge, you're making me box with one arm tied behind my back."

"No. The way I see it is, *the law* ties *both* your arms behind your back, and I'm letting you have one free. Mr. Dolinar is the one who has the right to object here."

"And I do object," Dolinar said.

"Noted for the record."

Hartley said, "I renew my motion to admit the lie-detector evidence. That's additional evidence of the corrupt origins of this prosecution."

"Denied."

"Exception. And I move for a mistrial."

"Denied."

CHAPTER ❧ 44

HARTLEY RESUMED HIS opening. And the trench warfare continued.

"As I was saying, the evidence will show that these children were effectively brainwashed during a series of intense interrogations carried out by intimidating authority figures, including"—he pointed toward the prosecution table—"the District Attorney's office in the person of Ms. Tarwater, the police in the person of Officer Hicks, and the lead investigator in the entire state for Child Protective Services, Mr. Brinkley.

"*Not* at the prosecution's table: Doctor Carlyle, the physician, and Betsy Mortimer, the so-called therapist, both employees of the Children's Clinic. Who were hired and paid for by the authorities, Child Protective Services. But as the evidence will show, they might as well be at the prosecution's table.

"The evidence will further show that Ms. Mortimer has little to no education, training, or experience in the identification and treatment of child sexual abuse. The limited experience she does have has all occurred in the last two years and all of it at the behest of and paid for by Mr. Brinkley's employer, Child Services, the agency that initiated this investigation and prosecution. No education, no training on the subject, but she does have some *notions* about it. And they're trying to put people in jail based on *notions*—notions the evidence will show are just wrong. They were bent on finding abuse, and so they brought to bear every coercive technique at their disposal—"

Dolinar exploded. "Objection!"

Hartley shrugged and followed him to the bench, but with the hint of a smile.

"This is exactly what you told him not to do, Your Honor." Dolinar said, loud enough for the jurors to hear him.

"I don't understand," Hartley said, feigning innocence. "I'm just telling them what we intend to prove."

Snyder, also at a volume that could easily be heard beyond the bench, said, "Come off it, Mr. Hartley. Brainwashing? So-called therapist? Intimidating authority figures? Coercive techniques? No. Simply describe the techniques, or the therapists' qualifications or lack thereof. Drop the inflammatory adjectives."

Hartley turned back to face the jurors. "Where was I going next? Oh, Dr. Carlyle. They are touting his experience. His experience, ladies and gentlemen, has been for decades to do the bidding of this prosecution office and others in this state, making his primary living testifying in literally dozens of cases on behalf of the prosecution. Never, not once, for the defense. His relationship was so close with the prosecutors that when it came time to move on from his not very extensive private medical practice toward retirement, they arranged with the Children's Clinic to employ him as their medical officer. We believe the evidence will show that Dr. Carlyle's findings are unsupported by any credible *medical* evidence and that he is acting here, as he has for his entire career, as a rubber stamp for whatever the prosecution wanted to prove in a sexual abuse case. We believe the evidence will show he is not worthy of belief.

"The evidence will further show that the prosecutors, the police, and the Child Protective state bureaucrats and therapist communities—all of them—had been prepping for months. Attending conferences on so-called Satanic crimes and ritual child sexual abuse. Participating in a recently formed local task force chasing after any hint or rumor that these things might be afoot— somewhere, anywhere.

"But they had a problem. *They didn't have a crime.* Not a single one in the whole metropolitan area. Not until a situation came along that allowed them to pounce—"

"Objection," Dolinar bellowed.

"Sustained. No more, Mr. Hartley."

Hartley continued as if nothing had happened. "They'll admit in open court what I'm about to say. The case that originally provoked all of this is no longer even being prosecuted. It was in the original indictment, but once we exposed some things—"

Dolinar sprung out of his chair and headed toward the bench. Hartley held his position until Snyder beckoned him.

"Your Honor, he's getting into the details, which he's not supposed to," Dolinar said.

"No details," Hartley responded. "I said 'some things.' How can I be more general than that?"

"Okay," Snyder said. "But that's it. No more."

"No more?" Hartley said. "You said we'd be able to get into the conversation between Heidi Lowe and Virginia."

"Inadmissible hearsay," Dolinar said.

"It's not inadmissible."

"Mr. Hartley," Snyder said, "I didn't say I'd let you do it in opening statement. I said we'd look at the issue when it came up. Do you really want us to stop your opening statement for however long it will take for both sides to brief the issue and me to decide it?"

"It's an easy issue," Hartley said. "It shouldn't take long."

" And how do we know you're even going to put your client on the stand? The evidence may never come in . . . for a lot of reasons."

"Move for a mistrial."

"This is getting disgusting. Now you're just manufacturing phony claims of error."

"While we're up here, Your Honor, I wish to make an offer of proof."

Snyder's face coiled into disgust. "Offer of proof? This isn't evidence. It's an opening statement."

"I'm not exactly sure what to call it, but I should be able to discuss the lie-detector situation that was the subject of my previous motion. It's critical to our case that we be allowed to introduce that evidence at trial and discuss it in my opening statement."

"No."

"So my motion is overruled?"

"Well, I'm not sure it's a motion or what it is, but I assure you that if you mention it, I'll both silence and sanction you."

Again, Hartley returned to the podium table and addressed the jury. "As I was saying, once we exposed some things about that original accusation, they dropped it from the indictment. Then, without carrying out any further investigation of these mere accusations against a young woman who has dedicated her life to educating children, and never been associated with any scandal or misbehavior of any kind, they sent out a letter to *every* parent of *every* child they could find who'd ever gone to the school."

He held up a copy of the letter with two fingers, as if it were on fire, and waved it. "I'm going to read from it now, but this letter will be in evidence, and please read it carefully for yourselves when you get the chance."

He began to read. "It says: 'Based on complaints we have received from several parents, we have initiated an investigation involving alleged child abuse, including child sexual abuse.'"

He looked up. "And yet there had been no investigation at all. The authorities had accepted the so-called complaints at face value. And I emphasize again, those initial complaints have now been dropped from the indictment. What does that say about the accusations that started all this? Virginia Montrose will get up on this witness stand and tell you what really happened."

Dolinar looked up at Snyder. Snyder shook his head. Not now.

"And then there's this: 'Please question your child about whether they may have been witnesses to or victims of such crimes.' Notice the language—how the 'allegations' have now become actual 'crimes.' And after terrifying the parents with lurid descriptions of those supposed crimes, ones so detailed that the parents couldn't help but know exactly who the targets of the investigation were, they then turned the parents into deputized investigators, a sort of posse with no law enforcement or other professional involvement, even though the parents likely had no training in such delicate matters."

He continued to read from the letter, explaining how the supposed indicators of abuse were normal aspects of growing up, and that an expert would testify to that and confirm there was no scientific basis to support it.

"You will also learn that every one of the children initially denied that they'd been abused, but their interrogators kept at them, using puppets and naked dolls equipped with real-looking sexual organs, asking these small children questions that signaled the answers these powerful authority figures wanted. Why? To lead the children to the answers the interrogators wanted. And they emphatically expressed their disapproval of the kids that kept denying and praised the kids who finally gave in.

"We will call to the stand a witness with extensive experience and expertise in these matters who will tell you that such techniques are at best improper, and at worst can lead to false memories."

He went on to describe how most of the parents were initially skeptical until they took their children to Betsy Mortimer at the Children's Clinic, who proclaimed that the children had been molested, in most cases right after the very first interview, and even though the children had denied it, "then she actually enlisted the parents of any 'uncooperative' children to badger their kids—"

"Objection," Dolinar said, and again headed to the bench, but he didn't have to say anything there. Snyder said, "Mr. Hartley, you were duly warned."

He turned to the jury. "Ladies and gentlemen of the jury, the opening statements are not supposed to be argumentative. They are supposed to be an essentially dispassionate description of what counsel believes the evidence will show. Mr. Hartley has violated that principle several times. You are to ignore the phrase 'badger their children' and any other inflammatory language, whether by Mr. Hartley or Mr. Dolinar."

Showing no repentance, Hartley returned to the point. "The evidence will show that Ms. Mortimer persuaded some of the parents to question those so-called 'uncooperative' children. So these powerful authority figures—the therapists, their parents—were questioning them continuously, and all the while refusing to accept their denials. As the trial date came closer, the prosecutors came on board, rehearsing the children, reinforcing the stories, maybe even embellishing them—"

Dolinar sputtered an objection.

"—*Unintentionally* embellishing, of course," Hartley said.

"The jury," Snyder declared, "should understand that it is conventional for both sides, if they're doing their job properly, to rehearse and otherwise prepare their witnesses for a coherent presentation of their testimony."

Hartley nodded and looked at the jurors. "Yes. But our expert, who's spent years in private practice treating child victims of abuse and is now a senior professor at a prestigious university, will tell you two things. One, that a child will figure out what an authority figure wants them to say. And two, the child will eventually not only repeat it but actually come to believe it."

He let that sink in for a moment, then continued. No, the defense would not be arguing that the children were lying in the usual sense of the word. Rather, they would show that, through no fault of their own, the children were not telling the truth. They are simply repeating what the adults coached them to say.

"*That* is what the evidence will show, and when it does, I will be back here suggesting to you that anything other than a verdict of innocence will be worse than wrong. It will be an American tragedy."

As Rockwell rose to address the jury on behalf of Marvin Smith, O'Keefe looked behind him. Many of the media reps had left the courtroom, hadn't even bothered to listen to most of what Hartley had to say. Now they wouldn't hear Rockwell tell the jury what a fine person his client had been—born into poverty, a budding star athlete until he had to drop out of high school to support his mother, his father having never been around. How, yes, Marvin had gotten into a little trouble after that, nothing serious, just a teenager acting up a little, but he'd risen above it, put it behind him, and he'd been working hard ever since to make a decent life for his family. Also how he'd worked at Operation Go! from the start. How he always made a special effort with the kids, often joining them on the playground to toss around a pee-wee football or helping them learn how to dribble a basketball. Consigned to a dingy boiler room, he'd made it more pleasant. Yes, the kids had visited him there sometimes, when they were down there for nap time or a music lesson or some other project. And he hadn't discouraged that. But nothing bad had ever happened to any child in that room. Only Marvin Smith's gentle goodness had been experienced there.

Rockwell stressed that his client hadn't even been mentioned in the first wave of accusations. But, eventually, one child had mumbled his name in an off-hand comment. Now there was supposedly a male involved as Virginia's partner in crime. "And, conveniently, that male was of a race despised and feared by many white people."

"Objection, your Honor," Dolinar said. "There's no evidence anywhere that race had anything to do with this."

"I only said it was 'convenient,' Your Honor," Rockwell said.

Snyder said, "Do you have any actual evidence that race was a factor?"

"It's obvious."

Turning to the jury, Snyder said, "The jury is instructed to disregard Mr. Rockwell's implications about the race of defendant Smith. At least so far, there is not evidence that race was a factor in the investigation or the prosecution."

Rockwell, chagrined and showing it, resumed. "We will show how Marvin became ever more prominent in the stories the children were telling. Even those who'd initially not mentioned him began to include him in their narratives."

Yes, Marvin had a close relationship with Virginia. She was nice to him and treated him not as a servant but as an equal human being. Yes, he'd done work at her house to earn some welcome extra money. But the suggestion that they had ever indulged in or would ever even *consider* a sexual liaison was "viciously false, as his loving wife well knows," and Rockwell pointed to where she sat in the front row behind the defense table.

O'Keefe hoped that the calm, measured cadences of Rockwell's speech had registered positively with the jury despite the constant distraction of rustling sounds, of footsteps, the opening and closing of the double doors of the courtroom as the lions of journalism made their exits to get something on file for the evening editions.

CHAPTER ཞ 45

IT WAS 3:30 P.M. by the time the lawyers finished their opening statements.

Judge Snyder scanned the courtroom. "I'm thinking maybe the jury and all the rest of us could use a little TGIF. So let's adjourn until Monday morning," provoking a smattering of applause in the audience and even from several jurors. Snyder tapped his gavel and smiled. "There'll be no more such joyful outbursts in this courtroom," which produced light laughter, quickly suppressed, as if anything more boisterous would distract from the grotesque content of the proceedings.

"Mr. Dolinar," Snyder said, "who'll be your first witness?"

"Dr. Norman Carlyle."

Startled, Hartley lurched up and asked to approach. Snyder flashed him a "surely-not-this-soon" look and said, "Well, maybe it's not so TGIF, after all."

"They can't do this without a foundation," Hartley said. "The children have to testify first. There has to be some evidence that abuse actually occurred."

Snyder seemed not to understand. He looked at Dolinar, who said, "Of course we'll lay a proper foundation. But the defense can't control the order of our proof. Plus, as you'll hear, the medical evidence will be part of the proof that the abuse occurred. It's no different than bringing in the doctor who treated a gunshot wound. It shows that the victim was shot."

That satisfied Snyder. "If what you intended was an objection, Mr. Hartley, it's overruled. I hope this isn't a portent of things to come."

Hartley returned to the defense table and set himself down hard and angry in his chair. His team stared at him, surprised by the vehemence of his reaction. He explained, "Putting the medical on first is very bad for us. It puts an expert stamp on everything right from the start … before we've had a chance to show on cross the weaknesses, contradictions, and downright lies in the children's and Betsy Mortimer's stories."

"All rise," the bailiff announced as Snyder left the bench. Ralph Merkel and Perry Slotkin made their way to the prosecution table. On his way Merkel tried to stare down O'Keefe, then shook hands and patted the backs of Dolinar, Tarwater, Hicks, and Brinkley, then hustled toward the exit, probably anxious to meet the media representatives surely anxiously waiting to meet with him. O'Keefe watched Merkel on his way out. As Merkel passed Annie and Kelly making their way to the defense table to try to say something to Ginny before they took her away to her cell, he brushed Annie's shoulder, though there had been ample room for him to have avoided any physical contact. She tendered him the "Annie look," contemptuous and recklessly fearless, but by then he had moved on.

O'Keefe's typical reaction to such things was an instant acceleration to violence. He lunged forward to charge Merkel but stopped when he looked at Annie, who well knew his propensities, and her eyes ordered him not to. Instead, he turned to Hartley and said, "I'm gonna walk my two to their car. Annie said the crowd jostled them a little out in the corridor while they were waiting for the doors to open, and Merkel almost ran into her just now."

Distracted, Hartley said, "So what'd you think?"

O'Keefe hesitated, wondering whether he should give his honest reaction and unsure whether his reaction was worth anything anyway, given his lack of experience.

"I really don't know," he said.

"Did you watch the jury?"

"As much as I could without offending them. But I couldn't read anything in any of their faces except grimaces when they heard the abuse details."

"I want you to be honest with me, even cruel. How'd I do?"

"Well … I don't know shit, but I don't know how you could've done better. All those interruptions."

With a rueful look, Hartley said, "Yeah, I'm afraid it didn't stick very well with the jury. How 'bout Lou?"

"I know you don't like him—"

"I don't dislike him. I've known him a long time, and I like him, you know, as a person. But I just don't trust him. I'm afraid he'll find a way to lose the case for us."

"I think he did just fine. That Columbo style of his pairs well with your intensity. Hot and cool. Yin and yang."

"Well, let's hope he doesn't yang us all into oblivion."

By the time Annie and Kelly got to the table, the bailiffs had whisked Ginny to the side door of the courtroom that led to the jail. Annie tried to smile. Kelly looked desolate. All Ginny managed was a forlorn glance.

"I'll walk you guys to the car," O'Keefe said.

"We'll be fine," she said, and Kelly chimed in, "They come after us, they'll have to deal with Karma."

"Maybe I just want to spend a few minutes with you two."

Annie looked reluctant but let him tag along. "By the way," she said, "I like that outfit. You clean up pretty good."

He hoped he had successfully concealed how happy that remark had made him.

CHAPTER ❧ 46

DOLINAR AND TARWATER had seemed to Ralph Merkel insufficiently concerned about O'Keefe's daughter and former wife testifying.

Tarwater reportedly had said, "The jury won't pay any attention to them." But that was short-sighted. It made Ralph angry. He wondered about the real motives of these O'Keefe people and others like them, even showing up in court sitting there conspicuously, even proudly, right behind the criminals. Why would they ally themselves with evil? They must be paying O'Keefe a lot of money. Greedy bastard. Or was it even worse? Maybe these O'Keefes were part of it somehow, maybe even gave their daughter to it. That's what had happened in *Michelle Remembers*. Why else would they go to such lengths? Were there dark secrets there? If he could expose them somehow…

He had checked out O'Keefe. A one-time drug addict, maybe even a pusher. Supposedly straight now. Maybe. A Vietnam vet. So what. Half the ones that came back from there were nut cases. And even the military elite weren't exempt. Child molestation by daycare workers had been exposed on the very grounds of the U.S. Military Academy, West Point itself, and what better proof could there be of a pervasive conspiracy than that?

Ralph had also investigated O'Keefe's skirmishes with the local underworld. Some of that seemed suspicious as well, especially his relationship with Rose Jagoda. How and why had he gotten involved with her anyway? Maybe it went back to his drug-dealing days. Maybe he was some kind of double agent—Mafia soldier and government informant at the same time. It wouldn't be the first time that had happened. How much were government people involved in this Satanic invasion anyway?

Now, on the first day of the trial, here on the wrong side of the courtroom they were, the whole O'Keefe family. More like the *un*holy family, Ralph thought, smiling sourly at his pun.

He joined his group on the sidewalk, sweating bullets and shriveling in the scalding sunlight, a ragged gauntlet that people leaving the courthouse were forced to wend through. The O'Keefes pushed through staring straight ahead, the crowd around them hovering on the edge of violence. Ralph unobtrusively separated himself from the rest of his group and, lingering back at what he hoped was an inconspicuous distance, followed the O'Keefes as they made their way to what turned out to be the wife's car.

On impulse Ralph hustled—jogging, then flat-out sprinting down the block to his van in the self-parking lot, jumped in the driver's seat, and lurched out of the lot, sweat flooding from seemingly every pore. As he banked left across traffic into the far lane, he narrowly avoided a collision with an oncoming maniacally honking car. By the time he arrived at the wife's car, O'Keefe was walking back to the courthouse, and she was pulling out into traffic. Ralph followed her, passing close by O'Keefe on the sidewalk, hoping the P.I. wouldn't recognize his van. For all Ralph knew, O'Keefe might be surveilling *him,* just as O'Keefe had done with the Lowes. But O'Keefe didn't even look up.

Ralph trailed Annie through the stop-and-go traffic, jotting down her license plate in the notebook he had Velcroed to the console lid, kept constantly open for situations like this where he needed to write something down quickly with the pen he'd also Velcroed to the lid next to the notebook. He also sometimes used a Dictaphone in situations where writing was too difficult or when he was struck by more complicated ideas too extensive to write down while on the move. He'd accumulated several tapes full of his musings.

They arrived at a small house in a neighborhood close to O'Keefe's place and also uncomfortably close to the inner city.

Respectable, but Ralph certainly wouldn't want to live there. Females loved to talk, he mused, so maybe this house would be the best place to install some sort of recording device. He had studied everything he could find on electronic eavesdropping and longed to employ it somehow to obtain valuable intelligence by bugging one of the principal adversaries in the case. What a coup that would be. And nobody would suspect a bug being planted here of all places.

Access would be difficult and high risk because the house was situated in the middle of the block. No alley. He circled the block and drove by the house a second time. He noticed a neighbor staring at him. Time to move on. But he added the O'Keefe woman and daughter to his drive-by roster. To his chagrin, during subsequent visits he discovered that O'Keefe's German Shepherd sometimes stayed at the wife's house. The damn dog seemed to be unpredictably everywhere—O'Keefe's house, his office, his wife's house …

School had started again. If the weather was decent, the daughter would walk home on her own, often dawdling along the way, and would be at the house alone for two to three hours until her mother arrived home from work.

LOSSES FROM THE SAVINGS & LOAN DEBACLE ONCE AGAIN EXCEED $3 BILLION.

CHAPTER ⅋ 47

DR. NORMAN CARLYLE took the stand.

He had a rooster's comb of white hair and a face etched with more than wrinkles—deep creases, virtual rivulets carved there over a long life. He wore black horn rim glasses, a bolo tie, white shirt, and a dark, somewhat baggy suit as if he had shrunk while the suit retained its original size and shape. His voice was full of gravelly authority.

Dolinar took him quickly through his credentials and experience, prompting him to describe the large number of sexually abused children he had examined and the numerous cases he had testified in.

Then he took Carlyle's pro-prosecution history head-on. "Doctor, why have you so often testified for the prosecution in these cases?"

"Because, in my long experience, they are always or almost always in the right. Children don't lie about these things. They don't know enough to lie about such things."

Dolinar then moved to Mortimer's interviews of the children, beginning with Misty Haynes, age five. "How did Misty come to be in your office for examination?"

"She was referred to me by the Children's Clinic, who had interviewed her and concluded—"

"Objection," Hartley said.

With a disapproving frown and a gesture of his right hand, Judge Snyder summoned counsel to the bench and said, "I know where you're going, Mr. Hartley. It's a dead end but go ahead. I'm sure you want to make a record."

DAN FLANIGAN ⤳ 193

"Your Honor, he's going to say that the Children's Clinic concluded that the child was molested. That's hearsay, actually double hearsay—once from the child to Mortimer, and then from Mortimer to Carlyle. It's extremely prejudicial and isn't necessary as a foundation for his testimony. The witness was supposed to determine whether the child had been abused, not what Betsy Mortimer had concluded."

"I also know what *you're* going to say, Mr. Dolinar, but please say it for the record so we can move on."

"First, it's not being offered for the truth of the fact that the abuse occurred, only why the child was in the doctor's office, so it's not even hearsay under the rule.

"Second, it fits perfectly into hearsay exception number four, a statement made for medical diagnosis or treatment.

"Third, Betsy Mortimer will be testifying and will be subject to cross-examination.

"Fourth, so will each of the children be testifying and will be subject to cross examination.

"Fifth, he's a medical expert, and experts can rely on hearsay as a basis for expert opinion.

"Sixth, the history of the case and the findings of the therapists are crucial to the medical diagnosis itself."

Snyder smirked. "At least one of those reasons has to hold up, doesn't it, Mr. Hartley?"

"It's highly prejudicial," Hartley said. "It gives the imprimatur of this physician to a statement that is, at best, a mere conclusion without foundation, and at worst, a fairy tale invented by Mortimer and Brinkley and injected into the child."

"Overruled."

Hartley, again with that apoplectic look, returned to the defense table, and Dolinar continued. "Do you recall the question and the answer given before Mr. Hartley interrupted you?"

"Yes. The Children's Clinic sent the child to me after concluding that she had been molested. They asked me to conduct an examination of the genital areas. Which I did."

Over Hartley's objections on hearsay grounds, summarily overruled, Dr. Carlyle then testified that the child herself confirmed that she had been abused.

Dolinar continued: "Were the clinic's findings and the child's confirmation important to your examination and findings?"

"Yes, the history is of great importance."

The prosecutor clicked on a remote device. A huge photo flashed up on a giant screen. "Dr. Carlyle, can you identify this image?"

"Yes. That's a photo of Misty's vaginal area, taken by my assistant under my supervision, with a colposcope, which is a photographic device that allows us to detect and reveal abnormalities that wouldn't be visible to the naked eye."

"What type of abnormalities?"

"For example, unnatural enlargement of the hymenal and anal openings or scars in the vaginal or anal walls, sometimes very small but still observable ones.'"

"What did this picture reveal to you, Dr. Carlyle?"

"It revealed a vaginal opening that was abnormally large, scars in the opening and on the outer edges of the interior wall. It had been subjected to blunt force trauma."

"And did you arrive at any conclusion concerning the cause of the child's condition?"

"The condition of the vaginal area was consistent with sexual abuse. Specifically, penetration by an object."

"What type of an object?" Dolinar asked.

"It could have been—"

Hartley objected. "Pure speculation."

Overruled.

Carlyle continued, trying to correct his wording to remove any possible objection, "It was an erect penis or some other object such as a wooden or plastic utensil. Consistent with sexual abuse."

He proceeded to provide similar testimony with respect to the vaginal and anal areas of each child named in the indictment.

CHAPTER ❧ 48

APPALLED WAS THE expression on most of the jurors' faces, now staring at the defense table with open hostility.

Hartley remained in his chair for a moment that seemed too long, and O'Keefe wondered what the rest of the courtroom probably wondered. Was he frozen in place, intimidated by the daunting task before him? Or maybe he was simply trying to heighten the suspense? But finally, he stood and proceeded grimly about his task.

He first established Dr. Carlyle's history, which was exactly as Hartley had described it in his opening statement.

He also brought out that Carlyle had never before used a colposcope.

"And this colposcope instrument was developed in part through experiments in the death camps during the Holocaust, right?"

Dolinar jolted forward, as if he intended to object but then thought better of it.

"I'm not aware of that," Carlyle said.

"And," Hartley continued, "it's only recently begun to be employed in sexual-abuse examinations, and still isn't widely used, right?"

"I'm not aware of the extent of its use," Carlyle said.

"And it magnifies by a power of thirty, correct?"

"Yes."

"Thirty! So the pictures you showed us on that screen were thirty times larger than what could be a seen by straight visual observation, right?"

"Yes, obviously."

"I assume they could not be seen if it had magnified them by only ten, or twenty, or twenty-five times, right?"

"I'm not sure."

"And how do you know what the"—he made air quotes—"'normal' size of a vaginal or anal orifice is? And what is that based on?"

Dolinar objected. "Argumentative."

"It certainly is," Judge Snyder said. "And compound too. Two questions at once. The jury will ignore Mr. Hartley's second question."

"So how do you know?" Hartley said.

"The literature."

"What literature?"

Hesitatingly, uncertainly. "Articles."

"And which articles are those?"

He could only recall one. "The article was written by a pediatrician. It stated that a normal hymenal opening was no more than four millimeters and that anything larger was consistent with molestation having occurred."

"Are you really saying, sir, that every child with a hymenal opening of more than four millimeters has been abused?

"I'm not sure how many, if any, there are with that condition, but I recall thinking the article was very convincing.

"An article by a pediatrician. What do you know about him?"

"Nothing … other than that a respected medical journal was willing to publish his article."

"Are you aware, Dr. Carlyle, of the study carried out at Harvard Medical School, completed a couple of years ago, which found *zero difference* between the genital areas of abused and non-abused girls?"

"I'm generally aware of it, but I disagree with it."

'Have you read it?"

"No."

"Then how can you disagree with it?"

"It's been criticized."

"By whom?"

He thought for a few moments. "I can't recall right now."

"And you're not contending, are you, that the article by the pediatrician you've cited has *not* been criticized?"

"I don't know either way."

"And you can't tell us the source of this alleged criticism of the Harvard study, correct?"

"Correct. I don't recall right now."

"But, whatever it is, you've chosen to reject the Harvard Medical study and accept the article by the pediatrician."

"That's what I said. Harvard isn't perfect."

"But I guess the pediatrician *is* perfect?"

"I found him to be more persuasive and consistent with my own observations after doing this for decades."

"More consistent than what? The Harvard study that you never read?"

"That's what I said."

"What was his name and what was the name of the journal the article was published in?"

"I don't recall off the top of my head."

"What year was it published?"

Carlyle didn't remember that either. Hartley continued to probe for details that Carlyle couldn't come up with.

"And you can't say for certain, can you, Doctor, that these abnormalities that you claim to have observed, were not caused by something other than molestation?"

"I don't understand your question," he said.

"They could have been caused by any number of things, like, for example, injuries from playground equipment or riding a bike…"

"I think I can say they weren't."

"On what grounds?" Scott asked.

"Based on the Children's Clinic findings and the children's statements."

"All hearsay," Hartley said, scowling at Snyder.

Snyder sustained the objection before Dolinar made it and instructed the jury to disregard Hartley's comment.

"You say that you relied on the Children's Clinic findings and the children's statements. None of that is medical, is it, Doctor?"

"The history is part of the medical analysis. In fact, it is critical, essential, decisive to the analysis."

"So why then even bother to do a *medical* analysis?"

"To establish whether the medical analysis shows consistency with molestation?"

And your specific finding, sir, your exact words are, "'Consistent with molestation having occurred.' Interesting wording. So you're not saying that what you observed was *caused* by molestation, but only that it was consistent with the *possibility* of molestation."

"That's true, but—"

"That's a yes or no question, Doctor, and you've answered in the affirmative. A speech isn't appropriate or necessary."

Dolinar stood. "He should be allowed to explain his answer."

Watching, O'Keefe was shocked when Snyder disagreed with the prosecutor. "You can get that explanation on redirect."

"And," Hartley continued, "you didn't consider whether some or all of these could be hereditary conditions, did you?"

"No."

"And in the case of some of the children, isn't it correct that these photos and colposcopic magnifications were taken more than two years, sometimes much longer, after the abuse is alleged to have occurred?"

"Yes."

"As much as six or seven years, right?"

"Yes."

"And isn't it undeniably true that all kind of incidents could have occurred in those intervening years to cause the conditions you observed?"

"Not in my opinion."

"But nothing in these photos themselves allows you to pin down or even estimate the time that any of these so-called abnormalities, if that's what they are, occurred, correct?"

"Correct."

"What if these children were brainwashed by someone?"

"I don't believe you can persuade a child to state there was abuse if it didn't occur."

"Do you believe children never lie?"

He paused, then said, "Of course some children lie about some things, but—"

Hartley held up his hand. "You've answered the question. Here's another one. If a child tells you that Santa Claus or the Easter Bunny exists, do you believe them?"

"That's not about sexual abuse."

"Do you believe them or not, Doctor?"

"No."

"And they haven't made those things up, have they? Adults have told them they exist, correct?

"Yes."

"And even if molestation did cause these abnormalities, it doesn't prove at all that *these* defendants molested these children, does it?"

"Yes, it does. Based on the clinician findings and the children's own statements and the fact that my findings were consistent with those."

"But none of those findings and statements were products of your own medical exam, were they? They didn't derive from your observation, your colposcope, or anything else that's actually medical in any traditional sense of the meaning of that word, correct?"

"The observations made in the medical examination, with and without the colposcope, determined that the physical condition was consistent with molestation, as I have consistently said."

Rockwell's cross focused on only one issue: the cause of the so-called abnormalities.

"You said that, and I quote, 'an erect penis or some other object' was inserted. But nothing about those colposcope images, or your examination, allows you to conclude exactly what the object was, isn't that correct?"

"Correct. I cannot."

"So you can't say that a male sex organ was the object inserted, correct?"

"Not with absolute certainty."

"It could have been many other things, isn't that right?"

"Unlikely, but possible."

"Unlikely? You have no basis for using that word, do you?"

Dolinar objected. "Argumentative."

Sustained.

"And if it was a male sex organ, you can't say *whose* it was, can you?"

"I think I can, based on what Ms. Mortimer and the children told me."

Rockwell, infuriated by his constant resort to what Mortimer told him, raised his voice several notches. "What someone, a non-physician, told you. But you can't say it based on any physical, medical finding that you made in your examination, correct?"

He slowly nodded his head.

"We need a verbal answer."

He seemed to have a hard time bringing himself to say it, but out it finally came. "Correct."

Dolinar stood for redirect. Was there anything *in*consistent with an erect penis being one of the objects that had produced the condition? No, Carlyle told him.

Did children lie? Occasionally, Carlyle said, but never about abuse. "I believe the children. Always."

"Mr. Hartley interrupted you when you tried to explain your answer as to whether the abnormalities were caused by molestation. Please explain."

"I had the history, which told me there had been abuse."

"And thus can you say with reasonable medical certainty that these children were abused by the defendants?"

"Definitely."

Enraged by the last question and answer, Hartley argued that they had exceeded the scope of his cross-examination, and he should be entitled to re-cross on that point. Again, surprising at least to O'Keefe, Judge Snyder agreed.

"Isn't it true," he asked, "that your so-called medical certainty isn't based on any medical findings, Doctor? As a physician, you are not contributing anything at all here, are you?"

Dolinar objected, the jury was instructed to disregard, and Snyder added, "This is an official reprimand, Mr. Hartley."

Hartley didn't respond, seemingly satisfied that Snyder's scolding couldn't erase from the jury's minds the point he had made.

After Carlyle stepped out of the witness box, Hartley and Rockwell approached the bench. This time, Rockwell did the talking.

"What we just experienced, Your Honor, was a textbook example of junk science. Actually, *no* science. Utterly worthless. The guy was really no more than a bystander. Even less than that. He was at most a tape recorder, regurgitating back what someone told him. We move that Dr. Carlyle's testimony be stricken in its entirety and the jury instructed to give it no credence whatever. We're prepared to file a detailed brief by tomorrow morning supporting our motion."

"Save your time, gentlemen. Motion is overruled."

CHAPTER ❧ 49

"**S**EEMS LIKE YOU and I might share a knack for snagging secret tapes."

"Does that mean you got it?"

"It certainly does."

"Meet?"

"Yes."

"Harvey's?"

"I'd prefer on this one we meet out in the open. How about Langhorne Park at 3 p.m.? The bandstand."

"Done."

On the phone Paschal had sounded quite pleased with himself, but here on the steps of the bandstand he didn't look that way. More like a hunted creature.

"I know you think Harvey's is safe," he said, "but I'm not trusting any place inside on this. You're not recording this, are you?"

"What's the world coming to?" O'Keefe said. "You keep not trusting me. You're welcome to frisk me."

Paschal waved him off. "I don't want to be stroking your pecker. We might both be shocked by what happens."

O'Keefe laughed. "Spare me, please."

Paschal grunted something in the vicinity of a laugh, but it quickly evaporated, and his cheeks squinched as if he were in pain. "Let's hope this tape produces as good a result as yours ultimately did."

"Let's hope," O'Keefe said, recalling the illegally recorded conversation that only a few weeks earlier had been maneuvered into the hands of a U.S. Attorney resistant to receiving it at all. But once the contents of the tape were communicated to the right parties in both the Mafia and law enforcement, good things had happened.

Paschal continued. "I'm not sure how to handle this. It could be big trouble for me and my source. I'm not even sure I'll give it to you."

"How 'bout you start with just telling me about it?"

Paschal explained that it was one of the first interviews done with a child at the Children's Clinic. Someone in the District Attorney's office got wind of that and promptly ordered the Clinic to stop recording. "Apparently, the DA's office took possession of the tape and made sure there were no copies."

"Hartley's asked for all that kind of stuff," O'Keefe said. "They've never delivered a tape."

"I hear they're not always very good at complying with that *Brady* requirement."

"Have you listened to it?"

"Watched. It's a videotape."

"And?"

"It reveals some pretty heavy-handed interrogation techniques."

"Nice," O'Keefe said. "And critically important, I'd bet. How and when can you give it to me?"

"Not so fast. I need to protect my source. They—"

"'They'? How many sources are there?"

"—One."

"Only one? 'They'?"

"Hey, dipshit. 'They' can be singular as well as plural, and it's gender neutral."

"Sorry to be so grammatically ill informed."

"So *their* ... that is, my *singular* source ... their conscience is tormenting them. They've waited until the last minute here, and they feel they have to do something before it's too late, but they're worried about getting fired, or worse, a criminal prosecution, for leaking it. If I give it to you, you'll have to testify where and how and who you got it from. That puts *me* on the stand. When I refuse to disclose the source, I go to jail for contempt."

O'Keefe groaned. "And now that I know this, I owe it to my client to do whatever I can to get that tape."

"Hasty action could still cause that tape to disappear."

"I feel guilty enough already. I have to tell Hartley. Now."

"What if I tell you I'll deny that I ever heard of such a tape or said a word to you about it?"

"You'd perjure yourself?"

"You put a rat in a corner, he'll leap for your face."

"This is gonna get ugly," O'Keefe said.

"How 'bout you try to figure out a way to force them to turn it over without identifying me or my source?"

O'Keefe thought for a moment. "I've got an idea, but I have to take it to Hartley, and he'll press me hard for the full story."

"Well, do what you can. I'm not kidding when I say a wrong move could make that tape go bye-bye forever."

Paschal reached inside his jacket and extracted what O'Keefe hoped would be the tape, but it was a half-full, half-pint bottle of Jim Beam. "Surely even you can't grudge me this one." And it was a very long one indeed. When he finished, the bottle was empty, and he said, "They sentenced Zola to a year in prison for publishing 'J'accuse!' And he was a world-famous author allowed to depart for exile in England. I'm a pissant with nowhere to go into exile. I don't even have a place to publish."

O'Keefe met with Hartley and suggested they file an emergency *Brady* request for any and all exculpatory items, specifically interview tapes, transcripts, summaries, etcetera.

"We already asked for all that in the first round."

"Try again," O'Keefe said.

"Why? What are you up to?"

"I can't say."

"What the fuck does that mean?"

"It wouldn't be good for the cause for you to know right now."

"How can that be? This is the weirdest thing ever." Hartley folded his arms and dug his feet into the floor. "You can't do this."

"Don't make me do this, Scott. It's not good for us."

"I'll be the judge of that."

Shit. "Okay. There might be a tape. But that's all I can tell you. I've been assured that if I tell you anything else, it'll vanish. Let's not risk it. Just file that request."

"That's crazy."

"Trust me."

But O'Keefe wasn't at all sure that he could be trusted.

CHAPTER ⌁ 50

HARTLEY ARRIVED AT the courthouse early.

As was his custom, he took the stairs. An unsmiling bailiff stood guard outside the courtroom. Hartley grinned at the bailiff, entered the empty courtroom, and placed five copies of the *Brady* request on the prosecution's table, then exited, nodding to the bailiff, this time without a smile. He walked a few steps down the hall to Judge Snyder's chambers. In the front room, the courtroom deputy pecked at her keyboard while a law clerk scratched furiously on a yellow legal pad. Hartley approached the deputy, placed copies of the request on the desk, and handed one to the clerk.

The clerk was alert, the deputy displeased.

"What's this?"

Hartley told her.

"So late?"

"We think they may not have given us everything. It's almost too late. We need to make sure."

"His Honor will enjoy this. He loves surprises first thing in the morning."

Hartley returned to the courtroom. O'Keefe was standing just inside the door. He cocked his head toward the prosecution table, where Dolinar and Tarwater were bent over reading the document. Tarwater looked up as Hartley and O'Keefe took their own seats and said, "What is this shit? We gave you everything long ago."

"We don't think so," Hartley said. "We think you'd better take another look."

"Games. Stupid games."

Once Rockwell arrived, the law clerk came out from chambers and beckoned for the lawyers to follow. Hartley grabbed O'Keefe by the arm. "You too. You definitely need to be there for this one."

In chambers, despite an unfriendly glance from Judge Snyder, O'Keefe's presence wasn't challenged.

Snyder sighed. "Okay, Mr. Hartley. What is it now?"

"It's a critical moment, sort of the point of no return. We want to make sure they've given us everything. It wouldn't be the first time a prosecutor had … let's say, *overlooked* something."

Dolinar raised his hands in exasperation. "We complied with our *Brady* obligations fully. Ages ago. This can't have any basis except to create a false issue to harass and distract us. It's just a fishing expedition in a puddle with no fish in it."

Hartley gave O'Keefe an "I told you so" look.

Snyder brushed the back of his right hand across the document he held in his left as if flicking it away. "You've got to give me something more concrete if you want me to do anything with … whatever this is."

"Can I have five minutes with Mr. O'Keefe in the hallway?" Scott said.

Snyder winced.

"Your Honor," Dolinar said, "this is so out of order, so improper."

"Five minutes," Snyder said. "Not a second more."

In the hallway, Hartley said, "I told you so. We look like idiots. You've taken me out on thin ice and stranded me. We have to tell him something."

O'Keefe said nothing.

"The client," Hartley said. "The client is who we have to think about here."

O'Keefe looked up at the bare, gray walls of the hallway but found no answer there.

"Clock's ticking," Hartley said.

"Okay, but I'm keeping it lean."

"You're making this too damned hard."

Without revealing McKenna's role, O'Keefe quickly told him there was a strong possibility that a videotape existed of one of the initial interviews of one of the children. Hartley was delighted about that news but enraged that O'Keefe would tell him nothing else. "You keep this up, and I'm gonna cut you loose and let you twist solely in the wind."

They returned to chambers, and he apparently wasn't quite ready to abandon O'Keefe yet. "We believe," Hartley said, "based on what we understand to be a source in the DA's office, that there may be one or more contemporary reports, memoranda, or even recordings of interviews with one or more of the child complainants."

Dolinar held up a finger, a silent request for a few moments of delay, had a whispered consultation with Tarwater, then said, "Assuming that such a thing exists, which neither Ms. Tarwater nor I can confirm or deny at this point, though we believe Mr. Hartley's statement is flat wrong, I would remind Mr. Hartley that *Brady* only requires turnover of exculpatory evidence—*evidence favorable to the defense, in the judgment of the prosecutor.*"

"*Reasonable* judgment," Hartley corrected him.

"I'm sure," Dolinar said, "that Rhonda and others in our office who assembled the *Brady* material made appropriate determinations."

"Well, there you have it, Mr. Hartley," Snyder said. "Your motion is denied."

As they made their way back into the courtroom, Hartley said, "Okay, I tried to do it your way. It didn't work. We need that tape. Any more fucking around and I'll make sure your ass gets so roasted you'll never want to sit down again."

Then something struck him. His face changed to amusement. "Did you notice how Dolinar set Tarwater up for the fall if that tape shows up somehow?

The media quickly picked up on the new *Brady* request, and the reporting must have had an influence on Paschal and his source. When he and O'Keefe met that evening, again in Langhorne Park, and O'Keefe recounted what had happened in the chambers conference that day, it seemed to tip Paschal all the way over. He reached in his coat pocket, and this time extracted not a half pint of Jim Beam but a package the size of a VHS tape.

"And you'll protect me if you can?" he said.
O'Keefe gave him his word, "If I can."

JURY ACQUITS LOCAL PRIVATE INVESTIGATOR OF UNLAWFUL WIRETAPPING BECAUSE HE ACTED ON FAULTY LEGAL ADVICE.

CHAPTER ⚡ 51

THE NEXT DAY, Friday, during the morning session, the prosecution presented evidence relating to the course of their investigation, and Hartley's cross examination made O'Keefe think of the old Zorro television show where Zorro was always fencing against two adversaries. In this case, it was Hartley vs. both Dolinar and Snyder. He tried to raise the Lowe issues, but Snyder allowed him very little leeway. He did manage to clearly establish that the Lowe complaint and nothing else provoked the original investigation and that no parents came forward whose children had not first been interviewed, sometimes multiple times, at the Children's Clinic.

His voice charged with outrage and contempt, he dragged Myra Hicks through almost every sentence of the letter she had signed and sent to the parents and extracted a concession that Betsy Mortimer had played a significant role in drafting it.

"So, Ms. Mortimer was actually part of the investigative effort, wasn't she?"

"No. She only consulted occasionally at our request."

"Did you give any thought to the reaction this letter might cause?"

"What reaction?"

"Do you have children?"

"I do not."

"Did you ever try to imagine the terror and hysteria this letter would provoke?"

"My duty was to uncover crimes against children."

"And you decided to do that by shouting fire in a crowded theater when you had no idea whether there was a fire or not, right? It was like you were trying to *start* the fire yourself, right?"

Dolinar's objection was sustained.

At the mid-day adjournment, Hartley asked Snyder to hold a chambers conference after lunch.

"What about?" Snyder asked.

"What we discussed yesterday in chambers. It's a recording of one of the children's interviews."

Snyder, startled, said, "Let's do it now."

Gathered in front of the judge's desk, and all looking expectantly at Hartley, he held up the tape. "Here it is."

Dolinar and Tarwater looked at each other. O'Keefe could detect only surprise, no guilt.

"Where'd you get it?" Snyder asked.

"It was given to Mr. O'Keefe."

"By whom?"

"It was given on the condition that Mr. O'Keefe wouldn't reveal the source."

Dolinar was the apoplectic one now. "Ridiculous," he spat. "We're entitled to that information. I mean, who knows where it came from?"

A tremor ran across Hartley's face, and his voice broke high. "I suggest we watch it. You'll recognize Betsy Mortimer and Ken Brinkley. The child is Robert Putnam, one of the children named in the indictment."

Snyder seemed flummoxed and looked at Dolinar, but the prosecutor seemed suddenly bereft of oratory.

"Please, Your Honor," Hartley said. "We can all watch it right here."

"How?"

"Judge Markowitz keeps a TV and VCR in his chambers. He's agreed to let me borrow it."

Snyder looked again at Dolinar. "Why don't we? Let's see if it's real and what it says."

Dolinar, with the look of a man who'd been maneuvered into a tight corner, said, "I guess we ought to, Your Honor, but it has to be understood that we're reserving all rights, waiving nothing."

"Of course," Snyder said. "I assume you won't contest that aspect, Mr. Hartley?"

"They can reserve all the rights they want."

Tarwater touched Dolinar's arm, conferred with him. He took a step back, yielding to her and indicating she should proceed.

"The defense claims it came from our office," she said. "Which means it's our property. And if it's our property, it's been stolen. Mr. O'Keefe conspired in the theft of property and has knowingly received stolen property. Those are crimes."

"How hysterical, how absurd," Hartley said. "The tape itself is worth nothing. It's a cheap medium for conveyance of information, and the information is not the government's property."

Snyder's smile was laced with malice. "We'll see about that. But Mr. O'Keefe should understand that he's potentially at risk on this."

O'Keefe hoped he was successfully disguising that his heart was drumming hard and fast.

A few minutes later, Hartley had set up the VCR and loaded the tape.

Mortimer opened with her brightest "Hi, Bobby," told him his parents were so proud of him, and mentioned "yucky things." Brinkley complimented Bobby on his "neat boots," established that he'd attended Operation Go! from age four, was now "almost seven," and promised him a real badge, "just like the policemen wear," if he did "a good job today." Bobby's head bobbed enthusiastically multiple times.

> Bobby: [Looking eagerly around the room.] Will I get to play here?

> Mortimer: Yes. With the dolls and puppets first, then maybe some other things.

> Bobby: I don't play with dolls.

> Mortimer: Well, these are special dolls. We just want you to show us some things, not really play with them…

> [They establish that his parents have removed him from the school.]

Bobby: They said Miss Ginny was bad.

Mortimer: Yes, several kids, including some of your classmates, have been telling us about those bad things.

Bobby: Who?

Mortimer: Do you remember Nancy Mangan? And Paul Skinner?

Bobby: Uh-huh.

Mortimer: Your friends told us some bad, yucky things about Ginny. And also Mr. Smith.

Bobby: Mr. Smith?

Mortimer: The school janitor. A black man. Do you remember him? [Bobby looks confused but nods.] Yes? Your friends said that some of those bad things were done to you.

Bobby: What things?

Brinkley: You tell us, Bobby. What bad things happened to you?

[A long pause.]

Bobby: She put me in Time Out sometimes.

Brinkley: That's all? Really? Are you telling us everything?

Bobby: I don't remember...

Mortimer: That's what we're here for, Bobby. To help you remember.

Brinkley: You know that Miss Ginny and Mr. Smith can't hurt you anymore. The police are watching them all the time.

Mortimer: We're wondering why you don't remember what the other kids remember. Sometimes, when really bad things happen to children, they have a hard time remembering. See this doll? Really, it's just a big puppet. It's a boy, see?

Bobby: [Giggles.] He has his own little peter.

Mortimer: And a bum too … What do you call it?

Bobby: Butt.

Mortimer: Did Ginny or Mr. Smith ever touch you on your penis or your butt? [Bobby's eyes widen, and he shakes his head vigorously.] No? You don't remember what other kids remember? Surely, you're as smart as they are. Did Ginny and Mr. Smith ever put their mouths on your penis or anything in your butt?

Bobby: Oh, no.

Brinkley: How about a plastic knife, or a spoon, or a fork? Like these. [Brinkley shows him the utensils.] No? … I want you to think really hard because we think the same thing happened to you that happened to other kids.

Bobby: I don't think so.

Brinkley: Yes, it did. Tell us.

[Another long pause. Bobby looks around the room, as if for an escape route. He begins to cry.]

Brinkley: Don't cry. Be a big, brave boy. We know it's really sad and scary to remember.

Mortimer: [Manipulating a puppet in each hand, one a frog, the other a boy. Roughing her voice slightly, but still plaintive.] This is Detective Froggy, and this is Bobby. Detective Froggy thinks Bobby knows something he isn't telling. If she didn't do it to you, what other kids did she do it to?

[A long pause.]

Brinkley: Who else?

Bobby: I guess Nancy and Paul, like they said.

Brinkley: What other kids?

Bobby: I don't know. I guess … I wasn't there.

Mortimer: And Detective Froggy says we have to make sure no other kids get hurt. He's begging. "Bobby, please help us. You're the only one in the class who won't tell. You want to earn the badge, don't you?"

Brinkley: How 'bout you show us where Ginny *might* have touched the kids or put things in them?

[Mortimer puts down the puppets, picks up male and female anatomical dolls, and lays them in front of Bobby. Long pause. Finally, Bobby points to the dolls' genitals.]

Mortimer: And who did she do that to?

Bobby: Nancy and Peter said so.

Brinkley: Did she ever take you over to the boiler room where Mr. Smith hung out?

Bobby: Once or twice.

[Brinkley and Mortimer look at each other knowingly.]

Brinkley: What did they do to you there?

Bobby: Just showed us all his stuff.

Brinkley: Did he ever show you his peter?

Bobby: No.

Brinkley: But he showed it to other kids. Didn't they tell you that?

Bobby: I don't remember that.

Brinkley: Did Miss Ginny ever help you go potty?

Bobby: Yes.

Brinkley: She touched you then, didn't she?

Bobby: I guess. Sometimes.

Brinkley: With her mouth?

Bobby: No.

Brinkley: Did your peter ever get longer or harder when that happened?

Bobby: [Eyes bulge.] Yes.

Mortimer: Good boy. Detective Froggy thinks you're doing a lot better.

Mortimer: Miss Ginny had you over to her house sometimes, right?

Bobby: Yeah, babysitting. We played lots of games.

Mortimer: Were you wearing your clothes when you were playing?

Bobby: Sometimes just pajamas.

Mortimer: What would Ginny have on?

Bobby: Sometimes pajamas.

Mortimer: Did she ever wear a robe?

Bobby: She did.

Mortimer: Was there anything special about it? Like a drawing or picture of any kind sewn into it? … No? I bet you saw her sometimes without any clothes on.

Bobby: I don't think so.

Mortimer: Were there candles?

Bobby: Yes.

Mortimer: Was there an altar. You know what that is?

Bobby: A table.

Mortimer: Was Mr. Smith ever there?

Bobby: [Thinking.] One time, maybe.

Mortimer: And what was he doing with Ginny?

Bobby: I don't remember.

Mortimer: You don't remember? You're not stupid, are you? Did they ever dance with each other?

Bobby: Maybe … When can I play?

Mortimer: You can play when you tell us like the other kids did. We know you're not as dumb as you're acting now, Bobby.

Brinkley: We know you must've been touched, or at least saw others get touched. We think you're a lot smarter than you showed us today. We don't want to tell your buddies that you wouldn't help them.

[Long pause.]

Bobby: Janie said something happened back in the cloak room … and in Mr. Smith's room.

Brinkley: Mr. Smith's room?

Bobby: She said Miss Ginny took her there.

Mortimer: What is Janie's last name? You don't remember? Janie Carter maybe? She's been here.

Bobby: That's her.

Mortimer: When did she tell you this?

Bobby: Last week. We play together sometimes. Our parents are friends.

Brinkley: And what happened in those places?

[Long pause.]

Bobby: I can't remember.

Brinkley: I'm thinking you just don't want to remember.

Mortimer: We know how hard it is, Bobby … how scary it is.

Brinkley: Clothes taken off? Touching? Fingers? Spoons? Did Mr. Smith show his thing? Miss Ginny her thing? Rubbing? Licking?

[Long pause.]

Bobby: Maybe.

Mortimer: To Janie, and Nancy and Peter? Yes? So, yes to Janie, Nancy, and Peter? How about others … Yes?

Bobby: [Hesitantly.] Yes … I guess.

Mortimer: Are you sure some of those things didn't happen to you, Bobby?

Bobby: I don't know. I'm tired. When can I go?

[Pause.]

220   ⇝ **AN AMERICAN TRAGEDY**

Mortimer: We'll meet again soon. Meanwhile, will you think about these things? Try to remember. Talk to your parents. They helped us, and they need your help back.

Brinkley: And don't be afraid any longer of the bad people—Miss Ginny and Mr. Smith or any of the others that might have done these things.

Bobby: I'm not afraid.

The tape ended.

CHAPTER ❧ 52

HARTLEY EJECTED THE tape and snatched it out of the VHS recorder as if someone might be tempted to grab it away from him.

"So there we are. Clearly Betsy Mortimer and Ken Brinkley of Children's Clinic. Clearly this case. Clearly one of the alleged victims named in the indictment. And somehow they managed to manipulate him from this initial interview to the allegations in the indictment that he was sodomized in various ways on several occasions by Virginia Montrose in the bathroom and the cloak room, and by both Virginia Montrose and Marvin Smith in the boiler room and in Virginia's home."

Dolinar looked angry, but fearful too. His voice cracked as he spoke. "Your Honor, there's so much wrong with this, I don't know where to start. He's accusing us of outright dishonesty, but there's no showing where this tape came from. He needs to tell us where it came from, how he got it, establish a foundation. And it's all BS anyway. Why? Because nothing on that tape is exculpatory. By the end, the kid's admitted he was abused and—"

"Nonsense," Hartley said. "There was no admission there. He was just floundering around, trying to get them off his back. It's a perfect illustration of the brainwashing process they employed, which is the whole crux of our defense. You saw it. Bobby denies it and persists in his denials, even after they wheedle, pressure, beg, reward, insult, and threaten him, and suggest time after time what they want him to say. The puppet lady is turning the kid into her own living, breathing, flesh-and-blood puppet. And observe the difference between the very vague admissions at the end of that tape compared to the horrific stuff that ends up in the indictment.

"And this is just the one tape we were lucky enough to find … so far. Who knows how many others there are? Who knows how much other exculpatory evidence hasn't been turned over?"

"I'm not sure whether I agree with any of that," Snyder said, "but first things first. Where did that tape come from?"

"I don't know. Only Mr. O'Keefe knows, and he won't tell even me."

"Mr. O'Keefe." Snyder said. It wasn't a question, it was a demand.

O'Keefe looked at Hartley, but the lawyer wasn't coming to his rescue. It was twisting in the wind time. After a painful silence, he said, "I'm not at liberty—"

"Liberty?" Snyder scoffed. "I don't see a gag in your mouth or a gun to your head."

"I made a promise, so I won't tell."

"Oh, I bet you'll tell eventually, my friend."

Dolinar said, "Let's put him under oath right here. He'll have to answer under pain of contempt right now."

Snyder, not to be buffaloed even by his favorite prosecutor, took a moment, then smiled, proud of himself. "No, I think we'll give him a little time to think about it and discuss it with Mr. Hartley and maybe his personal counsel. Mr. Hartley, I assume you'll advise him that this isn't grade school. He'll have to tattle-tale."

"I'll discuss it with him."

"Won't do any good," O'Keefe said. "I won't reveal it. Might as well put me away right now."

Snyder looked about to blow, but Hartley said, "Please give me a chance with him, Your Honor. Over the weekend."

Dolinar said: "They don't deserve any time. The duty's clear, especially where they've made such heinous accusations against our office."

"I agree," Snyder said, "they don't deserve it." He looked out toward the courtroom where the importunate press and militant parents were waiting. "But I'd like to avoid a public brouhaha if possible. We'll adjourn until Monday. First thing Monday morning, we'll hold a special hearing here in chambers. I think that's within my authority. I don't want the jury or the press or the parents to witness this circus if I can avoid it. And, Mr. Dolinar, your people need to spend the weekend turning over every rock to make sure there's nothing you've overlooked, or, God forbid, deliberately held back. I'll be expecting an affidavit on that. I try to avoid issuing formal gag orders, but I will be very unhappy if any of you say a word to the press about this. The only word is 'Mum.'"

As they stood up and turned to leave, Judge Snyder added, "Mr. O'Keefe, if you make a circus out of this, I'll make sure you're the one playing the clown."

CHAPTER ⇝ 53

THE MEDIA PELTED them with questions about what was going on.

"Just TGIF," Hartley said, "a good time for a break. We're all gonna go have a beer or two."

Out on the street, Hartley said, "Let's get in my car and drive around a bit. I'll drop you back off."

O'Keefe slid into the passenger seat while the lawyer got behind the wheel and switched on the engine. But only to put the air conditioner on. They went nowhere.

"You have to tell them."

O'Keefe stared through the windshield. "Not gonna do it."

"We have to lay a foundation, or he'll never let it in."

"He'll find a way not let it in anyway. You heard what Dolinar said about it not being exculpatory."

"But that will be error—"

"Maybe. It's not so clear, and you know it. You lawyers can make anything unclear."

"If he doesn't let it in, and they're convicted, that error will give us a good chance of getting a reversal on appeal. But if we don't lay a proper foundation to get the evidence in, we won't have done our part, and the appellate court will tell us to pound sand."

O'Keefe said nothing and Hartley continued, "You've got a duty to your client here, and that trumps ... no, it fucking *overwhelms* whatever stupid promise you made. Like Snyder said, this isn't grade school."

"Find another way."

"There *is* no other way. You've got an ethical duty. You can't escape it, so quit fucking around."

O'Keefe opened the car door.

Hartley said, "And I'm pretty damn sure I know who your source is. He'll be found out anyway, and you'll have gone to jail, gotten fined, and violated your ethical duty to Virginia, all for nothing. See you Monday … Wear your clown costume."

It was only two days but threatened to be one of the longest weekends of O'Keefe's life.

If it had been simply a case of reconciling his obligation to Paschal with his clearly superior duty to Ginny, it would've been easy. But Paschal had implied that there might be more tapes and other exculpatory evidence that hadn't been turned over and could be at risk if O'Keefe made the wrong move.

It should have been his weekend to take Kelly. They'd have figured out something to do outdoors, maybe take off with Karma for the lake country downstate for some hiking or canoeing and camping. But he called Annie and told her that his duties in the case were overwhelming at the moment, and he needed to push Kelly's visit to the following weekend. Of course she agreed. It wasn't like the old days when his word on such matters couldn't be trusted.

That evening a violent thunderstorm broke the oppressive heat. The sunlight welcomed him next morning to a day like no other that summer. Warm, but not too warm, and not at all humid, the air crackling with a freshness that could be mistaken for an invitation to hope. It was almost an act of cruelty, and he thought he might for the first time somewhat understand Eliot's line, "April is the cruelest month."

On his way to the kitchen, he noticed the yard through the windows. Large enough almost to be called "grounds," lush with trees and other flora that needed constant attention but had received none since the spring. It wasn't because of the demands of his work on Ginny's case—he hired people to do the yard work—but a sort of inertia had set in, and he had not even bothered to engage the gardeners for this summer.

The mirror was no kinder than the windows. He'd gained several pounds that seemed to make all the rest of his pounds look flabbier too. He had stopped exercising and compounded the ill effects of that by wolfing down unhealthy food at the anxiety-loaded lunch breaks, the fast-food dinners at the late afternoon or evening post-mortems and planning sessions at Hartley's office, and salty snacks and sugary desserts later at his own office as he tried to contribute something to all that he was neglecting there.

There was something about a long trial. The self-help gurus talked about living for the moment. This was living for the moment with a vengeance. Like traveling through a funhouse all day long, every sense attuned to what was happening *right now* and what dangerous thing might next pop out or up, below, or to either side. When the trial was over for the day, you had your own moments and space back, but they were already mortgaged to what would or might be happening the next day or week and how to anticipate it, plan for it, be constantly poised, as in a boxing match, to land, ward off, or duck the next punch or counterpunch. Not the healthiest life to be living. Trial lawyers like Hartley and Rockwell did this all the time. And, at least in their cases, it showed. Rockwell, sloppy and dumpy. Hartwell, almost anorexically skinny. Certainly it demanded some extraordinary level of will and concentration not to neglect everything else—yard work, personal health and fitness, family, the life of the mind, everything.

Karma, moving undetectably as always, appeared at his bedroom door. Another thing to feel guilty about. This dog had saved his master's life. His reward? His master's neglect.

He loaded Karma into the Wagoneer and headed an hour north of the city to an infrequently traveled footpath that ran along the river and up to the high bluffs above. With Karma scouting ahead, he hiked slowly along the trail, moving now with only a slight hitch in his step from his prior injuries. As he often would at times like this, he tried to open himself to whatever insight or wisdom the natural world and his non-human companion might provoke him to attain. This did not happen today because he already understood his overriding duty, but it did help him to make peace with it. He'd been willing to be fined, or jailed indefinitely, for Paschal's sake, but not if it put Ginny at even more risk. Now, he could only hope that the reluctant Hartley would over the weekend manage somehow to pick up the gauntlet that O'Keefe had thrown down before him—find another way. But what that was or whether Hartley would even try, he couldn't predict.

He returned home. The phone rang. He let it go for three rings but then forced himself to answer.

"I hear you're headed to jail for me." His friend's voice was dry, cracked. The familiar whiskey rasp.

"What? How do you know?"

"The whole thing's leaked," Paschal said.

"To you?"

"Hell, no. I'm so far out of it, I might as well be in Siberia. To Karen Todd, of course. She's writing a front-pager for tomorrow's paper. I'm afraid it's not favorable to your position."

"No surprise there. But how's that affect you?"

"I can't let them go to press without 'fessing up."

"About your source's identity?"

"Hell, no. Just that *I'm* the one who gave the tape to you."

Silence as O'Keefe tried to calculate the possible consequences. Failing to figure it out, he said, "I need to tell you that today I made a decision—that my duty to Ginny trumps mine to you. I have to 'out' you."

"No surprise there. And I hope you believe that I wouldn't let you go to jail for me. I already called the managing editor and told him. I'm surprised you didn't feel the tremors from the earthquake when I delivered that news. I'm meeting with the whole Politburo tomorrow evening, including Bruce Nelson, the owner."

"Oswald?"

"No. They don't want anyone there who might defend me. Not that he probably would anyway. He's had it with me."

"Maybe they'll have to support you. It's a helluva scoop."

"But the wrong scooper, the wrong poop in the scoop, and deposited in the wrong place."

"Maybe they'll feel they won't have a choice."

"I doubt it," Paschal said. "They don't like me, and I have no respect for them."

"Well, let me know tomorrow how you want to handle it. I'll try to do it the way you want … Know who leaked it?"

"No idea."

O'Keefe hung up and thought about who might have had a special interest in leaking the incident.

He called Hartley at home. His wife answered. "Why in the world would you think he might be home with his family on a Saturday night?"

Hartley was indeed at the office. O'Keefe told him the story, concluding with, "You might want to grab your Sunday paper early."

Hartley didn't react much.

"So what do you think?" O'Keefe asked.

"I suspected it was McKenna. It had to come out, one way or the other."

Hartley seemed too casual. That seemed suspicious. "Were you the leaker?" O'Keefe asked.

"Fuck, no. Why would you think that?"

"Because I know you wanted it all disclosed, and your reaction just now seemed pretty blasé. Forced casual."

"No way did I do that."

They were silent for several seconds, until Hartley said, "Don't you believe me?"

"I do. And I hope you believe this from me. I decided this morning, before I knew about the leak, that I would 'out' him."

"I believe it. I knew you would. Tough position you were in. But there really wasn't a choice. Not ethically anyway."

"Say … when you finally get home tonight—"

"Tonight? Fat chance. Ben, my senior associate, resigned today. Too much on his shoulders with me swamped and drowning in this case. Too much controversy, too many people asking him why he works for a creepy defender of pedophiles. He got a job offer. More money, less work."

"Nobody else to hire?"

"I don't even have time to breathe, let alone do that."

Hartley's little world was fraying or worse. O'Keefe called Maura and filled her in while her little girl babbled in the background.

"I knew Ben was slipping down the slope," she said. "It's been really hard around there."

A silence. Like she wanted to say more. And if he knew Maura Davis as well as he thought he did, he knew he wouldn't have to wait long for her to say it.

"He missed our last paycheck." Her breath caught. She was crying. "This case is swamping all our sad little boats."

As he hung up, he wondered if she was longing for some comfort, just as he was. It would be simple to pick up the phone one more time…

But not an option.

DIRTY HARRY & DIE HARD OPEN IN THEATRES.

PRESIDENT REAGAN'S POPULARITY WITH 18 –
24 YEAR OLDS IS A GREAT ASSET FOR GEORGE
BUSH. "REAGAN DREW THEM IN AND BUSH IS
HOLDING THEM TOGETHER." ONE STUDENT
SAID, "[REAGAN] CHANGED THE WAY PEOPLE
LOOK AT THE COUNTRY. WE HAVE PRIDE
IN AMERICA AGAIN. I WANT THE REAGAN
REVOLUTION TO KEEP ROLLIN' ON WITH BUSH."

CHAPTER ❧ 54

ON SATURDAY NIGHT the *Herald* fired Paschal McKenna and on Sunday he was arrested and jailed for obstruction of justice and knowing receipt of stolen property, a certain video recording of an interview with Robert Putnam, one of the child victims and a prospective witness in the pending criminal case of Virginia Montrose and Marvin Smith.

On Monday, Judge Snyder, on hearing of the leak, was said to have "gone ballistic," an explosion heard even in the hallway outside his chambers. He suspended the trial proceedings scheduled for that day and set a special hearing for the following morning and arranged for McKenna to be delivered there from his jail cell.

A Legal Aid attorney was hastily appointed to represent McKenna at the hearing. On a visit Monday night with his new client, the attorney learned that McKenna refused to disclose his source, relying on the First Amendment to the U.S. Constitution and a somewhat similar provision of the state constitution. McKenna claimed that those provisions, which guaranteed the freedom of the press, conferred on him as a journalist a privilege that protected him from forced disclosure of his confidential sources. The attorney and his colleagues scrambled to research the issues, which revealed some basis for McKenna's position, but it was less than strong.

On Tuesday morning the court convened, and McKenna's lawyer asked to meet in chambers. Judge Snyder refused. "This sideshow has already consumed too much time and energy. It threatens to divert us from the profoundly tragic situation we're dealing with here, the accusation that trusted caretakers of these children abused them in the most heinous fashion. Everyone involved—the parents, the public, the defendants too—deserve not to be distracted by this nonsense. In that regard, does defense counsel intend to continue to press your contention that this tape is somehow exculpatory and your motion accusing the prosecution of failing to disclose this and possibly other similar evidence?"

The defense confirmed that indeed they did. Rockwell was the one to respond, he and Hartley having concluded that Judge Snyder might be developing something even more serious than distaste for both Hartley and his investigator. "We certainly do contend that the tape is exceedingly relevant and exculpatory. We really must persist in order to properly represent our clients. And to be clear, we want, just as much as the prosecutor—actually far more than the prosecutor—that Mr. McKenna reveal his source. We believe identification of the source can only benefit the defendants, perhaps decisively so."

Snyder recognized Dolinar next, who said, "We've held back nothing that we were obligated under *Brady* to provide. We agree with you that this whole thing is a waste of time and a travesty of justice and are eager to dispose of this issue as soon as possible."

Turning to McKenna and his lawyer, who had been squeezed into the defense table and sitting area immediately behind it, Judge Snyder said, "Let's get Mr. McKenna on the stand and under oath."

McKenna stood and wobbled toward the witness stand, passing by O'Keefe on his way without acknowledging his friend or anyone else, and smelling strongly of cologne and booze. Leftovers from Saturday night? Or a smuggled-in stash during his Sunday in jail? Which would have surprised no one familiar with the system. But once on the stand, he didn't slur his words, though his voice, posture, halting gestures, and general demeanor evinced only discomfort and defeat.

His lawyer, barely out of law school, looking determined not to be overwhelmed by the drama in which he'd been abruptly cast as at least a character actor if not a leading man, asked McKenna questions to establish his background and present circumstances: a reporter at the *Herald*, assigned to local crime reporting; obtained the tape while acting in that capacity; and promised his source confidentiality. In conclusion, the lawyer asked, "Are you now willing to disclose the identity of your source?"

"With utmost respect for this Court," McKenna said, "but with even more for the U.S. Constitution and the principle of freedom of the press ... no. Not under any circumstances."

Counsel for the defendants declined to ask any questions.

Taking his turn at the podium, Dolinar said, "You didn't tell us about your job before the *Herald*."

With a bitter smile but a twinkle in his bloodshot eyes, McKenna said, "Making license plates."

Laughter erupted from those who got the joke. Even Dolinar smiled. Not Judge Snyder.

"Tell us about that," Dolinar said.

"I was in prison for armed robbery."

"And now you're in jail for knowing receipt of stolen property."

"True."

"And now you're *not* a journalist, are you?"

"I'm no longer employed by the *Herald* if that's what you mean."

"In fact, when on Saturday the *Herald* discovered your role in this, they fired you."

McKenna confirmed that, which gave Dolinar all he wanted. They proceeded to oral argument. The young man from Legal Aid traced the emergence in the 1970s of the idea that the First Amendment included the concept that a "free" press required the recognition of a journalistic privilege to protect sources. Dolinar countered by calling the concept "a mere notion" and citing instances where the Supreme Court and state courts had rejected it.

Snyder interrupted, clearly impatient, and a little smug too. "Both of you, let's just cut to the chase. What neither of you have apparently found is a provision in our statute books that controls the issue and ends the debate. It says that no privilege, other than the attorney-client privilege, shall apply to situations involving known or suspected child abuse or neglect. No other privileges apply ... not the clergy privilege, not the doctor-patient privilege, and certainly not this perhaps non-existent journalist privilege."

His words crashed down on the room with the emotional weight of a collapsing steel bridge. He turned to McKenna. "You understand what I just said, sir?"

McKenna nodded.

Snyder responded with a loud and stern command: "You must answer verbally, not with a gesture of the head."

McKenna flinched as if he had been slapped but quickly recovered himself and said, "Yes. I do."

"Now that you've been made aware of what our laws provide and what they instruct that you *must* do, will you now disclose who gave you that tape?"

"Most respectfully, I understand that no state law can override the U.S. Constitution, which is the supreme law of the land."

"And which the U.S. Supreme Court has not interpreted in the way you contend."

McKenna's lawyer rose hesitantly to his feet, but Snyder waved him back down and continued with Paschal: "I'll give you one more chance to disclose your source. If you don't, I'll hold you in contempt, and you'll go to jail until you answer the question. And, Mr. McKenna, I'm not kidding you, that might be forever, because we cannot tolerate the undermining of our justice system. It's up to you, and only you."

There was quiet, the spectators transfixed.

"My landlord's about to evict me anyway," McKenna said. "I'll need a place to stay."

Laughter convulsed many of the spectators, spreading even to some of the parents in the Save Our Children! group.

But not Judge Snyder. "Amusing, Mr. McKenna, yes, but that's just more contempt. It'll cost you a thousand dollars, which I order you to pay within thirty days after your release from confinement—that is, if you're ever released—and subject to return to confinement if you fail to pay timely."

Watching the bailiffs handcuff his friend and take him away, O'Keefe felt a surge of the old PTSD he'd hoped he'd conquered, but there it was—the flaming rocket across the night sky of his overwhelmed mind—and it took some force of will for him to restrain himself from quixotically rushing to his friend's rescue.

CHAPTER ❧ 55

"CONGRATULATIONS, MR. O'KEEFE," Snyder said after the brief commotion of McKenna's removal had faded. "It looks like you're off the hook."

Hartley stood, but Snyder waved him down, "Yes, Mr. Hartley, we still have the issue of the tape—"

"And," Hartley blurted without rising again, "other items that may not have been turned over."

"I realize that," Snyder said acidly, "but haven't you read the Dolinar and Tarwater affidavits filed this morning?"

Hartley and Rockwell both looked surprised. "If we got copies, we missed them," Hartley said.

After a few moments of flutter at the prosecution table, Tarwater approached the defense table and handed the affidavits to the defense lawyers. She turned back to Snyder and said, "I'm sorry, Your Honor. In all the excitement of the past few days and scrambling to deal with McKenna's appearance this morning, I forgot."

Hartley and Rockwell glared at her.

"Understandable," Snyder said. "I'll summarize them for the defense … One, the DA's office states emphatically that the tape contains nothing favorable to the defense. In fact, it supports at least some of the allegations in the indictment regarding Robert Putnam. The DA's office has completed a thorough new search, and they are unable to find the original or any copy of this tape.

"Two, the tape is an authentic recording of the first in a series of interviews between Betsy Mortimer and Ken Brinkley, and Robert Putnam, one of the victims named in the indictment.

"Three, Robert Putnam was the first witness interviewed. No other tapes of Robert Putnam or any other students of the Operation Go! school were made. The Children's Clinic no longer has the original or a copy of the tape. It believes it turned over the original or a copy of the tape to the DA's office, but in their words, 'we could not swear to that.'

"Fourth, the DA's office may have had the tape in its possession at least temporarily at one time. But their records indicate it was either not delivered to them, or if delivered to them, they don't know what happened to it thereafter. All of their current employees have been pointedly asked and state that they had no knowledge of the existence of the tape before Messrs. O'Keefe and Hartley disclosed it last Friday."

Rockwell stood. "Those affidavits raise more questions than they answer. We should be allowed to do further discovery including depositions of everyone in that office from the D.A. himself, and down to Mr. Dolinar, and down to Ms. Tarwater, and on down the chain. Whether there are more tapes or not, this one alone is plenty damning, and the foundation has now been laid for its admission."

Dolinar rose, but Snyder said, "Foundation, yes. Relevancy, not necessarily."

"It exposes their brainwashing techniques," Rockwell said. "Nothing could be more relevant."

"It does no such thing," Dolinar said. "It's a tape of the *initial* interview of *one* victim very early on, at the very beginning of the case."

The judge paused, looking weary, then stared down at his desk as if an answer might be found there, and after several seconds, lifted his head and said to Dolinar, "When do you intend to call Betsy Mortimer?"

"Soon."

As if thinking out loud, Snyder said, "So this issue won't come up until the beginning of the cross, right Mr. Rockwell and Mr. Hartley?"

"I guess so," Rockwell reluctantly conceded with Hartley sullenly and silently not protesting.

"Let's sleep on it. I want two business days' notice before you put Mortimer on, Mr. Dolinar, so we have a day to resolve this ahead of her testimony."

Following adjournment, the defense team retired to a witness preparation conference room off the corridor. "They're still covering it up," Hartley said, "I know they are. I hear there's a reign of terror in progress over there."

He fixed on O'Keefe. "Your friend McKenna seems like a good man. I'm not sure he realizes that he's protecting someone who doesn't deserve it … certainly doesn't deserve it when the fates of our clients might rest in his source's unclean hands. These people's lives are at stake. Surely that trumps this bullshit journalistic confidentiality stuff. And the sacred freedom of the press isn't exactly at stake here. This ain't exactly the Iran Contra affair or Watergate or the Pentagon Papers. What if that person knows something that could be decisive for our clients in this case? What worthwhile value would your friend be upholding if he stood by and let their lives be destroyed?"

"He believed in our clients' innocence and wanted to help. That's why he's in jail right now."

"And he can get himself out of jail and do the right thing in one swoop just by letting loose a couple of words."

CHAPTER ⋈ 56

THE JAIL ALWAYS induced thoughts of self-harm in O'Keefe.

The place was demeaning to all who entered, the inmates' shame, carried here by them and imposed here on them, almost tangible. He feared it was daily corroding Ginny's spirit, the King James Bible notwithstanding. He had hoped he would not have to endure the place again himself, at least on this case, except perhaps as part of a welcome-home celebration on Ginny's release following a verdict of innocence. Once the trial started, he no longer needed to visit her there, either for professional purposes or to offer her personal comfort, which she didn't seem to welcome anyway, overwhelmed as she was by the shame of being there at all. Annie and Kelly visited her, which had gradually devolved mostly into long silences until she'd asked them not to come anymore. She didn't want to be the cause of them having to endure the foulness of the place. Beneath that soft, compliant persona was an iron streak of pride that refused to bend, a quality that, both Hartley and O'Keefe worried, might not be serving her well in the tragically complex circumstances she now found herself enmeshed.

And now, here he was, visiting another who refused to bend.

Somehow, the incarceration had improved Paschal's looks and disposition. He moved confidently, even smiled now and then, an expression he favored his face with infrequently.

"You're looking up," O'Keefe said.

"As you might recall, this isn't an entirely unfamiliar environment to me."

"You're actually starting to look healthy."

"No more insults, or I'll ask them to take you away."

They laughed, and Paschal added, "Sober ain't so bad if you don't have a choice to feel otherwise."

Silence descended, neither man good at making small talk.

"Just spit it out," McKenna said. "I'm pretty sure I know what you're here for."

"Don't think I wouldn't've come anyway."

"I don't and won't. Are you wired?"

"No, damn it," O'Keefe said, laughing at what had become a regular inquiry.

"I can't frisk you. Tell me why I should believe you."

"Because I've never lied to you," which O'Keefe thought was a pretty lame response but all he could come up with.

Paschal said nothing, seemingly intent on maintaining silence, so O'Keefe went on.

"Ginny's fate might be in your hands. Say two words, maybe only one—a last name—and you might save her."

"Well, that depends on a whole bunch of things that are unlikely to happen. First, that there actually is another tape—"

"It doesn't have to be a tape. Who knows what else your source knows about evidence they've supposedly lost."

Paschal shook his head. "Quite a stretch there. The source tells me there's nothing else. Plus, the tape or other evidence would have to support your case."

"Ginny's case, Marvin's case," O'Keefe said, refusing to allow Paschal to focus on anyone or anything other than the defendants themselves.

"Whatever. The tape I already got for you got you exactly nowhere. Snyder won't even let you use it. All this"—as he gestured around the room—"for nothing."

"But new evidence might show something else, something he'd have to let in. And the more he doesn't let in, the better chance we have on appeal."

"As I said, I don't think there's anything else. I got all there is. That tape was it."

"But you don't know that, and there's two lives at stake."

"There's no way one thing like that decides the case, and you know it."

"You're defending an abstract principle, and a fuzzy one at that. You'll elevate that over a human life?"

"That's not it at all. It's not the First Amendment. There's another person's life involved. Not mine. My source's. And a promise was made."

"So we have two innocents facing long jail sentences for something they didn't do versus your source, who's too cowardly to come forward and face justice."

"Now you're just being stupid and cruel. Coming forward was brave, not cowardly. If that hadn't happened, where would you be? Bravery doesn't require them to put their head voluntarily on the chopping block, sharpen the axe, and pay the executioner. It's a gamble whether the source has anything else. They talk about believing the children. I believe the source."

O'Keefe leaned forward. "And the other side of the bet is that there's something else and it would actually make a difference. What about the straw and the camel's back? This might be the straw."

"Talk about an abstract principle. I never met that fucking camel. Or the straw either. It's the source's future life, which could now include a criminal charge, plus ostracism from their chosen profession, some version of those being a near certainty, against a speculative bet on whether there's any other hidden evidence, and if there is, whether it'll do the defendants any good."

Dogfall. O'Keefe had no more to say.

"Do you hate me now?" Paschal said.

O'Keefe hesitated, then said, "I need to ponder that, but I don't think so."

"You're an honest man, O'Keefe."

"I hope so. It's pretty much the least I can do in the world. Will you think about it?"

"Unfortunately, I won't be able to help thinking about it."

CHAPTER ⇝ 57

 THE NOTICE ARRIVED.

The prosecution would call Betsy Mortimer to the stand in two days.

But the notice letter contained an additional one-sentence paragraph: "We are also filing a motion today to amend the indictment to drop all charges relating to Terry Merkel and Robert Putnam."

The next morning, Judge Snyder summoned the parties to his chambers. Asked if the defense still intended to use the tape in Mortimer's cross-examination or otherwise, Rockwell said, "Certainly."

"It's hearsay," Dolinar said.

But Rockwell was ready. "We're only using it for impeachment of Betsy Mortimer, certainly not for the truth of the statements, most of which were false anyway. But that's not the point. It's not hearsay if used only to impeach. It falls squarely into that hearsay exception."

"Hearsay or not, it's irrelevant," Dolinar said. "If our motion to amend the indictment is granted, that child is no longer in the case."

"They're trying to drop him from the case for no reason other than to keep us from showing that tape to the jury," Rockwell said.

"Note, Your Honor, that we're also dropping the charges related to Terry Merkel."

Rockwell snorted his disgust. "A feeble attempt at a smokescreen to obscure their real purpose."

"As you well know," Snyder said, "because we dealt with exactly this issue in the Randy Lowe situation, it's at the prosecutor's discretion which crimes to prosecute and which not to."

"Not," Rockwell said, "if it's through an amendment to the indictment that prejudices the defendants. And it will greatly prejudice us if the result is that you won't allow us to use the Putnam tape to establish it as the model approach for all the interviews."

Dolinar said, "If asked that, the witness will deny it. She'll testify that all the interviews were individualized."

"Let her deny it," Rockwell replied. "The jury should have the opportunity to draw its own inferences about what that tape shows along with all the other evidence."

"So," Dolinar said, "now we're going to allow juries to receive irrelevant evidence to draw inferences from? What a disastrous precedent that would set."

Rockwell wagged his head back and forth, as if shaking off Dolinar's statement. "It's not irrelevant because it speaks to their interview process. The only reason we don't have more of these tapes is because the prosecutor's office told them to stop recording."

"That," Dolinar said, "is hearsay three or four times removed and from an unknown source, and doesn't matter anyway. You cannot establish a process from one incident."

"Your Honor," Hartley took over. "We should at least be allowed to show particular questions and lines of questioning from the tape that are the same as or very similar to what the children still in the indictment were questioned about."

"No," Dolinar said. "That would be highly improper. The jury could hear something on the tape that it considers improper but that didn't happen with any of the other children."

"What about the indictment amendment on the Merkel kid?" Snyder asked.

"We have to object to that too," Hartley said, "because who knows what diabolical motive the prosecution has to deprive us of even more defenses? Who knows what secrets that family is harboring or what crazy stunts Ralph Merkel has been pulling that we don't yet know about?"

Snyder said, "Diabolical? Interesting word choice, given the context."

"The only thing devilish in this case, Your Honor, is on the prosecution side of the aisle."

Dolinar's face reddened, his legendary cool slipping from his grip. "This is intolerable. He's completely out of line."

"I agree," Snyder said, "but it was part my fault," Snyder said. "I provoked it with my comment. And Mr. Hartley just can't help himself sometimes. In any event, the motion to amend the indictment to drop the charges against Robert Putnam and Terry Merkel is granted."

Dolinar and Tarwater began packing up their briefcases as if they were finished.

"And…" Rockwell said.

Snyder and the prosecutors looked at him quizzically.

"The tape," he said.

"I thought that would go without saying," Snyder said. "Irrelevant. One interview doth not a process make."

They left him smiling with satisfaction at his clever aphorism.

CHAPTER ❧ 58

O'KEEFE HAD TO admit, Betsy Mortimer was a formidable witness, at least on her direct examination. Articulate, sincere, exuding genuine-seeming friendliness.

Surprisingly, it was Tarwater, not Dolinar, who put Mortimer on the stand, and O'Keefe wondered if for some reason Dolinar wanted to distance himself from her testimony. Or maybe he'd decided that two women talking to each other about this delicate subject would better resonate with the jury.

Tarwater began by establishing Mortimer's background. After graduating college with a major in Childhood Education, she thought she was headed for a career as an elementary school teacher, but in her hometown, teachers' jobs were non-existent with a daunting waiting list. She ended up stuck for a few months in a clerical job while also serving as a volunteer with a local domestic-abuse hotline, which, in turn, led to a paid position at a residential center for victims of domestic abuse. She attracted the positive attention of the state child protection agency, and a job soon followed. From there, she moved across the country in a series of similar but ever-ascending positions with child-service agencies, both governmental and private non-profit, increasingly specializing in child abuse and then child sexual abuse. She took related university courses on a part-time basis and found the means to attend conferences on the subject. Pleasant, pretty, socially forward, and hardworking, she made many connections including well-positioned academicians and practitioners for whom she volunteered research, proofreading, and similar services, even agreeing to type manuscripts on occasion. From those grateful and prominent people, and each of her several prior employers, she assembled a batch of enthusiastic recommendations.

The Children's Clinic had been established with some of the gush of funds that had flooded forth from the federal government in the wake of the newly perceived epidemic of child sexual abuse in America. Mortimer applied there for the position of deputy director, and that batch of enthusiastic recommendations earned her the job.

Up until then, Mortimer had essentially no therapeutic training or experience. Still, at the busy and chronically understaffed Children's Clinic, she began working directly with children, first as an observer, then as a participant, and finally as a lead interviewer. She had picked up many cutting-edge ideas emerging in her discipline and had some special ones of her own. Her marketing efforts produced a stream of referrals, primarily from the state Child Protective Services Agency. When less than a year later the Clinic's director resigned, she was appointed director *pro tem* while the board searched for a more experienced candidate.

"What happened then?"

"After a series of interviews with other candidates over a period of several months, the board decided to offer me the director position on a permanent basis, and I've held it since then."

She personally handled all the interviews that led to the charges in this case, often with Ken Brinkley of Child Protective by her side, sometimes with Officer Sally Hicks as well. Although some of the children had initially been "unsurprisingly" resistant to admit what had happened to them, all eventually disclosed, and Mortimer had no doubt that every one of them had been abused, in all cases by Montrose, and in some cases by both Montrose and Smith as alleged in the indictments.

Tarwater then took her through the detailed and graphic particulars regarding each child, including what the children had told her. While Rockwell and Hartley remained on high alert, trying to observe Mortimer's demeanor and take notes at the time, O'Keefe alternated between anger and despair and tried to disguise both feelings while the defendants sat like statues, frozen in shock.

CDs HAVE NOW EFFECTIVELY REPLACED LPs.

CHAPTER ⍥ 59

ON CROSS-EXAMINATION, HARTLEY first established that Mortimer had only the most meager credentials, education, and experience in the areas of child abuse, sexual abuse, or counseling or interviewing techniques of any kind other than those she had more or less haphazardly acquired or made up herself on the fly.

Her experience was almost all in administration. She was essentially just a bureaucrat.

In response, she emphasized, "I've been interviewing victims of child abuse intensively for the last two years."

"And you've never once concluded that a child had *not been* abused, isn't that true?" Mortimer shook her head. No, she said, that wasn't true.

"How many?"

She hesitated. "There have been instances where we've been unable to conclude that abuse occurred."

"How many?"

She hesitated again. O'Keefe guessed she was about tell a lie.

"I don't know off the top of my head."

"You say, 'unable to conclude that abuse occurred.' That isn't nearly the same as concluding, simply, that no abuse occurred, is it?"

"It's highly recommended that we never conclude there was no abuse," Mortimer said. "It can be devastating for the child."

"No matter what the evidence says?"

"It would have to be overwhelming to brand the child as a liar."

"That isn't exactly a widely held view in the profession, is it?"

"I believe it is."

"What experts are you relying on?"

"I've relied mainly on the work of Dr. Roland C. Summit."

"Who else?"

"I can't recall any others right now."

"We'll talk more about Roland Summit later … You work almost exclusively for law enforcement, right?"

"No. Our primary client is the state Child Protective Agency."

"No? The Child Protective Agency investigates complaints of child abuse, brings actions in court to take children away from their parents, makes referrals to the police and prosecutors, and works with them on the ensuing prosecutions, as they did here. Correct?"

"Among other things."

"And you don't consider that to be law enforcement?"

"I do not. They have no authority to initiate prosecutions for molestation."

Hartley picked up two of the anatomical dolls used in the interviews, one in each hand. His back to the witness, facing the jurors, he held the dolls at shoulder height for several seconds. The dolls had wild hairdos, black faces, and maniacal facial expressions.

Once he seemed satisfied that the jurors had a thorough look, he turned back to the witness. "You used these in your interrogations of the children, right?"

"Argumentative," Tarwater said without bothering to rise, "to the word 'interrogations.'"

"Sustained."

"But you used these dolls?"

"Yes. And others."

"Wouldn't you concede that use of anatomically correct dolls, with actual sexual organs, is suggestive?"

Another objection. "Argumentative."

"Sustained. Rephrase your question."

"Alright. Did you consider that use of dolls with sexual organs *might be* suggestive?"

"Suggestive of what?"

Hartley looked toward the ceiling as if praying for deliverance. "Sexual behavior of course."

"Only if it occurred."

"These dolls were supposed to represent Ms. Montrose and Mr. Smith, yes?"

"Or others. There were other school personnel under investigation initially. And we've used those dolls in other cases."

"How did you find such ugly dolls?"

Tarwater rose to object, but Mortimer answered quickly, before Tarwater could get any words out. "I don't think that's a fair description."

"Well, they aren't exactly Ken and Barbie, are they?"

Most of the jurors and some of the audience laughed. Even Judge Snyder had to catch himself and suppress a smile.

"Objection!"

But before Snyder could sustain, Hartley said, "Withdrawn. I guess the jurors can decide for themselves. Now, can you tell me"— as he held up the dolls for the jurors to further observe—"why are they black-faced, Ms. Mortimer?"

"That's just the way they came to us."

He set the dolls down on the table and slipped a sock puppet over his hand. "And you also used these puppets?"

"Yes. This is a commonly used technique."

"But a controversial one, yes?"

"I'm not aware of that."

"You're not aware of articles by experts published in learned journals that say the use of dolls and puppets is counter-productive and prejudicially suggestive of sexual conduct that may never have occurred?"

"I'm not sure there are any such articles, at least that condemn it in the way you're describing."

"We'll see about that. And your method was to sheath your own hand with one of these, give it a name like Detective Froggy, speak in a character voice, talking as the puppet, and ask the children to tell Detective Froggy what happened?"

"Sometimes."

"And did you consider whether the use of these dolls and puppets, together with the whole party and fun atmosphere of your interview room, whether all that might encourage an atmosphere of fantasy, imagining, play-acting, game-playing, as opposed to a sober search for what really happened?"

"They're children. We try to communicate with them at their level."

"So if a child told you they saw Santa Claus coming down the chimney or the Easter Bunny nibbling grass in their front yard, would you believe them?"

Snyder again sustained Tarwater's objection.

"Isn't it true," Hartley said, "that you told the children about what other children had supposedly told you about improper behavior by Ms. Montrose and Mr. Smith?"

"In a few cases, yes, but as I recall, only if we determined that the child was being less than forthcoming … For example, children who had already made some sort of disclosure to their parents before coming to us but were now denying."

"But that was every child, wasn't it? Every one of them initially denied, correct?"

"I don't know that every one of them did."

"But in most cases, the children had *not* disclosed anything to the parents. In most cases the parents were just worried something might have happened and brought the children to you so you could help find out, right?"

"I'm not sure it was most parents," Mortimer said.

"And parents were especially seeking your advice after the letter was sent out to them, right?"

"I don't know about that."

"You did have something to do with that letter, didn't you?"

She hesitated again, looked at Tarwater, again telegraphing, at least O'Keefe so believed, that a lie, or prevarication, or at least equivocation, was coming.

"I saw it."

"That's all?"

"I made a couple of suggestions."

"And what were those?"

That hesitation again. "I don't exactly recall, but they were minor. Technical things."

"And you still claim that your role in this case isn't just as an arm of law enforcement?"

"I certainly do claim that. We are not."

"You said earlier that you would never make a finding that abuse had *not* occurred because it was a terrible thing to brand a child a liar, correct?"

"Absolutely."

"But there were instances where you did brand the children as liars, weren't there?"

"Of course not."

"Ms. Mortimer, isn't it true that if a child denied the abuse, you refused to accept the denial?"

"We've learned—"

"Not a speech, Ms. Mortimer. Yes or no. Did you refuse to accept the denials?"

"It's not a question that lends itself to a simple answer like that."

"When you refused to accept their denials, you were branding them as liars, weren't you, Ms. Mortimer?"

"Objection," Tarwater said. "That's both argumentative and states facts not in evidence. He is badgering her, keeping her from explaining her answer."

"Darned thing, Your Honor," Hartley said, "why do I feel like I'm the one being badgered?"

"Out of order, Mr. Hartley. And, Ms. Tarwater, I sustain your objection. Ms. Mortimer, you're allowed to explain your answer. Please proceed."

"Thank you, sir. We've learned that we must probe further. Initial denials in the huge majority of cases are actually evidence that abuse occurred. It's so horrible that the children suppress the memory. They can't bring themselves to acknowledge it."

Hartley tried to seize back control. "You say '*we*' have learned. Who is 'we'?"

"The profession."

"So are there scientific studies?"

"What do you mean by 'scientific'? This isn't chemistry or biology, Mr. Hartley."

"I mean empirical evidence based on actual experience. Long-range studies of outcomes. Experiments. Not someone sitting around noodling … spinning notions."

"As I said, I've relied on the work of Dr. Summit."

"And by his 'work,' you mean a paper written by him in 1983 called 'The Child Abuse Accommodation Syndrome.'"

"Yes."

"And that paper is fewer than twenty pages long, correct?"

"He also teaches and speaks at professional conferences."

"And that paper has been criticized within the profession, correct?"

"Somewhat, yes."

"*Extensively* criticized, right?"

"I don't know how to judge the word 'extensively,' but I know that his work has been widely accepted and broadly influential, and his critics are a small minority compared to those who follow his teachings."

"Isn't it true that Dr. Summit has never interviewed a single abused child?"

"I'm not aware of his actual interview experience."

"And you have personally had no training in interviewing techniques, right?"

"Not true. I've now had almost two years of actual experience."

"But no formal training."

"It depends on what you mean by that term."

"Classroom training from a qualified person or interviewing on the job supervised and advised by an experienced, qualified person."

"If you define it that way, no, but that's not the only way."

"Where did you learn that it was alright to badger the children until they give you the answer you want?"

Another objection, also sustained. The jury was ordered to disregard his statement. "And," Snyder added, "another warning to you, Mr. Hartley."

Hartley resumed quickly and without apology, but O'Keefe thought he was looking desperate. The lawyer was having to play Harry Houdini, shackled and padlocked in a strongbox by Snyder's evidentiary rulings, struggling to escape, the oxygen in the box seeping out all the while.

"All of the children initially denied the incidents occurred, right?"

Mortimer hesitated again, her mind seemingly searching for a way to avoid making the admission Hartley wanted. "I'm not sure. I don't remember."

"Well, certainly, in a huge majority of cases, if not every single one of them, which you have not contradicted and cannot contradict, the children initially denied that abuse had occurred."

"Objection. That's not even a question. He's testifying."

But Mortimer couldn't resist. Before Snyder had a chance to rule, she said, "No surprise in that. Denial is standard, expected."

"Let's take the case of Michelle Morrison," Hartley said, "almost age six now, four at the time of the supposed abuse. She initially denied that the abuse happened, correct?"

"Yes. Routine. Expected."

"And you interviewed her an additional six times, correct?"

"That sounds right."

"And a couple of those interviews lasted for more than two hours, in one case all afternoon?"

"Maybe."

"And Mr. Brinkley was there with you asking questions too?"

"Sometimes he would ask questions, yes."

Hartley continued, naming each child, showing a pattern of multiple and lengthy interviews.

"And you encouraged the parents to interrogate their children at home too, correct?"

Another hesitation. "I wouldn't say 'encouraged.'"

"But you certainly didn't discourage it?"

"Not at all. We wouldn't interfere that way."

"Even though the parents had no training in properly interviewing potentially abused children?"

"As I said, we wouldn't interfere that way."

"But you advised every parent that came to you, didn't you, that you'd determined their child had in fact been abused?"

"I'm not sure it was every one of them."

"So you can't say it *wasn't* every one of them, correct?"

"I don't recall exactly."

"And you so advised even when the kids were still denying it."

"Those were the conclusions I came to."

"And every single one of them denied it, correct?"

"Yes. As I keep saying, the denials are to be expected. Part of the process."

"Are you familiar with the literature in your field indicating that children will ultimately agree with an authority figure who persistently refuses to believe them and continues to ask them whether incidents they say have not occurred actually did occur despite their denials?"

Tarwater stood again. "Your Honor, he keeps citing these alleged published opinions and literature but never identifies them."

"What's the objection?"

"Speculative. Assuming facts not in evidence. Argumentative."

"This literature will be testified to and specifically identified by our experts when we present our case," Hartley said.

Snyder overruled the objection, telling Tarwater that if Hartley didn't deliver what he promised, he would then give appropriate instructions to the jury to disregard with a public admonishment of counsel."

"We just witnessed a miracle," Rockwell whispered to O'Keefe. "Snyder must have lost his mind for a second. Or maybe he forgot who was who."

Hartley continued. "And didn't you actually berate those children who persisted in their denials?"

"Objection. Argumentative."

"Sustained."

"Isn't it true that you *suggested* to at least one child that the child must not be as smart as the other children because he wouldn't admit that a sexual encounter had occurred?"

Clever, O'Keefe thought. Hartley was phrasing his question to mimic a statement Mortimer had made to Bobby Putnam on the suppressed tape. If Mortimer denied it, it might open the door to admission of the tape to impeach her.

"Objection. Speculative."

"Nothing speculative about it, Your Honor. Did she, or didn't she?"

"I'll allow it, but I'm not sure how much further I'll let this proceed."

The witness sat silent, as if she hadn't heard or didn't understand Snyder's ruling.

"Well, Ms. Mortimer, what's the answer?" Hartley pressed.

"I may have done that in one or a couple of cases when I was certain the child wasn't telling the truth and needed that kind of prodding."

"Don't you regard that as coercive?"

"I don't see how suggesting the child was not being as cooperative as other children would be coercive."

"Shaming the child as not being as smart as the others? You don't regard that as coercive?"

Another sustained objection.

"Alright. *Suggesting* the child might not be as smart as the others? You don't regard that as coercive?"

"No."

"And didn't you or the parents reward the children with small toys or other little prizes, trips to the ice-cream store and such, when they finally stated there was abuse?"

"I don't know about the parents, but in some cases, where the initial denial had been especially strong and the children had managed to overcome that, and the terror, the shame … we thought it right to encourage those children in small ways."

"And how about scolding or shaming children who persisted in their denials?"

Mortimer hesitated again. She had to know that this was exactly what had happened during the Putnam interview and somehow the tape might make its way into evidence.

"In cases where we strongly believed that the abuse had occurred, and the child was holding back, there may have been a very limited amount of that."

"Wasn't it your routine procedure to assure the children that Ms. Montrose and Mr. Smith would be going to jail or already were in jail because of what they had done to other children?"

"Yes. We believed it was essential that the children knew they were safe."

"You claim to be a therapy organization, don't you?"

"We don't *claim* to be. That's what we are."

"Then aren't you supposed to be treating the trauma of the abuse, helping the children to recover from it?"

"Yes."

"But isn't it true that you've done *none* of that in this case?"

"That's a long-term thing. The children can't even begin to recover until they acknowledge that the abuse occurred. It's part of the therapeutic process, the essential first step."

"Isn't it true that you were working for the Child Services agency, the police, and the prosecutors only to establish that the abuse occurred?"

"Not so. The parents brought their children to us."

"At the suggestion of the authorities, right?"

"In some cases, yes."

"In all cases, right?"

"I don't believe so."

"Who paid you for your services?"

"Child Protective ... They were the only ones with the budget for it."

"And isn't it true that you attended various meetings of the parents along with representatives from Child Services, the police, and the prosecutor's office?"

"A couple of those, yes."

"And at those meetings, didn't you join with the law-enforcement people in encouraging the parents to solicit other parents to examine their children's recent behaviors to see if they exhibited any of the supposed telltale signs of abuse?"

"Of course I did. That was the point of the meetings."

"And throughout the process you encouraged the parents to question their kids about what might have happened to them?"

"Yes, but—"

"You've answered the question, Ms. Mortimer."

Tarwater said, "She should be allowed to explain her response."

"Agreed," Snyder said.

"Alright," Hartley shrugged, making no effort to conceal his disgust. "Go ahead. Explain it if you can."

"I only did that once we established with certainty that extensive abuses had occurred, and we felt we needed to identify all possible victims ... who needed help, obviously."

"So you admit you became not a therapist but a hunter."

"I believed the children. I still believe the children."

"You mean you believe the human puppets you created."

"Objection. Outrageously improper. Request the jury be instructed to disregard."

No doubt in anyone's mind that Snyder would agree with that, and O'Keefe was certain Hartley knew exactly what reaction his statement would provoke. "The jurors are instructed to disregard defense counsel's last two questions or statements, whatever they were. Highly improper."

At the end of Mortimer's testimony, Hartley and Rockwell approached the bench and moved that all of her testimony be stricken as junk social science and hearsay. After that was abruptly and gruffly denied, Hartley made a final attempt to be allowed to play the tape, or at least segments of it, in order to impeach the witness.

"As I said, Mr. Hartley, one interview doth not a process make."

O'Keefe could have sworn that Hartley looked like he might scramble up the face of the judge's bench, grab Snyder by the tie, and smash his face into the desk. Or maybe that was just O'Keefe's purely private fantasy. In any event, Scott only sighed and walked back to the defense table.

O'Keefe gave him a reassuring nod, though he knew Houdini was still in the strongbox, and it was unclear how much oxygen he had left.

CHAPTER ✤ 60

THE WOODEN PEW on which Ralph Merkel was sitting—chafing, actually—might as well have been a throne of thorns as he was forced to sit and watch, not participate, in the much-anticipated climax of the prosecution's case, the testimony of the parents and the children.

They had shut him out. After all he'd done for them, the heroism he'd demonstrated, risking his very life to combat the Satanists. And for what? At this decisive moment, they'd left him out in the cold.

They'd said his prominent and aggressive involvement could compromise Terry as a witness. "That's a crock," Ralph had fulminated. "I could tell the jury so much, advance the cause so much."

"We just can't risk it," Dolinar mumbled.

"What a bunch of shit," Ralph said. "You'd better win this case. If you don't, I'll tell the world how you fucked it up by keeping your star player on the bench."

Literally on the bench. On this hard-ass bench. Forced to watch when all he wanted to do was act.

Ralph would have felt even worse if he knew the truth about the decision to drop Terry. The prosecution team had decided that it would look better if they included another child with Putnam in the motion to amend the indictment. "Let's get rid of Terry Merkel," Dolinar said. "His tales are too tall, and his old man's too ambitious. I'd like to let some of the air out of his balloon."

Ralph tried to take comfort knowing his testimony would surely be the centerpiece of the civil action that would immediately follow the verdict in the criminal case, and he renewed his private vow to do everything possible to ensure the success of that case, even if that called for his continuing efforts to assist the prosecution, ungrateful backstabbers though they were.

The original indictment had included charges involving fourteen children. Randy Lowe, Terry Merkel, and Robert Putnam had been dropped by the prosecution. Sherry Morgan and Drew Sheffield had announced, through tears and tantrums, their refusal to go forward. And two sets of parents had second thoughts about subjecting their children to the trauma of a trial.

Which left seven children. Three of them were now ages twelve, eleven, and nine. Nancy Mangan and Paul Skinner—classmates of Bobby Putnam—were a little younger, seven, and Misty Haynes and Michelle Morrison, five.

Tarwater had voiced her concerns about losing children from the case, but Dolinar said seven was enough. "It's just right. Call me Goldilocks." More would be geometrically more dangerous to their case. Too many kids had said not one word to anyone, and, at some point, that might strain the jurors' willingness to believe. Plus, the more kids' testimonies, the more likely the prosecution would be struggling to manage inconsistencies and meltdowns on the stand. "Too much whack-a-mole," he said.

"But there's so few *boys* left," she said.

"There's enough," Dolinar said. "Girls are more important anyway. Right or wrong, they'll incite more sympathy."

Hartley was also pleased that there were fewer children to deal with—the "vanishing victims" he called them. He might be able to make some hay out of those vanishings during closing argument, and fewer witnesses would ease his burden in the next phase. But he was under no illusions. He still dreaded that next phase above all else. The jurors' sympathy with the remaining parents and kids would be overwhelming. It would be almost impossible not to offend them during cross-examination. And no matter how gentle he was with them, if a kid started crying on the stand, it might be all over right there. Even masterful cross-examinations wouldn't be enough anyway. The defense would have to win a verdict of innocence mostly through their case in chief.

Tarwater handled most of the parent witnesses. Her line of questioning was essentially the same for each of them, as one by one she brought out that the children had exhibited one or more behaviors that the parents had been advised could be evidence of sexual abuse. Each had questioned their children about what might have happened, and the children had either denied it or given vague responses that did nothing to quell their suspicions. Two sets of parents took their children initially to outside therapists who made no specific findings, but all, at the suggestion of the police or Child Protective Services, were eventually referred to the Children's Clinic, where they were advised that their children had indeed been molested. The Clinic sent them on to Dr. Carlyle who confirmed the Clinic's findings ...

The defense lawyers renewed their challenges to the admission of the children's hearsay statements to the parents, but Snyder reaffirmed his rulings that they were part of the medical-evaluation and the criminal-investigative processes, in either case providing an exception to the hearsay rule. It would come down to their cross.

Hartley and Rockwell shared the cross-examination responsibilities, but as with almost everything else, Hartley handled most of it, carefully and kindly, but he was persistent too. Had they noticed any indications of abuse or significant changes in behavior before they received the letter from Detective Hicks? Had they consulted a doctor about any of these issues? The answer was "no" in every case. And not one set of parents had said or heard a single negative word about Virginia Montrose or Marvin Smith until they'd gotten that call from Heidi Lowe, read the letter, or consulted the Children's Clinic.

In each case, not only had the children never reported anything even close to molestation, but the kids initially denied, in most cases vehemently and defiantly, that any abuse had occurred. In most cases, the parents agreed, the denials continued even after the initial interview at Children's Clinic. The home-based interrogations had been as frequent as daily. Assurances were given to the children that they had nothing to fear. Eventually, the children had "remembered," though it had taken an incredibly long time, seven years in the case of the oldest child. "Bravery" was enthusiastically praised and rewarded with hugs, trips to the ice-cream parlor, and other treats and gifts. Throughout this period, the members of Ralph Merkel's Save Our Children! group had given each other extensive support, exchanging their children's respective stories and broadcasting developments in the case, reinforcing each other and their children's stories, keeping each other on message and on point. Representatives from the prosecutor's office, Child Protective, and the police had frequently attended their meetings.

So had Perry Slotkin, a top plaintiff's lawyer in the city, along with a PR specialist. Ralph Merkel had introduced them to the group. Yes, they had engaged Slotkin to file a civil suit once this criminal case was over. It was their understanding that the school was well insured. They didn't know how much they might ask for in damages, that would be up to Slotkin, but the children deserved— and the parents, too—all the compensation the law would allow for what might turn out to be a lifetime of harm inflicted on them by the defendants and the school that had allowed it to happen.

How about the run-up to the trial? It had been relentless. The parents had continued to discuss with their kids what had happened, repeatedly rehearsing the stories. That had been followed by numerous trial-preparation sessions with the prosecutors, some of them upwards of three hours long.

Rockwell worked hard to show that Marvin Smith was not even mentioned initially by any of the children. True, the parents said. But Betsy Mortimer and Ken Brinkley and Myra Hicks told them about him. And so they asked their children, who eventually "remembered" that too. After that, it became a cascade.

On re-direct, each parent testified that whatever doubts they initially had, they now unconditionally believed Betsy Mortimer, Dr. Carlyle, the other Save Our Children! people, and, of course, most of all, the children.

STUDY FINDS THAT MENTAL DEPRESSION IS SOARING IN U.S. AND HAS DRAMATICALLY INCREASED OVER THE LAST THIRTY YEARS, ESPECIALLY AMONG YOUNG ADULTS. THE STUDY SPECULATES THE CAUSE IS "SOMETHING ABOUT MODERN LIFE."

CHAPTER ⇝ 61

ON A THURSDAY morning Raylee called Maura.

"I'm faxing you a copy of a little hand-delivered gift I found in my mailbox this morning."

Maura read it, then sent a messenger to the courtroom with a note saying there was an urgent matter they needed to meet about as soon as possible after the court adjourned for the day.

"Have a seat," Maura said. "Raylee called. She said she found this document in her mailbox this morning. She's near panic. You'll see why."

She slid copies across the table. They read:

> We were shocked to see your name on the defense witness list. Surely that was just a bluff. You were so smart to run away. Surely you won't be stupid enough to come back. Of course you knew exactly what was going on. You were part of it too. You've been lucky to escape so far. If you come back and testify, you will be exposed. Or worse. We guarantee it.
>
> What will your parents do when you're gone? We know about their dementia. They won't remember you, won't even know you're gone, and for sure nobody else will miss you. You need to send a signal somehow that you're staying put. If not, we can assure you that you

will never set foot in that courtroom. Or anywhere else. You will be cast out like the devils Jesus cast out and drove into the herd of pigs. And they stampeded over the cliff into the waters of the sea below. Where they drowned."

Hartley finished first, set the paper down, and waited until the others raised their eyes, and said, "What did she say? Will this keep her from testifying?"

"She's beyond skittish," Maura said. "I told her we'd call tonight."

Maura centered the speakerphone and dialed.

Raylee answered on the first ring. "Why'd you put me on a witness list without my permission? And what's so important about my testimony that I have to deal with this?"

Hartley looked around. O'Keefe wondered if he was deciding whether he could lie to her in front of everyone.

Hartley looked back at the phone. "It's more about what it says if you don't testify. It will shout to the jury and the whole world that Virginia's guilty. That even her best friend won't stand up for her."

"That's bullshit, Mr. Lawyer. The whole world is just like whoever wrote this note. They all think I'm guilty too. You're sacrificing me on a gamble. And my odds suck."

"That's not so."

"How will you protect me?"

"We'll report it to the prosecutor's office, and to our Judge Snyder, and the police. You'll report it to your local police."

"What baloney. Not one of that bunch cares a shit about me. Whoever wrote that letter was on my porch. They were only a few feet away from me. You put me on that list. You owe me."

"We'll do our very best to provide you with protection."

"Forever?"

Hartley looked around again as if hoping for help.

Nothing was offered.

"All I can say is we'll do our best."

Still talking to Raylee but looking at O'Keefe as he did, "What if we sent someone down there right now?"

"Who would that be?"

Hartley muted the phone but still whispered to O'Keefe. "You? … Please?"

O'Keefe scowled but nodded.

O'Keefe unmuted the phone. "Raylee, this is Pete. I'll either get down there myself or send one of my security guys."

"I'd prefer someone I know, but I'll take what I can get. But that won't mean I'm gonna testify. You know good and well that my testimony might actually hurt her."

After hanging up, Hartley said, "She's too important to let go without a fight."

It was supposed to be his weekend with Kelly, so soon after he'd canceled the other weekend due to the crisis with Paschal. He called George. First, at home. No answer. He called the office. George seemed tired and irritable. "Long time no see, Boss."

"Sorry about that. Time to talk? Anywhere you like. Dinner? A drink?"

"I'm too tired. And I need to exercise Karma while it's still light. You remember. *Our* dog? … So what's up?"

O'Keefe explained what happened with Raylee.

"Who do you think did that? Someone from Save Our Children!?'"

"I can't think of any other candidates."

"Aren't a bunch of those people Catholics?"

"Yeah. Not all, but a bunch."

"They ought to be inspecting their own nests. The sacristies and the parish houses. If the truth about all those priests ever comes out, and the cover-ups … Remember when Father Mulligan suddenly disappeared and everyone pretended they didn't know why? He did a lot worse to kids than rubbing my altar-boy ass every chance he got."

True. But this was one of George's bête noires, and a rabbit hole O'Keefe didn't want to go down. So he got straight to the point and asked if his partner had anyone who'd like some overtime this weekend. "Better than walking around in a building all night," he said.

But George was shorthanded as it was.

"Anyone you can recommend I could hire?" O'Keefe said.

"You mean *Hartley* could hire."

"I think the guy's broke. He's having trouble paying his staff."

"Haven't we given enough to this cause of yours, Boss?"

O'Keefe couldn't think of a reply.

"Like you said, Boss, I've got an embarrassment of *riches*. But it looks like you've got an embarrassment of *witches*."

"Witty, George. Quite witty."

"You've always underrated me, Boss."

"Never again, George. Never again."

"Karma's looking awfully impatient with me. That's *our* dog I'm referring to. Remember him?"

"Thank you, George."

O'Keefe hung up and called the airline.

CHAPTER ❧ 62

HE CALLED ANNIE to give her the bad news about the weekend.

"I understand," she said, "but she'll take it hard. It's been rough at school lately. There's some bullying going on. Not from everyone, but some. And some of the people calling her a 'witch,' asking her where she's hidden her broom and boiling cauldron, that sort of crap. She seems very alone."

"Should I stop by on my way to the airport?"

"That would probably be good."

"Being Friday tomorrow, they'll probably adjourn early. TGIF. At least for some."

"She'll be home from school by four."

Kelly answered the door.

"What's that?" she said, referring to the small box he carried.

"Something your mom wanted."

They sat in the living room, both awkward. The "How's school?" opener wasn't an option. Not this time. They talked about how the case was going, and how unfair it was.

She said, "Surely they won't put her in jail."

"The world isn't always fair."

"No kidding," she said. He thought she might cry, but she looked too miserable for tears.

He searched for something positive to say that wasn't also fraudulent, and came up with, "But you've done the right thing. That's what's important."

"Not if it doesn't do any good. Not if they put her in jail."

He thought about repeating that the world wasn't fair but passed on that. "You're being a real hero, pal. That isn't always easy. Sometimes it hurts really bad."

Her look said that wasn't enough.

He shifted the conversation to next weekend, told her to think about what she wanted to do more than anything else—every day, every minute of it—and promised her that that would be exactly what they'd do.

She brightened slightly.

He handed her the box. She looked confused … "It's really for you," he said.

She opened it. "Walkman!"

"The newest version," he said.

Delighted, she started crying.

An odd female thing, he thought. *Crying when they're happy. Even this young.*

"Where's your mom?"

"Upstairs. Need to talk to her?"

"Yeah. If she can."

"I'll get her," she said, and ran up the stairs, happier about this little errand than for the Walkman. Probably her main goal in life was to restore her family, whether her parents liked it or not, a consummation devoutly to be wished.

Annie bounced down the staircase, barefoot and wearing a sundress. He wondered if she knew that every time he saw her in a sundress, it was a stab in his heart. She sat near him on the couch, crossed one leg under the other, and waited for him to state his business.

"She's not doing so well," he said. "How about you?"

Things were chilly at the office. She wasn't getting offers to partner up with people like she used to. She thought people were picking up bad vibes about her from her boss. "I may just be paranoid, but I feel like he's looking for an excuse to let me go." And it was squeezing her income. "Something similar for you?"

He was reluctant to admit it. "Sort of."

"Are they paying you anything on her case?"

"Theoretically. But I haven't sent a bill … How about your friends?"

She'd lost some. "There's a cost to all this," her voice catching mournfully at the end.

She was only an arm's length away. She had chosen that spot. He couldn't remember a time since they had parted when she had come so near him. And she had a look about her. Softer than he remembered. Softer than he'd seen for years. Might they be on the verge of that moment? That moment he was afraid would never come again. An arm's length away. Could he touch her, hold her, let her let it all go, maybe cry a little, out of happiness hopefully, look up at him with a tear-stained face. The first kiss in years … reach under her sundress … as he had done so many times, but the last time such a long time ago. If she consented, by opening herself slightly, lifting herself up slightly, into his hand, an affirmation and invitation…

He caught himself. Don't make a stupid move. He was probably imagining things. Wishful thinking. He had left her alone with a little girl. Whether you were religious or not, that was a sin, simple as that. He had come around to understanding that and what it had cost him. But what had it cost her? Was it irreparable? He had tried for a reunion, but she had refused. Maybe you could wound a person so deeply that for whatever reason—a special vulnerability or even a stubborn pridefulness—that wound could not be healed. She had taken a chance on him, made a precious commitment to him. And failing to understand that the gift was an undeserved blessing, he had—don't sugarcoat it—flung it back in her face.

But that sundress. Choosing to sit on the couch with him, a mere arm's length away. Was she ready now? To forgive? To take another chance?

But maybe it had nothing to do with forgiveness. Maybe it was, as she had hinted once, the violence in his life.

And here they were, all of them in crisis. If a reunion was ever going to happen, it needed to happen in a happier time than now.

CHAPTER ❧ 63

Ι T WAS LATE when O'Keefe landed.

He called Raylee to tell her he was on his way. She seemed relieved that he'd arrived, which elevated his mood about making the trip. He'd forgotten to bring any work or anything else to read to pass what might be an excruciatingly boring weekend, so he picked up a couple of guilty-pleasure potboilers from the airport bookstore. He rented a car. Another damned expense unlikely to be reimbursed.

He heard the chain lock clink and the dead bolt snap back.

"Installed those myself today," she said with pride, then pointed to a couch in the living room made up with a sheet, blanket, and pillows.

"Hope you don't have a bad back or something."

"Actually, it looks pretty comfy. Your parents?"

"In bed. They sleep a lot. Which is good. You want something to drink? Or eat? Have you had dinner? I could make something quick."

He declined all and sat on the couch. She perched on the edge of a leather chair opposite.

"It's only nights I'm worried about. You don't have to hang around during the day if you don't want to. And I guarantee you won't. They're a chore. I bring someone in to help during the week but not on weekends."

"I want to show you something," she said, left the room, and returned with something wrapped in a cloth. "It's my dad's."

He unwrapped it. It was a pistol. "Is it loaded?" he said. "You know how to use it?"

"Both."

"Be careful. You don't want one of your parents getting hold of it."

"You carrying one yourself?" she said.

"No."

"Really? You want this while you're here?"

"I've been trying to swear off firearms. Let's just keep it someplace where we can get to it but they can't."

She showed him around the small house, including a tiny, dusty basement and a door in the ceiling with a precarious-looking drop-down stair contraption that led to the attic. He made sure there was no way to enter the basement and that the attic contraption had a bolt on it, though it looked like it would break with a couple of good kicks from above.

Apropos of nothing, she said, "The one thing I've got going for me is that this house is free and clear. I'll probably have to mortgage it when I can't take care of them here anymore, which won't be long from now."

The parents had separate bedrooms. "Otherwise, they just fuss with each other." She cracked open the door to each one and whispered, "I don't want to turn the light on. If they wake up, there might be hell to pay."

She showed him her bedroom.

"What about the window?" he said, as much to himself as to her, "and for that matter, all the windows?"

"They have the original locks on them, and I've locked them all."

"Might have to take a more careful look at that," he said. "No alarm service, I assume?"

"It's on my list to check into tomorrow."

The kitchen was at the back of the house. She turned on a dim light that barely revealed the outline of a back yard where someone could be hiding right now. A detached and severely dilapidated garage to the left looked like it might collapse at any moment.

"I'll need the strongest flashlight you've got," O'Keefe said.

She retrieved it. It was lousy.

"I'll get a better one for you tomorrow," he said.

After she went to bed, O'Keefe turned on the front porch light and took a look around. Small front porch, hedges on both sides of it that blocked the view beyond. A metal mailbox with a hinged lid attached to the wall by the front door. Yes, the intruder had been that close.

How had the intruder approached?

O'Keefe walked down to the sidewalk and looked up and down the street. Her house had a driveway leading back to the dilapidated garage, but most of her neighbors had no driveway, so the street was crowded with parked cars.

Where would the intruder have parked? Though it was likely a man, since it could be a woman, O'Keefe found himself using Paschal's number-and-gender-neutral "they." Surely, they came in an automobile. But would they have wanted to risk some night owl noticing the car? Or would they have parked on an adjacent street and walked here, which, if they were noticed, could be an even bigger problem for them—walking down the street in the middle of the night?

O'Keefe thought about how he'd have done it. His license plate covered, drive slowly but not too slowly down the street. A quick scout to make sure no or minimal lights were on and the coast was clear. Then a second pass. This time, cut the car lights, pull into her driveway, check that the car's interior roof light was off. Leave the car running and the door open. A few steps across the yard to the porch, stick the item in the mailbox. Flinch and want to vamoose when the hinges squeaked. Stride a few steps back to the car, shut the car door very slowly and quietly, back out, lights still off until well down the street or maybe even a block or two away.

O'Keefe walked around to the back of the house, the pathetic flashlight barely illuminating his way. Stay away from that pile of rubble that used to be a garage. The black hole of a back yard adjoined its neighbors with no fence or other obstacle between them. An easy point of entry. A special vulnerability.

Back in the house, he checked to make sure there was a lock on the kitchen door to the outside and turned on that anemic light for what it was worth. Nothing more to do tonight.

The next morning, he stayed around the house long enough to be overjoyed that she had given him the daytime get-out-of-jail-free card. He listened to her gamely chattering at her parents, as if they were now the children, but provoking little response from them other than disjointed complaining and berating her and each other for one thing or another and asking the same questions over and over.

The father looked toward O'Keefe once, but more through him than at him, as if he were invisible.

The mother, noticing O'Keefe, panicked, tried to rise from her wheelchair, and sputtered, "Who's that? How did he get in here?"

Raylee rushed to her, patted her shoulder, reassured her that O'Keefe was a friend, pressed her back down in the chair, and turned her around so that he was no longer in her line of sight.

He found a coffee shop with a conveniently positioned pay phone inside and compiled a list of local security services and detective agencies from the Yellow Pages.

Then he called Harrigan to get any recommendations he might have.

"Uh-oh," Harrigan said. "Bad time for me to be called in off the bench."

"No, but your ass must be getting sore."

"Not a bit. Quite comfy here."

By the end of the day, he had identified promising candidates. The security firm was intrigued by the situation and interested in charging him a hefty premium until he told them it was a pro bono case and he'd be footing the bill. Having convinced them to move down to their regular rates, he briefed them. They'd be parked in Raylee's driveway all night, every night. Without a break. Diligence and trustworthiness were essentials. They needed to take this threat very seriously. "I'm not shittin' you. A life might really be at stake."

By Saturday evening, he'd scheduled three interviews for the next day, explaining to Raylee, "You know I have to get back to the courtroom ASAP. But I've arranged some interviews tomorrow."

She started to protest, but he convinced her to keep her mind open. She would not have to let the guy into her house. He would be required to stay outside all night unless she became comfortable enough to let him in.

"Both of us will interview them," he said.

"You move fast, big fella. Maybe too fast?"

"They come well recommended, and I've done some diligence already, and I'll do more tomorrow. And if you're not comfortable after the interviews, we'll consider alternatives."

But what those alternatives might be, he had no idea.

CHAPTER ⚜ 64

THE FIRST CANDIDATE showed up fifteen minutes late.

A guy in his twenties who'd graduated from junior college and thought a job as a security guard might be a good way into law enforcement. "But I'm not so sure now," he said sadly. His answers to their questions were laconic at best, and his own questions focused not on Raylee's situation but on working conditions, such as meals, refreshments, and bathroom breaks.

"Flake," Raylee said. "Did you really diligence that guy?"

The second candidate was in his fifties, with some law-enforcement experience. He scoffed at their concern for Raylee's safety and wondered why her parents weren't in a nursing home "where they could be cared for properly." He expressed incredulity that there was no neighborhood watch system. "There damn well should be. What's wrong with these people?" Instead of spending money on a bodyguard, she should invest in a good security system and a pit bull. "Likely cheaper than me. But I'll take your money if you want."

When he left, O'Keefe shut the door and turned to Raylee. "Don't say it."

"I'm saying it anyway. He and I would last about eight seconds."

As they waited for the third candidate, after giving O'Keefe a look somewhere between skepticism and outright disdain, she disappeared into her parents' area of the house, where he could hear her chattering away as she attended to their needs and demands while he mentally groped for other possible solutions that wouldn't involve him personally bedding down on this couch indefinitely.

The third guy was fortyish with a close-cropped haircut, the squarest of jaws, and a judgmental gaze. Only his light-blue eyes softened the spit-and-polish aura. He sat on the edge of the couch as if prepared to spring into action at any moment.

"I grew up trailer trash and badly educated and had a few scrapes with the law. But I wasn't completely stupid and thought the military might do me some good. Joined the Marines, survived two tours in Vietnam, decided to re-up, advanced to the rank of master sergeant, hung in there for twenty years, and retired one day after my twenty-year anniversary."

O'Keefe decided not to share that he too was a former Marine and a Vietnam vet, guessing he might have a much different view of both those things than the master sergeant.

"Seems like you were successful. Why quit?"

"Too narrow a world to be living my whole life in it. At the ripe old age of thirty-nine, I'd earned a lifetime pension, not much of one but not complete chump change either. And I used the GI bill benefits to enroll in the university here in town. I'm working toward a degree."

After he left, Raylee seemed enthusiastic. "Obviously, Dudley Do-Right there is the man for the job. Very professional."

"Very handsome too," he said, winking.

"You're a shithead, O'Keefe."

She insisted on cooking for him, and over a late dinner he asked how she was feeling.

"Safer, but not safe."

"And about testifying?"

"Still no promise. I told myself I'd never set foot in that shit town again unless they dragged me back there in the rear of a paddy wagon. But forget about me. If I don't believe I can really help her, I won't show up, and no lawyer's gonna tell me otherwise."

After an interval in which O'Keefe considered whether to argue with her, she said, "Last time you were here, you asked me if I was a lesbian. Am I gonna get asked that on the witness stand?"

"If they ask you that question under oath, will your answer be the same one you gave me?"

"Yes. As long as they don't get more detailed."

"Like, have you ever had intimate sexual relations with Ginny?"

"I'd say no."

"Interesting wording. And you don't look or sound sincere."

"Hey, we went to a girls' college. There were no boys within miles. The joke around there was L-U-G. You know what that means?"

He squinted and shook his head.

"Lesbian Until Graduation."

He smiled.

"We were roommates. We played around some. But that was it."

"Really? No ongoing relationship … that kind, anyway?"

"Might be hard to believe, but no. We were just both born to be old maids. Not that we didn't try out a couple of boys, but all that was too complicated. Like I said before, sisterhood was a lot less complicated."

He was quiet, though he wanted to ask questions.

"So if they ask me if I'm a lesbian, I think I can say no. If they get more detailed, I don't know what I'm gonna say. If I lie, are you gonna report me?"

"Not unless they put me under oath and ask me the right question."

But was that true? He wasn't so sure what his duty might be in that instance. If it came up, he might have to ask Hartley instead of "having a fool for a lawyer."

She said, "I'm gonna do whatever I think might help her, truth or perjury, whichever."

"But she's innocent of all this satanic and molestation stuff, right?" O'Keefe said.

"Hell, yes. You have doubts?"

"I've learned to take nothing for granted."

The next morning, she got ready to leave for work and he to catch his plane back home.

At the front door, he said, "You okay, at least for now?"

"I think so. Until the next crazy-ass thing comes along."

Her face seemed so much softer this morning than before—maybe, he thought, because with whatever grudging reluctance and for whatever selfish motives, someone other than Ginny had for once shown a little care for her instead of just leaving her to contend with the world all by herself. Eleanor Rigby. All the lonely people.

Maybe she and Dudley Do-Right would fall in love and live more or less tolerably ever after.

At the airport, O'Keefe called Harrigan to ask him to put in a good word with his banker buddies to help O'Keefe secure a personal loan so he could pay for this latest round of expenses.

100,000 AMERICAN CHILDREN ARE HOMELESS.

DISGRACED STOCK TRADER IVAN BOESKY, THE CHEERLEADER FOR THE "GREED IS GOOD" DECADE, ACCUSES JUNK BOND KING MICHAEL MILLIKEN OF INSIDER TRADING.

CHAPTER ❧ 65

I T WAS THE children's turn in the witness box.

Each recounted the horrors inflicted on them. Given the age of the children, and despite the defense lawyers' vehement objections, Judge Snyder allowed the prosecutors ample freedom to ask leading questions whenever a child got lost or their attention wandered.

Some of the accusations were against Ginny alone. Some involved Ginny and Marvin together. None involved Marvin alone, Ginny always the alleged procurer and impresario.

Many of the children were barely three years old when they arrived at the school and not all had mastered potty training. Even the older ones sometimes had accidents or difficulties in getting clothing items on and off, perhaps soiling them to some degree in the process. Ginny was accused in several cases of fondling boys and girls in the bathroom.

The prosecution then turned to the basement multi-purpose room where art and music activities and daily naps took place. Ginny was accused of taking certain children into a cloak room, a room with no doors, and removing some or all of the children's clothing, and sometimes her own, and subjecting her victims to fondling, mutual oral copulation, and most bizarrely, on at least a few occasions the insertion of plastic forks, knives, and spoons, and in one case even a metal knife, into vaginal and anal orifices.

Ginny was also accused of taking children across the hallway to Marvin's lair, where the children were made to engage in everything from watching Ginny and Marvin performing various sexual acts on each other to being forced to participate themselves, including oral copulation in various configurations. Beyond that were alleged incidents that everyone in the courtroom, especially the defendants, reacted to with visible horrified disgust—a gel or ointment rubbed on vaginal and anal areas, followed by penile penetration by Marvin Smith, enthusiastically orchestrated and egged on by Ginny.

Finally, there was the babysitting. Similar activities to those in the boiler room were described but allegedly also accompanied by satanic rituals. Several children claimed that Ginny would perform odd, dance-like gestures and utter prayer-like incantations, often in a strange language the children didn't understand. They said that when present, Marvin cavorted naked except for a smiling devil's mask.

One child described being taken to the basement where he was warned that devils gathered there and would spear tattletales on the prongs of their pitchforks and fling them down into the bowels of Hell. The same child claimed that Ginny and Marvin sometimes killed baby bunnies and other small animals by slitting their throats and drinking their blood. Another said that Marvin had bragged about drinking the blood of human infants.

When Hartley rose to cross examine, O'Keefe thought he looked the opposite of confident. He looked like a novice skater venturing out onto ice of unknown thickness.

Hartley and Rockwell had agreed they would not focus at all on the details of the alleged acts of molestation even though many of them were preposterous. Unless, of course, one actually believed in demonic possession as portrayed in movies like The Exorcist, which all the jurors on the panel had denied when questioned about it on voir dire. Dwelling on those details would only emphasize what the lawyers wanted at all costs to avoid emphasizing and also risk a dreaded emotional breakdown by a child on the stand. So Hartley began by taking each witness through their histories of multiple denials. Rockwell rang his own changes on that theme by showing how Marvin Smith had been entirely absent from the initial narratives even after the children finally admitted they'd been molested.

But somewhere in their trial preparation, the prosecution had hit upon a possible answer for that. One after another, the children said something like, "Yes, I didn't remember, but Miss Betsy and my mom and dad helped me remember." Which of course fit perfectly with the idea that the incidents were so painful the children suppressed memories of them, memories that could only be recovered through persistent efforts by skilled clinicians. And, in turn, the recovered memories supported the notion that initial denials by the children actually constituted proof that the abuse had occurred.

O'Keefe recalled his initial conversation with Betsy Mortimer in her conference room. *Catch-22 come to real life,* he thought now as he listened to the testimony.

The defense lawyers then focused on the interview process with the clinicians, police, and parents—their frequency and length, the leading questions, the rewards offered and disapprovals expressed—culminating in several multi-hour sessions with the prosecutors as they prepared for the trial.

Questioning the nine-year-old, Hartley gently coaxed out of the boy that it had been four years since he'd attended Operation Go!, and he couldn't recall how old he'd been when the alleged abusive incidents occurred.

"And you had no memory at all of any of those things until your dad discussed them with you when you were nine, correct?"

The boy nodded.

Judge Snyder snapped, "You need to answer yes or no, not just shake your head."

"Yes."

Hartley resumed, "And at that point, you denied it, right?"

"I guess so."

"But your dad persisted, right?"

"What's that mean?"

"Sorry. Kept it up. He kept asking you about it."

"He did."

"Over and over again?"

"Well, a lot."

"But you kept telling him that nothing had happened?"

"Yes.

"Until you went to Children's Clinic, right?"

"Yes."

"And you didn't want to go?"

"No."

"And even after you went there, you denied it happened, right?"

"For a while."

"How many times did you visit the Clinic?"

The boy scrunched up his face, thinking hard it seemed. "I don't remember exactly."

"Four, five, six?" Hartley offered.

"Maybe."

"And how long before you remembered the nights at Miss Ginny's house?"

"I don't remember."

"You've said here that your parents, the people at the clinic, some of your schoolmates and friends, the police, and the prosecutors all told you that things like that had happened to other kids, right?"

"Yeah. Everyone's been talking about it."

"And that was before you remembered being there yourself, right?"

The boy looked at Tarwater and then out to the courtroom audience as if an answer might be found somewhere out there. "I think so. I'm not sure. I don't remember."

The twelve-year-old, Susan Martin, testified in detail about gropings in the bathroom, fondlings in the cloakroom, and sessions with Miss Ginny and Mr. Smith in the boiler room that had occurred seven or eight years earlier. She recited all this as if she had memorized a script word for word and with an incongruously peppy affect.

Hartley asked her how she was doing today.

"Good," she said, bobbing her head emphatically.

"Had you forgotten about these incidents that happened to you when you were three or four at Operation Go!?"

"Yes."

After covering the many sessions with Mortimer and Brinkley and her parents, Hartley asked, "How many times did you meet with the prosecutors to go over your testimony?"

She gave some consideration to that, then said, "Three."

"How many hours did each meeting last?"

Again, she thought about it. "First one was longest."

"How long?"

"All of one afternoon."

"And the others?"

"Two to three hours, maybe."

"Did they tell you how they thought you should answer the questions?"

"Sometimes."

"Even the specific words for the answers?"

"Sometimes."

"Did they have written questions and answers for you to follow?"

"Yes."

"Did they show them to you?"

"Yes. We followed along with that."

"You seem to have absorbed it very well."

"Thank you."

"Do you have a copy of those written questions and answers?"

"No, they had me leave it there."

"Did they talk to you about this cross-examination, my talking to you, Mr. Rockwell talking to you, and how you should handle that?"

She nodded.

Snyder started to correct her, but she sensed her mistake, as if she remembered him snapping at the previous witness, and blurted, "Yes."

"What did they tell you?"

"To be brave, and not let you trick me or trap me."

A smattering of laughter, quickly stifled, as if the audience had recognized again that, however desperate they were for comic relief, nothing of the sort was appropriate in this trial.

Hartley smiled. "I have no intention of tricking or trapping you, Susan. I don't want any more or less than the truth. Do we agree on that?"

"Of course."

"You only went to school there for two years, right?"

"I think so."

"When you were four and five?"

"I think so."

He asked her about various other things she might remember from that time, such as the names of other teachers, how she got back and forth to the school, daily activities in the classroom and on the playground. In each case, she answered, "I can't think of anything," or "I don't remember."

"But you ended up remembering vividly these particular incidents you've talked about today, right?"

"Yes."

"Is it fair to say that the *only* things you remember about school in those years are the things you testified to today?"

"Pretty much, I guess. They all helped me remember those things."

"I'll bet they did," Hartley said.

Tarwater was on her feet. "Objection. That's grossly improper, and he knows it."

"The jury will disregard," Snyder said. "And we'll stand in recess for thirty minutes. Counsel, I want you in chambers immediately."

Hartley returned from the chambers conference with a look of resigned amusement and a thousand-dollar fine, "Which," he said, "will be reviewed for possible increase, along with other possible sanctions, when the trial is over according to Judge Snyder. Fuck him. I've got to level this goddamn playing field somehow."

Only two witnesses were left. The prosecution had saved them for last.

"The scariest of them all," Hartley said.

CHAPTER ⌇ 66

AMANDA DRESSED FIRST.

Long brown hair shining. Only a touch of makeup. A light layer of lipstick for a slight gloss. No fingernail polish. Small, barely noticeable (but still deliberately noticeable) golden hoops in her ears. No necklace, a very thin bracelet on one wrist, a small, tasteful watch on the other. She had polished her wedding ring until it sparkled in the sun's rays. The summer heat outside was stifling, but the courtroom was freezing, so she wore a lightweight but long-sleeved dress that she'd purchased especially for this occasion. A simple but elegant black dress, neither too long nor too short, falling straight from shoulder to knee. Hosiery that made no statement but enhanced her long legs. Black patent high heels, but not too high, so no danger of a wobble as she made her way to the witness stand. The impression she was seeking to make, after discussion with Donovan: subdued elegance; a gentle but serious woman not to be trifled with, and definitely not a hysteric.

"Are you ready to go?" she asked.

"Oh, yes," Misty said, eager and smiling.

Misty looked like her mother's child in every respect including the matching barely visible rows of three freckles on each side of her nose. Amanda had made sure to also dress Misty according to Donovan's instructions. "Young and soft, but not like some doll." A simple black dress with a white lace collar and black patent Mary Janes.

Bow or no bow? Amanda had a hard time deciding. Misty didn't usually wear bows, at most a clip on one side. She decided that adding the bow just wouldn't be right.

The other, younger children had taken a comfort item with them to the stand—a doll, a tattered old blanket. Amanda thought that was a bit much, an obvious show for the jury, when their innocence and vulnerability were clearly evident without the need for props. But she asked Misty anyway, who immediately darted to her bedroom and returned with the Care Bear she took to bed with her every night, holding it out to her mom with both hands. The bedraggled thing had once been bright pink but was now faded, splotched, dirty. Amanda regretted asking but felt she had to honor the choice.

Mitch had left for work earlier than usual, telling her with a tone of irritation and resentment in his voice, "I have to get some things done before I spend all day in that damn courtroom," as if she and Misty were somehow the ones imposing this burden on him. Here they were, on one of the most important, maybe *the* most important, days of their family's life, and he was acting this way. But he had acted that way all along. He hadn't helped her at all to coax the truth from Misty. Acted in fact like he just wanted it all to go away. Could he really be so callous and uncaring? Surely not. Surely it was just the shock of it, some inner shame that his beautiful little daughter had been abused in such a horrid and disgusting way. Dealing with it all on her own hadn't been easy. But she did not flag, not in the least.

They had inserted their little girl into this terrible situation. And for what? Yes, Amanda had believed that socializing with peers would be good for Misty, even at such an early age, to say nothing of the educational advantages provided by daily exposure to a real learning environment instead of just dawdling around in her playroom. But there was pure selfishness in play as well. She'd wanted more time for her volunteer activities, for reading, for staying in shape. The shame that suffused within her felt almost physical, the knowledge that she may have sacrificed her daughter to her own self-centered agenda. Her only chance at redemption would be to do everything she could to help heal that grievous wound.

At least Mitch wasn't late. He was waiting for them on the courthouse steps, standing with the other Save Our Children! parents, and thankfully, so thankfully, he was beaming, welcoming them with, "Here's my two girls. Beautiful and brave."

Misty's smile was huge. Mitch could be so charming when he wanted to be. He had come through after all.

They entered the courtroom, Misty in the middle, each of her hands in one of theirs. After the first day of trial, they had visited the courtroom only one other time, the other evening in fact, so Donovan could explain things to Misty. It had been empty then. Now it was near full, and a quiet rustling increased in volume as people turned to look at the star witnesses.

Rhonda Tarwater had presented the testimony of the other parents, but Donovan, which was how Amanda referred to him now, had taken a special interest in her and Misty, adopting them as something like his "pet" witnesses, fondly shepherding them through the process with special attention. He must believe they constituted an especially powerful component of the prosecution's case, which imposed a responsibility on her that she took on with utmost seriousness.

Honoring the rule excluding witnesses who had not yet given their testimony from being present in the courtroom during the testimony of other witnesses, Mitch took Misty into the corridor while Amanda testified. She described what she called her "terrible journey" from initial disbelief and emphatic rejection of the idea that a wonderful teacher like Miss Ginny or the always friendly and seemingly good-hearted janitor, Mr. Smith, could commit such heinous crimes to the belief that the two had actually committed those very crimes.

Donovan had advised her to downplay aspects of that journey, even leave some bits out.

Like Mitch, and his refusal to get involved.

Like the letter from Myra Hicks—even though it was the letter that had punctured the first chink in her armor of doubt that such things were even possible. Because surely, they wouldn't send out such a letter to so many people if they didn't have the strongest evidence of guilt.

And of course she shouldn't lie, but unless pressed by the defense attorneys on cross, she should stay away from things like the fact that not once when they picked Misty up after a night or weekend of Ginny's babysitting did Misty show any sign of anything bad or even odd having happened to her. And Amanda should most certainly not volunteer that she gave Misty a bath every day and never saw any physical indications of tampering.

If possible, also avoid references to Ralph Merkel. After she received the letter and called a few of her friends and acquaintances to ask their opinions, he called her. On that call, and subsequent calls and visits, he was adamant that, just like his son and *hundreds* of others over the years, Misty had been molested. Few, if any, had escaped. They had been snatched up in a nationwide, likely worldwide, Satanic conspiracy. He even brought her some books like *Michelle Remembers.* He said that Gloria Steinem believed in cult ritual child abuse and had donated money to the cause. He introduced her to Save Our Children!, at whose meetings she renewed old acquaintances and made new friends. There were no doubters there.

He also introduced her to Perry Slotkin and encouraged her to take Misty to the Children's Clinic. There, and this she could and should testify to, that impressive young woman, Betsy Mortimer, who'd worked with so many other children, had told Amanda unequivocally that Misty had been molested though Misty still denied it. At Betsy's recommendation, they sent Misty to Dr. Carlyle, whose physical examination also indicated abuse. Amanda and Betsy agreed to work together to bring Misty along, gently but insistently and firmly, to bring out the truth.

Though still not entirely convinced of the molestation, she kept working on it with Betsy until it finally began slowly coming out. "One night, I was tucking her into bed," she testified, "and I was just overcome with all of it, this beautiful, innocent little creature subjected to those things. Everything I'd been told and read said you just had to get this kind of thing out in the open or it could blight a life forever. And here I was, unable to persuade my own baby to trust me enough. It was just too much. The tears just started trickling down my face and then I broke down all the way. And Misty looked up at me and said—"

The defense lawyers objected on hearsay grounds. Donovan didn't bother to respond to what was now a tired refrain, leaving it to Judge Snyder, who said, "You know the answer to that."

"—She looked up at me and said, 'Mommy, what's wrong?' And I told her how much I wanted to help her, but I couldn't if she kept secrets. And she asked what secrets I was talking about. And I said, 'School. Miss Ginny's house. What happened to you there? Did someone touch you in your private places?' Then she started crying and shook her head yes. And it started coming out then, and after a few more sessions with Betsy, it all came out. At least I think it's all. I hope it's all."

Donovan proceeded in a low gentle voice as Amanda struggled to hold back sobs. "And what is it that came out?"

Amidst sobs, Amanda described what Misty had told her and Betsy about the fondlings in the bathroom and the cloak room and the sessions both in the boiler room and at Ginny's house where Mr. Smith had penetrated her "down there."

"AN UNFORGETTABLE SUMMER DRAWS TO ITS DREARY END. THE DROUGHT OF 1988 HAS LEFT A LEGACY OF CHAOS, SUFFERING, AND DEATH ACROSS AMERICA: PRELUDE TO A FALL WITHOUT HARVEST, A WINTER OF POVERTY OR BANKRUPTCY, A NEW LIFE OFF THE FARM."

CHAPTER ~ 67

Gently, gently, Hartley rose and on oratorical tiptoes addressed Amanda Haynes.

Softly, softly, probably barely audible beyond the jury box, he said: "The alleged occurrences you've described here occurred over a period of almost two years, correct?"

"Yes. What I know about anyway."

"And it's true, isn't it, that during that time, those two years, Misty never reported any of those traumatic incidents to you?"

She hesitated a moment, considering, taking care. "True."

"And you did not during that period notice any departure from Misty's normal behavior, correct?"

"No."

"And as you testified, you didn't initially believe that Misty had been molested?"

"No."

"That was despite the fact that you were attending the parent meetings and hearing about other children supposedly being molested, correct?"

"No. I didn't understand then the way it worked."

"And how did you learn about the Children's Clinic?"

"Ralph Merkel initially."

"And who is he?"

"One of the parents. He's pretty much the leader of the parents' group."

"Is he in the courtroom today?"

She answered yes and, at Hartley's request, pointed him out. Dolinar and Tarwater scowled, but it seemed to go by them faster than they could articulate an objection. Ralph sat up straight, proud, defiant.

"Did you learn about the Clinic from anyone else?"

"That's where all the parents in the group had sent their children. And Betsy came with the police and Child Services people to a couple of meetings."

"And when you came to understand 'the way it worked,' as you call it, your teacher on that was Betsy Mortimer, right?"

"Mostly. Mr. Brinkley from Child Services attended the sessions too. And I did some reading on my own."

"What did you read?"

"Well, there was *Michelle Remembers*."

"And that is a book about a young girl whose *family members* were supposedly members of a satanic cult, right?"

"Yes."

"Not teachers. Family members, right?"

"Yes."

"Are you aware that many believe that the stories in that book are all lies?"

Dolinar objected. "Argumentative."

"Sustained."

"Are you aware that several experts have questioned the credibility of the stories in that book?"

Dolinar objected again. "He needs to establish some foundation that these so-called experts actually exist."

"It's probably irrelevant anyway," Snyder said, "at least in this context, but I'll allow at least this question."

"I'm not aware of that," Amanda answered.

Hartley continued. "Ms. Mortimer recommended that book?"

"She may have, but I'd read it earlier."

"Who did you hear about it from?"

"Ralph Merkel."

"How about Perry Slotkin? Did he recommend anything?"

Dolinar squirmed, but Amanda said quickly and decisively, "No."

"And even at Children's Clinic, Misty continued to deny that any abuse had occurred?"

She looked wary this time. "Yes."

"How many sessions did Misty attend at Children's Clinic where she continued to deny the alleged abuse?"

"Three."

"And Ms. Mortimer reported those denials to you but also told you that, in her opinion, Misty had been molested?"

"Yes."

"But you didn't believe her, right?"

"I wouldn't say that."

"Well, what word would you use to describe how you felt? Skeptical?"

"Somewhat."

"And, as I understood your testimony, at the last of those three sessions, Ms. Mortimer enlisted you to closely question Misty to persuade her to admit the abuse."

"Yes, but she didn't characterize it that way. It was to uncover the truth of whatever might have happened to Misty."

"But Misty continued for a period of time to deny it despite your continued questioning, right?"

"Yes."

"How many times did you question her?"

Amanda took a while to answer, at one point seeming to look to Dolinar for help.

"I don't remember."

"More than five? Ten? Twenty?"

Amanda looked at Dolinar again, seeming to beseech him for assistance, but he only tightened his jaw.

"I'm not sure. Maybe between ten and twenty."

"But you're not sure. It could have been more?"

"Possibly. I'm not sure."

"And she kept denying, right? And finally one night you broke down and wept while you were questioning her, right?"

"Yes. It was so frustrating."

"In all those sessions, especially that last one, you were *begging* her to tell you that something bad had happened, right?"

"I wouldn't characterize it that way. Probing, making sure. Everything I was hearing indicated that terrible things had occurred there. I had the opinion of a professional that she'd been violated."

"By 'professional,' are you referring to Ms. Mortimer?"

"Yes, and—"

"Did you ever check her credentials?"

"I didn't think I needed to. She was head of the Clinic. I had put Misty in that situation. And it could have wrecked her whole life. I thought I had to make sure—"

"You were feeling guilty?"

"Somewhat."

"And so you were begging her, entreating her? What word would you use?"

"I wanted to make sure she wasn't so ashamed that she was repressing it."

"And she didn't tell you about any details at that time, did she? Just said, 'Something bad happened.'"

"That's right."

"You didn't at any time contact another professional, only Ms. Mortimer, right?"

"I did. Dr. Carlyle."

"The doctor who worked with Ms. Mortimer at Children's Clinic, yes?"

"Yes."

"Other than those two, did you ever consult any professional concerning Misty's situation?"

"No."

"And after the session where you were in tears, and Misty said something had happened but without any detail, you then took her back to the Clinic for a number of sessions?"

"Yes."

"And you participated in some of those?"

"Yes."

"But not all?"

"I only participated in a few."

"And more came out of those sessions, right?"

"Right. It all slowly came out."

"Over how many sessions?"

"I think four or five more."

"Ms. Mortimer used the dolls and the puppets?"

"Yes."

"Do you know what a leading question is?"

"Maybe. It's a little confusing."

"Would you agree with me that one aspect of a leading question is that it suggests the answer that the questioner wants?"

"Not exactly. I would say it might suggest the answer that the questioner believes is the truth."

"And did the two of you use that type of question to bring these things out of Misty?"

"Oh, yes. After all, she's only five years old."

"And the three of you did that for four or five sessions?"

"Yes."

"And before that as well?"

"Yes."

"How long were these sessions?"

After a few seconds, she said, "Several hours."

"Did you have her repeat the incidents in these later sessions?"

"Yes. Betsy wanted to test her."

"Did you have a problem dragging her through all that over and over again?"

"I understand what you're saying, but no. I thought it was for the best possible purpose. Helping her remember, the beginning of healing according to Betsy, and punishing the people who did these awful things to her."

"How did Misty act when she was telling these things over and over?"

"I'm not sure I understand."

"Was she sobbing, hysterical, matter-of-fact?"

"More matter-of-fact as we went on. She's so innocent. I'm not sure she realizes how awful it was."

"Have you taught Misty nursery rhymes?"

"Sure."

"Has she memorized them?"

"Yes, several," Amanda said with pride.

"Could it be that she was so matter-of-fact because she'd just memorized what you two adults had told her, like she'd memorized those nursery rhymes?"

"Objection," Dolinar said. "Calls for speculation."

"Sustained," Snyder said, scowling even more fiercely than usual at Hartley, and added, "Mr. Hartley…" It was a warning.

"Does Misty believe in Santa Claus?"

"Objection," Dolinar yelled.

And while the prosecutor fumbled for a reason why he was objecting, Hartley added, "You've told her about Santa Claus, I assume?"

"Irrelevant," Dolinar had finally come up with something. "Suggesting that Santa Claus and sexual abuse are anywhere close to equivalent is an abomination."

"Sustained. The jury will ignore." And in a rising voice, another warning, "Mr. Hartley…"

Strike two. But Hartley wasn't done yet. "After the four or five times with you and Ms. Mortimer, how many times has Misty met with the police and prosecutors?"

She paused. "Five or six."

"So, all in all, Misty was questioned about these things three times in the first phase by Ms. Mortimer, ten to twenty times or more by you, four or five more by you and Ms. Mortimer, and five or six with the police or prosecutors, correct?"

She didn't want to say it, but her champion failed this time to come to her rescue with an objection. When she realized she had no alternative, she said, "Seems right."

"So she's been questioned about these matters at least twenty-two times, maybe as many as thirty-four times."

"I guess so, yes."

When Amanda finished, Snyder announced a brief recess and called the lawyers into chambers.

Ten minutes later, Hartley returned with an additional three-thousand-dollar fine. "And Snyder intends to file a formal complaint about my behavior to the bar association after the trial.

"Don't look so proud of yourself, Scotty," Rockwell said.

CHAPTER ❧ 68

AMANDA LEFT THE stand, met Misty and Mitch at the gate
to the bar, leaned down and kissed Misty on top of the head and
stroked her back.

She passed Misty to Dolinar, who took Misty's hand and led
her to the witness stand. Misty was tiny, even for a five-year-old, and
Dolinar had to help her onto the booster seat.

Misty looked around. O'Keefe would swear her features
unmistakably brightened when her eyes rested on the defendants.
He hoped at least some of the jurors had noticed that. Dolinar had
definitely noticed it and quickly moved to block Misty's view of
Ginny and the jurors' view of Misty.

Once he'd diverted Misty's attention away from the defendants,
Dolinar wasted no time in pleasantries. He asked her if Miss Ginny
had ever touched any of her "private parts."

Yes, the first time was in the bathroom. When Misty asked to
go, Ginny took her there. They were alone in a stall. Ginny locked
the door, then took Misty's pants down and felt her in the place she
went potty and put her fingers in there, then her mouth on there.
This happened more than once, she couldn't say how many times.

At nap time, Miss Ginny sometimes led her to Mr. Smith's
room. He took his pants off, and she saw his "thing," which "stood
up straight." Ginny took some of her own clothes off, and she and
Mr. Smith "did things" to each other that involved their "private
parts." After that, Miss Ginny said, "Let's play doctor." They put
Misty on the cot and Mr. Smith touched her with his "thing."

"Did that hurt?"

"It started to. I made a noise, and he stopped."

"Did it happen again?"

It had. He did it again and this time was more careful and it didn't hurt.

Dolinar left it to the jurors' imaginations how far he had penetrated her.

"And did that happen other times?"

"Sometimes," she said.

Similar things had happened at Miss Ginny's house. "We would have parties with cake and ice cream."

"Soft drinks, too?"

"Coke."

"After she gave you the treat and the drink, did you ever feel dizzy or woozy?"

"Sometimes."

Then things would happen like in the boiler room.

Misty looked past Dolinar at her mother and said, "Right, Mommy?"

That was an awkward moment.

Dolinar quickly intervened. "Your mom helps you remember?"

"She does," she said, nodding eagerly.

"Did it hurt when Mr. Smith did that to you?"

"I don't think so. Or only a little bit." As if she had just remembered, she said, "And he put something on his thing that made it not hurt like that first time."

"Did anything come *out* of his 'thing' sometimes?"

"Yes."

"Can you say what that was?"

"Gooey."

Amanda sobbed audibly.

"Mommy?" Misty cried out.

The look on Marvin Smith's face was beyond O'Keefe's power of description. He was afraid to look toward the jury box …

"When these things were happening," Dolinar said, "did you ever tell your parents about them?"

Craning to try to see her mother, she said "Un-uh."

"Is that a 'no'?" A voice from somewhere, not Mr. Dolinar. Misty looked up with alarm, unsure where the booming voice had come from.

The booming voice again. "Little girl, you have to answer with a word. Is it 'no'?"

Misty froze and Dolinar hurried to help. "No, you didn't tell them, right Misty?"

This time, Misty both shook her head and said no, then looked back up warily at where the God-like voice had come from.

"Why not?"

Her face was blank.

"You said you didn't tell your parents about it. Did you not do that because Miss Ginny and Mr. Smith told you something?"

Hartley objected. "There has to be some limit on how much he can lead her, Your Honor. He might as well be a ventriloquist."

As they argued at the bench, Misty moved to get down from the booster seat. Tarwater hurried to stop her, saying, "Not yet, Misty. Not yet."

After Snyder overruled the objection, Dolinar moved very close to her and asked her again if she hadn't told her parents because Miss Ginny and Mr. Smith had said something to her, and added, "Did they tell you not to? That something would happen to you if you told?"

"They said the devil would come and hurt me if I told."

Hartley tried to be gentle, but Misty was clearly afraid of him.

"These things in the school bathroom," he said, "and the boiler room and Miss Ginny's house … at first you said they didn't happen, right?"

"Until I remembered."

"How were you able to remember?"

"They helped me. They told me."

"What did they tell you?"

"The things that happened."

"Who is they?"

"Mommy. Miss Betsy."

"Did they use the dolls to show you what they thought might have happened?"

"Sometimes."

"Were there other kids in Mr. Smith's room when these things happened to you?"

She looked confused but didn't answer.

"Did Betsy and your mom tell you what other kids said Miss Ginny and Mr. Smith did to them?"

She nodded her head vigorously.

"Little girl," Snyder said, "you have to say 'yes.' You can't just wag your head."

Misty eyes grew large as she looked up at the bench.

Hartley continued gently. "What did they tell you?"

"Just asked me things."

"Did they ask you specifically if Miss Ginny took you to the bathroom and did some things there?"

"Yes."

"And did they describe what they thought happened in the boiler room and ask you if that's what happened?"

Misty didn't respond.

"Do you understand what I'm asking you, Misty?"

She shook her head.

Snyder barked, "You have to say 'yes' or 'no.' You can't just shake your head like that."

At first there was no sound, just tears streaming down Misty's face, then she sobbed, then she wailed. And wailed more, her chest heaving, struggling to catch her breath.

Hartley looked around helplessly.

Amanda stood and moved toward Misty.

"Mommy!"

Hartley hung his head and walked over to stand by the defense table while Amanda, followed closely by Mitch, embraced Misty who continued to wail inconsolably.

"Can we take her out?" Mitch asked Snyder.

"Yes, we'll take a short recess," Snyder said.

Mitch gathered Misty in his arms and carried her out of the courtroom.

Hartley sat down and leaned back in his chair. "I really think she was going my way."

"Do you think Snyder did that on purpose?" O'Keefe whispered.

"No. He's just an asshole. Can't help himself. He probably talked to his kids that way their whole lives. Probably even his grandkids."

It took almost an hour before they were able to coax Misty back into the courtroom. Now she sat on Amanda's lap. Snyder climbed down from the bench and tried to ingratiate himself with her, but she turned away and buried her face in her mother's chest. Hartley whispered, "I don't think the dumb ass even understands what he did."

At the break, Hartley and Rockwell had agreed that Rockwell would take over when Misty returned to the stand.

"Hello, Misty. My name is Lou. I represent Mr. Smith, over there, sitting at the table. Do you remember him?"

She nodded, looking straight at him, showing no fear or hostility.

Rockwell rushed to say, softly, "Is that a yes?"

Again she nodded.

Rockwell quickly said, "Your Honor, may the record reflect that the witness is nodding in the affirmative?"

"Alright," Snyder said.

Misty looked up, still fearful.

"What you said about Mr. Smith rubbing you with his thing, were those your words that you told your mom and Miss Betsy, or were they your mom's or Miss Betsy's words?"

Misty looked at him with incomprehension, shrank back into her mother and looked up at her face.

"Do you understand, Misty?" Rockwell said. "Should I ask you another way?"

She frowned and shook her head, then said crossly, "I don't know."

Rockwell hesitated, trying to conjure up the right wording, but before he could manage it, Misty said, "Mommy, I want to go home now."

Rockwell looked over at Hartley, who shrugged and raised his hands in a gesture of helplessness. Marvin Smith turned away.

Ginny shook her head and mouthed the words "No, No, No," to Rockwell.

"I wanna go home, Mommy," Misty wailed and again buried her head in her mother's chest.

O'Keefe felt a strange silence descend on the courtroom and in that moment the world seemed to stop, no movement at all, the exhausted warriors frozen in place, as if they had punched and lurched and stumbled and slogged, mud up to their shins—in a closed, dark room—in some contest whose rules they had never but slenderly understood—and now no longer understood at all—and had no idea what to do next.

That was the end of the cross-examination of Misty Haynes.

CHAPTER ༺ 69

WHEN THE PROSECUTION RESTED, Judge Snyder gave everyone a day off before the defense put on its first witness.

That was the day Billy Bitson returned to town, sponsored by several local evangelical churches and Save Our Children!. They sold tickets, and O'Keefe had Dagmar buy one for him, using a fake name.

"What if they recognize you?" Dagmar said.

"I doubt they'll do more than throw me out."

She rolled her eyes. "Should I call the ambulance now and get them ready?"

His response to Dagmar may have been cavalier, but it would do no harm to take precautions. Despite a lifelong aversion to both sunglasses and hats, he wore both. Tan shorts and a plain white T-shirt too. Just an ordinary guy. He showed up a few minutes after the proceedings had started and found an aisle seat in the back row that would enable a quick escape if necessary. He was not in good position to survey the crowd but was able to locate a few of the Save Our Children! people that often attended the court proceedings, various media representatives, including Karen Todd from the *Herald,* and Rhonda Tarwater in the front row. One Save Our Children! person easy to identify was Ralph Merkel, one of only three people on the stage other than Reverend Bitson, the other two O'Keefe guessed to be local preachers.

Bitson elaborated on his usual themes: the erosion of family values; the decline of religious observance; the pernicious effects of the 1960s: free love, free sex, and free everything else, and the accompanying decline of authority, responsibility, and the other character traits that had made the country great.

"Why should we be surprised at the spread of Satanism," he bellowed, "when the so-called intellectuals are shouting from every rooftop that God is dead?"

Bitson came to the front of the stage and leaned forward. "You have right here in this city this disgusting day-care scandal, these children cruelly molested over all those years, and nobody came to their rescue. I think we have now learned, unfortunately in the hardest way possible, that we cannot oust our children from the bosom of home and family and thrust them into the often unclean hands of total strangers whose beliefs, politics, and morality we have no idea about.

"In Russia and other Communist, Godless countries, parents are *forced* to give up their children in this way. We should not do the same thing *voluntarily* in this free, though increasingly unfree, land. In this regard, I so much appreciate Ralph Merkel and his group not just for sponsoring my trip here, but much more so for carrying the right message at this decisive moment in our history. For sounding an alarm, a warning to all of us that we must awake, and like Jesus, cleanse the temple of the infidels."

O'Keefe's knowledge of the Bible wasn't great, but wasn't it the moneychangers, not infidels, that Jesus drove from the temple? In any event, Bitson closed on that note, and handed the microphone to Ralph Merkel, red-faced, eyes darting and dancing with angry ambition, thanking everyone for coming. Not to be outdone by Bitson in the realm of scriptural exegesis, he said, "Please, all of you who believe the children, get off your duffs, rise up, and help us, like Our Savior Jesus in the Bible when he cast the devils out of that possessed man and into the herd of pigs and stampeded them over the cliff and they drowned in the sea below."

Now there was a familiar turn of phrase.

CHAPTER ⚜ 70

Hartley woke, sopping wet with sweat.

Thick smoke was pouring in through the bedroom window above the front porch. His wife's hacking cough had doubled her over, and visibility was near zero. He helped her struggle through the billowing smoke to the kids' bedrooms. They yanked the kids out of their beds. Each parent, with a kid in arms, found their way down the stairs as fast as they could but stepping carefully in fear of tripping and tumbling down. They dodged the flames that had engulfed the front door and stumbled to the back of the house and out the back door. The fire department arrived minutes later. An insomniac neighbor had noticed the flames and made the call. They figured it out right away. A Molotov cocktail.

Someone tipped a local television station. They interviewed Hartley, naked except for his boxer shorts, a neighbor's blanket around him, his terrified wife and young children beside him.

"All I have to say," he told the reporter, "is that I'll be in court tomorrow morning. Business as usual."

O'Keefe was unaware of the incident when he arrived at the courthouse. Maura breathlessly passed on the news.

"Where is he?" O'Keefe said, "What's he gonna do?"

"He told the television reporter on the air this morning he'd be in court."

Five minutes before the usual starting time, Hartley marched into the courtroom where everyone but Snyder and the jury were in place. He strode over to the prosecution's table and in full declamatory voice addressed all sitting there as well as the Save Our Children! group in the audience.

"My children were in that house. Do you hear me, child savers? My children were in that house."

"Cool it, Scott," Dolinar muttered.

"You brushed off the threat to my witness. Are you gonna brush this off too?"

The bailiff approached and said, "How about taking this into chambers, Mr. Hartley?"

"What the fuck good would that do?"

He walked back to the defense table where his colleagues were as shocked as everyone else in the courtroom, sat down, and said to the bailiff, "Please tell Judge Snyder that the defense is ready." He turned to O'Keefe and whispered, "No way will Raylee show now."

Snyder adjourned for the day. Scott went off to deal with his family, his insurance adjusters, and the police.

O'Keefe called Annie and asked if she'd heard the news.

"Yes. Horrible. What's wrong with these people?"

"Where's Kelly?"

"At school of course."

"I'm worried about you guys. I'm gonna set you up with some security."

"What exactly does that mean?"

"Bodyguards. Pick her up from school, drive you to work and back."

"No. We're having enough unwanted attention without that."

She could be damned irritating. "Then I'll personally pick both of you up," he said.

"Come off it. We're just witnesses. Maybe you're a more likely target. Maybe we should stay out of *your* way."

"Raylee is just a witness too. She got a death threat."

"A little different kind of witness than we are."

"You're being stupid."

"You're being hysterical."

"I can't force *you,* but I'll be waiting for Kelly after school."

He slammed down the phone before she could protest.

He was fed up with law enforcement. They had reported the threat to Raylee to the prosecutor's office and the police in their city and hers. Tarwater's only comment was, "Are you sure she didn't send it to herself?" The police in Raylee's town interviewed her but did nothing else. It had always seemed certain to O'Keefe that the author of the letter was not from her current city but her old one, yet as far as O'Keefe could tell, the local police were doing nothing. Now this attack on Scott and his family.

O'Keefe called his sort-of-friend in the force, Lieutenant Steven Ross. He didn't need to say anything. Ross knew why he was calling. "I'm surprised I haven't heard from you before now." They agreed to meet at what Ross called "the old meeting place," otherwise known as O'Keefe's driveway, which was the last place they had furtively convened in the midst of O'Keefe's escapades earlier in the year.

O'Keefe sat sweating on his front stoop, cursing the suffocating humidity that had smothered the city and the country at large all summer. Ross pulled into his driveway on time. O'Keefe stood up to shake Ross's hand as the detective sauntered over to him.

"Is there any pile of shit in this town you don't find a way to step in?"

O'Keefe offered a rueful smile.

"Okay, I need to frisk you," Ross said. "For a wire. You understand, I'm sure."

"So you don't care if I shoot you as long as I don't record you."

Now it was Ross's turn to smile. "Yeah, that's it."

As Ross quickly and expertly finished the pat-down, O'Keefe said, "So, can I assume you've heard about our witness-tampering problem and the attack on Scott Hartley last night?"

"Try as I might, I can't seem to do anything but hear about it."

"Our theory is that the department not only doesn't care enough to follow up but is even cheering these bastards on."

"Nah. There's that element in the force, but it's not the consensus. Most of us have tried to keep our heads down, stay as far away from this thing as we can. It won't pay to stick your neck out on it. We can't wait for it to end."

"Why don't you do something to help it end?"

"You should note that despite all the hullabaloo and the accusations that every day-care place in town is a Satanist nest of child molesters, there's only been your case. We think we've done a good job of maneuvering through the panic. We've been the opposite of witch hunters."

"Tell that to Sally Hicks."

"You're just one contrary fucker, aren't you, O'Keefe? We can't be perfect."

"What about the attack on Hartley?"

"It's under investigation. Not by me."

"Will they really try or just let it go?"

"I think they'll be in good faith on it."

O'Keefe gave him a look.

"Alright. I'll try to make sure they're diligent about it."

"Seems like someone could do at least a little bit of work on this tampering situation if only to cover your asses. What if some harm really comes to that lady? For example, why wouldn't some brilliant and enterprising policeman set about checking the commercial airline flight manifests ... maybe check for all flights from here to there the day of the mailbox deposit and a day or two before and after?"

"It's a pretty easy drive."

"That's not a good excuse for not doing the obvious."

"Alright. I'll make sure it's looked into."

"Do you know who Ralph Merkel is?" O'Keefe said.

"'Fraid so. Royal pain in the ass. He's in our face weekly if not daily with tips on Satanist activities and demands that we round up the whole crowd and, I guess, burn them at the stake."

"It would be nice to know if he was out of town when Raylee Reynolds received that death threat."

"Okay. If I can check that quietly enough, I will."

"Appreciated."

"Yeah, I think you might be on the right side on this one. For once."

Janice Braverman, a Cincinnati photographer, arrived in Irvine, Kentucky to begin a one-year photography project funded by a $10,00 grant from the Kentucky Arts Council.

Her project focused on kids "who might not do well in school and get discouraged and skip classes or drop out entirely."

When she went to visit principal Russell Bowen at Estill County High School, she encountered four girls in a restroom skipping class. These were just the kind of kids her project was focused on.

She photographed the girls and showed them how to take pictures.

Earlier in the summer, six persons had been arrested locally for a grave robbery said by the police to be related to devil worship.

By the weekend, rumors were circulating that a woman representing a Satanic cult was taking pictures of blonde-haired, blue-eyed girls as potential candidates for human sacrifice.

On Monday she went to Principal Bowen's office again. He came out of his office "yelling and screaming, threatening her arrest and removal from school grounds."

Fearing for her safety, she fled town.

CHAPTER ᪥ 71

NOT JUST THE SPECTATORS but the courtroom itself seemed to take a deep breath when Hartley announced, "I call as my first witness Virginia Montrose."

Hartley felt he had to buck the received wisdom that the defendant should be kept out of the witness box if at all possible. But Hartley believed it was essential here, and neither Rockwell nor any other of his human sounding boards disagreed. Too much was riding on the jurors' perception of the kind of person she was. She could not hide in the shadows like a guilty thing surprised. She could not just proclaim her innocence, she had to reveal it. Seeing and hearing directly from her might engender reasonable doubt all by itself.

Of course it was her decision, not his. But she had no doubts, and would likely have refused to follow any other advice.

Amplifying the risk, he also kicked to the corner the received wisdom that if you do make that high-risk choice, the defendant should be the last, not the first witness. Certainly she would make a good impression on direct, and if she survived the prosecution's onslaught on cross, the defense would be off to an excellent start. And if things didn't go so well, he would have a large chunk of time and a number of potentially stronger witnesses between her and the end of the defense case to try to repair any damage.

As usual, she was soft spoken, composed, and unemotional except when she talked about her love for children and for teaching. That was why she had made the personal financial sacrifice to take and keep the low-paying Operation Go! job for all those years. (Listening, O'Keefe thought, *And this is your reward.*) She volunteered for extra duty at the school, such as handling the daily naps, in part to make a little extra money, but mostly because she enjoyed spending that different kind of time with them. It was the same for the babysitting. The additional money had been welcome, but she loved doing it, probably would have done it without pay if asked, and it had the additional benefit of helping out the parents.

Yes, her relationship with Marvin Smith was friendly. They had both started work when the school opened and had spent many years there. Yes, for years he'd done work for her and her housemate, everything from minor repairs to their cars to especially heavy yard work, painting, and fixing all the things that go wrong with household appliances and the infrastructure items the landlord refused to do or did so badly it made things worse. He too had welcomed the chance to earn a little extra money. And he was a good guy, always happy to help out, and fun to have around. She locked eyes with Mrs. Smith, sitting in the gallery immediately behind her husband, and, deviating from her customary calm delivery, poured angry contempt on "the snide and vicious" accusations of a romantic or sexual relationship between them. It was "preposterous." She couldn't recall ever even touching him.

And, yes, she often assisted the children in the bathroom—the youngest ones were often barely potty trained when they arrived at the school—and of course when she babysat them. But she never touched one inappropriately at any time in any place.

After taking her through a series of denials and accompanying details tending to show the impossibility that the accusations against her could have occurred, and especially could not have occurred without discovery and outcry, Hartley moved to the incidents involving the Lowe family.

"Objection. Hearsay."

The defense knew this moment would come. They also knew they were well prepared for it.

Maura handed Hartley copies of the brief. He gave one to Dolinar and another to Snyder, who received it as if he'd been handed soiled toilet tissue. "This is likely to take a while, I assume?"

"Probably," Hartley said, and Dolinar agreed.

They took the jury out. "Don't get comfortable," Snyder told them. "You'll be back soon."

"It's not hearsay," Hartley said, "because it's not being offered to prove the truth of the statements. We are not offering them to prove that Randy Lowe's parents abused him. We are offering it solely to show that the incident provoked the investigation in the first place."

"It's being offered for the truth that the statements by the defendant and Mrs. Lowe were made," Dolinar said.

"He's obfuscating," Hartley said, "trying to create a smoke screen. "I repeat: It is not hearsay at all unless it's offered to prove *the truth of the matter asserted.* We are not offering it to prove that the Lowes abused their son. We are offering it show how and why this investigation started. And if you want another reason, as we elaborate in the brief, it's also offered to impeach, which is also not hearsay."

"Impeach who?" Dolinar said. "Impeach what?"

"The entire investigation, the entire prosecution. To show that its origin was simply vengeful slander."

An epistemological and jurisprudential conundrum indeed. Snyder's face reflected his anguished confusion. Clearly, he didn't fully understand the issue and was likely worried about looking moronic to all eyes in the courtroom, and thanks to the media, outside the courtroom as well.

"Your Honor," Hartley said, "we've been heading to this moment since the beginning of the case, since they amended the indictment to drop Randy Lowe. You ruled that we could get into this issue in a general and careful way. You let me talk about it generally in my opening statement. You let me generally cross-examine the detectives about it. Mr. Dolinar is asking you to change your mind at this most critical point. We're asking only that you stay good to your word."

"This isn't general," Dolinar said. "It's a whole other level."

Snyder looked at the brief as if it were a summons to his own execution. "Mr. Dolinar, I think I have to let him do this. Up to a point. Maybe I was wrong to let any part of it in. But here we are.

If it gets out of hand or bounds, I'll rein him in, instruct the jury to disregard, or something."

"I take exception," Dolinar said.

Snyder's eyes narrowed. His favorite prosecutor had managed to irritate him. "If you think it's false testimony, damn it, bring that Lowe women in on rebuttal and contradict it." Catching himself, he darted a look at the court reporter—a silent instruction to keep his profanity out of the transcript. Then he looked out at the media. Those were reporters he couldn't control.

Time to end this embarrassing colloquy. "You're getting a gift here, Mr. Hartley. Keep it simple. And get it over with quick."

The jury returned and Ginny testified in general terms to her suspicion that the child had been physically abused, that she'd warned the child's mother that any further suspicious incidents would be reported to the authorities, the angry reactions of Randy's parents, and that she later learned that Heidi Lowe had called other parents and the police and accused Ginny of sexual molestation.

Tarwater's opening cross was indirect, allusive, suggestive rather than a direct assault. Many of the questions seemed routine, on their own unobjectionable, but together they amounted to something more. Hartley objected but could not convince the judge that these "background" questions, taken as a whole, were irrelevant and unduly prejudicial. So Tarwater was allowed to emphasize that Ginny had attended a girl's college, Raylee Reynolds had been her roommate, and they had shared living quarters ever since, and Reynolds had moved out of the city immediately following the indictment, though Ginny managed to add that this was to care for her parents, both of whom suffered from dementia.

She acknowledged that she had seldom gone on dates either in college or out.

"Have you ever dated a black man?"

"What?!"

Hartley and Rockwell rushed to the bench.

"Do I really have to point out that this is irrelevant, Your Honor?" Rockwell said, "And disgustingly racist too."

For a change Snyder looked more irritated with the prosecution than the defense but said, "I guess it's sort of relevant given the accusations in the indictment."

"But," Rockwell said," that's because Marvin Smith is a man, not because he's a black man."

Snyder allowed it anyway but urged Tarwater to use caution.

"No," Ginny said, curt and clipped.

"Have you ever had a steady boyfriend?"

"Not really."

"Have you ever had sex with another female?"

Hartley shot up from his chair, but before he could say anything, Snyder called a short recess, kept the jury waiting in the courtroom, and ordered counsel to his chambers where Hartley paced angrily and glared at Dolinar who seemed to be looking for the woodwork to melt into.

Snyder, twice in a row exasperated with the prosecution, and not a fan of female attorneys anyway, growled at Tarwater, "How in the world can you justify asking that question?"

"Simple, Your Honor. If she is sexually deviant in one way, why wouldn't she be in others?"

"Deviant?" Hartley said, "This is 1988, not 1888. The whole world has decriminalized same-sex relations."

"Not so," Tarwater fired back. "It's still illegal in several states here in the U.S., including this state, and the Supreme Court upheld those laws just two years ago in *Bowers v. Hardwick.*"

"Plus," Hartley said, "no foundation. There would have to be some expert testimony that it's even 'deviant,' and that one type of deviancy actually makes another more likely."

"Polymorphous perversity," Tarwater said.

Snyder appeared to be clueless.

Tarwater continued. "It's a famous book of the 1960s by Norman O. Brown. *Life Against Death.* Polymorphous perversity. It advocates every kind of sex with everybody imaginable. We found a dog-eared copy on Ms. Montrose's bookshelf. Once you go in that direction, like Dostoyevsky said, then 'everything is permitted.'"

"Please wake me when this is over," Hartley said. "This has to be the first and hopefully the last time Norman O. Brown and Fyodor Dostoyevsky have been cited as authorities in a courtroom. I don't know why I have to dignify this crock of dung with any response at all."

Snyder shifted some of his irritation to a more familiar target. "Keep yourself under control, Mr. Hartley."

"And I assume the next step," Rockwell said, "is to claim that interracial sexual relations constitute further deviancy that somehow follows from same-sex relations. It's so crazy it's hard to deal with it. I guess I need to point out for the record that *Loving vs. Virginia* was decided way back in the 1960s."

Bypassing Tarwater, Snyder said to Dolinar, "I can't let you do this without a ton of expert testimony that we'll first have to take in chambers on a voir dire basis."

Dolinar, managing to muster a contrite expression, said, "Of course, we'll accept your ruling, Your Honor. If you sustain his objection, we'll just move on."

Hartley, fuming, "All this and none of it's true anyway. It's all hogwash. But they've already poisoned the well. The question itself was the poison. What's the jury gonna think when the question isn't answered?"

Snyder, slyly, "Well then, do you want to withdraw your objection and let her answer?"

"That's not fair. This is gross prosecutorial misconduct. I have to ask for a mistrial. I don't want to because I don't think the case is going in their favor at all, but we can't risk this."

"And I join in that request," Rockwell said.

"That's too harsh for one question, gentlemen. We'll come up with some kind of jury instruction to handle this."

Hartley reported later to his team that he could swear he saw Tarwater and Dolinar slyly smirking at each other on the way out of chambers. "The fuckers knew exactly what they were doing. They knew it didn't need to be answered to embed it permanently in the jurors' minds."

Back in the courtroom, the judge stated simply that the objection was sustained, and Tarwater moved on to address the Lowe issue.

"Isn't it true, Ms. Montrose, that you were obligated under state law to report your suspicion that Randy Lowe had been abused.

"Possibly, I guess. I'm not a lawyer."

"But you didn't report it, did you?"

"No. I hoped a warning would be enough. Reporting it when I couldn't be sure about the black eye, or whether the yanking was just a one-time impulsive thing, could have led to unforeseen consequences, possibly tragic consequences, especially for the boy himself. Foster care is often a terrible alternative."

"But the law doesn't give you the right to make that kind of judgment, does it?"

Ginny hesitated. Tarwater filled the gap. "And assuming your suspicions were justified, the result of your decision not to report was to leave that little boy in a home where he was being abused, correct?"

"My hope was that the warning would stop it."

"Or was it just a lie that you concocted later to counter the parents' complaint that *you* were the one abusing their son?"

"No."

"Or could it be that you didn't report it because you were afraid that an investigation would have"—her voice laden with sarcasm—"'*tragic consequences*,' to use your words, for you and Marvin Smith, including the consequence of uncovering the abuse you and Marvin Smith had been inflicting on children for years?"

Rockwell and Hartley stood together and objected.

"Argumentative and no foundation," Hartley said.

"And calls for speculation," Rockwell said.

"Sustained."

Rockwell said, "Will you please instruct the jury that the question was improper and should be ignored?"

"The jury is instructed to disregard."

"And that the question was improper?"

Snyder said nothing.

Tarwater said, "No further questions."

"It's prosecutorial misconduct," Hartley said loud enough for the jury to hear. "I move for a mistrial."

"Denied."

CHAPTER ⇌ 72

As O'KEEFE TURNED recent events over in his mind, his fear and anger grew apace, and voices of danger and warning in his head grew louder and louder until they were screaming at him.

He had finally convinced Annie that one of them needed to drive Kelly to school in the morning. Since he was always tied up in court until late afternoon, someone—one of his security people, but if she would not countenance that, then Annie herself—should be picking Kelly up after school. Kelly should never be alone—anytime, anywhere. "And you should never be alone yourself, and even the two of you together shouldn't."

"I won't live that way. If you make too much of this, you'll terrify the school people, and they'll ask her to leave."

You might die this way, he thought. *If this woman gets something embedded in her head, you can't dynamite it out.*

"I'm through fucking around with you," he said. "If I have to go to court, I will."

She hung up on him. He wondered why he was trying so hard to reunite with this woman. Was he wishing for a lifetime of this?

He felt he had already delayed too long. He could just grab Kelly, just show up at school to pick her up and keep her until Annie capitulated. Kelly might not react so well to that, not the cops either. He guessed he had a decent chance to obtain an emergency court order for temporary custody. He didn't want to involve either Hartley or Harrigan. He called one of the city's prominent family lawyers, who was in court, but his secretary said she would get a message to him to return the call. "He'll be very interested in this," she said …

But within a couple of hours, Annie called back to grudgingly relent. Not for herself, no security guard for her, but for Kelly. "Let's do *this*," she said. "I'll pick her up whenever I can, and if for some reason I can't, you do it or send one of your goons. But they've got to be discreet. I think maybe I'll have her stay in the classroom after school for a bit so your guy won't be sitting in the pick-up line with the moms in their minivans."

"Since when do you care so much about what people think?"

"I don't, but Kelly doesn't need any more spotlights on her."

He also convinced her, this with no resistance at all, to have Karma with them whenever possible, especially at night. Either Dagmar or O'Keefe himself would shuttle the dog back and forth as necessary. "And don't misinterpret this, but just say the word and I'll move there temporarily and sleep on the porch or the basement or the back yard."

"No, it's all too crazy. Now isn't the time." (Later, he devoted much pondering to that last sentence of hers.)

"Well, you can't stop me from having a guard sitting in a car outside your house. That's non-negotiable."

"The neighbors'll go crazy with all this. They'll be carrying signs in front of our house. We'll be pariahs … like you."

"Tough shit. Remember, this one is your and Kelly's project, not mine. I'm just your humble servant here. But I'm not gonna let her get hurt, or even you, just because you insist on being a goofy bitch."

She hung up on him again, but a little later called back—to apologize for being stubborn about the protection. The age of miracles was still at hand. "Sorry" was something she offered rarely and only under the most severe duress. *Annie Hawthorn O'Keefe: Often wrong but never in doubt.*

"I'm sorry for calling you that," he said. "You really aren't goofy."

Showing she got the joke, she laughed. "Just a bitch, huh?"

"You said it."

"This thing's made me crazy," she said. "This town's become a goddamn nuthouse."

Nuthouse or not, the town definitely had some nuts in it, and one or more of them was doing ugly, dangerous things. It seemed he had spent the last several years trying to keep his only child from harm, but it seemed to find her anyway, no matter what, and even when he wasn't the cause of it.

He called Ross.

"Anything to report?"

Ross didn't answer for such a long period of time that O'Keefe wondered if the call had been disconnected somehow. "Are you there?"

"Yes, I'm here. We've made some progress."

"Yes? Meet? Usual place?"

"No. I've thought about it, and given the situation, including your track record, etcetera, I don't think I should be reporting to you on this."

"But you said—"

"That was before I gave it the thought it deserves. And I shouldn't have to tell you why the police shouldn't be sharing information with a civilian on a pending investigation ... especially a civilian with a vital interest in the matter ... even more especially, a civilian who's a private investigator for the defense in a criminal case that the department actually initiated—"

"Okay! Enough!"

"...And especially a civilian who has a history of occasionally taking the law into his own hands."

"I understand completely. Really."

"I hope so."

He did understand, and it would be very stupid to piss Ross off when Ross was in the right. But these cops never seemed to leave him an alternative. He knew what to do. Whether Ross intended to or not, he had told O'Keefe exactly what he wanted to know.

As on so many other nights, he was still in his back office, trying to catch up, as darkness began to fall. It was getting harder and harder to juggle all the balls—actually more like crystal goblets—without dropping one or more. There was trying to maintain his business and keep the pipeline somewhat full through his sales and marketing efforts, which could not be delegated. There was operating the business on a daily basis. There was devoting actual face time to his family. There was serving as the organizer, leader, and public face of the Save Our Children! movement locally and beyond. And there was his investigative work to try to help the police with not only this case but other cases in the city that more than *screamed out* to be investigated.

A man was walking through the office door. *I'm sure I locked the front door.* Something at the man's side. A dog.

"What…what are you doing here?"

"We need to have a talk."

As O'Keefe sat down in the chair in front of Ralph's desk, Ralph focused not on the man but the dog whose eyes had locked onto Ralph.

Ralph started to stand up.

"Don't," O'Keefe said. "One word from me and this dog will rip your face off."

As he sat back down, Ralph's mind leaped to his van where he kept the tape recorder and wished he had it here with him now, wished he had also obtained one for his office as well. You could never be ready enough.

Easing back down, Ralph said, "How'd you get in here?"

"The door was unlocked."

He's lying. I know I locked it. Or did I tell Jane to do it before she left?

The dog didn't move. Kept staring. Didn't blink. Did dogs have eyelashes?

"I let it alone," O'Keefe said, "when I caught you following me around, which you're no good at by the way. Because it was a way for me to keep my eye on you. But you've gone way over the line. You're out of control, asshole … a danger to people better than you."

O'Keefe slid a paper across the desk. "I'm guessing you didn't keep a copy of this for yourself,"

Ralph studied it, trying not to show that he knew exactly what it was.

"I know you wrote that. I know you went to Raylee's house and deposited it in her mailbox. I can prove it. You're in deep shit, Mr. Merkel."

"Get out," Ralph said, still eyeing the dog and wondering if he should, if he could, grab the pistol in his desk drawer.

His eyes must have involuntarily glanced there.

"Don't do that. You'll regret it more than I will."

A standoff silence for several seconds, until O'Keefe said, "I'm also pretty sure you had something to do with Scott Hartley's house."

"You broke in here. That's a crime."

"The door was unlocked. My word against yours."

"I'm an upstanding citizen, not a former drug dealer. A Satanist."

O'Keefe managed to resist the urge to dive over the desk and beat Ralph senseless. "You won't be upstanding when I show them what you've done. You, Ralphie, are one handwriting analysis away from a jail cell."

He had deliberately not used cursive but printed in block letters. Could they somehow still identify it as his? Maybe he had left fingerprints on something—the letter, the envelope, the mailbox. Even if his wife Lori lied to them or refused to talk, his employee Jane knew he had been out of town that day. What other traces might he have left? He had paid cash for gasoline.

O'Keefe was talking again. "I have a simple … I won't call it an offer, or a proposal, or a proposition. It's more of a promise, a threat, an instruction, a directive, an ultimatum—from one vigilante to another. I'm gonna leave you alone, and you're gonna leave me and mine alone. And 'mine' include not just my family and my employees and my dog but every person on the defense side of the case. Witnesses, lawyers, paralegals, all of them. If you don't comply, I might not kill you. But I might. Think what I could've done to you just now, think what Karma here could've done to you, instead of sitting gently down here to peacefully discuss this situation. But whatever it is that I and my best friend here do, it *will* ruin your life. If you're not dead, you'll wish you were dead every remaining day your miserable self can keep from blowing your idiot fucking brains out of your concrete skull."

O'Keefe stood up abruptly. Ralph thought he was about to be attacked and started for the pistol in the drawer, but O'Keefe had turned and was walking out, the dog by his side. He could shoot the bastard now and claim self-defense. But he would be shooting him in the back … But could he get both the dog and O'Keefe before one of them could get him? . . .

And then they were both gone.

Raylee said hello on the first ring again. Seemed to be her thing.

"How's your bodyguard doing?"

"Still very professional."

"And still very handsome, I'm sure."

"Shithead."

"I've called for two reasons. I want to go over Ginny's testimony with you."

"Good."

After he described Ginny's testimony in as much detail as his notes and memory would allow, she said, "Well, seems like some good and some bad."

"More good than bad."

"As my dear old grandmother used to say, you wouldn't shit me, would ya?"

"Never. Isn't that obvious by now?"

"Checking and testing."

"One more thing. I hesitate to tell you this at all, but I want you to have all the facts, however murky they are."

"'Murky' is my life now."

"There's a decent chance that progress has been made in solving the situation that has caused you so much recent concern for your safety."

"Really? Somebody's not on the way here with a firebomb?"

"Really. Substantial progress."

"That's good to know. But I still can't promise. Who knows what else might happen? Like I've said all along, I'll let you know the day before."

CHAPTER ❧ 73

Hartley wanted Rockwell to put Marvin Smith on the stand right after Ginny.

Lou looked glum. "He hasn't decided yet whether he's willing to testify."

"What? Goddamn it, Lou. It's a little late to be up in the air on that."

"Believe me, I've badgered and besieged him about it. But it's a big decision. He wanted to watch Ginny first. That unsettled him, I'll tell you. Now he wants to decide after Raylee."

"You need to tell him that now that Ginny has testified, it will look bad for all of us if he doesn't. That by itself could convict both of them."

"I'll try. Up to a point. But I won't twist his arm. It's his call, not mine."

"Could he be hiding something in his background? Jesus, I wonder if the prosecution has some bad info on him that we don't."

"I've checked him out every way I know how," Lou said. "I'll ask him again."

In the meantime, Hartley said, they'd put up a strong bridge witness between Ginny and Raylee.

That is if Raylee even showed up.

He suggested to Rockwell that he handle the next witness to give both Snyder and the jury a respite from "Hartley-all-the time," as the two lawyers had previously discussed. But Rockwell demurred, provoking Hartley to say, "What's the deal, Lou? Hedging your bets or what?"

Rockwell shrugged. "You're in better position to do this one."

Hartley gave him a suspicious look. Rockwell turned and moved away.

The bridge was Principal Marie Dreyer, a woman who'd dreamt of following in the footsteps of her heroine, Maria Montessori, and making pre-kindergarten more than a babysitting service. She'd drafted Operation Go!'s curriculum accordingly—a professional and age-appropriate educational program. No one was more enraged by the scandal than her. It had resulted in the closure of the school and the obliteration of her life's work.

The prosecutors and phony "child savers" from Child Protective and the Children's Clinic were, as far as she was concerned, all driven by a corrupt ambition intent on destroying the lives of the defendants—dedicated members of a staff she'd handpicked—and anyone else in the path of their fanatical juggernaut. And she had no sympathy for the parents who'd sprinted into the arms of the Save Our Children! lynch mob. While a few may have believed the insane fantasies cooked up, most were just greedy hogs, noses in the malpractice damages trough. And it wasn't the school or its employees who caused damage; it was the authorities and parents who'd embarked on this insane crusade.

So great was Marie's ire that during preparation Hartley had frequently needed to ask her to tone down the diatribe. Now she was in the witness box. He took a breath and asked his first question, his fingers mentally crossed.

"Can you start by telling us about Virginia Montrose and Marvin Smith's qualities as employees?"

She looked out to the gallery, directly addressing the Save Our Children! parents. Of the highest quality, she said. Ms. Montrose had not one single blemish on her employment record. Mr. Smith

328 AN AMERICAN TRAGEDY

was occasionally late, but Marie had always let that go, because he had a large family, lived a long way from work, and was stuck with an old and undependable vehicle that sometimes left him hustling to catch a bus in the morning. "And he always made up for any tardiness by staying longer that same day."

"Were there ever any complaints from any parent, child, or other employee about Mr. Smith's conduct?"

"Not one."

"How about Ms. Montrose?"

"Not one complaint in the all the years she worked at the school. On the other hand, there've been innumerable written and oral statements highly praising her work."

Marie went on to describe in grim detail the "damnable tragedy" that had spiraled from one parent's false accusations into a "shameful witch hunt" involving an intense and hysterically publicized investigation, parents withdrawing their children from the school in droves, and a deluge of claims for damages, which led to cancellation of the school's insurance, a wrongful cancellation in her opinion, but she could neither reverse the cancellation nor replace the policy. All that had culminated in the school's closure and the loss of eleven jobs.

It had gone well, Hartley thought. Now they had to get through cross.

Dolinar stood and sauntered toward the witness stand. "And one of those jobs lost was your own, correct?"

"Yes, but that was the least of it. It's the others I care most about. Some of them are still out of work."

"Your Honor, I object to the answer," Dolinar said. "It was nonresponsive. All I asked was whether she too had lost her job."

"Which," Hartley said, "was a phony if not bad-faith question. He knows good and well that Ms. Dreyer lost her job. We all know. And surely the jury does. What's irritating him is that he didn't get away with the stunt he was trying to pull."

Snyder chuckled. "Alright, gentlemen. You're both right. It was nonresponsive, Mr. Dolinar, as you say. But yours, Mr. Dolinar, was a 'baiting' sort of argumentative question, as Mr. Hartley said. So let's call it a dogfall and move on."

"Were you aware," Dolinar continued, "that Ms. Montrose was making money on the side by providing babysitting services to some of the parents?"

"Not much money. And on the side of what? There was no side."

"Ms. Dreyer, I know you understand my question."

"There were no secrets at our school," Marie said. "No secrets at all, Mr. Dolinar."

"So you think that was an appropriate thing for you as principal to permit?"

"I didn't consider it my place to interfere. To the extent I thought about it at all, I believed it might draw the parents and children's teacher closer, and that could only be a good thing."

"Did you consider the children's safety?"

"I left that to the parents. They made the arrangements, not me."

"Did you, Ms. Dreyer, ever institute a program for your staff, the children, or anyone else that dealt with the issue of child molestation, including what types of touching, etcetera, were appropriate with children?"

"I'm not aware that any such program exists, and even if it does, I don't believe that our well-educated, well-trained, honest, and good-hearted staff would need such a program. Mr. Dolinar, surely, you're aware that this witch hunt came out of nowhere, to the shocked disbelief of all of us in the childhood-education and day-care worlds."

"Your Honor, that's the second witch-hunt comment. Nonresponsive and argumentative."

"The jury will disregard the witch-hunt comment," Snyder said. "It was highly improper. Ms. Dreyer, you're warned not to repeat it or anything similar again."

The witness didn't seem to give a care what Judge Snyder's opinion might be.

Dolinar resumed. "You're very angry about what happened to your beloved school, aren't you, Ms. Dreyer?"

"I am."

"And you blame not the defendants but the authorities—people like me, and Ms. Tarwater, and the Child Services people, and the Children's Clinic?"

Marie Dreyer paused, seeming to be considering her answer, then took the plunge. "The only thing you people are serving are your own ambitions."

Dolinar started to object, but Snyder's look said, "Don't bother, you asked for that one."

"And you believe even the parents are to blame?"

"Some of them."

"And, Ms. Dreyer, I want you to assume that some of the children have come to this witness stand before you and have testified that the defendants sexually molested them in numerous ways. You don't believe *any* of that?"

"I don't believe any of it."

"So they're lying?"

"If lying means telling falsehoods, yes, they're lying. Children do lie, you know. Do you have children, Mr. Dolinar?"

"I'm the one who asks the questions here, Ms. Dryer. And you believe that every single one of these falsehoods, as you call them, has been entirely concocted and forced into their heads by the police and the Child Services and Children's Clinic people?"

"Yes."

"You weren't present at the scene of any of the incidents of molestation described in the indictment, were you?"

"There were no incidents for me to be present at. That indictment is a work of fiction. Trashy pulp fiction."

"So you cannot say they didn't happen, can you?"

"I sure can."

"But you weren't there, right?"

"Who was the writer that said 'there's no there there,' Mr. Dolinar? There was no there to be there at."

Dolinar hesitated, as if he would object to the answer and persuade Snyder to impose a tongue lashing or worse on this pugnacious lady. But he just said, "No further questions."

It wasn't hard for Hartley to conclude that no redirect was necessary.

FIVE INCHES OF RAIN BREAK THE DROUGHT. FLASH FLOODS FOLLOW. MOTORISTS STRANDED ALL OVER TOWN.

CHAPTER ⚓ 74

"**P**ETE, YOU'VE GOT to talk to Paschal again."

O'Keefe groaned. "I thought only kings had fools."

"What's that mean?"

"It's a fool's errand you're sending me on."

"Gotta try. It's gettin' past the point of no return. Might already be past it."

"I hate that fucking jail. It always makes me think of that poet's line: 'Shades of the prison-house begin to close upon the growing boy.'"

"What's that supposed to mean?"

"It's too profound for the likes of you, Mr. Hartley."

"Get the fuck out. Pull out all the stops."

When they brought Paschal to the visiting area, O'Keefe noticed that, unlike most prisoners, Paschal looked healthier, much healthier, than when he went in.

"Sorry to tell you, but you keep looking better every time I see you," O'Keefe said.

"Being a former jailbird, I know how to make the best of this."

"It ain't the grub, Paschal. No booze, right? Can't get it in here."

"Oh yes, I can. Drugs too. I've just put my substance abuse on pause. To see what it's like. And I gotta tell you"—he leaned forward and smirked—"I'm not sure I like it."

"You will eventually."

"Doubtful. Meanwhile, I can guess why you're here."

Time to pull out all those stops. "The clock's ticking. Almost too late. You can save some innocent lives."

"Don't make it more dramatic than it is."

"And you shouldn't minimize it. You're sacrificing real flesh-and-blood people. For what? A principle? A promise?"

"A promise that got you the tape in the first place. A promise that a real flesh-and-blood person with nothing personal to gain risked a lot to rely on. Just like I told you before, I think we have all the source has to give. I know it."

"Godlike, eh? You have that much trust in your own judgment? It's been so good to you in the past?"

"It's all I have. Plus, fuck you."

"There was a certain Roman official once upon a time who thought he could wash his hands like that. History hasn't treated him so well."

"Fuck you again."

"Why not let it out in the open? Let the system operate on it, make sure there's really nothing else."

"You want me to trust the system that put me here today, and my roommates, Virginia Montrose and Marvin Smith, where they are today? You want me to betray the source so your boss discovers there's really nothing else, or gets nowhere with it, or the system finds another way to negate it, so your client gets torched anyway? Can you guarantee me that my source won't be exposed and ruined, maybe even end up in jail on some bullshit theory … for nothing? Does this case have to crush every single person that gets in its way? I'll be damned to hell with the Satanists before I feed anyone else to this monster, especially someone who's tried to do some good."

Nothing. That's what O'Keefe had to say. He could make no such guarantee. And odds were strong that Paschal was right about the likely outcome.

O'Keefe stood up. "Can I get anything for you? Food? Books?"

"Forgiveness would be plenty."

CHAPTER ❧ 75

DESPITE ALL THE drama over it, it wasn't clear that they should put Raylee Reynolds on the stand.

Hartley was wrestling with himself, Hamlet-like, "to or not to." Both O'Keefe and Maura Davis assured him that Raylee appeared to be more than tough enough to keep from wilting under cross examination.

"But there's that 'L word' issue still hanging around," Hartley said.

"I think she can handle it," O'Keefe said. "Maura and I asked her straight up, and she said 'no.'"

"All that means is she might be willing to lie about it. And they've already put it in the jury's minds. They'll be at the innuendo again even if they can't take the direct route. If we don't put her on, they won't be able to insinuate that yet one more time. And she's got that lean and mean look if you know what I mean."

"You know, Scott," Maura said, "the jurors may not be quite as redneck as the prosecutor thinks they are and that you're afraid they are."

O'Keefe wondered if Scott hoped Raylee would refuse to come and thus spare him the anxiety of making a decision that could blow up in his face. But she called early the morning before and said she would be there.

On the following morning, Hartley asked for a chambers conference, at which he said, "I assume we won't see a repeat of what we experienced on Virginia's cross examination."

"This is insulting," Tarwater said.

"It's certainly intended to be," Hartley said.

Snyder said, "I'm sure Ms. Tarwater understood my prior ruling. You didn't need to do this, Mr. Hartley."

"I think it *was* necessary. You saw how they poisoned the well with their questions, making sure an objection would be too late to keep the harm from being done."

Hartley also announced his intention to introduce the threat letter that Raylee had received. The prosecution objected and Snyder said he wouldn't allow it. Reporting to his team at the defense table, Hartley said, "I knew Snyder wouldn't allow it, but one more thing to appeal. Who knows what'll stick in the end?

You're a smart one, and clean up pretty good yourself, O'Keefe thought as he turned with the others to watch her move through the gallery, into the well of the court, and stand ready to take the oath, wearing more than a chip on her shoulder: a snug blue dress that was not daring but short enough to advertise that her legs were thin, tan— and shaved. She had even applied a light touch of makeup and fluffed her hair somehow to make her boyish bob bounce jauntily as she walked.

Her direct testimony was simple. She had known Virginia since college, and her friend had not once expressed any sympathy with Satanism or any unorthodox religious opinion whatsoever. Not being the "motherly type" herself, Raylee didn't hang around during the babysitting sessions, staying late at work, as she often did anyway, or on the weekend attending a movie and returning after the kids had been put to bed. During those nights, or any other times she was in the house, she had never witnessed anything strange at all, especially anything remotely like the "ceremonies" alleged in the indictment.

She had left town, yes, but mainly because her parents needed her. They had needed her for quite a while, but she had been happy in her job and kept putting off facing the defeat and surrender that moving to another city and in with her parents would mean. But when it seemed like the whole town was going crazy, and she was locked out of her house for weeks because it was supposedly a crime scene, and the "Save Our Children!" people were constantly driving by the house, her neighbors avoiding her, her boss and co-workers directing suspicious glances her way, and they had put her roommate in jail without bail and apparently intended to keep her there until the trial was over—she decided she might as well do now what she'd needed to do for a long time—go take care of her parents.

"It's been said in this case that Virginia at least once slit the throat of a baby bunny."

"Impossible."

"Why do you say that?"

"She wouldn't even step on a spider. She'd gather it up alive in a dustpan and toss it out the back door."

Tarwater took the same tack on cross as Dolinar had with Marie Dreyer. She finally got Raylee to admit, after much resistance, that the witness could not say definitively, "with your own eyes and ears," that any of the things in the indictment had *not* happened because she was not present on the scene when the alleged abuses occurred. Tarwater also re-emphasized Mr. Smith's many visits to their house, especially his presence there on many evenings and at times when Raylee was not at home. Tarwater also worked the lesbian insinuation angle—the girls' college, no boyfriends, few dates. But Raylee did better than Ginny on that. "We had men over there often, for dinner or drinks or whatever."

"But not for romance, right?"

Hartley started to object, but Raylee had a certain look on her face that caused him to hold back.

"What do you mean by romance, Ms. Tarwater?" she said, daring the prosecutor to probe further on that subject.

When Tarwater failed to respond, Raylee said, "A little, not much. We were just a couple of old maids trying to make our way in the world, Ms. Tarwater. How about you?"

Tarwater looked toward the judge, but he wasn't rushing to help her out on this by scolding the witness. In fact, it looked like he was trying to conceal amusement. Dolinar also was avoiding her gaze. She looked at the witness, seemingly searching for an appropriate retort, but not finding it, sat down.

Again quite satisfied with precisely where things stood at the end of the cross, Hartley said, "No questions. Thank you, Ms. Reynolds."

As she passed the defense table on her way out, she glanced at Ginny, warily and barely detectibly, but intensely and with the slightest nod, as if hoping to will something out of herself and into her friend. The whisper of a smile passed over Ginny's face and quickly disappeared. O'Keefe thought he and perhaps Maura might have been the only ones in the courtroom to detect that exchange. It overwhelmed him with sadness.

CHAPTER ∻ 76

IT WAS 3 P.M.

Raylee was the last witness scheduled for the day, so the court adjourned early.

Hartley drew Rockwell aside. "This is it, Lou. Your man needs to testify next."

"He's not ready."

"Unacceptable. Can we meet? Can I talk to him ... right now?"

They asked the guards to hold back Smith until they could arrange a meeting there in the courthouse, which was soon set up, and Hartley, Rockwell, O'Keefe, and Smith gathered in a witness waiting room while two guards stood outside the door.

O'Keefe tried to make eye contact with Smith, but Smith avoided his gaze. Smith had always been thin, but he had lost even more weight in prison. His bones were starting to show where they weren't supposed to. And O'Keefe could swear that the gray—even white—in his hair had advanced considerably since the first time he had seen him. Marvin Smith was aging in front of their eyes. He was also looking angrier and more desperate by the day as the stories he had to listen to about him took their toll ...

"Marvin," Rockwell said, "we've discussed at length and a number of times whether you should testify. As you know, even though I have some concerns about it, I've recommended that you take the stand. You're reluctant. Scott believes not only that you should testify but that you should testify right now ... that it would be a great mistake to wait any longer. Because we've got some strong witnesses coming up, and we want to close as strongly as we can."

Smith pressed back into his chair.

Hartley, gentle in manner and voice, said, "Marvin, I understand you're afraid. Do you mind telling us what you're afraid of?"

"Look what they did to Ginny. And she's a lot more well-spoken than I am."

Hartley, distressed, "You really think it was bad? I sure didn't think so. Lou?"

"I thought it was way more positive than negative."

Smith rubbed his cheeks up and down like his skin was burning. "Nah, they made her look like a lesbian who either didn't care about reportin' child abuse or is just lyin' about it. Plus they made her look way too comfy with a black man. But that ain't really it. It was that little Misty. Even I had to fight back tears, and I *know* it didn't happen."

"Don't you think we showed how they brainwashed her to say that?"

"Not enough. Like they say, 'believe the children.'"

"Sorry to ask this, but I have to: Is there something in your past that you think they might know about that we don't? Something that might hurt you? I don't think those juvenile troubles of yours are gonna hurt at all. That was so many years ago."

"The only thing in my past that's hurting me is I was born black. I'm just a convenient nigger for those asshole prosecutors. A black man supposedly fuckin' a white woman and little white kids too."

"But we managed to get a black juror on."

"What you got on there is one nice, older Baptist, 'Negro lady,' as the judge called her." If a bunch of white people on that jury pressure her, can she resist, especially if she falls for that 'believe the children' stuff and especially if she's a bit suspicious and offended about that 'diddlin' with a white woman' stuff? Then maybe I just become a 'nigger' to *her* too."

"You're thinking the very worst. That lady is a great opportunity to hang the jury."

"And you're thinking the very best. That nice lady will have to stand up to eleven white people. Too much to ask."

"You're proving right here in this room that you can handle yourself in that witness box. And you've got two lawyers telling you that you'll be worse off if you *don't* get up there."

Rockwell leaned forward, put his hand on Marvin's arm. "You know we're right, don't you? You know there's not really a choice."

Smith shook off Rockwell's hand. "All that means is I'm screwed either way. I'm done talkin.' Tell 'em to take me back."

"Will you at least think about it?" Hartley said.

"What else have I got to think about?"

"We need an answer soon. Actually, we need it right now."

"Well, you ain't getting it now. And no promises for the future."

After they led Smith away, Hartley said, "I'll get the other witnesses ready, but we've got a weekend here. I want you to ask him again on Saturday and again on Sunday. If he changes his mind, we'll get together and get to the jail and prep him. If he keeps saying 'no,' I want to ask him again on Monday morning."

"I'll do all those things, but I'm not gonna twist his arm."

"That would be a stupid choice, Lou. You need to *break* his arm if necessary."

O'Keefe and Hartley walked out together. As they made their way down the corridor, Rhonda Tarwater entered from a side hallway carrying an unwieldy looking stack of papers in one arm and pulling a wheeled catalog-style brief case with the other. O'Keefe offered to carry one or the other for her.

"No, thanks," she said with a dismissive air and kept looking straight ahead. As the threesome walked along a few steps in sync, she turned her head slightly and said, "Say … thanks for putting the bull dyke on today. We'll do our best to return the favor sometime."

Hartley put on the brakes and O'Keefe did the same, as she walked on.

"Hey, Pete," Hartley said, "I think I see a fox and some grapes. Sour ones. Raylee looked great, didn't she? Talked great too."

Tarwater emitted a contemptuous snort of a laugh. "Lipstick on a pig," she said and walked on.

As they watched her go, Hartley said in a low voice, "We've wandered with Alice into Wonderland. Into the realm of the Queen of Hearts herself. Abandon all hope, ye who enter there."

It was past rush hour as they walked toward their cars in the twilight along the barren street of the emptied-out business district, crowded during the day, a ghost town at night.

"Assuming Marvin doesn't change his mind," Hartley said, "we'll be going with Annie and Kelly and then our other parents, then the medical, then the shrink. Then we're done, unless we can get Marvin to change his mind."

O'Keefe said, "Ol' quiet Marvin's been sitting there burning and seething and smoldering inside. Must be hell to have to sit there and listen to that and can't defend yourself."

"I'll do everything I can to try to persuade him to testify, but I can't blame him even if I try to. Race in this country. It blights everything."

"You think they really targeted him that way?"

"No. But I think he's right. Once it came up the first time, the sharks smelled the blood in the water, and like he says, he became extremely 'convenient.'"

On Saturday, Sunday, and again on Monday, Marvin Smith continued to refuse to testify, and would give no indication whether he would ever do so. "And you lawyers quit bothering me about it. If I decide to testify, I'll let you know."

CHAPTER ❧ 77

Tuesday, October 25, 1988.

A day the defense team had been dreading. Scheduled for broadcast on NBC that evening: Geraldo Rivera's two-hour documentary special, *Devil Worship: Exposing Satan's Underground.*

"The one thing you can be sure of," Hartley said, "is that he'll sensationalize the whole damn thing. And there's nothing sensational about the *non-existence* of Satan worship, Satanic crime, and Satanic and other ritual sex abuse in day care centers. If the jurors even hear about it, never mind watch it, it can't do anything but hurt us. Maybe doom us."

"They've probably already seen plenty," Maura said. "He's not the only one. Oprah and Sally Jesse Raphael have been at it for years."

Judge Snyder had refused at the beginning of the case to sequester the jury or to issue a general gag order, although he had consistently throughout the proceedings warned jurors not to read, listen to, or watch anything about or related to the case in the media. Hartley had protested. "The media is out of control on this. The coverage is one-sided in favor of the prosecution and it's extremely prejudicial. I think they need to be sequestered. The trial won't take that long. I'm not comfortable they'll obey your order or warning."

"Mr. Hartley, I think you greatly misjudge the integrity of the typical juror. They're a lot more honest and trustworthy than some lawyers I know."

Hartley almost took umbrage, thinking Snyder was passively aggressively insulting him. But that wouldn't do his client any good, so he joked, "Given what people think of lawyers, Your Honor, I'm not sure that's a very high standard for a juror to live up to."

But that still got him nowhere, and he put his objection on the record.

The question now was, should they ask the judge to instruct the jury not to watch this particular show even if it didn't mention this case? That could act as a veritable *TV Guide* for the jurors who weren't already aware of it. Worse, it might signal the defense's fear of it and thus validate it. "But," Hartley said, "we can't afford to leave it alone. If we don't try for the instruction, we won't be able to argue about it on appeal. He'll probably deny the request, and that'll be just another chance for us upstairs."

Judge Snyder did indeed deny the request. As always and ad nauseam, Hartley made a record of his exception, prompting Snyder to say, "How many objections and exceptions have you made so far, Mr. Hartley? It might be a world record for number of objections per trial transcript page."

After the close of the courtroom proceedings on the day of the broadcast, an exhausted-looking Hartley assembled his group and repeated his invitation, which was phrased more like an instruction, to meet in his conference room that evening to watch the program. O'Keefe arrived only five minutes before the start. Hartley and Maura were there, but not Rob Nugent, Hartley's sole remaining associate after his senior associate Ben Lerner had quit.

"Rob couldn't make it," Hartley grumbled. "Family obligations," he added with obvious skepticism, then gestured for O'Keefe to take a seat.

The program opened with a teenager who'd been sentenced to death in Oklahoma for killing his mother. He'd now found Jesus but assured the viewers that the devil had made him do it, blaming heavy-metal music laden with Satanic overtones and often accompanied by Satanic costuming and ritualistic posturing.

Ozzy Osbourne, the British rock star, followed, offering a rambling, incoherent defense of the music that served more to evidence his own fatuousness than anything else. Next up was a Catholic priest assuring viewers that possession by the devil was not only possible but still happening.

That was followed by a high school student claiming that he and his classmates, one of whom was the class president, had been driven by heavy-metal music and devil worship to beat another student to death. Seventy blows. One of the assailants claimed that heavy metal music and devil worship drove them to it. O'Keefe recognized it as the case George had been reading to him about from the newspaper at their breakfast several months before. "That case happened just downstate," O'Keefe said. "But one of those kids denied that devil worship had anything to do with it. I notice he didn't get interviewed."

The program next focused on sexual abuse in preschools, including at the storied U.S. Military Academy at West Point. "Well, there you go," Hartley said. "If it could happen at West Point, it sure as hell could happen anywhere else including at our own little Operation Go!."

Then Geraldo himself appeared and solemnly warned parents that if they had not done so already, "get your kids away from the TV for our next report." Upon return from the commercial, the report began with an eight-year-old boy in Mississippi, whose father had forced anal sex on him, then to a five-year-old girl in southern California sexually victimized by a trusted minister, dissolving into the infamous McMartin case in Manhattan Beach, California, a suburb south of Los Angeles where children said they'd been subjected to a long and outlandish litany of abuses at their preschool. A spokesman for the McMartin parents' group castigated law enforcement for not doing enough to expose the vast Satanic conspiracy that had engulfed their children.

At commercial breaks, Geraldo's warnings continued that the children must be kept away from the screen. The program focused next on serial killers Charles Manson, David Berkowitz, Henry Lee Lucas, and Richard Ramirez, the Los Angeles "Night Stalker." Ramirez was the only one of that group who was a professed Satanist, but the program failed to disclose that most of those familiar with the case believed that was a pose Ramirez only adopted at his trial to enhance his reputation for evil, an aura that apparently had excited many women young and old to propose marriage, or just unsafe sex, with the killer.

Geraldo and his guests, including retired FBI agent Ted Gunderson, attested that sacrificial infanticide was frequently practiced in Satanic rituals. Asked why not one body of one child or any other physical evidence of child sacrifice or other ritual abuse had been found, Gunderson assured viewers that was because the slaughtered infants had been chopped up, encased in concrete, dumped into the ocean, even eaten. Women were interviewed who confessed to breeding babies for sacrifice. A therapist in Denver reported that therapists like him, who had stubbornly resisted the skeptics and held fast to their beliefs in Satanic and other ritual atrocities, had received death threats.

In Kansas City, Robert Berdella had tortured and murdered a number of young men in his home in a well populated neighborhood in the middle of town, then buried them in his backyard. Although signs and symbols of Satanism were close to non-existent, and there was no evidence that Berdella was anything other than a lone predator, Geraldo interviewed a local politician and a couple of city police officers who claimed law enforcement wasn't doing enough to pursue the Satanic conspiracy angle. Geraldo fulminated that "many in the community are outraged that the investigation did not go further," and vilified the local authorities for their indifference to the evil that had invaded their town. This included a combative interview with the local prosecutor, who held to his belief that there was no evidence whatsoever supporting the Satanic conspiracy claims.

As the show neared its end, Geraldo waffled slightly about whether there was any real proof of any of these things, but by the final frame, he had recovered his militancy, pronouncing definitively and not to be brooked, that "these children are not lying."

At the end, the stupefied group in the conference room sat silent for a few moments, until Maura said, "You think the jurors are watching?."

"They weren't forbidden to. Why wouldn't they? Everybody else in America probably is."

As O'Keefe and Maura walked to her car, she said, "I'm worried about Scott. The firm is falling apart. He's broke. He missed our paychecks again last week. He managed to catch them up this week, but people can't afford that. We all live paycheck to paycheck. Ben Lerner quit. Now Rob is looking. Note that he didn't show up tonight."

"How about you?" O'Keefe asked.

"I'll stick it out, at least through the verdict. I don't know where I could get this much experience at this level anywhere else, stressful and depressing and terrifying as it is."

Two days later, the *LA Times* would report that the show had been watched in 19.8 million homes, one-third of the number of people watching TV between 8 and 10 p.m. Eastern time that evening.

CHAPTER ❧ 78

TWO DAYS AFTER the Geraldo broadcast, Rockwell called Hartley.

"Sorry to call so late, but I wanted to let you know as soon as I did. We won't be in court tomorrow."

"What?"

"Marvin's taking a plea."

"WHAT?"

"You heard it right."

"What is it?"

"Ten years."

"And exactly what did he plead guilty to? I hope not conspiracy with Virginia."

"Not at all. It's an Alford plea."

"Small favors."

"I insisted," Rockwell said. "And Marvin insisted that under no circumstances would he testify against Virginia."

"Whoopie-doo and fuck you. How long you been negotiating this?"

"A while."

"That's why he wouldn't testify. Giving us that racism stuff. And you two dummyin' up on me in that meeting."

"No, Scott, that 'racism stuff' is deeply and honestly held. Which was exactly why he was willing to listen to Dolinar in the first place. He held out a long time, but that Geraldo show tipped him over."

"He watched that? How?"

"You know, they've got a TV in the prisoners' common room they can watch until nine o'clock. The other inmates, white and black both, almost lynched Marvin on the spot.

"Those jailer assholes. They probably showed it on purpose. Dolinar and Tarwater are probably behind this. And you didn't bother to say one word to your co-counsel."

"They conditioned the talks on keeping them secret. Marvin wanted to go along with that. And I never thought when we started that he'd agree to a plea. Plus, what good would it have done except put another big bag of shit on your shoulders, maybe for nothing?"

"Among many other things, it would've given me a chance to talk some sense into both of you. It's a stupid move. Idiotic, Lou, goddammit. You should never have let him do it. I knew you'd somehow fuck me in this case."

Rockwell was silent, well used to Hartley's belittling.

"Dolinar demanded secrecy?" Hartley said, as if thinking out loud. "Because of who? Me?"

"The parents."

"You bet. They'll skin him alive. Nothing less than life imprisonment will do for them ... We need to meet. Will Marvin talk to me?"

"Probably. But you won't talk him out of it. Remember last time. And that was pre-Geraldo."

"It's an insane move for Marvin, and it'll doom Virginia."

"You'll get a mistrial."

"With Judge Roy Bean? No chance. Especially if your deal's conditioned on no mistrial."

"It's not. Dolinar wanted that. I fought hard against it. Eventually, he gave in. I'm not as stupid as you make me out to be."

"Which means," Hartley said, "Dolinar must've thought there was no chance of a mistrial. Damn, could he have talked to Snyder?"

"You think they're that unethical?"

"In this case, who knows? Anything is possible. We're in the realm of the Queen of Hearts now."

DAN FLANIGAN ⇒ 349

Hartley called O'Keefe with the news.

"It's what they call an Alford plea. He maintains his innocence of the crime but admits they have enough proof to convict him."

"Are we fucked?"

"Unless I can turn Lou and Marvin around, hell yes, we are … So we won't need Annie and Kelly today. They'll deal with Marvin's plea before any more testimony. We have a meeting first thing at the jail with Marvin and Lou. You'll meet me there and give the ladies the news?"

"Marvin," Hartley said, "do you realize what those parents are gonna do when they find out about this? They're gonna dump shit all over Dolinar and the whole DA's office."

"Why would I care?"

"Two reasons. First, Dolinar would never have risked bringing that down on his head if he hadn't been scared shitless he was losing this case. So you fucked yourself. Surely you don't believe that if we get an acquittal, they'll let you off the hook on this plea? Lou, you haven't told him that, have you?'

"I told him just the opposite."

"Marvin?"

"I don't see it that way."

"Put some glasses on, Marvin. Your vision is seriously impaired … Second, they may just raise enough hell that Snyder won't approve the plea. Then you've admitted your guilt publicly for nothing."

"It's an Alford plea."

"Nobody believes that's anything but an admission of guilt."

"I like my odds."

"What about your wife and kids? What are they gonna do when you're rotting in prison?"

"I'll only be rotting for ten years—probably less, with good behavior. If I get convicted, they'll give us the max on every count. It'll be life."

Rockwell nodded. "Scott, you know that's true."

"Wife and I," Marvin said, "have talked it all the way through. She's a hard-workin' woman. The kids are good kids and know I'm innocent. The older ones'll work to help her out. And her relatives are good people. They'll help too."

Hartley played his last card. He knew it was feeble but had to try everything.

"How about those civil rights people that stuck up for you? Aren't you stabbing them in the back?"

"They ain't facin' life in prison. And they know. They know how it is."

"That prison sentence will hang over your head for the rest of your life."

Marvin laughed. "You really think where I come from they give a fuck about that?"

"So you and yours'll be stuck in the ghetto forever."

"I guess it didn't do me much good to be hangin' around white folks, did it? It's always been the same and it'll always be the same. Our function in this world is to take shit … and take shit … and take some more shit … That's the deal, honey."

"And Virginia? You don't care about her?"

"Fuck you, Shyster. You were just tellin' me how you were gonna get her off while I rot in jail. All you want me in in this case for is so that 'Negro lady' might hang the jury … And if Ginny gets off and I rot, good for her. She deserves it. She's the sweetest of hearts."

He turned to Lou. "This meeting is done. Get me out of here."

CHAPTER ❧ 79

ALL HALLOWS EVE.

Dolinar and Rockwell filed separate motions for approval of the Alford plea. Hartley filed an objection to the plea and a motion for a mistrial. The parents prevailed on Perry Slotkin to file an objection to the plea with a request to be allowed to speak on behalf of the victims at the hearing (though Slotkin was not at all sure it was a wise move, since a finding of guilt was exactly what he needed for the civil lawsuits he would soon be filing). Judge Snyder said that the only thing that made sense at this turn of events was to suspend further testimony in order to hear the motions. The jury was told to stay home for the day.

On the courthouse steps that morning, Ralph Merkel made a statement on behalf of the Save Our Children! group, whose members attended in force with signs with slogans like:

DOLINAR = JUDAS ISCARIOT

OUR CHILDREN MOLESTED AGAIN
BY THE PROSECUTOR'S OFFICE

"In the strongest possible terms," Merkel said, "we object, violently object, to this disgraceful surrender by the prosecution. This man who violated our little children should at a minimum be put away for the rest of his life. Even the death penalty would be too good for him. But he gets only ten years? That's a travesty. And the idiots will probably let him out of jail in a week or two 'for good behavior.' He doesn't even have to admit his guilt. This is betrayal, plain and simple. At least Judas got thirty pieces of silver. These idiots got nothing at all. Satan is smiling today."

At the hearing, Dolinar and Rockwell had little to say beyond summarizing their respective motions.

Slotkin took the podium and asked to make a statement on behalf of the parents.

"Which parents?" Hartley demanded. "Not all parents by any means. We'll be hearing soon from parents who aren't part of Mr. Slotkin's civil lawsuit group, who consider it a shameless money grab and are incredulous that this beloved teacher has been victimized in this way."

"Mr. Hartley," Snyder said, "let's keep the hyperbole and grandstanding and eloquence-waxing to a minimum today, please. I don't know what audience you're playing to, but it doesn't help your cause with me. It hurts it. Please sit down and wait your turn.

"As for you, Mr. Slotkin, I want first to state, in the strongest possible terms"—pointedly quoting Merkel's speech on the courthouse steps and looking directly at Merkel when he did so—"that the group you're purporting to speak for does not have any *legal* standing in this matter, and from that point of view, I should not allow you to speak."

From the gallery, grumbling and protests, loud talking but not quite shouts. Snyder pounded his gavel. "And if there's one more voice raised in disruption of these proceedings, Mr. Slotkin will definitely not be allowed to talk."

Ten seconds later, the room had quieted, and he continued. "However, I'm very sensitive, as everyone knows, to the suffering of the children and their parents in this situation, and as victims"— then catching himself—"or potential victims … I think they should be allowed to express their point of view."

Slotkin's speech sounded to O'Keefe like a more elaborate, elongated, and diplomatic version of Ralph Merkel's statement on the courthouse steps.

On his turn, Hartley said, "With regard to the plea, I'm constrained to object to it … first, because it is simply false." Marvin Smith is guilty of nothing. The evidence is not even close to sufficient to convict him or anyone else. "The evidence here is a box with a fancy ribbon on it, *but there's nothing inside it.* Yet our hysterical media in this town will paint it as something else entirely. And it's absurd to think that the jury will not observe and know why Mr. Smith and his lawyer have suddenly disappeared from the courtroom. It's hard to see how it won't wound my innocent client, perhaps fatally."

As for the mistrial motion, he said that he felt especially sad to have to file it, "because I believe we were winning this case, hands down, at least we were until"—he looked at Lou Rockwell— "this incredibly ill-advised decision on the part of Mr. Smith. He's exactly like the drowning man who panics and takes his rescuer down with him."

Dolinar stood and Snyder acknowledged him. "Mr. Hartley is trying to manufacture a controversy where there is none. A guilty plea during a trial by a co-defendant is not an unusual event, here or anywhere else. It's handled very simply by giving the jury an instruction that a plea by one defendant absolutely cannot be considered as proof of any guilt whatsoever of the co-defendant. End of story, move on."

"You have got to be joking," Hartley responded. "An instruction isn't nearly enough, not within miles of enough. We need to start over and pick a jury that's untainted by any of this."

"But" Snyder intervened, "wouldn't the next jury surely already know, or will certainly learn one way or another, whether we like it or not, that Mr. Smith has pled guilty?"

"They might. Frankly, I don't know how we'll ever effectively remedy this, but we deserve at least a chance. Respectfully, Your Honor, we've ended up in this terrible situation because you denied my original motion for severance and separate trials."

"Well, you'll just have to take that up on appeal with all the other errors you've alleged I've made here with your world-record number of objections. Anything else, Mr. Hartley?"

"All I can say is, I object, I object, I object."

"You certainly do," Snyder said, which provoked a few cheers from the gallery, and once more Snyder waited for silence to re-establish itself. O'Keefe braced himself while the judge talked at length about victims of crime being entitled to "the greatest sympathy," but "our system is not a vehicle for the enforcement of private vengeance." There was an overriding public interest in the fair and proper functioning of our justice system. Our laws have given the prosecutor broad discretion in these matters, and "we must trust their judgment unless there is a very clear showing that they have made a mistake.

"The simple truth is that our adversary system can sometimes present extremely confusing situations that pose difficult problems for jurors. They can't, and don't, always get things right, for either side. The prosecution is often best advised to eliminate the risk of a guilty person walking free because the jury doesn't believe the prosecution has satisfied the very high standard of no-reasonable-doubt they must satisfy to convict.

"Given the parent group's strong feelings about this case, how would they feel if someone they believed guilty got off scot-free, a not guilty verdict, with no further ability to punish an atrociously guilty offender due to the constitutional prohibition on double jeopardy?"

Blah, blah, blah, O'Keefe thought, *get on to the inevitable.*

And there it finally arrived: Plea accepted. Mistrial denied.

"I'll expect the defense to be ready to go with their next witnesses first thing in the morning. Who will that be?"

"Annie O'Keefe, then Kelly O'Keefe."

O'Keefe thought he detected a significant decibel spike from the grumbling gallery when they heard the names, which, in turn, spiked his adrenaline and sparked his heart to a rapid beat. Hartley appeared not to notice. He was glaring at Rockwell's back as his former co-counsel hustled out of the courtroom.

"I told you he'd kill us," Hartley whispered.

O'Keefe thought he should offer at least a mild corrective. "Not sure that's fair, Scott."

Hartley's return glance seemed to say, "Have you gone nuts too?"

As the courtroom cleared, Dolinar separated himself from his group and beckoned Hartley to join him. "I'll bet you're wondering why I agreed to this stupid deal."

"I am. I guess any idea you had of running for office is done. They're probably waiting out there with tar and feathers."

"I'll deny I ever said this, but I did it because you guys stuck me with that black juror. It was too big a risk she'd hang the jury if the janitor was still in the case at the end. So I guess the devil made me do it. Happy Halloween. Trick or treat."

A SHAREHOLDER CLASS ACTION LAWSUIT IS FILED AGAINST LA PETITE ACADEMY, A DAY CARE CENTER OPERATOR WITH OVER 600 FACILITIES NATIONWIDE, WHOSE STOCK HAS SHARPLY DECLINED RECENTLY DUE IN LARGE PART TO ITS LOSS OF INSURANCE FOR SEXUAL ABUSE CLAIMS.

CHAPTER ◈ 80

SOME COURTHOUSE EMPLOYEES were whimsically costumed to look like Little Red Riding Hood or Bugs Bunny, some gruesomely as ghouls or ax murderers, reminding O'Keefe of the Halloween night two years earlier when he and Kelly had been attacked while trick-or-treating.

Outside the courthouse, the Save Our Children! crowd, Ralph Merkel front and center, were gathered in force along with the media brigade.

"Shit," Hartley said, "we should've gone out the back."

"I don't think they're after *us* today" Maura said, pointing to the signs. "It's Dolinar's and Tarwater's turn."

A ragged line of police separated them from the hostile crowd as they walked the gauntlet. Ralph Merkel looked re-energized, triumphant even, despite Snyder's approval of the plea agreement. He tried to stare O'Keefe down. Not a good sign. Had any fear he'd managed to instill in the guy already drained away?

"GUILTY," Merkel yelled, and the crowd picked up the taunt. "GUILTY—GUILTY—GUILTY—GUILTY…" and in lower registers words like "bastards," "motherfuckers," "bitch," "slut."

Once in the parking lot, Hartley said wearily, "Hard to remember in this business you've got a family. Gotta get home for trick-or-treating."

O'Keefe sat in his car, thinking about the look on Ralph Merkel's face and the crowd's slurs. That and Hartley's comment further stoked the memory of Halloween night two years ago. He couldn't believe he'd been so thoughtless, so careless then. And now Kelly was exposed again, and Annie too, and here he was dawdling in the face of a likely new danger on the same day two years later.

He called Annie who said, "Please don't tell me they've put us off again."

"No. What're you two planning to do tonight?"

"Nothing different. Your man will be outside, and Karma's here. In fact, I'm trying to figure out how to keep him from barking at all the little kids without *me* barking at *him* every five minutes."

He told her about Ralph Merkel—all of it about Ralph Merkel, including his conclusion that Merkel was the author of the threatening note to Raylee, his recent *tete a tete* with Merkel, and Merkel's militant re-emergence today. "And even if I'm wrong about him specifically, there's all kinds of angry people out there who're now on the edge of crazy over this plea deal."

She seemed different tonight, more appreciative of the danger. Maybe it was because of this day, the anniversary of the day two years before when she had almost lost her daughter. "Trick or treating needs to be before dark," he said, "and I should go with her—"

"Not sure how safe that is. You sure nobody's after *you* lately? You haven't pissed anybody off recently?"

"Nobody but Ralph Merkel. You should go with us. Nobody should be alone tonight. We'll take Karma. And don't answer the door."

"I always hated people that did that."

"Put a couple of big bags of candy out there and a sign that says 'Take One. Just One, Please.'"

"Your guy'll be out front. Isn't that enough?"

"That's too far away. He might not be able to react fast enough."

"Okay," she said, hesitantly, reluctantly.

"Promise?"

"Promise."

He called Maura. After six rings, the answering machine kicked on. "Hey," he said. "This is Johnny-Come-Lately. Call me back asap."

But when he hung up, it occurred to him that the ambiguity of that message might signal the wrong thing to her. He called back and added, "I'm worried about everyone's safety tonight, all of us."

He called Hartley, apologized for being "asleep at the wheel," and suggested Hartley take special precautions on this night of marauding monsters.

"I've taken care of that," Hartley said, "We're staying with Marsha's cousin tonight and trick or treating in that neighborhood, and only before it gets dark. I'm not very popular around this house right now … or anywhere else for that matter."

"Isn't that what happens to crusaders for Justice? They become martyrs for Justice."

"Remember the Alamo."

O'Keefe thought a moment about that but couldn't quite get it. "I don't know about the 'Justice' part, and they all died."

"But we remember 'em. Victory or Death!" And Hartley laughed. A bit manically, O'Keefe thought, sounding like one of those mad scientists in the movies, and O'Keefe wondered if Hartley might be precariously teetering on the edge of a mental cliff with only the Gulf of Psychosis below. He'd been in the trenches too long.

Annie called back. "Your daughter says, 'It seems like Dad wants to ruin all my Halloweens,' and she further states that it is absolutely too uncool for an almost-twelve-year-old to be trick or treating before dark, and especially with her parents. That's for little kids. She thinks you should take us out to dinner and a movie instead."

He said, hesitantly, barely audibly, "Are you willing?"

"I guess so. But no pizza. You live with that girl too long, you never want to eat, see, smell, or even think about pizza ever again."

The next caller said, "Hey, Johnny." Her buoyant self despite a difficult day. "I may be an airhead but not totally stupid. We're trick or treating only before dark and staying at my brother's house."

Raylee was his final call on this mission. Again, a message machine. His message: "I hope you're being careful tonight. Stay close to Dudley." But hanging up, he regretted that last misguided smart-ass non-witticism. Stupid. It would probably just make her feel more alone.

They had experienced nothing like this in years. No sundress tonight. Too cool for that on a full-out autumn night. But she had not neglected to look good. He'd been afraid it might be awkward, but it wasn't, maybe because they had plenty to talk about with their testimony coming up the next day. He avoided discussing anything about the substance of what they might say—Hartley had already prepared them thoroughly—but they were curious about the way the courtroom operated, the personalities of Snyder and the prosecutors, what the jurors were like, and whether the Save Our Children! people in the gallery were still so aggressive and intimidating.

The movie, a romantic comedy, ended at 9:30. Thankfully. As they left the theatre, he said, "I think I deserve a big positive checkmark on my side of the ledger having to sit through that." He pulled into their driveway, waved at his operative parked out front, walked them to the door, said hello to Karma, and checked the house thoroughly. "My guy will periodically check the back, but put Karma on the porch out back tonight," he told them. He thought about giving his operative a "tonight of all nights" speech but didn't want to suggest there was any night that was *not* a special night on this particular assignment.

Approaching his house, he remained on high alert. All the trick-or-treaters had disappeared, but who else might be waiting in the darkness to treat him to a trick? Karma was exactly where he needed to be tonight, with Annie and Kelly, but O'Keefe wished he had a clone of the guy with him now. His headlights fully illuminated the interior of the garage, and he was more careful than his usual "lost in thought" distractedness to observe that nothing was there but the things that should be there. He took the large flashlight he kept in the car and trained it all around the back of the house and yard. His footsteps crunching on the gravel driveway spooked him. He stopped and listened. There were some crickets still alive. They seemed louder than usual, especially at this time of year. The dog a couple of doors down barked. Probably at O'Keefe. Maybe a reassuring sign.

Starting at the back door, he walked around the house, checking all the windows, ending up at the front door. Haunted by memories of previous attacks, he flinched as he opened the outer screen door, then unlocked the inner door and pushed it open with his foot, shining the flashlight on the entryway. Checked the alarm system. On. Entered the code. Inspected every room, every corner, the basement too. Opening the closet door, then the dresser drawer, putting his weight on the bed as he sat down to undress—simple, everyday moment-to-moment actions for most people seemed for him ridiculously high risk.

And then an insight. An unwelcome one. He found it odd how it surprised him, how it had escaped him until this moment. Had he now joined the ranks of the accursed? Would this be his life always now, a life of constant exposure to life-threatening danger, and how could he in good conscience allow, let alone entice, Annie and Kelly to live it with him?

CHAPTER ❧ 81

A REGAL QUALITY.

The way she carried herself. A quality that for years he had sensed barely consciously and couldn't quite pinpoint until over and over again he'd observed other people's reactions to her. When she moved through an airport or other crowded public space, she would attract an inordinate number of stares, and more from the women than the men, as though they thought she must be a movie star or some other celebrity but couldn't recall the name. Today her shoulder-length auburn hair shone in the sunlight streaming through the courtroom windows. She wore a black dress with a stiff mandarin collar. A slit of an opening at the throat revealed a thin gold chain beaded with small onyx stones. A row of striking large white buttons lined the front of the dress.

O'Keefe's mind drifted to their first years together. She was more beautiful than he deserved for sure, long-haired, small-breasted but ample enough there and elsewhere, sassy with a dictatorial tendency, a cool customer but with a wild streak always trying to break through. Delighted, for reasons neither of them quite understood, to have discovered each other, they drank and danced and made love and immersed themselves in themselves.

And they fought. A lot. Too much for him, who had endured a childhood in a household of drunken disputation that too frequently surged to violence. And there he was, disgustingly re-creating what he had vowed would never happen to him. He blamed both of them, but her more of course. Somehow, he got lost in that. And in all the other things. The drugs and the drink and whatever in him caused him to get lost and want to stay lost in those things. He had wasted a lot of his life up to this point, and wasting her had been the worst of all the wasting.

"Please state your name."

"My name is Anne Hawthorn O'Keefe. I'm usually called Annie."

Which she didn't like, O'Keefe thought, but she was stuck with it. At one point, she had tried to persuade O'Keefe and others to call her Anne, but it didn't take. She was an "Annie," whether she liked it or not. And she was a hawthorn too. "Hey, Thorns," he would say when she was jabbing at him, "give me a break."

As Hartley had instructed, she looked nowhere but at her questioner and the jury and answered just loud enough that those inside the bar would be able to hear while the courtroom audience beyond would strain.

"Are you familiar with the accused in this case?"

"I'm slightly acquainted with Mr. Smith and very well acquainted with Ms. Montrose."

"How so?"

"My daughter Kelly attended Operation Go! preschool for three years. Miss Ginny was her primary teacher."

"As a mother, did you develop an opinion about her teaching during those years?"

"I'm no expert in evaluating teaching skills, but I cannot imagine anyone doing better with my daughter. She was way ahead of where we expected her to be in everything from learning the alphabet to reading, to arithmetic, even to things like geography. She knew things by the time she was five that I didn't know even then as an adult."

"Did your relationship go beyond just a parent-teacher one?"

Annie described the close relationship that had developed and continued after Kelly had left the school. And that, yes, Ginny had babysat for the O'Keefes frequently including overnight.

Had Kelly ever reported any incidents, or ones even remotely like those alleged in the indictment, when in Ginny's care?

"Never."

Had Annie ever had reason to believe that Ginny had perpetrated those acts on her daughter?

"Never."

What about in relation to other children under Ginny's care?

"Never."

Had she ever heard anything from a parent or anyone else that had caused her to suspect that such things had been done to Kelly or any other child in Ginny's care?

"Absolutely not," Annie said. "Nothing whatsoever."

"Given all you know today, including your reading of the indictment, including all you may have learned in the media or otherwise about this trial and the accusations against Miss Ginny, have you altered your view in any way?"

"In one way, yes."

Scott looked surprised. "And that would be…"

"I've visited her a few times in jail"—Annie looked directly at Ginny—"and I admire her more than ever for the bravery and grace she is showing in this horrible situation that has been viciously forced on her."

Annie choked back tears. And for the first time in the entire ordeal, O'Keefe saw Ginny cry. He hoped the jurors had seen it too. If they had, they were quickly distracted by a derisory groan from the spectator gallery. Hartley turned and stared angrily at the crowd. Snyder struck his gavel lightly, a gentle warning.

Hartley turned back to the witness. "Now, your daughter's father is your former husband, Peter O'Keefe, sitting over there at the defense counsel table, yes?"

"Yes."

"Is your testimony here today in any way motivated by a desire to help him out?"

"We've been divorced for several years. He left me. He's not exactly on my gift list these days."

Light laughter rippled through the courtroom. O'Keefe felt the heat rise in his cheeks.

Rhonda Tarwater stood for the cross.

"Mr. O'Keefe continues to pay child support, correct?"

"Yes."

"And alimony?"

"Yes."

"Does he help you out financially in other ways?"

"In a few extraordinary situations, yes, but not regularly."

"So it's important to you that he prosper financially, correct?"

"Prosper or not," Annie said, "he has a court-ordered obligation to make those payments, and I assure you I'll hold him to that obligation."

Again, laughter in the courtroom.

"We've heard what you have to say about your daughter's experience with the defendant, but you can't say what did or did not occur between the defendant and any other child including those named in the indictment, can you?"

"I guess not … except it's like the dog that didn't bark."

Snyder called a recess, and as Annie left the witness stand and walked down the aisle toward the back of the courtroom, there was the customary staring. O'Keefe wondered how many of them were thinking what an idiot he must be to let such a woman get away from him.

He asked Hartley, "Did you rehearse that little gem about the gift list?"

"You bet. We thought we deserved to have a little fun."

CHAPTER ❧ 82

WHILE NOT WITHOUT a certain quality of poise of her own, the next witness did not exhibit quite the same level of self-assurance as the previous one, and did exhibit a certain amount of uncertainty about where exactly to go, where to stop to take the oath, and how exactly to climb into the witness box.

Once installed there, she could see her dad at the defense counsel table, right where he said he would be, and her mom in the first row with that little smile of hers, almost a smirk, that seemed to say, "All is well. You've got it, girl. I have no doubts."

Her mom had been adamant that she wear her school uniform—blue plaid skirt; blue knee socks; black and white saddle shoes; a crisply starched; impeccably white blouse; and, instead of the usual navy blue sweater, a short navy blazer her mom had bought her for this occasion. "Yes," Annie had said that morning as she surveyed her daughter up and down. "Just right."

Her mom had warned her not to trouble herself looking at those hostile people on the other side of the courtroom. Kelly quickly scanned past them until she located toward the back, sitting on the aisle, Mr. Harrigan beaming a smile at her. She had known him forever, her forever anyway, knew him before she even knew what knowing was. He had been in the pictures they took when she and her mom were leaving the hospital a few days after her birth. His kids went to her school—Rachel very sweet, Robbie not so much. "She's her mother and he's her father," her mom had said. As she sat in the hallway with a courtroom bailiff waiting to be called in, all of a sudden he was there, standing above her.

"Aren't you something?" he said and sat down.

"You have a case here?" she said.

"No. I came to see my hero."

She was confused. "Dad, you mean?"

"No. You, silly."

She blushed.

"You're the Champion. The Champion for Justice."

She didn't know what to say.

"I mean it. That's what you are."

She blushed more.

He opened his palm, which held a gold Shamrock pin. "This is the Irish good luck charm," he said, and pinned it up near her shoulder above her heart.

"Not that you need it. You've got the truth on your side."

"I do," she said.

"But it will make you even stronger. If you get confused or afraid, or just want a little lift, just reach up with your right hand and touch it."

The called her into the courtroom and the bailiff signaled that she should follow him. At the courtroom door, she turned back and said, "Are you coming in?"

"Of course."

But now Mr. Hartley was talking to her, asking for her full name.

"Kelly Caitlin O'Keefe.

Hartley took her through a similar sequence as her mother, eliciting answers like, "The best teacher I ever had;" and

"Yes, when she babysat me, she helped me dress and undress, and every once in a while gave me a bath, and there was not one touch ever that was even close to wrong or that made me uncomfortable;" and

"Not one other kid ever said that anything happened like they are saying here, including the ones I knew then that are saying it now;" and

"The only time I was ever in the boiler room was a couple of times when some of us sneaked in and looked around when Mr. Smith was gone;" and

"The only time Mr. Smith ever touched me was to hold my hand while he was walking me to the car;" and

"It's all lies."

When Hartley switched the subject to Kelly's meeting with Mortimer and Brinkley at the Children's Clinic, Dolinar and Tarwater seemed surprised and began whispering.

"What happened first?" Hartley said.

"They asked me—"

"Objection," Dolinar said. "It's hearsay."

"These statements," Hartley replied, "are not being offered to prove their truth, so they're not hearsay. Even if they were, you've ruled that hearsay statements made by the children in these interviews are admissible because they were made in the course of a medical diagnosis process, which is an exception to the hearsay rule. These statements were made in that very same connection."

"But these are statements made by the clinicians, not the children," Snyder said.

"Doesn't matter. They're statements made in the course of attempting to carry out a medical diagnosis of Kelly O'Keefe. They were trying to get to the same place with Kelly as they had with the other children. If she'd gone along with them, she'd have ended up in Dr. Carlyle's office under the colposcope."

"Seems to turn things on their head," Snyder said.

"Moreover, Mortimer and Brinkley are obviously available for cross-examination. In addition, the statements are being offered to show the effect of those statements on Kelly's state of mind, which is another exception to the hearsay rule."

Dolinar interrupted. "But this witness's state of mind is *irrelevant*," Dolinar said. "And that's the real objection here. Kelly O'Keefe is not one of the children named in the indictment. You ruled on this same issue in the Bobby Putnam situation. Whatever happened at his interview is irrelevant because he isn't in the case anymore. Kelly O'Keefe was never in the case at all."

"And," Hartley said, "I was about to add, before I was rudely interrupted, it's being offered for impeachment purposes. These people denied on the witness stand that they engaged in this kind of interrogation, and Kelly is about to tell us that's exactly what they did."

"It's still not relevant," Dolinar persisted. "There's no tie between Kelly O'Keefe and the other children. It was an entirely different situation. There's nothing this witness can say to contradict the testimony about the interviews of the children named in the indictment."

"It's a pattern," Hartley said. "It's a practice. We showed that through the Putnam tape and in other ways. You wouldn't let us introduce those things. Now this. Showing their techniques, their pattern and practice is critical."

"I'll sustain the objection."

Hartley shook his head and looked up at the ceiling as if praying for guidance. "May I ask, Your Honor, How *many* interviews *doth* it take to make a process?"

A smattering of laughter including from O'Keefe, thinking, *Ching Ching. That fine amount just went way up.*

Snyder fumed, and Hartley rushed on. "I want to, and I have a right to make an offer of proof. Right now. The witness is on the stand. There's no reason to drag her and all the rest of us in here later. It'll only take a few minutes. You can give the jury a short break, and we'll be done PDQ."

Dolinar started to protest, but Snyder cut him off, muttering, "Might as well allow it. One less thing for him to appeal. But it better be super quick, Mr. Hartley."

The jury left and Hartley repeated his last question to Kelly: "What happened first?"

"They asked a lot of questions about my family, my mom and dad's divorce, whether I wet the bed and had nightmares. Stuff like that."

"Then what?"

"They said they hoped I'd help the little kids, like some of the big kids were doing."

"Big kids?"

"My age. Kids who were in my class."

"Did you understand what 'help' meant?"

"I thought they wanted me to tell stories about Miss Ginny and Mr. Smith doing 'yucky things'—that's the way she said it— to kids."

"Were they specific about any of those 'yucky things'?"

"Very much. They talked about fingers and spoons and forks and knives ... and Mr. Smith's"—she couldn't seem to bring herself to say the word—"thing ... being put in front and rear ends."

"And what did you say?"

"I said those were all lies."

"What was their response to that?"

"They just kept trying to get me to say things like that Miss Ginny took kids into the boiler room and things like that. They asked me if Miss Ginny gave me baths, if my dad gave me baths, and if either of them had touched me ... down there."

"Your dad?"

"Yeah, they did. I told them none of that happened."

"Did they accept that?"

"No. They said children sometimes bury bad things really deep, but that I should be 'honest and brave', those were their words, like the other kids had been. They wanted me to go home and think real hard and try to remember things like that. They asked if there were weird ceremonies at Miss Ginny's, whether I slept in the same bed with her, and whether she and her roommate slept in the same bed."

"How did it end?" Hartley said.

"They asked me to go home and think about it all, 'and please be brave,' they said, and come back and help the little kids."

On the cross-examination portion of the offer of proof, Dolinar asked whether any other children had been questioned in the way she had, and Kelly conceded that she couldn't say because she wasn't there.

"In any event, Kelly, nothing Ms. Mortimer or Mr. Brinkley said in the interview caused *you* to change your story, did it? You denied it going in and also coming out, right?"

"I sure did."

Hartley announced that his offer of proof was over, and Snyder ordered the jury back in.

"One final thing," Hartley said. "Kelly, you know of course that your dad has been working with me to defend Miss Ginny in this case, don't you?"

"Yes."

"Are you here testifying because he asked you to and because you want to help him?"

"Just the opposite. It was me who begged *him* to help her. She was the best teacher I ever had."

Kelly left the witness stand, and Dolinar asked for a sidebar. "I know the jury's not supposed to read or watch anything in the media, but it would be a travesty if one or more jurors learned of the irrelevant testimony in the offer of proof because the media reported it."

"I can't order them not to publish."

"How about just a courteous request?"

"Ridiculous," Hartley said. "Judge, I remember what you said to me at the beginning of this case about the honesty of the typical juror."

But Judge Snyder made the courteous request anyway, and nothing appeared in any media concerning Kelly O'Keefe's testimony about the techniques used by Betsy Mortimer and Ken Brinkley in her interview.

CHAPTER ☙ 83

"**I**'M SORRY," THE assistant told O'Keefe, "but Doctor is swamped for the next few months, and there's just no way he could take a trip there."

In the run-up to the trial, O'Keefe had hustled to develop a small network of correspondents who had previously participated or were then still engulfed in the flood of day-care molestation cases that had inundated the country beginning in the early 1980s. Through those contacts, he identified a doctor who had recently participated in a study of hundreds of child and adolescent subjects that produced results contrary to Dr. Norman Carlyle's testimony in this case and so much of the other so-called expert medical testimony delivered up to that time in the nation's courtrooms in similar cases, all of which had been based on no clinical study at all but only anecdotes and notions.

The new study revealed that it was rarely possible to tell the difference between vaginal and anal areas that had never suffered trauma from such areas that had undeniably been traumatized. Moreover, the specific physical source or cause of any particular trauma was somewhere between extremely difficult and impossible to identify after any significant time lapse between the trauma experience and the medical exam. Consequently, the doctor was much in demand, not just by defense counsel but also by organizers of medical and forensics conferences around the country. In a bid to protect his thriving medical practice during a period of new-found and possibly fleeting fame, he hired a special assistant whose sole job was to shield him from having to deal with the many requests for his participation. Inexperience as an expert witness made him particularly skittish about trial testimony.

"What if we came there to take his testimony by deposition?" O'Keefe said, having no idea whether that could be done, but he didn't want to give up on what he thought was buried treasure.

The assistant asked how long it would take.

"Half a day at most, probably less."

"Can you guarantee that?"

"Yes," he lied.

The doctor agreed. But Judge Snyder did not. Any testimony whatsoever in this case had to be live in the courtroom.

O'Keefe left a pleading voicemail with the assistant, begging the doctor to ride to the rescue of the beleaguered defendants. She called a day later and said it just wasn't possible, but "Doctor" had given her the name of a physician in O'Keefe's city, William Latham, who "Doctor" had met at a conference and been impressed with the young physician's keen interest in and knowledge of the subject, including the findings in the study that "Doctor" had participated in. O'Keefe, now desperate, contacted Latham, and the doctor enthusiastically agreed to testify.

Latham was young but had substantial experience with routine examinations of children, and even some experience, though not much, in abuse cases. But aside from his limited experience, the daunting barrier they had to surmount was the fact that he had never examined any of the children in the case, and Judge Snyder had prohibited additional examinations or interviews.

"So what we'll do," Hartley said, "is just focus him on Dr. Carlyle's testimony and do our best to destroy it."

And that's what they did. Unlike so much of the defense case, Latham's testimony came through like a knife through soft butter. Hartley took Latham through his credentials and experience and his familiarity with the most current developments in the field, especially the most recent and much discussed study that "Doctor" has been involved in. Latham testified that Carlyle's opinion that the physical examination and the colposcope images were "consistent with abuse" was meaningless. None of what he relied on was any more "consistent with abuse" than "consistent with *no* abuse." Especially devastating, Hartley and O'Keefe thought, was Latham's unqualified opinion that, based on his review of the facts stated in Dr. Carlyle's reports and testimony and the colposcope images, there was no medical evidence that any abuse had occurred.

On cross, Dolinar avoided probing the details of the findings reported at the conference, instead focusing on Latham's weak spots, starting with his limited experience in examining suspected victims of child abuse, and ending with, "But have you actually examined any of the children involved in this case? Yes or no?"

"No."

On redirect, Hartley asked, "Did you have any opportunity to examine the children?"

"No."

"Why not?"

"It's my understanding that the court refused to allow any additional medical examinations."

"Mr. Hartley," Judge Snyder intervened, "let's ask him if he knows *why* the court ordered it ... Dr. Latham?"

Latham looked at Hartley who could do nothing but shrug, so Latham answered, "It's my understanding that the court thought it would be too traumatic for the children to undergo another exam."

Hartley pounced. "And you were not consulted about that, were you, Dr. Latham?"

"No."

"In your *medical* opinion, would an additional exam have caused additional trauma to the children?"

"My opinion is no, it would not. Not at all."

Snyder's face turned purplish red. "And I'm sure the prosecution would have presented an equally or better qualified expert who'd have contradicted *you*."

After the jury was dismissed for the day, Hartley renewed his motion to allow an additional medical examination of the children remaining in the case. "Judge, you now have the only expert medical opinion admitted in this case that an additional examination would not harm the children."

Denied.

He then moved that Dr. Carlyle's testimony be stricken in its entirety as junk science and that the jury be instructed to give it no credence whatsoever.

Denied. Just another addition to his "world-record number of objections" and grounds for appeal.

**WHITE SUPREMACISTS IN IDAHO ARE
RESPONSIBLE FOR A SERIES OF ROBBERIES AND
BOMBINGS INCLUDING A PLOT TO BOMB THE
FEDERAL BUILDING IN COUR d'ALENE, IDAHO.**

CHAPTER ❧ 84

O'KEEFE HAD LESS difficulty finding a psychological expert.

This group seemed to almost relish controversy and disputation. O'Keefe, who was personally skeptical of the therapy profession, suspected that this inclination toward internecine conflict stemmed from how fuzzy and speculative all of it was despite its wrapping around itself a thin and threadbare and perhaps entirely illegitimate "scientific" cloak. And when he found Ellsworth Becker, he thought that perhaps he had found the best expert the defense could have asked for.

Becker was a Nebraska farm boy who somehow made his way into the profession of clinical psychiatry with a specialty in child psychiatry and had earned wide recognition as an expert on trauma and abuse including sexual abuse of children. During a long career in private practice, he had been privately and publicly critical of many prevailing psychiatric doctrines and methods. He'd also become an expert on trauma and abuse, including child sexual abuse, and had frequently served as an expert witness. After retiring early from private practice, he'd taken a dual appointment in the departments of Psychology and Psychiatric Medicine in the medical school at one of the most prestigious universities in the region, one that would be well known and respected by the typical Midwestern juror. Neither he nor his university employer would be suspected of promoting East Coast gobbledygook or West Coast New-Agey airy-fairy pipe dreams.

He spoke with the slow, near drawl of the Midwestern Great Plains states. The more critical he was of an idea or a practice, the slower and flatter he got. "The problem with my profession," he said, "is the lack of both objectivity and humility. Going all the way back to Freud, we usually have no provable basis for what we're saying, but that doesn't keep us from saying it quite dogmatically."

At first it didn't go so well. He had some sympathy for the case but insisted on reviewing certain pleadings and testimony before agreeing to testify. And his fees were steep, and the retainer account was apparently depressingly low. O'Keefe pulled out all his oratorical, rhetorical, but especially guilt-inducing, stops trying to persuade Hartley to spend the money.

A conference call with Becker won the lawyer over. Hartley agreed to Becker's fee schedule.

"But what the hell are we gonna have him testify to?" Hartley mused, mostly to himself. "Like Latham, he hasn't and won't be allowed to examine the children. At least Latham had the colposcope images. We have no recording of the interviews."

"Except the one," O'Keefe said.

They agreed that Becker would review any parts of the trial transcript that revealed the interviewing techniques, the Putnam tape, and Kelly's testimony. "I'll try again to get them in," Hartley said, "but we're kidding ourselves."

Formidable was the word that came to O'Keefe's mind when Becker entered the courtroom. Tall, dignified, elegantly dressed, stern of face, steely of eye, firm of jaw. He strode to the witness box as if he were the commanding officer of the entire gathering. Hartley took him through his credentials, emphasizing his long history in private practice and clinical environments.

"Doctor, we've heard it said that children never lie about sexual abuse. Do you agree with that statement?"

"No."

"Why not?"

"I have personally had young patients who lied to me about sexual molestation."

"How did you know they were lying?"

"Either they later credibly withdrew their accusations, or all the rest of the evidence conclusively demonstrated that the abuse could not have occurred."

"Are there reasons other than outright lying that could lead a child to falsely claim that abuse occurred?"

"Yes. And the most significant development, one that's emerged in the past five or ten years, is misguided and dangerous interview techniques that lead children to make false statements."

Hartley prompted Becker to elaborate how in the last decade the sexual abuse of children had garnered a huge amount of attention and attracted a gush of federal funding. The result? A proliferation of public agencies and non-profit organizations focusing on and publicizing the issue. All of this was enthusiastically, even fanatically, supported by strange bedfellows, from militant feminists to evangelical Christians to both liberal and conservative politicians. And in 1979 the federal government had imposed funding caps on all social service programs *except* child protection.

All this extremely generous funding of this single area, while other programs were struggling with severe budgetary limitations, led to a major transfer of personnel and new programs to this field. But that new money was not spent on training or certification programs for these new recruits to the cause.

"This huge influx of money and people and … let's call it 'enthusiasm,' … has unfortunately led to all kinds of poorly educated, poorly trained, and abysmally unqualified so-called 'therapists' doing this work.

"Along with that, certain ideas have gained a following unsupported by evidence or the experience of those of us who've worked in the area for years. Those include a newly advanced notion that a child's allegations should *always* be believed except in only one instance: when a child initially denies or when a child recants, that is, later denies that the abuse occurred. Worse, that a child's denial that abuse occurred is *actually evidence that it did occur.*

"A companion of these doctrines is that therapists should be constant advocates for the child, always believing them, never making a finding of non-abuse—"

"I object," Dolinar interrupted. "This long lecture is not responsive to the question."

"I think I agree," Snyder said. "What's your basic point, Doctor, if you have one?"

"My conclusion, which needed the context in order to be properly understood, is that the current governing doctrine in this field is that the child protector interviewer/inquisitor is always the child's advocate except in one instance: when the child refuses to admit that molestation occurred when the inquisitor believes it has occurred. At that point, the interviewer believes it's their duty to break down the child's defenses against admitting the abuse. This justifies, in the interviewer's mind, using some techniques that were previously considered inappropriate, such as not letting the child tell their own story. The interviewer should be asking open-ended questions, not leading ones, especially not highly suggestive questions."

"Can you give some examples of leading questions you've heard or read in this context in this case?"

Becker cited examples of what he could glean from prior testimony and other evidence.

"What about telling a child what the child's schoolmates have said about being molested or witnessing molestation of others?" Hartley asked.

"Highly prejudicial. It both sets the stage and gives them a script to follow when they eventually figure out what's expected of them."

"Doctor, what is your opinion of children being intensely questioned by investigators, therapists, clinicians, parents, and prosecutors as many as ten or twenty times or more?"

"I have never," Becker said, "seen a situation where more than four or five sessions were needed to draw out what the children accurately and truthfully had to say. If adults keep pounding at them, kids figure out what they need to do to get them off their back. They'll eventually go along with the story their authority figures want them to tell."

"What about using dolls and puppets?"

"Very bad idea. It creates an atmosphere of fantasy, of make-believe. Children live in that world most of the time anyway. It's a thin line. They're very suggestible. Think about Santa Claus, the Easter Bunny, and the Boogeyman."

"Brainwashed?"

"That may be too strong a term. But something like that. Maybe seeding, planting, watering—and a story sprouts."

"What about deputizing a parent to interrogate a child?"

"Like homework?"

"Sort of."

Becker shook his head. "So, we have unqualified or only marginally qualified therapists deputizing an even more unqualified lay person, who is a powerful, sometimes terrifying figure in the child's life? No. It's a very pernicious, very bad practice."

Asked about the so-called behavioral markers of sexual molestation—bed wetting, masturbation spitting, and the rest—constantly trotted out by everyone from Betsy Mortimer to Myra Hicks in the infamous letter to the parents. "Those indicate nothing about sexual abuse. Welcome to growing up."

Hartley marched the witness through all the rest of it. Social and peer pressure, browbeating, criticism, insults, threats, promises of rewards, actual rewards, social and peer pressure.

The final question: "And anatomically correct dolls, Dr. Becker. Ones with realistic male and female sex organs. What is your opinion of those?"

"I consider their use by the interviewer to be a form of child abuse by the interviewers."

Dolinar stood and began his cross-examination. "You haven't examined even one of these children, have you, Doctor?"

"I haven't been allowed to."

"I repeat the question, to which I'm entitled to a straight answer. You have not examined even one of these children, have you, Doctor?"

"I have not."

"Are you saying that the techniques you deem objectionable occurred on a wide scale in this case?"

"I believe that is the case. The examples I gave were taken from the record in this case. But it's hard to say because the interviews weren't taped, which they absolutely should have been."

"Believe. You say you 'believe.' But you don't *know*, do you? You can't say how much or even whether those techniques you object to were used at any other time in the case other than in the few examples you gave?"

"No, but I would bet a large amount of money they were."

"Objection to the response after the word 'No.' It's nonresponsive."

"Sustained," Snyder said. "The jury will disregard that comment, and it will be stricken from the record."

"The bottom line, Doctor," Dolinar continued, "is that you don't believe the children."

"I don't have enough information to answer that question, if that's what it is."

"But based on the information you have, you don't believe the children, correct?"

"Based on the information I have, and some other information I have seen but has been ruled irrelevant in this case, I do not believe the children."

"Object again," Dolinar said.

"Sustained," Snyder barked. "The remark about other information being ruled irrelevant will be stricken, and the jury will disregard it. And, Doctor, you are a blink of my eye away from being held in contempt."

Dolinar looked quite satisfied with himself and his world. "You and Mr. Hartley talked about leading questions. But you only gave a few examples. I think I counted four. Were there any others?"

"I'm sure there were."

"That's another 'believe,' isn't it? You don't *know* that, do you? You can't say there were any more leading questions asked of these seven children, in all these hours and hours of interviewing, than the four you specified, right?"

"No tapes. No transcripts."

"I repeat my question and ask the court to direct you to answer yes or no."

"I cannot say there were more than the four."

"No further questions," Dolinar said.

"Any redirect, Mr. Hartley?" Snyder said, though it seemed to O'Keefe more a threat than a question.

"Dr. Becker," Hartley said, "do you believe there were more leading questions than the four you mentioned?"

Dolinar smiled. "Objection. Mr. Hartley's question is leading and there's no foundation.'

"Sustained."

"A final question, Doctor. Do you believe the children are lying?"

"Not necessarily lying in the usual sense of that word. I think they are just not telling the truth even though they may believe what they're saying."

After Becker's testimony, the defense rested.

The prosecution said it did not intend to call any rebuttal witnesses. The next day would be devoted to working out the lengthy and detailed instructions that would be given to the jury, with plenty of opportunity for disputation in that process. On the day after that, the jurors would return to receive the instructions and listen to the opening and closing arguments.

Dolinar again signaled Hartley to step aside for a conversation. "I wonder if he's planning another poke in my eye," Hartley muttered to Maura and O'Keefe.

"Can we meet, say, in our office in a couple of hours?" Dolinar said.

"To discuss the instructions?"

"That. Plus we might as well see if we can make a deal. It's definitely the point of no return now."

CHAPTER ◈ 85

DOLINAR AND TARWATER on one side of the table, Dolinar with an insincere smile, Tarwater looking even more pugnacious than usual.

Hartley, Davis, and O'Keefe on the other side, all warily expectant, Hartley with his drafts of proposed instructions in front of him.

But Dolinar didn't bother even to address the instructions. "I'm authorized to make you an offer. I'll spare us all a long speech. Eighteen years. A chance for parole only after ten years. That's it. No negotiation, and I'm not bullshitting you on that. It really is take it or leave it."

Hartley's head tilted, as if he were struggling to process what Dolinar had just said. "Why so much more time than Marvin Smith?"

"She hurt more kids than he did, and she was the ringleader."

"And she's white," Maura said. "No civil rights groups harassing you about her. And no special worry about a black juror."

"Children," Tarwater said, "best be seen and not heard. Go play with your dolls, little girl."

O'Keefe watched his sweet-natured friend pass into what looked like homicidal rage, but before that particular exchange could degenerate further, Hartley intervened.

"Alford plea?"

"No way," Dolinar said.

"You're putting on a real puffed-up, hard-ass show here, but you must be worried about whether you've met your burden."

"No concern at all."

"Then you must be worried about a juror or two or three holding out for not guilty."

"I couldn't care less. You know the stats, Scott. We win the second trials in most cases, and our win percentage in third trials is even better. And we don't give up. You and your client will be broke, and we'll have every single one of our resources still available to us, and more. The offer is good through tomorrow. The moment I deliver the first word of my closing, it's off the table."

"Aren't you hot shit? Do you really believe she did these horrible things? You have to know your case is nothing but snake oil you're selling to the jury and the world."

"Thing is, Scott, I don't really care. That's for the sociologists, philosophers, and politicians. The grand jury indicted her. They assigned me the case. My duty is to prosecute that case to the far limits of whatever talents and diligence I can apply to it. End of story."

"You forgot your duty to do justice, Donnie."

Dolinar laughed in mockery of that idea while reddening in anger at the disfavored nickname.

Tarwater, looking at Dolinar as if saying, "a plague on your house too," addressed the group, "I'll tell you what I think—"

"I didn't ask you what you think," Hartley said.

"I'm telling you anyway. I believe with every fiber of my being that your client is a monster. I believe she did many horrible things to these children and others. I believe she should be punished to the furthest limits of the law, and beyond that if it were possible. I opposed making this offer. I hope you and your client are stupid enough to reject it."

"Think about that," Dolinar said. "Are you willing to risk a jury that might feel like my partner here?"

Ginny listened impassively as Hartley explained the offer. "It's very hard to know what to advise you," he said, "but I believe that at your age, with the opportunity for parole after ten years, and it is highly likely that you'll achieve that…and you won't be forgotten…

we and others will be working for your exoneration all the while. And don't hate me for saying this, but, you know, prison isn't the worst thing a person can experience. People in prison have achieved some remarkable things, spiritually and otherwise. So I have to say, if I were you, I would take the deal."

While O'Keefe was wondering how justice had become so much like a trip to the casino, he felt Maura squirm next to him, an involuntary physical protest, and for the second time that day, he saw his bubbly friend turn angry. She looked at Hartley as if she might slap him.

Ginny's response was quick, abrupt, clearly final. "Never."

"You don't even want to think about it?" Hartley said. "We've got a little time here."

"Never. I would never admit to any of that."

"What if we could get an Alford plea like Marvin's?"

"That's no better."

"What if we could get less prison time or an earlier chance at parole?"

"Never."

"Alright. I respect your answer. If you change your mind, and I'm not saying you ever will, but if you change your mind, we have until the beginning of the prosecution's closing argument to accept it."

"Never."

"I believe in your innocence one hundred percent, and I'll fight for you all the way. But though they call it a system of justice, it doesn't always do justice, so I was obligated to make that recommendation."

Her face didn't change. It was as if she were looking through him, and through all the rest of them, and through the prison walls as well.

CHAPTER ᪣ 86

IN AN AMERICAN criminal trial, the prosecutor gets the last word.

The prosecutor speaks first, the defense next, then the prosecutor is allowed extra time for "rebuttal." The prosecution is given this advantage because it has the burden of proving its case beyond a reasonable doubt. Hartley considered this advantage "maybe the single most unfair aspect of the trial process for the defendant."

Although it is seldom done, the prosecutor can elect not to separate its argument into the two stages but require the defense to go first, reserving all its time for the final "rebuttal." It surprised everyone when Dolinar announced that this was the procedure the prosecution would elect in this case. Hartley was crushed. "That Dolinar is an evil genius. Now he'll have all his time after hearing what I have to say. He knows Snyder won't rein him in. He'll be able to say any damned outrageous thing he wants, and I won't be able to answer any of it."

Scott Hartley stood and paused, taking a long look at the jury, trying to shut out everything else in the courtroom and the world except the twelve people he hoped would devote the same intensity of concentration to him and the story he had to tell.

"Day after day, I keep wondering when I'll wake up from this nightmare I'm having. In this nightmare, a kind, dedicated young

8

woman has given up the chance of a more financially rewarding career in order to dedicate her life to the youngest of children … helping to boost them along at the dawn of their lives . . . helping them develop the skills to make their way in a world that is seldom easy and is often rock hard to navigate.

"She toils for years, earning few dollars but much love from her students and praise from the adults who know her. Her supervisors, her fellow teachers, parents, not one ever gives her a harsh review or says a single bad word about her. Until, one day, there's a knock at her door. It's the police, come to throw her in jail for committing unspeakable acts of sexual violation on the very children she's done so much to help and care for.

"What has happened? Do they have physical evidence of these unspeakable acts? No. Do they have disinterested witnesses to any of these acts or even any suspicious behavior on her part? No. Do they have even any circumstantial physical evidence to support these allegations? No.

"What they do evidently have—shockingly, unbelievably— is several children who say that she's done horrible things to them. Attention must be paid to that of course. We are not saying that sexual molestation of children does not occur. We are not saying that caregivers are never guilty of such crimes. Such allegations must be taken very seriously. Our children must be protected against such predators.

"So we listen. We listen very carefully to what the children are saying. We try to apply our reason to the statements they're making. We investigate the history and background of those statements. We ask why they never reported these crimes at the time they were occurring. Some of the crimes alleged involve penetration of the tender private parts of young children including, incredibly, spoons, forks, knives. Surely that would have caused pain and injury. But none of the children reported any pain or injury. None of the parents, who gave them baths and undressed and dressed them every day, reported any injury or any sign of abuse whatsoever.

"So why are a few of the children saying these things, we ask? And it *is* only a few. Please remember that. Hundreds of children who went to Operation Go! have never reported such things, even though every single one of them who could possibly be found was hunted down by the police and have been prodded and pulled to tell whatever they might know. Or not know.

"That letter. Sent out to every parent they could find of every child who had ever attended Operation Go! and invited every one of them to turn over every rock. Yet hardly any of them have come forward. I suggest that you can infer from the evidence, and the lack of evidence, that most of the children are like young Kelly O'Keefe, who took the stand there and said that nothing like that had ever happened to her at the school…that Miss Ginny was the best teacher she's ever had…that these accusations must be lies. 'All lies,' Kelly says. That Miss Ginny could never have done those things. That none of her fellow students, including the ones the prosecution put on the witness stand, said a word at the time.

"So why, we ask, are these few children making these accusations? Certainly attention must be paid. And we do pay attention. The closest attention. We investigate further. What do we discover? That it all started with an accusation by a mother seeking to divert attention from her own, or her husband's, physical abuse of her son.

Virginia's testimony about that was uncontroverted. You can draw your own inference about the truth or falsity of those accusations by the fact that the child is not even included in this indictment and that they did not bring the mother in here to claim to you that Virginia was lying. Please think about that long and hard. They never brought her in here to tell you that Virginia was lying about what happened.

"But when that mother went to the police with her slanders, the police, instead of approaching the situation with the proper reason and intelligence and open-mindedness citizens have the right to expect from them … they punched the hysteria button and sent out that letter.

"That letter. I told you about that letter in detail in my opening statement. Please take it back into the jury room and read it carefully and consider the effect of that letter on the parents who received it.

"We the defense, through our own investigation and our cross-examination of their witnesses, have learned and shown you here that every single one of the children initially denied that these things happened to them. But these people—not that many people, a very few people, basically just three people: Ken Brinkley from the Child Protective Services agency refused to take the children's 'no' for an answer; Myra Hicks from the police department refused to take the children's 'no' for an answer; and Betsy Mortimer from the Children's Clinic refused to take the children's 'no' for an answer.

"How ironic. But that's too tame of a word. How insane that they demand that *you* believe the children. And yet *they* refused to believe them. In fact, they scolded and made fun of the ones who continued to deny. Instead of believing the children, they planted ideas in the children's heads in the form of leading questions. They enticed the children into a world of fantasy with their dolls and puppets, rewarded the ones who finally gave in and adopted the required storyline, shamed the ones who didn't, and convinced most of the parents to act as additional interrogators on a constant daily basis.

"All of that—the suggesting, the badgering, the demanding, and yes, the brainwashing— finally brought some of the children around. Like our witness Doctor Becker said, the children figured out what was being demanded of them by adult authority figures and ultimately provided it, and even came to believe it themselves. Santa Claus. The Easter Bunny. The Boogeyman. Missy Ginny. Mr. Smith."

He went on to discuss in detail the charges in the indictment involving each of the remaining children and how the prosecution had not supported any of those charges with believable evidence.

He closed by reciting all the "preposterous things" the jurors had to believe in order to render a guilty verdict.

"To render a guilty verdict, first, you must believe that not one child—not one—told anyone else that these things were happening to them at the time of their occurrence. The children say—in my opinion, were 'coached' to say, like they were coached to say everything else—that Virginia threatened them with horrible consequences if they told. But is it believable that not one told *anyone,* in *all the years* between the time they attended the school and when they met up with Betsy Mortimer? To vote for guilt, you must believe that every single one kept that secret for all those years, even after they were *long* away from the school and Virginia. And if you don't believe that, then how can you believe there was ever such a secret to keep? That alone constitutes reasonable doubt.

"Second, you must believe that it was possible for these molestations to occur but that not one child showed any injury from the gruesome assaults on their sensitive private parts. These are tiny children we're talking about. Three, four, five years old. Yes, Doctor Carlyle made claims about what his colposcope had supposedly revealed, but none of those injuries were recognized or detected prior to his entry on the scene at the behest of his employer Betsy Mortimer. Surely you agree with me that the recent study that Dr. Latham discussed in his testimony and Dr. Latham's review of Carlyle's reports and colposcope images thoroughly discredited Carlyle's testimony. That alone constitutes reasonable doubt.

"Third, not one parent noticed any change or disruption to their child's behavior at the time. A couple of them say that they now recall such behavior. Convenient memory. But they didn't say it then. They didn't notice it then. That alone constitutes reasonable doubt.

"Fourth, you must believe that in an environment in which parents and teachers were coming and going from the school and the various classrooms throughout the day, often unannounced and at random, nobody detected anything suspicious when this"— he made the air quotes he was so fond of and gestured toward Ginny—"'criminal mastermind'" supposedly cavorted naked with the children in a cloak room. Not even a room. An alcove. *With no doors on it.*

"And that she was shuttling children back and forth to the boiler room, spending enough time there to engage in orgies, and shuttling back again. And that all of that went unseen by anyone. Not by a child. Not by another teacher. Not by a parent who came a little early to pick up their child and found the children alone in the nap room. All of that defies belief, and that alone constitutes reasonable doubt.

"Fifth, you must believe that this dedicated woman was for all these years a secret Satanist though not once did anyone who came into contact with her suspect that. That alone constitutes reasonable doubt.

"How is it possible that this prosecution could even be considered, let alone filed, let alone pursued all this way? I've thought and thought about it, night after sleepless night, and I cannot figure out what has happened in this country, what kind of hysteria or panic has produced this. It's mind-boggling to me. But here we are commanded by law and justice to leave all that insanity behind and consider nothing but evidence. And the prosecution not only failed to prove these crimes beyond reasonable doubt. They proved *nothing at all.* The truth is, ladies and gentlemen, that it's not just that *Virginia Montrose* is innocent of any crime. It's that no crime happened here. Except, that is, the atrocity of what these fanatics have done most viciously—not only to Virginia Montrose, but also to these children and their parents and all the rest of us who've been forced to wallow in this filth for all these days.

"Through these vicious accusations, they have destroyed Virginia's good name, they have annihilated her teaching career, and they've scarred her heart and soul. But they want you to do worse. They want you, they really want you, to send this dedicated, sincere, self-sacrificing woman to what will amount to life in prison based on *nothing—nothing* but new, unprecedented medical and psychological theories that our experts, Doctors Latham and Becker, *real* experts, not fake self-proclaimed ones, have told you are completely false—*nothing* but fantasies cooked up by fanatics and planted in these poor children's heads.

"*They*, not Virginia Montrose, are the child abusers. Please, please don't be misled. We all know the ninth commandment, don't we? Thou shalt not bear false witness against thy neighbor. That is exactly what happened here. False witness. Seven times. False in every instance. If they can persuade you to do this to Virginia Montrose, then who is safe? None of us, once they decide to come for us. Please deliver a verdict that will wake us, deliver us, rescue us, and most of all Virginia, from this nightmare. That verdict must be innocent on every count of this vicious pack of lies they call an indictment."

Hartley looked at the jury, imploring them with his gaze, as if seeking to move beyond words and pass the emotional energy of his unshakable belief in the innocence of his client from himself to the jurors. Then, to O'Keefe's surprise—and, he thought, probably to the surprise of everyone else in the courtroom—Hartley turned to face the Save Our Children! people. His expression wasn't what O'Keefe would have expected. Not defiance. Not at all. It looked more like a plea for mercy.

Judge Snyder announced a short recess. Hartley sat down and stared ahead. For an uncomfortably long time. O'Keefe wasn't sure what to do, so he just remained seated himself.

Finally, Hartley said, "Are they gone?"

"Who?"

"The parents."

"Pretty much, yeah. Out to the hallway."

"I'll be so relieved when they're not there behind me all day, every day. Sometimes I have a hard time taking the next breath. They're like a huge weight bearing down on me, all the time, pressing me into my chair. I have to struggle to stand."

CHAPTER ⇾ 87

"IT'S SIMPLE, YOU either believe the children or you don't," Dolinar said.

"The defense had a huge problem here. They knew it would be impossible for any normal, common-sense person to believe that the children had made these things up. Children the age these were when they were assaulted and molested by Virginia Montrose and Marvin Smith don't know enough about sexual things to make things like that up."

That was the first of many references to Marvin Smith. Dolinar mentioned Marvin Smith more times in his closing than he mentioned Virginia Montrose. At one point, Hartley leaned over and whispered, "Marvin Smith, Marvin Smith, nothing but Marvin Smith. He's completely overcome that limiting instruction."

"Yes, that was a huge problem for the defense. So what did they do? They pursued the only angle available to them, the brainwashing theory."

He attacked the theory in a number of ways. "Mostly," he said, "the defense has just made unsupported assertions. They did not, could not show, in testimony, either through their own witnesses or their cross examination of Betsy Mortimer, that all these so-called suggestions and leading questions and putting words in the kids' mouths *actually happened*. You heard Doctor Becker. He could only come up with four leading questions. They kept saying it happened, but there is no evidence that the kids were pressured in that way. If you doubt me at all, I urge you to ask for and review the transcript of the testimony on those subjects. You'll see that I'm right."

Hartley whispered, "There's his reward for keeping the Putnam tape and Kelly's testimony out."

Yes, that was it, O'Keefe realized, as it hit him harder than it had before. The prosecution had succeeded in suppressing or blunting almost all the evidence that the defense had tried to offer to show the coercive techniques—the Putnam tape, Kelly's testimony, and Becker's. The defense had launched assault after assault on the citadel, all thwarted. Now they were left with just a few of the nuggets Hartley and Rockwell had managed to extract in their cross examination of the parents and children and Mortimer. Would that be enough?

Hartley objected. At the bench Dolinar said, "Your Honor, I didn't interrupt him once."

"I had to, Your Honor. Both the Putnam tape and Kelly O'Keefe's testimony established they did exactly those things. The refusal to let the jury hear that evidence is doubly prejudicial given his misleading closing argument."

"Not the children named in the indictment," Dolinar said. "They established nothing as to them."

"What would you have me do, Mr. Hartley?" Snyder said.

"Stop everything. Re-open the evidence. Let the Putnam tape in. Let Kelly O'Keefe's testimony in. Let us cross-examine Mortimer again based on that evidence. Bring Dr. Becker back and let him comment based on all that. "

"Absurd," Snyder said.

"Then I have to ask for a mistrial."

"Denied."

Dolinar resumed. "All that lawyer talk from the defense but no evidence. The greatest writer in English, William Shakespeare, expressed it perfectly: 'It's a tale told by an idiot. Full of sound and fury. But signifying nothing.'

"And isn't it just common sense that a child would initially deny that a shameful thing like that had happened to them? Dr. Becker had some different opinions about how to recover buried memories, but he in no way conclusively demonstrated that Ms.

Mortimer and the experts she relied on were wrong. He just had a different opinion. And we know about opinions and what they're similar to and how everyone has one, right?"

Muffled laughter in the audience and the jury box.

"And isn't it common sense to believe that the children were terrified of the threats to send the devil to kill them and their families, to slit their throats just like Montrose and Smith had slit the throats of those bunnies?

"And how do we know that Betsy Mortimer and Ken Brinkley got to the truth? Because the children eventually told their stories. Not just to Betsy and Ken, but to their parents. You heard Amanda Haynes. This was not some bad-cop intimidating interrogator with a rubber truncheon in one hand and brass knuckles in the other. She refused to believe at first, kept not wanting to believe, but finally she couldn't suppress it any longer and came to believe only after she basically had no choice but to believe.

"But the most important thing is that the children got up on that witness stand, in this intimidating environment, having the abusers sitting right in front of them, and told those same stories to *you*. And they were subjected to cross- examination. Intense, careful, well-prepared cross-examination. That's where the defense had the chance to get them to change their minds. But they and their stories withstood that cross-examination. None of them changed their stories. How? Why? Because they were true. Because children wouldn't, couldn't lie about such things.

"I'm sure you noticed how the defense tried to make the parents look greedy because they were talking to a lawyer about civil actions to seek financial redress. Surely you won't fall for those cynical, snide innuendoes, as if they don't deserve to obtain some redress, some recompense for the horrific wrongs done to their children.

"Mr. Hartley says the defendant didn't do these awful things to every one of the children she taught. Of course she didn't. She would have been caught long ago. And I urge you to think about all those children we couldn't find, couldn't identify, all those children who are still repressing the nightmare memories of what happened to them, or who just can't bear to admit it, and are out there living with the consequences. Yes, Kelly O'Keefe, the defense investigator's daughter, testified that nothing happened to her. We never said that it happened to her. Her testimony was irrelevant in every respect. We didn't charge that it happened to every child or even most of them, just that it happened to way, way too many and these remaining courageous seven children are here as representatives of all the other victims still out there. Maybe predators like Virginia Montrose and Marvin Smith have an instinct for choosing the most likely victims, the most vulnerable among us.

"Mr. Hartley tried to appeal to your emotions, your good natures, tried to make you feel sorry for the defendant. But what does the evidence show? Most importantly, what does the uncontroverted testimony of the children show? I repeat: Uncontroverted testimony. The children were entrusted to her care, and she violated that trust, betrayed the children in the most despicable ways. All those years when she was fooling her superiors, fellow teachers, and the parents. Talk about a wolf in sheep's clothing. A devil-worshipper in sheep's clothing. The very essence of evil. The ones who deserve your consideration are the children and their parents, who have suffered these atrocious wrongs, these sickening assaults on their bodies and souls. And they will continue to suffer from them for the rest of their lives. What about *their* life sentences, the life sentences inflicted on them by Virginia Montrose and Marvin Smith?"

"They say we presented no evidence. Who do they think they're kidding? Do they think you didn't hear those seven children come to the stand and tell what Virginia Montrose and Marvin Smith did to them? Uncontroverted testimony. The defense cannot overcome that evidence. Mr. Hartley kept babbling about reasonable doubt, reasonable doubt, on and on. Those children's testimony is way beyond reasonable doubt. It eliminates *all* doubt. 'Out of the mouths of babes the truth will come.'

He walked to the prosecution table. Tarwater handed him one of the bound volumes of trial transcript. He read Misty's testimony about what Virginia and Marvin had done to her, then snapped the book shut.

"The defense uses lots of evasive words, but they all amount to calling little Misty a liar. You saw and heard that poor little girl. A not-guilty verdict will be worse than a slap in her face. It will be an assault, another grievous wound, a knife in the heart. A not-guilty verdict will crush these parents and their lovely children who have come before you seeking justice. Please believe the children. Save our children."

CHAPTER ❧ 88

Guilty, GUILTY, GUILTY, GUILTY, GUILTY, GUILTY.

Again and again and again. All counts of the indictment. O'Keefe heard a moan. Recognized the voice. Kelly. But the great mass of the gallery exploded in cheers, stomped their feet, stood, applauded. Tarwater squeezed Dolinar's shoulder and grinned toward the defense table, gloating, the first smile O'Keefe had ever seen from her. Snyder kept pounding his gavel to no avail. Annie wept. Kelly wept. Strangely, Maura did not, just stared straight ahead. Not shocked. Angry. Hartley looked like he might scream or that his head might burst. And O'Keefe—he was a boy once more. In church again. Good Friday. The Stations of the Cross. *He was condemned to death ... The cross was laid upon him ... He fell the first time ...*

Fools. They had dared to hope. It was like your own death, a reality inevitable but still too overwhelming to believe and accept, deep down, that it would actually happen.

The calmest person in the room seemed to be the defendant. The pundits would misinterpret this as sociopathic remorselessness when it actually stemmed from a grief so powerful it strangled the words before they could even form to be spoken, the tears before they could even well up. The guards rushed forward and grabbed her—in unseemly haste, O'Keefe thought, and too roughly—and he had to restrain himself from leaping to her rescue. "We'll win on appeal, Virginia," Hartley called out to her as they hustled her out, provoking a disapproving stroke of Snyder's gavel.

After the tumult faded, Snyder thanked the jury for their service and dismissed them. O'Keefe looked over his shoulder. Annie and Kelly were gone. He wanted to escape himself and wondered if Maura and Scott felt the same way, but a rigid decorum and protocol was expected in the playing of this part of the game. They were even expected to mouth bullshit phrases like, "We respect the jury's verdict…"

But they would not do that. Not in this case.

"Clear the courtroom," Snyder told the security personnel lined along the back and sides of the room. Occasional whoops and hollers could be heard as the crowd shuffled out. Ralph Merkel was not interfered with as he made his way against the crowd to the prosecution table. He first hugged Dolinar who complied but remained rigid, unenthusiastic. It wasn't just that Dolinar despised Merkel. This was over now, his duty done. Time to move on to the next assignment, the next batch of prisoners to be condemned. But Tarwater, Hicks, and Brinkley responded eagerly, gleefully to Ralph's embrace.

"I have to go try to interview the jurors," Maura said, without her usual lilt, all steel. "Fucking idiots."

Snyder stood behind his chair until the courtroom had cleared. Only Hartley and O'Keefe remained within the bar, sitting, still stunned, at the counsel table. Could that actually be a look of compassion on his face? O'Keefe thought of Captain Vere in *Billy Budd*. But surely not…

"Let them stay," he told the bailiff and disappeared into his chambers.

Hartley sat staring ahead. O'Keefe didn't know whether to remain or leave and kept trying to come up with something helpful to say.

"Scott," a voice said.

Hartley looked up toward the speaker standing beside him. "Here to gloat, Lou, you piece of shit?" He dove from his chair, spit flying and fists flailing, into Rockwell's chest, tackled him, pinned him to the floor, and pummeled at him, trying to drive his fists through Rockwell's arms crossed protectively in front of his face. O'Keefe tried to pull Hartley off. The bailiff followed close behind, took over from O'Keefe, yanked Hartley up, slammed him back down in his chair, and hovered over him to make sure he stayed put.

Hartley seemed dazed, not quite in mental touch with what he had just done.

Rockwell sat on the floor, mopping at his bloody nose with his necktie. "I just wanted to offer my condolences … try to comfort him … He's my friend."

O'Keefe helped Rockwell to his feet and led him out of the courtroom while Rockwell kept looking back at Hartley. At the door Rockwell said, "Just tell him all I was trying to do was offer some help. If he wants me to, I'll help … with the appeal … or whatever."

He left then, and O'Keefe returned to the counsel table. The bailiff still stood over Hartley.

Hartley, as if hypnotized, stood and waited for someone to tell him the next thing he should do.

"Am I under arrest?"

"No, sir. But I need to close up here. I have to ask you to leave."

O'Keefe walked slowly a few steps ahead, which prompted Hartley to follow.

Snyder's courtroom was located off a side hallway that niched off from the main corridor. They sat on a wooden bench built into the wall, Scott still in a trance-like state.

O'Keefe let him be for a few minutes, then said, "What's next?"

Still locked in his straight-ahead stare, Hartley said, "Nothing. That's what. Nothing. I'm so sick of this shit. Just about everyone I've ever defended was guilty. Some of them I got a good deal on a plea they didn't deserve. Some of them I won their cases, which they didn't deserve. And here I had someone completely, entirely, one hundred percent innocent, the most deserving person in the world. And that asshole Snyder will pile it on her. She'll never get out. Or she'll be so old it won't be worth getting out."

"You'll turn it around on appeal, right?"

"Somebody might. Not me. I need to get out of the way so they have a clear shot at an ineffective assistance of counsel claim."

"No."

"Yes. They have to. I've argued it myself, I don't know how many times, on an appeal. It's very effective. Trash the guy who tried the case. Now I'm the trash. The last time I'll appear in the law books will be for that."

"Only if you quit. And this is all bullshit. You were valiant, man. What could they possibly pick on that you did wrong?"

Hartley's face went from trance to contempt. "You've been around lawyers too long to say something stupid like that."

"The deck was stacked," O'Keefe said. "I understand what you're going through," O'Keefe said, "but buck up, boyo. Won't do you any good to feel sorry for yourself."

"It's her I'm sorry for. Nobody else. She's all that matters. Me? I'm done. With all of it. I'm broke anyway. Might as well close up shop and find something more useful to do."

It seemed there was no consoling him, so O'Keefe said, "Let's go. I'm tired of this ugly-ass building."

The old Hartley would have chuckled at that. This one just looked up at the walls and the ceiling as if he were seeing the place for the first time. "No. I'll stay here for a while."

O'Keefe stood up, trying to figure out whether and how to leave.

"Where's Lou?" Hartley asked.

"Gone."

"I need to apologize."

O'Keefe made his way out of the courthouse, hoping he would not encounter Rhonda Tarwater there again. He might do something quite ungentlemanly.

The bailiff, going home for the day, rode the elevator with him. "You might want to know," he said, "the judge lifted the contempt order on your reporter buddy. He's already been released."

GEORGE BUSH DRUBS
MICHAEL DUKAKIS IN THE 1988
PRESIDENTIAL ELECTION.

CHAPTER ❦ 89

PASCHAL MCKENNA COULD not help thinking of one of his favorite poets, William Blake ("There we wander, there we weep"), as he was himself near weeping as he wandered along the streets near the jail, wondering where he might sleep that night.

Large flakes of wet snow danced madly in the swirling wind. Luckily, it was early in the season and they wouldn't stick, but he was still damn cold in his thin leather jacket and knew the flakes would ultimately soak him if he stayed outside too long.

He carried in his left hand a small bag with a few personal items they had thrust at him on his release and in his right hand a crumpled sheaf of writings he had composed during his incarceration. Included in these writings was his own five-page "J'Accuse" on the Montrose-Smith case.

J'ACCUSE (I ACCUSE)
BY
PASCHAL MCKENNA

I write of an American tragedy.

Virginia Montrose ("Miss Ginny" to her students) will soon surely be sentenced to a horribly long prison sentence for sexual molestation of children under her care (likely thirty-five years, five years for each of the seven children she was found guilty of molesting). This action completed a legal lynching of an innocent woman and her co-defendant. While one can hope that someday the appellate courts will rectify this injustice, her life is in ruins. If her conviction is overturned, it will likely occur only years from now and after the expenditure of much blood and treasure—someone's anyway; not Ginny's, as she has lost everything and will now be dependent entirely on the kindness of strangers.

If her conviction is overturned, it will not release from prison her co-defendant, Marvin Smith, the African American janitor at the school where both defendants worked. The two were accused of falling into a sexual relationship, and with Miss Ginny as the impresario, sexually abusing some of the children including in Satanic rituals. Mr. Smith, looking ahead in the midst of the trial and foreseeing and fearing the likely outcome, chose to plead guilty (without, however, admitting guilt, a so-called "Alford plea"). As a result, he is serving a prison sentence of up to ten years. So far, his gamble seems to have paid off. But this is a long game. If somehow Ginny's conviction is overturned, Mr. Smith will not be released unless he is able to persuade the governor to exonerate him.

Their trial featured not one but two of the hysteria-inducing issues—Satanic panic and moral panic—that have bedeviled us (please excuse the irresistible pun)— in this "low, dishonest decade" (W.H. Auden, "September 1, 1939") that has now descended so much lower and more deeply corrupt with this trial and others like it sprouting like festering plague sores all over the body politic. The different races of the defendants also offered a miscegenation overlay that surely disturbed and brought to surface lingering but powerful strains of racial paranoia buried not so deep in our national psyche.

This has reminded me of another trial, this one in France in the late nineteenth century, when a Jewish officer in the French army named Alfred Dreyfus was framed, convicted, and imprisoned by his military superiors for treason. As the disturbing facts of the case were slowly publicly revealed, the great French writer, Emile Zola, wrote a notorious open letter to the President of the French Republic, in which he publicly accused ("J'accuse") various French officials of high crimes for their roles in the persecution of Dreyfus.

While this author is about as far from possessing the status and talent of Emile Zola as can be imagined, and the chances of the President of our own Republic (or perhaps hardly anyone else for that matter) reading this are nil, one must do his duty when (however belatedly), where (however obscurely), and how (however ineptly) that one can.

What caused this American tragedy?

Child sexual abuse is a serious problem in our country that was long ignored. But we know that the overwhelming number of those crimes occur within the family circle or family acquaintances, not in our day care and preschool facilities.

I ACCUSE: The authorities, our so-called "public servants," including the police department, the local

Task Force On Satanic Or Other Cult-Based Or Ritual Crimes, and our state's Child Protective Agency for ignoring the real problem and inventing non-existent crimes supposedly committed by day care providers and preschool teachers and workers like "Miss Ginny" Montrose and Marvin Smith. (Such crimes may indeed sometimes be committed in childcare facilities, but we shall never know how many actual such crimes have gone and will in the future go undetected due to the energy and resources diverted to false accusations. And, later, when the inevitable backlash from those false accusations inevitably occurs, the resulting distrust of the authorities will make it more difficult to identify and pursue actual culprits.)

I ACCUSE: The vaunted Task Force and other law enforcement of bowing to the sensationalistic tabloid press and the pop culture purveyors of hysterical and mostly false stories of so-called Satanic crimes. Failing to find any real such crimes, they desperately set upon the respected, respectable, and entirely innocent Operation Go! school and its employees.

I ACCUSE: The social workers and so-called therapists, grasping for their share of the flood of federal dollars pouring into the sector during his decade. Fueled by careerist ambitions and the hunger for publicity and praise for their "crusading" efforts to protect children, they (1) covered themselves with an aura of social "science" when there was no scientific basis whatsoever, only mere speculative notions, supporting the theories that underpinned their efforts to ferret out abuse, (2) blighted the lives of many children by convincing them, including by means of so-called "recovered memory" therapies, that they had been sexually abused when they had not, (3) planted false stories in children's minds and persuaded them through now-discredited techniques (techniques that were themselves in many instances abusive to the children they were purporting to "save") to regurgitate those stories to snare and prosecute and imprison innocent caregivers, and (4) shattered so many lives of those they falsely accused.

I ACCUSE: The aforementioned authorities and therapists of broadly publicizing their doctrines and supposed "findings" to a too-eager sensationalistic media.

I ACCUSE: The mainstream media that became no better than the tabloid media by eagerly accepting, casting all journalistic professionalism aside and eagerly accepting the salacious stories that were fed them, then broadly spinning them to a prurient public with no concern for the presumption of innocence, due process, or fair trials.

I ACCUSE: The prosecutors in the Montrose-Smith case and many other cases of failing to do their primary duty of "seeking justice." Whether to advance their careers, pander to the howling mob, or out of a misguided fanatic zeal, instead of seeking justice, they merely sought convictions, and turned our criminal justice system into something closer to the Spanish Inquisition or the Salem witch trials than a tribunal to discover truth and do justice.

I ACCUSE: Those Judges, like Judge Harold Snyder in Virginia Montrose's case, whose function in our theoretically even-handed system of justice, is to ensure a fair trial but, instead, cowardly pandered to the mob. In Judge Snyder's case, he made so many rulings hamstringing the defense that a not-guilty verdict would have been miraculous if not utterly impossible. He is likely now to steep his hands deeper in Miss Ginny's blood with the viciously harsh sentence he is almost certain to impose. Instead, may mercy move him to do otherwise.

I ACCUSE: Those elements of the public that eagerly seek out, beg for, and greedily devour the garbage produced by the fanatical, the prurient, the purveyors of outlandish rumors, half-truths, conspiracy mongering, and outright lies. The embrace of such baseness degrades our world and prepares us to believe the worst and do the worst.

I ACCUSE: Every person who knew or sensed that something was wrong and simply shrugged it off, every person who neither did nor said anything to protest or counteract it in any way. The politicians, the media, the prosecutors, and Judge Snyder should have been inundated with objections to the obvious atrociousness of their proceedings. Our streets should have been full of protesters demanding due process and fair trials. Instead, the only voices heard were the shouts of the witch hunters.

I ACCUSE: Finally, and most of all, the author of this article, a man who was in a position to raise his voice to call attention to the injustice being perpetrated and perhaps even somehow alter its tragic course. But he had compromised his reputation and thus his effectiveness by living a life of too much self-pity and self-indulgence, this man who made no effort to control his addictions and other demons but let them control him. So, when the need arose, when the victims cried out and the opportunity to come to their aid appeared, the man lacked the status and stature to raise a voice of any power. One really must do so much better than that. One must live at least in such a way that he can be somewhat useful in dark times like our own.

He intended to take those pages that night to a large but shabby looking old Victorian house in town where *The Sentinel,* a local weekly newspaper with a "countercultural" bent and minimal readership maintained its "offices," such as they were. He was thinking that, after all, he had only recently been a well-regarded reporter at the major newspaper in the city, and if this piece excited them, they might publish it. And if they were sufficiently impressed, wanted more like this, they might even hire him, even pay him enough to have a leaky roof over his head and a few crusts of bread to eat. But given that he no longer had a place of abode, had now become "unaccommodated man," mainly he hoped they would just allow him that night to sleep in a back room, or if not that, on their front porch. He didn't have enough cash to pay for a cab, but he did have enough for a phone call, and a phone booth would also provide a brief respite from the cold, and the wind, and the snow.

CHAPTER ⇒ 90

DRIVING TO THE office from the courthouse, O'Keefe had to admit, guiltily, that despite this tragedy, his shoulders felt light, a burden lifted, and the road in the windshield before him seemed, despite the swirling snowflakes, wide, well lit, welcoming.

He could get back to real work now and was ready to immerse himself in it immediately. He felt better walking through his office door into his reception room than he had in months. It was after five, but all of them had gone, unusually early for this group, as if they knew he was likely coming and thought it best to leave him alone.

Sara had left a note on his chair. "I'm sure you are in pain. I don't know what to say except that my heart goes out. But we are glad (exceedingly) to have you back. There's a gift for you in the conference room."

Gift? He couldn't imagine. Opening the conference room door, he beheld his gift. Papers. Papers all over. Covering the conference room table and the credenza behind it. Stacked along the walls. Barely a path left to walk in. A four-by-four-foot banner pinned to the wall, hand printed with magic marker, said, "I'M DYING HERE!"

On the floor, a few steps from the door, she had lain a longer note, presumably so it would not be lost to his notice among all the other papers. The note listed briefly the many questionable transactions, suspected frauds, and fraudulent transfers bobbing to the surface in the wake of the failure of Enterprise Bank, the project she had started with Harrigan about the time he had disappeared into Ginny's case. This sorry mess of papers lifted his soul. They were as sturdy to him as the bricks in this building where he'd chosen to locate his firm. In these papers and papers like them was the world he wanted to grow into and the vehicle through which he could travel there.

He returned to his office. A blinking red light on his phone signaled voicemails. And for the first time in months he wasn't afraid to listen to them.

The first was from Maura. If she'd not said, "It's Maura," he might not have recognized her. No "Hi!" No lilt. No bubble. Bitter. She'd spoken to the jurors. In a contemptuous, mocking singsong she mimicked, "They believed the children. They thought some of it may have been made up, but something really bad must have happened. Kids couldn't make up stuff like that. Not all of it. And the police and Mortimer and crew may have been too aggressive, but that can't explain everything. Like that poor little girl Misty and her mom, who herself didn't believe originally. And why else would that Marvin Smith have plead guilty? ...Idiots."

The second one: "It's Grady from Global. Sounds snappy, doesn't it? Grady from Global. But enough of that. Sorry to hear it, man. And selfishly sorry too. Call me as soon as you can. I'll explain when you call back."

When O'Keefe called, Grady said, "First thing, who was Paschal's source?"

"Only Paschal knows.

"He won't even tell *you?*"

"Not even me."

"He's way down on his luck, I hear. Wonder how much he'd take for the information?"

"I know that's your M.O., Grady, but not everyone is for sale."

"How about if we gave him a job?"

"I don't think he'll accept that or any other currency including thirty pieces of silver."

"Okay..."

"Is that a surrender, Grady? I don't believe it."

"Hell no. My mind is buzzing with ideas. Perhaps kidnapping and holding hostage a loved one?"

"I don't think he has any right now. He probably hasn't been very lovable most of his life."

"Okay. For now anyway. I'm not giving up on Paschal and his source. I might need it for our case."

"'Our case'?"

"Yes, sir. Here's one for you in the realm of supremest—is that a word? supremest?—if not, it should be. In any event, supremist irony. What is 'irony' anyway? Is this irony? It turns out that we recently bought the company that carried the coverage on Operation Go!. Our so-good-friend Perry Slotkin wasted no time. He filed this very day, two floors down from your courtroom at the clerk's office, not more than minutes after the verdicts.

"And here's the most deliciously ironic dish of them all. They want to hire you for the investigative work. The very thing that made you a non grata persona, or however you say that, has now cleansed you thoroughly, and supremely ... *supremest* ... qualified you for the investigative work on these civil cases in which we find ourselves now embroiled."

It didn't excite him at all, only made him more weary. "No way. Can't do it."

"Surely you jest."

"Not a bit."

"Is this a grudge you're holding against us about Bart Yarborough?"

"I do hold one, at least a small one, but that's not it. I've been flailing around up to my nose in this shit for months. It's enough for a lifetime. Too much actually."

"Lots of work. Generous fees. Plus a chance to open the pipeline here wide and full. Can you really afford to pass that up?"

"Probably not. But there's a line in some book somewhere that I read a long time ago that stuck with me. 'The wish to hear such baseness is degrading.' No pun on your name intended."

"That's okay. Call me De-Grady. De-Grady from Global. I like the ring of that. But you're just having a bad day. I should have waited to talk to you. Wait a few days and give me your answer then."

"You'll be wasting those days, Grady."

"I can afford them."

"I never want to hear the word molestation or the words for sexual organs again. I never again want to see a beautiful little girl on the witness stand pathetically describing with heartbreaking clarity and unshakeable certainty a despicable violation —*that never happened.*"

"We're likely to settle these cases. Can't afford to go to trial and get tagged. But there'll be plenty of action before that."

"Slotkin won't let you off easy. It'll probably go all the way to jury selection before he's satisfied he's squeezed all he can out of you. "

"Right. That's why we need a great investigator."

"You know where that bullshit will get you. What you need is a great lawyer. Have you hired one yet?"

"Nope. Just got my list out."

"You ought to think about Scott Hartley. He's damn good and obviously has plenty of relevant experience."

"But he's just a criminal guy."

"He's done some civil. I'm telling you, he'd be a good choice, maybe the best."

"I'll think about it. He'd have a better chance if his investigator agreed to work on the case along with him."

He was willing to help Scott but not that much. "Not to change the subject, but to change the subject, and speaking of a grudge, how's Mrs. Yarborough doing?"

"Since we're still paying her per your idea, which remains a good one by the way, *she's* doing fine. *Us* not so well. Your friend Niles Panderman hasn't done much for us, though you'd think the opposite if you totaled up the bills."

"I'd definitely work on that one. I never knew anything about Panama before. Interesting place."

"Take on the other, and you might get it back. In fact, I can predict with nearly absolutist certainty that you will get it back."

"The word is 'absolute.' You're a foul capitalist corrupter, De-Grady. But I repeat, 'the wish—'"

"Keep that crap to yourself. I haven't read a book in decades. I'm waiting for you until next Monday at noon. High noon. Good movie, by the way. 'Do not forsake me, oh my darling.' That's my song to you."

He was at his door about to turn out the light and leave when the phone rang. He couldn't help himself. He returned to his desk and answered it on the fourth ring.

"They let me out."

"How are you?"

"Perfectly fine for a penniless pauper with nothing but this phone booth for a roof over my head."

"How can I help?"

"No help needed. Not right now anyway. Maybe later. The only reason I called is to tell you that I hope you know I'd've been glad to stay in there a lot longer if I could've traded that for a not guilty."

"I believe you. You're a natural prisoner."

"I'm wondering. Are you blaming me right now?"

"Not at all. Are you blaming yourself?"

"No. I'm one hundred percent sure my source had nothing more to offer. It was right not to expose them to the 'slings and arrows of outrageous fortune,' as some scribbler once said. But I'm still having trouble not blaming myself."

"You shouldn't … blame yourself, that is. Catholic guilt. It sticks even when you 'fall away,' as they say. But it can be useful. Keep thinking about it. It may not be too late."

"Sadly, we find ourselves enmeshed in an American tragedy."

"What's next for you?"

"I have a plan. Remember J'accuse? I've written my own version."

"Maybe you'll end up Zola after all."

"You ever read the *Sentinel?*"

"Once in a while, when I can find it."

"Watch for it the next couple of weeks. It might be in there."

"'Fraid that's like the tree falling in the forest. Nobody there."

"That's bullshit. The tree still falls."

"I'll give you that."

"I'm wondering why you haven't brought up what I know must be on your mind."

"I guess I'm afraid of the answer."

"Don't be. Not yet, anyway. A day at a time."

"Good. And I'll be here. Anytime, anywhere."

"Appreciated. Oh, one more thing. You know I've been trying to write the great American novel…well, *any* novel, really…and not getting anywhere. But I really think might have it now."

CHAPTER ⇗ 91

KELLY.

Without really knowing what he was doing, or at least not wanting to admit what he was doing, he had avoided thinking about her since he'd heard her cry out when the verdict was read. Yes, a lot had been going on, Hartley's attack on Rockwell only the start of it. Maybe deep down he wanted a small space of time away from this thing, this thing that had drained so much from him and ended so badly. And maybe also because he couldn't think of any real and honest comfort to offer her, couldn't conjure up even a drop of glue to help mend the crack in her heart that her outcry had made manifest. But he would at least need to try.

It bothered him that the heavy inner front door of Annie's house was open and the outer glass door unlocked. She still failed to appreciate the danger, which might still be lurking. He knocked instead of going straight in, not wanting to scare her or be presumptuous. It was not his right to be so familiar.

Karma was the first to answer the door. The dog might have normally been expected to greet O'Keefe with pricked ears and a tail wag or two, but today he seemed even more solemn and dignified than usual, as if this special animal had by osmosis detected, absorbed, and internalized the emanations of grief from the human occupants of the house. Annie came behind Karma, her face bloated from crying, and opened the glass door.

O'Keefe said nothing, but his face was a question mark. Annie answered, "She's upstairs. In her bedroom since we came home. Inconsolable."

"I only came because I suppose I'm supposed to. I have no idea what to say."

"Just be with her for a while. It can only help. She'll recover somehow. Don't we all? I'll go get her. I'll stay upstairs."

He stood in the living room, waiting for her. Karma stood too, alert, waiting to be called by someone to do something. He heard her footfalls coming slowly down the stairs. As soon as she saw him, she ran at him, lunged into him so hard she almost knocked him backward, buried her head in his solar plexus, crying, then sobbing in wracking, rising waves until she was convulsing against him. It scared him. He squeezed her hard as if that might tame her somehow, which it partly did, enough so he could lead her to the couch, awkwardly set them both down, her head in his chest, their arms locked around each other.

She finally cried herself out and leaned back from him and said, "How could this be? How could God let this be?"

"You did your best. We did our best. It's an ugly world a lot of the time, and all we can do is the best we can. You did that, the best you could."

She shook her head violently back and forth. "No, no, no. What about Miss Ginny and Mr. Smith? What about *them?*"

From the mouths of babes. From this little girl (for he still thought of her as a little girl). What about Miss Ginny and Mr. Smith? There was really nothing to be said to that, certainly not, "You did your best."

What about *them?*

All the rest was pablum and platitudes.

On the drive to his house, he struggled to find something more uplifting to say to her that was not in truth a shitload of phony wishful thinking. But there would be an appeal, and the appeal might even be won. The lives of Ginny and Marvin had been ruined. For now. Maybe forever. But maybe not forever. It was hard to imagine anyone that could have been more buried alive than Colonel Dreyfus on Devil's Island. That guy had *nothing* left.

Except Emile Zola.

Still driving, he called their house. Annie answered. He asked for Kelly.

"She may have fallen asleep."

"If she has, please wake her."

"Hello. Dad?" Her voice, weak, all cried out.

"I'm going to get you a book," he said. "It's about a man in France named Dreyfus who after his trial was in many ways even in worse shape than Ginny and Mr. Smith are now. He was sent to a horrible place called Devil's Island, under constant guard, and he was very ill, almost every creature comfort denied him for years. But certain people, including a great writer named Emile Zola, fought for him, and they ultimately vindicated and freed him."

"When?" she said, a slight lilt in her voice now.

"As soon as I can get my hands on it."

"Thanks, Dad."

Kelly hung up and turned to Annie standing near her and obviously curious about the call.

"He's giving me a book. About a man even worse off than Ginny and Mr. Smith are now. And people, including a famous writer, fought for him and saved him."

"Well, good. Does that make you feel better?"

"Maybe."

Annie escorted her up the stairs, helped her into bed, pulled up the covers. At the door, before she turned out the light, she said, "I was thinking. It's coming soon. I wonder if we should invite him to Thanksgiving dinner this year."

Kelly sat up. "Really? Let's call him now."

"Whoa there. It's just a thought. I need to do a little more thinking." And, she thought, *Maybe we can all together figure out something to be thankful about.*

It was full dark when he pulled into his driveway. He drove around the circle drive to his front door. He was so weary he was not sure he wanted even to bother to leave the car and go into the house. Why not simply lean his head back and sleep right there? He'd forgotten that morning, maybe for the last several mornings, to turn on the front light. Exhausted and shattered as he was, he still should be careful not to let his guard down. He moved quickly from the car to the house. When he stepped onto the porch, he stepped on something. Something oddly soft. He unlocked the door and turned on the light. A furry thing. He squatted down and examined it. A bunny, not much more than a baby. A congealing pool of blood underneath it. He pushed on it with his index and middle finger. Its open eyes bulged slightly from the pressure. Its throat had been slashed.

He picked it up. Not much blood. It was such a tiny thing. He took it into the kitchen, wrapped it in a paper towel and laid it in the refrigerator. He was not sure why he did that. Maybe he would show it to someone. Maybe to the police. They wouldn't care. Maybe to Lieutenant Ross at least. Maybe it would trouble his waters some.

How about Annie's waters? He hurried, a near run to the phone.

"Yes," she answered. He controlled the panic in his voice. He wouldn't tell her about the bunny. Treat it lightly. Just try to get her to be careful.

"Hey, Thorns, when I came there tonight, your damn front door was unlocked. You really need to be more careful. You always worry about Kelly being with me. What about when she's with you?"

He waited for her to jab him. But she said, "Fair point. I'll do better."

He hung up, feeling the same despair he had felt on Halloween. The bunny's was not the only death to mourn this night.

Signs and portents. What to do now? He could only come up with one thing. Start pushing the boulder back up the hill.

Hartley seemed to really mean that he intended to quit. Quit everything. A man of integrity in a system that had lost its way. Even if Hartley changed his mind about all that, he was broke, his practice plummeted to zero. He would need help.

It was too late to bother Harrigan at home, so he called his office and left a message on the voicemail, so Harrigan would have to think about it some before automatically saying no.

"Hey, brother knight. It's time to come off that bench. We need you … and you need us even more."

THE END

I want to announce publicly that as a firm believer of the Believe The Children movement of the 1980s, that started with the McMartin trials in California, I am now convinced that I was terribly wrong ... and many innocent people were convicted and went to prison as a result. And I am equally positive [that the] repressed memory therapy movement is also a bunch of crap.

Geraldo Rivera, 1995

Overzealous intervenors ... can include parents, family members, foster parents, doctors, therapists, social workers, law enforcement officers, prosecutors, and any combination thereof. Victims have been subtly as well as overtly rewarded and bribed by usually well-meaning intervenors for furnishing further details. In addition, some of what appears not to have happened may have originated as a result of intervenors making assumptions about or misinterpreting what the victims are saying. The intervenors then repeat, and possibly embellish, these assumptions and misinterpretations, and eventually the victims are 'forced' to agree with or come to accept this 'official' version of what happened. ... If the guilty are to be successfully prosecuted, if the innocent are to be exonerated, and if the victims are to be protected and treated, better methods to evaluate and explain allegations of "ritual" child abuse must be developed or identified. Until this is done, the controversy will continue to cast a shadow over and fuel the backlash against the validity and reality of child sexual abuse.

Kenneth V. Lanning, Supervisory Special Agent
Behavioral Science Unit, National Center for the
Analysis of Violent Crime, Federal Bureau
of Investigation, INVESTIGATOR'S GUIDE
TO ALLEGATIONS OF "RITUAL "CHILD
ABUSE, pp. 23, 40, January 1992

The greatest dangers to liberty lurk in insidious encroachment by men of zeal, well-meaning but without understanding.

Louis D. Brandeis, 1928

Whoever can make you believe absurdities can make you commit atrocities.

Voltaire, 1765

AFTERWORD, DEDICATION, ACKNOWLEDGMENTS

A NYONE FAMILIAR WITH my personal history and previous writings might be surprised by my choice of subject matter in this book. I have for some years been extensively involved with an international organization whose primary mission is the global eradication of child sexual exploitation. Villainous sexual predators of children were featured in *Mink Eyes* (Arjuna Books, 2019) (the first book in the O'Keefe series) and even more so in my novella *Dewdrops* (included in my collection of short fiction, *Dewdrops* (Arjuna Books, 2019)).

But I have found there can be another side to the child sexual-abuse story—the possibility of public hysteria, false witness, wrongful convictions, and long, crushing imprisonments of the innocent. My purpose in the Peter O'Keefe series is to tell stories that carry us from the mid-1980s to the present day, that try to shed light on such questions as, "What has happened to us and how did we get here?" by following the fictional lives and adventures of Peter O'Keefe and the assorted characters in his orbit as they navigate through the dramatic transformations and the scams, schemes, and scandals of our era. In pursuing this enterprise, I found it impossible to ignore what has been called the "Satanic Panic" and the related "Moral Panic" that gripped the U.S. in the 1980s and 1990s. This episode taught us many lessons then and may still speak directly and poignantly to us now, including offering cautionary tales for our contemplation as we struggle to comprehend, then mend, our shredding contemporary social and political fabric.

Although stimulated by certain actual events of the 1980s and 1990s, except for certain specific and obvious references to

424   ⇒ AN AMERICAN TRAGEDY

real people and events, such as the "news headlines" that appear at various points in the book describing somewhat random events that occurred in 1988, the description of the Geraldo Rivera broadcast of October 25, 1988, and a few other references to real people (for example, George Bush, Manuel Noriega), legal cases (for example, *Batson*, *Loving*), situations (for example, the McMartin trial in California and the Kelly Michaels trial in New Jersey), and conditions (the broiling heat of that cruel summer), this is entirely a work of fiction in which all of the characters, organizations, and events portrayed are either products of the author's imagination or used fictitiously. Unless expressly stated otherwise, any resemblance to actual events, locales, or persons, living or dead, is unintended.

Nevertheless, this fictional work, while always remaining exactly that, has been substantially inspired and informed by the nonfiction writings and other efforts of certain journalists, social commentators, researchers, therapists, lawyers, and others who sounded the alarm and came to the defense of the wrongly accused and convicted in the 1980s and 1990s, succeeding in many cases in overturning convictions and somewhat turning the general tide, establishing at least far greater caution and far more careful techniques and procedures in the identification, investigation, and prosecution of such allegations. This book will hopefully serve as a modest dedication to the work of those stalwarts including those identified below.

For those who wish to explore the actual history of what has been referred to as the "Satanic Panic" or "Moral Panic" or "Ritual Abuse Panic" of the era, I suggest the following book-length nonfiction works, which are listed by author in alphabetical order and with apologies to those worthy writers I have inadvertently omitted: Richard Beck, *Believe the Children;* Stephen J. Ceci and Maggie Bruck, *Jeopardy In The Courtroom;* Mary de Young, *The Day Care Ritual Abuse Moral Panic;* Paul and Shirley Eberle, *The Abuse Of Innocence;* Robert D. Hicks, *The Pursuit of Satan;* Phillip Jenkins, *Moral Panic;* Kenneth V. Lanning, *Investigator's Guide to Allegations of Ritual Abuse* and *Love, Bombs, and Molesters;* Matthew LeRoy & Deric Haddad, *They Must Be Monsters;* Debbie Nathan and Michael Snedeker, *Satan's Silence;* Debra A. Poole and Michael E. Lamb,

Investigative Interviews of Children; Dorothy Rabinowitz, *No Crueler Tyrannies;* Bernard Rosenthal, *Justice in Ohio;* Robert Rosenthal *State of New Jersey v. Margaret Kelly Michaels,* An Overview, *Psychology, Public Policy, and Law,I 1,* 247-271 [Robert Rosenthal was the lawyer who won the Michaels appeal and also that of Grant Snowden in Florida], Lawrence Wright, *Remembering Satan.*

There are also many superb journalistic pieces not cited here as well as numerous published legal opinions arising from the various prosecutions that are well worth reading.

It should be noted that Debbie Nathan and Dorothy Rabinowitz, for example, first raised the alarms on all of this as journalists, Nathan in *The Village Voice* and Rabinowitz, in *Harper's* and *The Wall Street Journal.* In addition to their efforts, deserving of special mention is the six-part series in 1988 in the Memphis *Commercial Appeal* by reporters T. Charlier and S. Downing that reported on thirty-six different cases across the country.

Cinematic treatments of the subject include the television movie *Indictment: The McMartin Trial* (1995) produced by Oliver Stone and Abby Mann and the especially poignant documentary *Freeing Bernie Baran* (2010).

Those who wish to explore "the other side of the issue" (one that in many respects I personally do not agree with) may wish to consult Ross E. Cheit, *The Witch-Hunt Narrative;* Patricia Crowley, *Not My Child;* Lisa Manshel, *Nap Time.*

The "headlines" appearing at various places in the text are derived from my review of *The Kansas City Times* and *Kansas City Star* for each day during the time period of the fictional events in the book, roughly June to mid-November 1988. They are roughly though not perfectly in chronological order.

As I have done before, I apologize to the comma sticklers of the world for not strictly following commas placement "rules." If I think a comma either interrupts the rhythm of a sentence or obscures a meaning rather than clarifies it, I don't use it. On the other hand, there are situations, especially in dialogue, where I use a comma where the "rules" don't require it as a momentary pause in the speech.

Also, as in previous books, there are occasional unattributed quotations from Shakespeare, Wordsworth, Dante and perhaps others that I have not attributed either because it would destroy the effect, or it should be obvious from the archaic language that it is not mine, or to allow those who enjoy such things to "catch" them.

Many thanks to my editors Ericka McIntyre, Louise Harnby, and Travis Tynan. They made this a better book in so many ways and cannot be blamed when I didn't understand or stubbornly ignored their advice, a comment that applies also to the following:

Rene L. Valladares, the Federal Public Defender for the District of Nevada and the author of the bestselling *A Defender's Guide to Federal Evidence* for reviewing and commenting on drafts of the trial portions of the book (which, of course, was most of it). I also note that, in October 2023, Rene was presented the National Association of Criminal Defense Lawyers Champion of Justice Award, bestowed on individuals "who—through legislative, journalistic, philanthropic, or humanitarian pursuits—have staunchly preserved or defended the constitutional rights of individuals in the United States and have endeavored to ensure justice and due process for persons accused of crime."

And thank you to my good and smart friends who were kind enough to read drafts of the book and provide me their insights: Ann Darke, Bill Hale, and Chris Parrott. A special appreciation in this regard goes to Gina Harman who had most at risk in delivering a candid assessment.

Thanks also to Miladinka Milic of www.milagraphicartist.com, Aimee Ravichandran of Abundantly Social, Mickey Mikkelson of Creative Edge, and Deena Rae of eBookBuilders for their respective "midwife" services in delivering this infant into the world.

My daughter has been an essential companion at arms in these late literary adventures that have now brought forth six books in the last few years. She was indispensable in every aspect of the creation of this book from notion to idea to numerous drafts to book design, proofing, final publication, and marketing. Meghan, I know of a certain lady that would be delighted and exceedingly proud of both of us. Thank you.

DAN FLANIGAN

Dan Flanigan is a novelist, playwright, poet, and practicing lawyer. He holds a Ph.D. in History from Rice University and J.D. from the University of Houston. He taught Jurisprudence at the University of Houston and American Legal History at the University of Virginia. His first published book was his Ph.D. dissertation, <u>The Criminal Law of Slavery and Freedom, 1800- 1868</u>.

He moved on from academia to serve the civil rights cause as a school desegregation lawyer, followed by a long career as a finance attorney in private law practice. He became a name partner in the Polsinelli law firm in Kansas City, created its Financial Services practice, chaired its Real Estate & Financial Services Department for two decades, and established the firm's New York City office and served as its managing partner until October 2022. His legal bio may be viewed at <u>https://www. polsinelli.com/dan-flanigan</u>.

Taking a break from the law practice for two years, he and his wife, Candy, established Sierra Tucson, a prominent alcohol and drug treatment center located in Tucson, Arizona.

Recently, he has been able to turn his attention to his lifelong ambition—creative writing. In 2019 he released a literary trifecta including *Mink Eyes*, the first in the Peter O'Keefe series,

Dewdrops, a collection of shorter fiction, and *Tenebrae: A Memoir of Love and Death*.

Tenebrae is a bracelet of verse and prose poems dedicated to his wife, Candy, to honor her last illness and death and their 40-plus years together, a work that has been described as "celebratory" and "heartbreaking and exquisite." It was a Finalist for both the 2022 IAN Book of the Year in Poetry and in the 2022 American Book Fest "Best Book" Award in the Legacy: Autobiography/Memoir category.

Dan's novella, *Dewdrops*, was originally written for the stage and enjoyed a full-cast staged reading at the Theatre of the Open Eye in New York. It was included in his short fiction collection, titled *Dewdrops*, which was a Finalist in the 2022 Independent Author Network's Book of the Year for Short Story Collection and a 2022 American Book Fest "Best Book" Award Finalist in Fiction-Short Story.

Dan followed this trifecta with the third and fourth books in the O'Keefe series:

The Big Tilt, the second book in the Peter O'Keefe series, was published in 2020 and has been described as "deft, hard-boiled, but literary prose that's reminiscent of Raymond Chandler's best work." *The Big Tilt* won the 2022 National Indie Excellence Award for Crime Fiction and was a Finalist for the 2022 Independent Author Network's Book of the Year in Thriller/ Suspense. In 2023, *The Big Tilt*, was awarded Honorable Mention in the Eric Hoffer Awards in the Legacy Fiction category, which included hundreds of books across all fiction genres.

On Lonesome Roads, published in 2022, is the third book in the series, and was a Notable 100 Book in the 2022 Shelf Unbound Best Indie Book Competition and 2023 IPPY Silver Medalist in the Best Mystery/Thriller eBook category. Most notably, *On Lonesome Roads* followed up *The Big Tilt's* 2022 NIEA Crime Fiction win with a finish as Finalist in the same contest and category for 2023. In the 2023 American Fiction Awards, *On Lonesome Roads*, finished with its own trifecta: winner for Mystery/Suspense: General; finalist for Mystery/ Suspense: Hard-Boiled Crime; and finalist for Thriller: Crime.

He has also written stage plays: "*Dewdrops*" (previously described); "*Secrets*" (based on the life of Eleanor Marx); and "*Moondog's Progress*" (inspired by the life of Alan Freed), which was awarded Honorable Mention in 2022 in the 91st Annual Writer's Digest Writing Competition for "Script."

He serves on the Board of Directors of Childhood USA, the U.S. arm of the World Childhood Foundation, established by Queen Silvia of Sweden, working to end child sexual abuse and exploitation everywhere.

He divides his time among Kansas City, New York City, and Los Angeles, and, whenever possible, visits the Catskills in New York and the San Juan Islands (off the coast of Washington state), as well as the Gulf Islands, Vancouver and Vancouver Island in British Columbia.

THE PETER O'KEEFE SERIES

How did we get here?

Dan Flanigan, after a long career as a finance, banking, and bankruptcy lawyer in which he was both a player in and witness to the dramatic transformations of our modern times, intends to provide at least a few of the answers to that question through a series of novels, recounting, from the 1980s to the present day, the life and adventures of his private detective hero Peter O'Keefe and the assorted characters in the O'Keefe orbit.

Welcome, then, to this chronicle of the scams, schemes, and scandals of the last four decades of American life. Flanigan hopes the series will appeal to every generation—from the Boomers, who lived all of it, down to Gen Z and future generations as well who are trying to learn the lessons the immediate past has to teach them and help them to play the hand dealt to them.

In the first three books of the series—*Mink Eyes, The Big Tilt*, and *On Lonesome Roads*, which are set during the period 1986 to 1988—Flanigan explores such themes as the disruption and decline of the traditional American Mafia; the Savings & Loan scandal that crippled much of the U.S. banking system in the 1980s and early 1990s; the fallout from the AIDS crisis of that era; the emergence of the surveillance society ("Who is watching? Who is listening?"); the corrosive effect of keeping secrets in both public and private life ("We are only as sick as the secrets we keep."); addiction and recovery; date rape and other sexual violence and the blighted lives that so often result.

In these stories, though teeming with plenty of villains, everyday people of mostly good will, confronted with extraordinary challenges, struggle to repair and heal themselves and others, and their world, from their wounds, self-inflicted and otherwise.

MINK EYES
(PETER O'KEEFE BOOK 1)

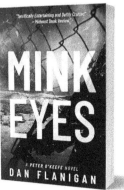

YOU DON'T SEND AN ANGEL TO DO A DIRTY JOB

It is the tarnished heart of the "Greed is Good" decade. Peter O'Keefe is a physically scarred and emotionally battered Vietnam vet. Struggling with life after war, O'Keefe tries to outrun his vices by immersing himself in his work as a private investigator. Hired by his childhood best friend, ace attorney Mike Harrigan, O'Keefe investigates what appears to be merely a rinky-dink mink farm Ponzi scheme in the Ozarks. Instead, O'Keefe finds himself ensnared in a vicious web of money laundering, cocaine smuggling and murder.

Mink Eyes is available in paperback, hardcover, eBook and audiobook.

"Terrifically entertaining and deftly crafted…"
–Midwest Book Review

THE BIG TILT
(PETER O'KEEFE BOOK 2)

NO GOOD DEED GOES UNPUNISHED

The war in Vietnam didn't kill Peter O'Keefe. Neither did his run-in with ruthless crime boss "Mr. Canada" in the Arizona desert. But chasing after justice in his own hometown just might.

A high school crush of O'Keefe's turns up dead, but the details don't add up. His pal, Mike Harrigan, has put his trust in the wrong people and now stands accused of crimes that could put him in the slammer. And O'Keefe? The mafia has put a price on his head.

The Big Tilt is available in paperback, hardcover, eBook and audiobook.

> "*...Flanigan manages to conjure deft, hard-boiled, but literary prose that's reminiscent of Raymond Chandler's best work. A gritty and eloquent crime novel.*"

–Kirkus Reviews

ON LONESOME ROADS
(PETER O'KEEFE BOOK 3)

SOME ROADS MUST BE WALKED ALONE

As private detective Peter O'Keefe continues to heal from the burns he suffered from the blast of a car bomb, neither he nor the police can prove who his assailants were. The media speculates that "The Outfit," a mafia group in the city, is to blame. O'Keefe isn't so sure, but he means to find out – and fast. Terrified of another attack, O'Keefe's ex-wife, Annie, won't allow his eleven-year-old daughter near him except under the tightest security, including an armed guard. He can't blame her. It isn't safe for Kelly, or anyone else he cares about, to be near him while his attacker is on the loose.

In a desperate effort to keep his family safe and restore his life to some measure of normality, O'Keefe becomes consumed with solving the mystery of who is hunting him. Along the way, he'll be forced to negotiate with The Outfit – a "devil's bargain" that just might cost him everything.

On Lonesome Roads is available in paperback, hardcover, eBook and audiobook.

"The further exhilarating adventures of an unbeatable detective, packed with tantalizing loose ends."

–Kirkus Reviews